Tim Waterstone was born in Glasgow in 1939 and educated at Cambridge University. He lives in London and has eight children.

He founded in 1982 the Waterstone's bookshop chain, now the largest specialist booksellers in the British Isles.

LILLEY & CHASE, published in 1994, was his first novel. He is currently working on his third.

Also by Tim Waterstone from Headline

Lilley & Chase

AN IMPERFECT
MARRIAGE

TIM
WATERSTONE

HEADLINE
REVIEW

First published in 1995
by HEADLINE BOOK PUBLISHING

First published in paperback in 1996
by HEADLINE BOOK PUBLISHING

A HEADLINE REVIEW paperback

10 9 8 7 6 5 4 3 2 1

ISBN 0 7472 4851 6

Typeset by Avon Dataset Ltd, Bidford-on-Avon, B50 4JH

Printed and bound in Great Britain by
Cox & Wyman Ltd, Reading, Berks

HEADLINE BOOK PUBLISHING
A division of Hodder Headline PLC
338 Euston Road
London NW1 3BH

For Rosie, who made my life

Author's Notes

The author has volunteered by private correspondence with Lee Young of Liverpool University that his inspiration for writing both the contents of Chapter Seventeen and the letter in the Epilogue came from reading Mr Young's most memorable article in the *Guardian* of 21 December 1993, entitled CRACK OF DOOM.

The author would like to acknowledge the author of the anonymous poem on page 78 which he first read in the 1973 edition of John Julius Norwich's anthology *Christmas Crackers* and understands originally appeared in a magazine in the 1960s. It has unfortunately proved impossible to track down the author.

The author would like to thank Mr James MacGibbon, the literary executor of the estate of Stevie Smith, for his kind permission to use *Not Waving but Drowning* by Stevie Smith on page 161 and J. M. Dent Publishers of the Orion Group for their kind permission to use *The Bright Field* by R. S. Thomas on page 163.

The author would like to make clear that the town of Bavancore, the Poonjee River and the State of Maduram are entirely figments of his imagination, as is any arrangement in the financing of a dam project between the Government of India and the World Bank or any other body, and any resemblance to real persons; events; places or projects is purely coincidental.

Prologue

The little boy, just six years old, stood on the main platform of the railway station. His hand was in his father's hand, his eyes looking up to him, the bustle and heat of the Ranchi morning all around them.

Every so often he smiled politely at his father's railway company friends, who were talking and laughing there with him. His father was dressed, as always, in his crumpled tropical suit, his khaki topee pushed back on his head. He chattered and called out in his excitable, musical Welsh voice, his hand resting proudly in its statement of ownership first on the boy's shoulder, and then on his head, running the coarse, oily fingers of his workman's hands through his son's soft, dark hair.

Before them stood the engine of the waiting Howrah Express; throbbing, wheezing its steam as it waited to leave at twelve noon precisely for Jamshedpur and Kharagpur, then Howrah and Calcutta itself, almost 300 miles away to the east. Ranchi station teemed, as it always did in the little boy's memories in later years, with cows and goats and hand-trucks and bicycles and people. Hordes and hordes of people; shouting, jangling, pushing, jostling... and then the whistles blew and the guard and the stationmaster waved their flags, and blew again, and the great engine lurched and jolted and was on its way.

Everyone struggled to get aboard; climbing up the doors and the windows and on to the roof, hands reaching down to grasp at the arms upheld to them from those below.

And the child's father then, in a sudden whoop of joy and abandon, seized him under the arms, and threw him up on to the footplate, then ran along beside him on the platform, knees high, arms pumping, trying, trying to keep pace. The little boy first laughed and shouted in encouragement, and then suddenly he was afraid, and he was crying and imploring and stretching out his hand. His father's fingers were just, just in contact with the handrail, and then he had it, and he was scrabbling and grasping, and desperately, desperately pulling at the iron grip, and then he was there.

There with the little boy, lying on his back on the footplate floor, the topee fallen and gone, laughing, laughing with his friend the engine driver, and with the little boy too. Except the child had his tears to wipe away, and he did so with the back of his clenched fist, looking down at his father as he lay there still, on the footplate of the Howrah Express.

And what was in Robert Luscombe at that moment was the dependence and the sudden pure ache of love. As if it was a glimpse of the transcendent. The shaft of sunlight on a small, dark field.

PART ONE

Chapter One

Mother Superior looked across at poor Douglas Tilton's daughter with a pleasure so intense that it felt as if it was the onset of a physical infatuation. She had never met her before that weekend, but there was about Sarah Tilton a simple, unaffected loveliness that stirred her heart.

Sarah was nineteen years old, but wearing, as she did, not a scrap of make-up, looked much younger. Her lovely hair, ash-blonde and gleaming, was pulled back into a severe bun, the style of a woman of much greater maturity. For all that, the bun set off her fine features in clear relief, and her high neck too, and this was as slender and graceful as Mother Superior thought she had ever seen.

The way she presents herself suits her so well, the nun sighed. What a blessing she must be to her father. What innocence there is in the child. Such simple piety.

Father Douglas came across with the teapot, and Mother Superior smilingly shook her head to refuse a third cup. She turned to Sarah and said, 'Are you excited, my dear? Are you pleased?'

Sarah clapped her hands together, and when she smiled the nun could see again the even white teeth, and the dimples, so deliciously pretty, that hollowed her cheeks.

'Am I *pleased*? Oh Mother Superior, this is what I've been waiting for all these months! It's what I prayed for all the time I was at college. Father will tell you that. To teach in the Mission's schools in India – there's nothing, Mother, *nothing* that I would rather do.'

And she laughed, and clapped her hands once more, and Mother Superior thought she saw in poor Douglas's eyes a little tear as he smiled too, then went over to lay his hand on his daughter's shoulder.

Sarah put her hand up to cover his, and though her smile was one of open joy, her thoughts at that moment were of something rather different. Mostly of regret that she would now be torn away from the little physical excitements and explorations she had been enjoying in recent weeks with the young garage mechanic from down the road. This offset by relief that she would no longer have to go through the misery of failed interviews with the dauntingly proficient women at the girls' private schools she had applied to for teaching posts. And that was worth a good deal.

This job with the Missionaries for India League was by no means what she wanted, but it would do until something better came along. And at least it would get her away from Folkestone for a bit. The trip out to India on the boat would be fun, anyway. Goodness knows whom she might meet. She could easily give the job up after a few months and come home again. In fact, that was exactly what she would do. Unless she met a really nice boy there . . .

She beamed up at her father again, and gave his hand a little squeeze, and Mother Superior watched them with such happiness. What a blessing for Douglas. All those years together in Folkestone; ever since his wife died in that influenza epidemic just after the war. Just the two of them together from when Sarah was tiny.

She'll get on so well with Sister Luke in Darjeeling, the nun thought. And then, who knows? Perhaps she'll take the veil herself one day, under Sister Luke's instruction. That would be a wonderful thing. How dear Douglas would love that. Of course the child is a little younger than the League usually likes, and her qualifications are somewhat thin . . . but I can see a nun when one's put in front of me. What a spiritual presence she has.

Soon it was time for Mother to catch the Sunday-night train back to London, and as she leant out of the carriage window for one last wave, she could see father and daughter standing there on the platform, their arms around each other's waists, each with a hand raised in farewell.

And to think Douglas tells me he used to worry that he was too possessive with her, she thought. How wrong he was. What a marvellous father he must have been. What a little angel he's brought up!

Chapter Two

The mission school in Darjeeling stands right at the top of the little town, beyond the planters' club and up the dirt track that leads away into the foothills of the Himalayas, twenty or thirty miles to the north.

From Tiger Hill, just outside the school grounds, sightseers stand at dawn to see the first rays of the sun strike the peak of Kangchenjunga, and then, moments later, the apparently smaller, insignificant Everest beyond to the north-west. These mountain tops seem to float unsupported in the sky like some miraculous vision in the rosy glow of early light, before, quite gradually, the shapes and contours of all the surrounding mountains slip slowly into view above the mist-filled valleys below.

It is all of a scale that would awe the most world-weary traveller . . . and when Sarah Tilton arrived in Darjeeling in 1962 to begin teaching in the Mission School, she was anything but that. Apart from a single trip to Paris in the company of a group of her father's parishioners, she had never been out of England before in her life.

She was now only a week or so past her twentieth birthday, and had been sent up to take her place at Sister Luke's school in Darjeeling after a month's training at the main Mission School in Calcutta. Sarah was by no means pleased to be dragged away from the city, where she'd found the company of a number of very promising young men. But she was obliged to go, and to put as good a face on it as she could, though the moment she arrived she knew her doubts were well founded.

From the very start, it was all too apparent that Sister Luke failed to find in Sarah the least trace of the saintly virtues that Mother Superior had most fulsomely described in the letter of introduction she had sent to Sister Luke in advance of Sarah's arrival.

It was the girl's lack of personal organisation and discipline that first irritated Sister Luke. She had taken the trouble to give her a bedroom right at the top of her own little house in the school's gardens, as she was anxious that Sarah should feel cared for and protected in her first stay so far from home. But within the week Sister Luke wished, fervently, that she'd put Sarah in with the other teachers in their hostel across in the main school. For the bedroom had quickly become a sea of dirty clothes and spilling suitcases, its adjoining bathroom littered with damp towels and bath-mats left on the floor, the basin still unemptied from whenever it had last been used.

There was a tradition at the Mission that the servants should not be asked to perform housekeeping tasks of this kind. The fact that Sister Luke had specifically warned Sarah of this on her arrival made her all the more annoyed that the girl had made no effort to clean up after herself.

She tended also to be late for meetings and class – another sign of indiscipline and immaturity, Sister Luke told herself, in an institution that the child must have seen prided itself on its sense of structure and efficiency.

'None of these things matters, my dear,' Sister Luke told her. 'In themselves they're insignificant. We're not presenting them to you as great icons of civilised life. But when they go wrong, they create strains in your relationships with other people. Trivial selfishness is like that. In itself it signifies nothing that touches at the heart of things, but it's the warning light for aspects of the personality that need correction and adjustment.

'Of course you're very young,' she went on. 'You've the capacity for development in so many ways as you mature. But your conduct in these trivial things indicates to me that you have not yet grasped that you've both a social and moral responsibility to put the needs of others quite automatically before considerations for yourself. And particularly your responsibility to the children. The very youngest of them are in your care. They depend on you to give them stability and security, and dependable, reliable care. At the moment you are too erratic in the discipline of your own life to provide that for them.'

It was at that point that Sarah knew for a certainty that she didn't want to spend the rest of her life in a Mission School, nor in any other form of institution of that type. All this was quite wrong for her, and she should never have come to Darjeeling. She was a free spirit, someone whose hidden destiny was for some adventure in life incomparably more interesting and important than the pettifogging restrictions forced upon her here by people such as these. She would seek to put herself now with people who could see that she was a girl of very unusual character.

The problem with her life, she thought moodily, was that no one had ever really wanted to help her. Her father had never worked with her sufficiently; never allowed her to find her true potential. He'd always held her back – smothered her with all that demanding affection. Perhaps he was frightened of having a daughter who was more clever and successful than he had ever been.

And another thing; she would have been far more successful at school if she had been better taught there. Her school had let her down as well. She'd needed much more encouragement than she'd received. The disappointments of her life had absolutely not been her fault. People didn't understand her. No one understood her secret destiny.

Sarah watched Sister Luke across the table with considerable dislike. This woman doesn't understand me at all, she thought. She doesn't know me. What she needs is someone who'll stand up to her – and she'll get that from me when the moment is right. I'll stand up to her. She's not going to get at me in this way. She's going to accept, as everyone else will, that I'm a very good and interesting person. And that I'm marked out for really special things.

She drew herself up in her chair, and looked Sister Luke firmly in the eye.

'I'm so sorry, Sister Luke. Of course you're right. I must pray for the success of my life here and the work of the Mission School. And for Mother Joseph. And for the sick and the dispossessed. And for all the children. And for you.

'May I leave now? I have some lessons to prepare. And I would like then to help Sister Matthew by sweeping out the chapel before evening prayer.'

Chapter Three

Sister Luke watched Sarah as she turned and left the room. Before I lose my temper with her, she thought, as I'm on the point of doing, I must remember that she has the intellectual and moral development of a small child; but, whatever the truth of that, I'm not comfortable with her, to put it mildly. I don't believe she has the inner strength and quality that we need, or ever will have. I doubt that this is the right place for her, and I doubt that she'll stay.

And in this Sister Luke was correct, for it was only a few weeks after this that Sarah met Robert Luscombe.

She found him walking along the path up from Darjeeling that passed the Mission grounds before winding up through the Himalayan foothills. She was coming down the path as he climbed it, and when he had reached her, he stopped and touched the brim of his hat and asked the way to the dhak bungalow some fifteen or so miles away up in the hills.

She knew that the map he was carrying marked quite clearly the route to the bungalow, but she went along with the fiction, and explained it all in sufficient length and detail to give him time to run his eyes over her face and body, which she could see that he wanted to do.

They sat down on a wayside bench and talked together, at first shyly and inconsequentially, and then with increasing freedom. Sarah learnt from him that he was staying at the Mount Everest

Hotel, and that he was on a week's holiday from the Calcutta office of the Moorgate & Mercantile Bank, for which he had worked since leaving University seven years before. And she told him about the Mission School, and Sister Luke, and her childhood in the Folkestone vicarage, and, because she sensed his devotion for India, she included some entirely false statements of ardour for Darjeeling and the local countryside.

When Robert returned two days later from his trek he found a message from Sarah waiting for him at the hotel. He contacted her, they met that afternoon, and walked together for an hour or more around Tiger Hill. Then they returned to the cavernous, deserted hotel, with its balconies and terraces furnished with broken wicker furniture and rusting metal tables, and the stools of its dusty lounges piled with ancient English magazines, and the grimy walls hung with crooked, stained prints of fox-hunting in the shires.

They sat together over drinks in the empty bar, with its forlorn relics of past days of the gay, sportive Raj, and when Robert asked her in due time to come to his room on some lame pretext or another, Sarah thought she could hear in his voice a tight, strangled sexual intensity.

And she was right. As soon as the door was shut, he stood up against her, and ran his hands over her breasts, then down her back. She brought her hands slowly forward from her sides and touched for a brief second, and feather-lightly, the hard lump that was pressing at her from his trousers. He started to pull and fumble at her clothes, and in time he undressed her, kissing at her, licking at her, feeling at her, and she at him.

She lay back on the bed with him, her breathing accelerating, whispering to him in urgent, repeated phrases. But it was all too much for him; too soon he was clutching at himself, staring, open-mouthed, wide-eyed, ejaculating, his hand pumping and pumping, and then it was all over.

And, absurd perhaps as it was, from this one frenetic meeting their lives together were set.

For Robert, who was now just short of his twenty-seventh

birthday, and deeply longing for a physical life with a woman, this was like a thunderflash upon him. Here was what he had been dreaming of, year upon year. Here was the girl he had longed for. This was love!

And for Sarah it was a sudden, exhilarating opportunity to be free of the life she had found herself trapped within. Free of Sister Luke, and of those uncomfortably precise judgements of her and her character. Free of the Mission School, and those remorseless, nagging tasks. Free too of her childhood, and the suffocating confines of the Folkestone vicarage, and all the expectations that were loaded on her there. And that was the point. Now she was free of any more need to prove herself in anything whatsoever.

Marriage would release her from all that; for marriage was the best, the most finite excuse of all. No one could say that she was walking away and failing. She was doing anything but that; she was getting married. This was success, not failure.

She was to have a husband. He was going to be responsible for her now. Her husband. She was going to be a married woman.

Chapter Four

They lay naked, face to face, and as Sarah opened her mouth and cried out in her pleasure Robert pulled away from her, staring at her face, stroking her back, wiping the sweat from her forehead.

The wooden shutters of the open window creaked and swung in the strengthening breeze coming up from the sea. Robert looked over Sarah's shoulder and lay quite still, gazing at the white, gaunt beach on which the little cottage fronted, glaring and stark in the blaze of the afternoon sun. A crow swung down to peck and worry at some morsel or other there on the sands, and as it screeched its rage at another bird trying to wrest the tidbit from its beak, the baby at the end of their bed awoke and cried.

Sarah pushed herself to her feet, and went to the cradle to pick the child up, holding it against her naked breast, rocking it slowly, singing to it, calming it back to rest. Robert could see the swell of her second pregnancy already showing in her belly as she stood in profile, and there came to him a wave of affection for her, and responsibility, and shame for the shortcomings of their marriage. Thank God we can make love, he thought. Thank God we can communicate in that way at least.

Sarah turned and smiled at him. 'Sophie's so sweet, Robert, don't you think? She's so sweet and innocent-looking. She's going to be such an angel, I know she is. And you do love her?'

And then; 'I'm so happy with you, Robert. So happy with you

and the baby, and now the next one too! Lovely little Sophie,' she said, snuggling her face into the baby's stomach, and rubbing it there. 'Boo, boo, Sophie.'

And as much to punctuate this as anything else, Robert got up to fetch Sarah's dressing gown and spread it over her shoulders. Then he wrapped a towel around his waist and went to the window to secure the shutters, which had begun to bang against the wall. While there, he stood and looked out across the beach to Puri over on the other side of the bay, its ancient temples rising above the shabby rooftops of the sprawling town.

After a moment he said, as if suddenly remembering that she'd spoken, 'Of course she is, Sarah. And of course I do. How could you think anything else?'

He smiled and shrugged, and turned once more to the window, now looking out to the surf rolling in on to the deserted beach, its solitude broken only by a mongrel dog, picking its way across the scorching sands with hopping, dancing feet.

Two truths perhaps, he thought. Her truth, and my truth.

His truth was of a marriage that had not so much started an early descent into failure, as had never really been a marriage at all; at least in the sense that a normal expectation of marriage would encompass a balanced relationship between two people mutually in love, and in harmony, and of a single mind and purpose.

When they were married, Robert had seen in Sarah an innocence, and a loveliness of face and feature, and an unformed but gentle character. He was infatuated with her. He longed for her, and could find in her nothing but all those things that he most fully craved. But that had sprung from loneliness, he realised now, without in the least admiring himself in the recognition of it. Loneliness and an acute physical passion. For turning no more depth of connection than that into a marriage for life, Robert admired himself even less.

They had never settled. After three years of living together their awkwardness was too extreme to have the potential for change. There was a brittle nervousness between them that could not be broken down. The courtesies were there, and the compliments, and the ritualised statements of affection, but there was not a hint of intimacy, nor humour, nor engagement, nor the search for common interests. After three years of marriage those should have been there. Now, he thought, they never would be.

And her truth? Because she had never discussed these things with him he had no certain knowledge as to what her feelings were. But she was proud of him at least; he knew that. That was so. Proud to be his wife, and the more so as his career in the bank accelerated away. And relieved and assured that he was a generous provider of her material needs.

All that he was sure of; but her indifference to him as an individual, as a person in himself, was painfully clear. She had no interest in his life, nor jealousies of him, nor concern for him, nor enquiry as to what filled his mind and his memories. She was affable, obliging and polite. But she cared not a scrap, and that he knew too.

And why should she? Robert thought. For neither did he. They had married because they had made love with each other one evening in Darjeeling. And made love again several times more over the course of the three days they were together there. Having done that, marriage was what was then expected to follow, in that time, and in those circles. So they had married.

But there was nothing between them. That was Robert's truth. He knew that the marriage was not only empty now, but was going to remain so all their days.

And perhaps that was Sarah's truth too. They had never talked about it, but surely she must have realised all that as well. But married they were, and there was a baby now in Sarah's arms, and another one soon to be born.

He turned from the window, tightened the towel around his waist, and smiled at her.

'She's adorable, my darling, she really is. And I'm longing for the new baby too. I can't wait. Well done. Well done.'

Chapter Five

Had Robert and Sarah been less obviously ill at ease with each other, then few would have thought more than that the imbalance in their intelligence and interests might at some time in the future cause difficulties between them. As it was, their uncomfortable aura of incompatibility led them to make no mutual friendships of any kind. To Robert (and for all he knew, to Sarah too) this was the most obvious symptom of their disconnection. But the children arrived in their lives so quickly that some of the more painful aspects of their mutual discomfort were lost in the busyness of parenthood.

For Sarah particularly that was a blessing. Motherhood gave her the protection of having a role to play in her group of acquaintances that was identifiable and acceptable. On her own, she was not a credible figure to anyone as the devoted, ambitious wife of a devoted, ambitious husband. She knew that, and Robert's developing self confidence and reputation as a professional banker served to widen the gap yet further. But in motherhood she was safe. Her demanding little daughters gave Sarah a social identity and a purpose, and she threw herself into this new life with an energy that she had never found in herself before.

As the girls grew, however, and found their own distractions and interests with their schoolfriends and peer group, this role for Sarah was no longer available or appropriate. Her problem now was that she had no idea of how to spend her time in a way that others would find acceptable. So, perhaps in despair, she was easily reassured and flattered into an affair with first one young man when they initially returned from India to live in London, and then another, and then more. Several times she wondered if she was in love. At least once she was certain she was, and was on the point of telling Robert, and leaving home, when the man changed his mind, and Sarah's heart was near broken by the experience.

There were attempts to fill her days with something other than trips to department stores, and spending there what always seemed to Robert, considering Sarah's modest dress-style, quite mysteriously large sums of money, but these were always short-lived. There were stops and starts, but that's all they were. Open University courses, applied for with such excitement, then abandoned almost as soon as the first material arrived through the letter-box. Bridge lessons at the Town Hall. Meals-on-Wheels occupied her for a month or two. The Pastoral Outreach to the Homeless scheme of Sarah's church lasted a little longer, but that too declined and faded away in two or three months, as the St Matthew's congregation, after an initial flurry of energy, failed to find any homeless in their part of London to outreach to. Apart from a single reclusive West Indian lady, who was indignant at her cherished isolation being ripped away from her by a bevy of church ladies offering her sandwiches and their spare room for the night.

One evening Robert took Sarah out to dinner in the brasserie near their house, and talked to her about the possibility of opening a charity shop.

'I think you'd love it, Sarah,' he said. 'You'd get a real sense of achievement out of it. The property people at the Bank will help you to find a site if you would like that. You might be able to raise quite a considerable sum of money through it for whatever charities you're most interested in. Your Church, and so on. Why don't you give it a go?'

The flush in Sarah's face told him that he had awakened an immediate enthusiasm in her. This was something that was entirely within the range of her ambition for herself. Doing good to others . . . nothing to do with a horrid office job . . . something she could set up immediately, without the need for training, or qualifications, or anything tiresome of that sort . . .

She looked across at him, and although she tried initially to sound prudent and measured, he knew that she was hooked.

'Where's the money coming from to set it up? It sounds a good idea, but with the children's school fees and everything else . . . It's all very grand . . . but it does sound a good idea, I suppose. In some ways.'

She flushed again, and he could sense the mounting excitement in her.

'Something I could be good at. You never think I can do anything. That's half the problem with me. You have no confidence in me at all. You have no idea what I'm capable of. And I'm certainly capable of that. And yes – it does sound a good idea in many ways. It really does.'

There was silence for a moment.

'But it would have to be big, mind you. And have lots of stock. You have no idea of the potential for these sort of things. It's not worth wasting my time with something too small. I could make it very big indeed. If I did it at all, I would intend to. I don't want to have some sort of half-baked operation that could never make any money for anybody. If I'm going to do it, then it's worth doing it properly.'

So Robert bought Sarah the lease on a premises in Notting Hill Gate, and she fitted it out to sell a range of ethnic goods made, or sewn, or donated by the public. She made a most enthusiastic start to it, but after a month or so the shop became overwhelmed by inappropriate stock, and almost no one at all came through the door. Sarah lost heart and commitment and interest, and Robert closed the place down one winter Sunday afternoon, quietly paying Oxfam two thousand pounds to take the entire inventory of ethnic bric-à-brac off his hands and do with it whatever they wished.

There followed some fitful participation in charity projects and the parish activities of St Matthew's, Wetherby Gardens; some love affairs; a rather desultory management of the various home-helps and handymen who came to run the house; and a daily round of departmental store shopping. That, from the time the two girls were of school age, was the compass of Sarah Luscombe's life. And the irony was that the more Robert's career progressed, and their prosperity grew, the less likely it was that Sarah would ever become self-reliant. Sarah widowed, or impoverished, might have had some chance of engaging herself with life, and thereby being fulfilled. Sarah as she was, drawing from a joint bank account whatever and whenever she wanted, was drowning in her lack of self-purpose.

But, for all that, there was Sophie, on whom all Sarah's emotional resources were focused. For Robert there was an immediate and perhaps over-heightened devotion towards their second daughter, Rowena. And that was how the marriage and the Luscombe family settled in its course. No more unhappy than many, perhaps. Robert had at least his career at the Bank, and that was becoming something of real success and power. But Sarah had only the shadows of things; there was a bleakness in her being that neither knew how to address. For both of them, in their own ways, had become emotional and familial cripples.

Robert could do nothing for Sarah, but wished that he could. It never occurred to Sarah to consider whether she could do anything for her husband.

He has his career after all, she thought. I have nothing. And a lot of that is because of Robert. I have absolutely nothing. And that's not my fault.

PART TWO

Chapter Six

As Sarah looked down from the verandah she could see the fishermen on the Bavancore beach.

They were pulling now at the heavy nets and chanting their rhythmic songs as they hauled together, their bodies pitch black, hard and muscular, gleaming with sweat and sea water. On their heads they wore the little pointed triangular basketwork hats that fishermen throughout India use to protect themselves from the surf, and around their waists were knotted loose white loincloths. Otherwise they were naked, and Sarah watched them silently and alone, her hair tied back in a bun behind her head, her loose cotton dress stirring in the breeze that came off the sea. A tray of tea, brought to her by the company servant Mustafa, stood on the wicker table in front of her. The teapot, as always in India, was wrapped in a thick down cosy, and with it on the tray was the plate of digestive biscuits that Robert had requested when they first arrived in Bavancore eight days before. And were now served as a matter of ritual, but eaten only by the servants when the tray had been taken down to the kitchen.

The house that the Luscombes were staying in was owned by the Indian affiliate of the Moorgate & Mercantile Bank, of which Robert, in his mid fifties now, had become Deputy Chairman. The affiliate, the Hindustan-Moorgate & Mercantile Bank, was formed at the time when the Government of India had legislated for foreign companies to divest majority control of their subsidiaries into Indian hands.

The house was kept for use by any of the senior officials of the Bank who required accommodation whilst in the town. It was situated in a part of Bavancore that acted as a quasi-suburban village for the managers of the banks and trading houses that had offices there. Thirty years before, in the 1950s, the occupants of the houses would almost all have been British, and the architecture and the feel of the place entirely reflected that.

Some knew the suburb in those days as 'Little Nettlebed', and not absurdly so, for there was a quietness and serenity about the place redolent of an idealised English village. There was even a cricket ground on the green, as if this tropical place was in Surrey or Sussex. The houses that stood around it were neat, well-ordered villas, with curtains in the windows, and cars drawn up in the front drives, and scrubbed, smiling children playing their games on the tended lawns.

But old Bavancore, real Bavancore, was sited away down at the neck of the river. There the fishing boats and the sleek naval vessels lay crammed together in the curve of the little bay, protected by the fall of the land from the storms and occasional mountainous seas of the monsoon months. This was India untouched by the British or by any other foreign influence. The noisy, quarrelling, bustling town was like a thousand others in the sub-continent; rickshaws, hooting taxis, cows wandering down the main streets, huge, jostling crowds, and children darting amongst the beggars, some of these hideously maimed, calling piteously for alms, their hands outstretched and their tin boxes rattling.

The Luscombes' house was more substantial than most, and had perhaps the best position. It faced on to the so-called village green, and backed directly on to the wide sandy beach that ran from Bavancore almost all the way down the Malabar coast to Cape Comorin, two hundred miles to the south.

The garden was pretty and well tended. A strictly rectangular lawn was bounded by three fine old frangipani trees and a border bright with dahlias and phlox and tall tiger lilies. Bougainvillaea, starred with tight clusters of purple flowers, climbed up and covered the verandah on which Sarah sat that morning, and, as she gazed away down the beach towards the fishermen and their nets, the gardener, the *mali*, came shuffling along the path below her, cackling with laughter and shouting back at another of the servants behind him at the front of the house.

The *mali* was carrying a broom under one arm and dragging a rake under the other. A mongrel puppy, that had adopted the *mali* as its owner, was chasing after the rake and snapping at it in a game which was repeated morning after morning, with neither the dog nor the *mali* seeming to tire. He stopped to unwind and turn on the hose, training the spurt of water on to the pots of bright red geraniums lining the steps up to the little sitting room that looked out over the garden.

Eight days more, Sarah thought, then Robert's three-week tour of the Far Eastern offices would be over, and they would be on their way back to London. She was longing to get back. She should never have come.

Sarah turned her head again, and looked out once more along the stretch of sand towards where the fishermen were working. At nearly fifty, she was still a most handsome-looking woman, particularly in profile. Her fair hair, barely touched with grey, was drawn as always tightly back into its bun, and helped thereby to give sharp definition to her features, which at that angle appeared to retain much of the fineness of her younger years. If in full face there was now a little coarseness perhaps, a little slackening and loosening of the skin, those striking violet eyes under the bold eyebrows still gazed before her, as they always had, with the innocence and delicacy of a small, lost child.

I wonder what time Robert will come back here from the office. I wish I was better at finding things to do in a place like this. Perhaps I can get someone to take me on a drive down to the town, and show me the synagogue that those people were telling me about at the dinner party last night. I could buy some more silk too to take home for Sophie and the parish bring-and-buy sale next month. Or some bracelets or something like that. But the noise and the bustle and the crowds in the bazaar are so oppressive. Perhaps I can go with Robert tomorrow if he'll make the time.

Mustafa came across the verandah to clear away the tea tray, and Sarah made some arrangements with him about her lunch. She looked at her watch. Still only just after nine o'clock in the morning. This heat, and still the whole day to go . . .

Mustafa was gone now, and was at the back of the house talking loudly to one of the other servants in a language she couldn't understand, and then they all laughed with him in some shared remark. She turned and gazed down to the beach once more, and watched for some minutes as the fishermen pulled at the nets and dragged them up the sand. The sound of their shouting and their laughter drifted up to her as she stood there, her thin cotton dress now damp with her perspiration and clinging against her body.

Then Sarah seemed to make an abrupt decision, and went down the steps into the garden. In her hand was the big key on the wooden ring that secured the tall wrought-iron gate leading from the garden to the path to the beach. When she reached the sands she took off her sandals and laid them neatly in the shade of a bush. With the *mali*'s puppy now running around her legs and barking his excitement, she set off to walk along the beach, playing in her hands with a piece of rope she'd found lying on the sand.

She picked up a stick or two, and threw these for the puppy as she walked slowly over in the direction of the fishermen. When near to them, she sat down on the beach, and put her hands behind her in support. Then she stretched her legs out in front of her, and pulled her cotton dress up so that her legs and then her thighs were bare to the sun, at that time in the morning not yet in its full intensity.

She remained in that position for some minutes, and watched as the puppy started barking at a vulture that was picking at a cadaver of a sea snake further down the beach, then flapped unhurriedly into the air as the dog went galloping forward at it. Sarah sat more fully upright, bent her trunk forward, and flexed her knees outwards, opening her thighs. Leaning forward, she drew a pattern on the sand with one of the sticks she had picked up as she was walking, moving her position slightly so that her body was now facing directly towards the fishermen. She made a movement to hitch her dress just a little further up her thighs, and forced her knees open yet further.

One of the fishermen bent down to rub his foot, saw Sarah, turned away, then back again, and, quite unmistakably, looked between her legs. She pretended to hold her gaze out to sea, but her peripheral vision enabled her to see the fisherman looking at her, and as he did so she strained her legs out yet further. She felt her pink cotton pants pulling tight now across the slit of her vagina; but she kept her neck and head bent downwards so that she could be seen to be absorbed in her game with her stick in the sand.

She heard the fisherman laugh, and say something to the others, and then laugh again. She remained with her head down, still drawing with her stick on the sand, and then in time she slowly closed her knees, and stretched her legs out, and she could feel the dampness of excitement down the crotch of her pants.

She called the dog, pretending a sudden urgency of concern about the vulture, got to her feet, and straightened her dress down her legs again as she rose. She turned back to face towards the fishermen, putting her hand to her eyes and gazing above their heads out to sea, as if she saw there something of interest. Then she turned back again to call the dog once more, and they moved off together up the beach, away from the fishermen and back in the direction of the house.

She was near there now, and she sat for a moment on the trunk of a dead tree that lay angled across the sand. She still felt her arousal, emphatically so, and she realised that she was quite breathless with it all. She was tempted to go back to the fishermen, and re-enact the scene all over again. It had been played out several times in the preceding few days, and she realised that the fishermen had come to expect her. Only last week, when she had started this daily ritual, she would struggle with herself to conquer the temptation. She would rush to her bedroom on her return from the beach, and sit on the bed with her knuckles clenched so tight that the skin was drawn white across them, and pound them in self-punishment against her temples. But daily the sense and focus of the shame had lessened, and although there was still guilt, she knew quite well she would do it all over again.

It was nearly finished now, whatever this strange need was that had overcome her. There was no need to fight it too hard, because within days, within hours almost, they would be on the plane for home, and there would be no more of this. No more ever of this sort of thing. When she was home, this side of her would be put away and finished for ever. She could allow herself one or two times more of it over the next few days, now that the game had been started, but then it would be stopped. For ever. It was an odd need in her, but it was there, and too much guilt over it would be self-destructive. And it didn't matter too much out here in Bavancore. As long as it was just a private thing, of course. As long as it was a secret.

There is always secrecy and privacy in these things. That's how life is – life for everybody. Everybody has odd little secrets. But just a time or so more, then it must end.

Sarah straightened her dress again, and rose to go back into the house. Mustafa was in the bedroom collecting some clothes which he had asked Robert and Sarah to put out for charity, and he caught sight of her with distaste as she crossed the lawn. There had been gossip about her in the market, and he hadn't liked to hear the ribaldry and the disrespect. It reflected on the dignity of the whole household. And that of the Bank.

'Time to go home now, woman, where you belong. Home. You're a bad woman,' Mustafa muttered to himself, then pulled a chest of drawers away from the wall, and picked up from the floor a cotton shirt of Robert's that he'd concealed there the previous week, and that Robert appeared not to have missed.

He put the shirt in the pile of garments he'd selected as being good enough to sell to that Dharmapuri rogue in the bazaar, and set off for the town.

Chapter Seven

Six days earlier, Robert and Sarah had been in Calcutta, and one evening Robert had caught the sleeper down to the seaside town of Vishakhapatnam, six hundred miles or so away to the south.

He would be gone for three nights, he said, and rather than risk the rigours of travel in one of the poorest regions of India, Sarah decided that she would stay where she was, in the dependable, air-conditioned surroundings of her international hotel.

There was business for him to conduct, but Robert had another reason for going to Vishakhapatnam, and although Sarah knew of it, she had never grasped its full resonance and significance in Robert's life. For in a cemetery at the far end of the town, in a section reserved for railway employees and their families, Robert's father and mother lay side by side in two simple graves under the shade of a huge old frangipani tree. Identical plain memorial stones marked their place. *Owen Thomas Luscombe, 1915–1951. Beloved husband of Rachel* said the one, and *Rachel Gwen Luscombe, 1915–1951. Beloved wife of Owen* said the other. And each of the three evenings he was there, Robert laid on their graves the little wreaths of lotus blossom and tiger lilies that he himself had prepared, sitting there to watch as the sudden Indian night dropped around him like a gauze shroud. He remembered their gentleness, and their uncomplicated love for each other, brought to an end one morning at the height of the monsoon, when a bridge collapsed over the Maharadi River, and the train in which they were travelling plunged down to the flooding waters below.

Robert was just past his fifteenth birthday when they died. He was back home in Wales at his grammar school, living in a back-to-back terraced house in Pontypool with his mother's sister, who was married there to a mining engineer. The news came by word of a reporter on the local newspaper, and when Robert got home from school he found the man sitting pink with embarrassment and bolt upright on the settee in the front room, opened only for visitors, the antimacassar behind his head and the cuffs on the arm-rests all freshly starched and pressed. A cup of tea, served in their best George VI Coronation china, was clutched on its saucer in his hand. Robert's aunt, her own cup of tea before her on the little white settle table, sat still and silent, her face white and drawn, a single tear staining down her powdered, shrunken, courageous face.

The railway company buried the Luscombes the following day. Only the local superintendent was there to accompany the minister as the two plain deal coffins were laid in the tropical, alien ground, far from the longed-for, serene place in the green Welsh valleys to which they had been bound on Owen's retirement, only a few months hence. And Robert, thousands of miles away, alone, went to the chapel at the end of the village, up beside the Temperance Hall and the Garden of Rest. There, unable as always to pray, he sat the whole day through, and remembered them, and started on the long and, as it turned out to be, indefinite process of mourning for their loss.

Owen Luscombe had been a dark, vital little man, bustling about his business at the railway. He had first gone out to India when he was barely twenty years old, but had already by then worked in the marshalling yards in Cardiff for fully five years, first as a general apprentice, and then as a relief shunting driver.

Owen came from Sprott, where he was part of a large family who lived in conditions of extreme poverty. Despite the purpose and determination of the boy, Rachel William's fond parents, who owned a haberdashery business down in Albany Road, and lived in relative affluence there in Roath amongst others of their sort, were dismayed to learn that their daughter had been much in his company. The two young people had met at the Tabernacle choir, and the choir was in regular and frequent rehearsal, and unless something was done about it, and done quickly, Rachel showed every sign of forming an attachment that might prove, if left to develop, next to impossible to break.

So Rachel was sent first to London, to stay with her grandmother in Hackney, and then to Bath, where there was an academy for governesses that her parents had arranged for her to attend. She would stay there until she had passed her twentieth birthday, and was old enough then to secure a position in a rector's family, or with an army officer and his wife, or something of that kind. But one night, having been at the academy for barely ten or eleven weeks, she looked out from her dormitory window and saw Owen Luscombe standing alone under the street-light, huddled in the drizzle of the autumn evening. His cap was pulled down over his ears, his arms hugged his overcoat around him, and a carpet bag stood beside him on the glistening pavement. He was looking up at the grey, gaunt buildings of the school, as if in the certainty he would see her there.

Rachel made her escape out of the back of the kitchens, ran to him across the street, and they stood there held tight in each other's arms, motionless, until a passing policeman moved them on their way. They walked the mile or so to shelter at the railway station, and sat there over a cup of tea at the buffet.

Owen showed Rachel the letter he had received from the Bihar and Orissa Railway Division, confirming him for a post as a junior engineer, and the steerage ticket to get him there. Eight days later they set sail together from Liverpool, his savings from the previous five years in the marshalling yard providing just enough for the marriage licence, and Rachel's passage, and a small suitcase of tropical clothes.

Robert was born to them fifteen months later, in a tiny cottage hospital in the heat and dust of the remote railway town of

Jharsuguda. The problems of the delivery were so intense, and the nursing competence of the place so inadequate, that it was a most dangerous moment for both the baby and the mother. The rupturing of the womb and the haemorrhaging that followed the birth were so violent that Rachel was told that she had been too badly damaged to have more children.

The experience for both of them had been such that they readily came to terms with the fact that their son was to be their only child, and they returned first to the tiny house that the railway rented them on the outskirts of the cantonment, and then, on the day of Robert's second birthday, they moved to a company bungalow at Ranchi, where they were to stay for the rest of their married lives.

It was a fly-ridden little house, and poorly ventilated, and in the hottest months the heat used to settle there like a leaden blanket. There was just a single room in which the family sat and ate, off it two tiny bedrooms to the rear, and an open shower in the dirt yard at the back. This was contained on three sides by a bare brick wall, on the other side of which was a single lavatory, barely concealed, inadequately roofed and, at certain times of day, directly in the blaze of the sun. The little stone and brick cooking stove was also out in the open, tucked against the side of the house, the pans and the irons hanging there on nails. Chickens and a single cockerel pecked and scrabbled in the dust for whatever grubs and scraps that they could find. The elderly servants shared a single hut just outside the courtyard wall. When Robert was a baby, and then a small child, these two were accompanied in a little lean-to shack by a woman from a nearby village, who acted as the *ayah*.

In the heat of the place, and the discomfort of it, some occasional quarrelling and stress between them all was inevitable, and it certainly occurred. One of Robert's earliest memories was of his father standing red-faced and pouring with sweat in the front doorway of the little house, shouting at Rachel as she arrived home later than expected from the town. There was in him on these occasions a sudden, unpredictable fury that would have frightened anybody, let alone a small child. And this despite the fact that for most of the time – for almost *all* of the time – Owen Luscombe was an affectionate, sweet-natured man, considerate to both his son and to his wife.

It was, as Robert realised and understood in later years, the effect on his father of drink. Owen seldom took it, but when he did, this harsh, crude violence would invariably be unleashed from him. There would be a breaking of furniture and a smashing of glass, and a shouting, sweeping rage would be in him. The child would hide beneath the bed, or outside among the little houses clustered together by the bank of the railway cuttings facing on to the scrubby edge of the surrounding jungle. Weeping could be heard from the house then perhaps, or sometimes a chilling, abrupt silence, but eventually it would be over.

Robert would crouch in the lee of the wall, or hide in the shadow of a tree, the chattering, rattling, shrieking sounds of an Indian night around him. After an hour or so he would creep back to the house, and the safety of his familiar, bare little room, and lower himself as soundlessly as he could on to his wooden bed, with its mosquito net and its single, threadbare cotton sheet.

Then he would wait for sleep, and the dawn, and the clank of the bucket and the pull and the rush of the cistern from the yard outside his window. His father would come morosely, slowly, back into the house, his head hanging, his wet hair standing up dark and spiky and glistening in the early sun of the day, a collarless cotton shirt spread open at his neck.

Peace would then be in the house for days, even weeks and months, and Owen, in the way he had in his contrition, would chatter with the child, and carry him perched on his shoulders down to the marshalling yards and the engines and the clanking, shunting, sweating bustle of the place. And Robert would know that all was well, and that his father was mended again, and that love and trust and certainty were back, at least until the next time, and who knows when, if ever, that might be.

Rachel would be waiting for them when they returned; on one, much remembered, beloved occasion, it was fully a day later before they were back with her. That time Owen, in an impetuous, gleeful decision, had thrown Robert up on to the footplate of the noon express to Howrah, and the pair of them had made the journey there, and come back on the overnight mail, sleeping the hours before dawn, huddled and clasped together on the driver's palliasse, as the train hurtled and whistled and roared its way through the tropical night.

It was those moments, and that journey, that stamped the most treasured images from his childhood on the private soul of Robert Luscombe. The journey on the footplate of the Howrah Express. And his mother standing there at the door of the house to welcome them home, the telegram of explanation from Owen fluttering in her hands, and her arms held out wide for the child to run into.

In all Robert's childhood, Rachel was always there, or so he recalled in later years; always gentle, always calm it seemed, always his mother, always ostensibly at peace. There was a school for railwaymen's families available to them at Ranchi, and Robert attended it for the sake of the company of other children that he would get there. It was Rachel, however, who taught him almost all that he knew, seeing in him from his earliest months what she construed as great promise of intelligence.

So books were sent out from Pontypool, where her sister had moved as a young married woman, and Rachel enrolled herself and Robert in a formal educational correspondence course. And each day when Robert arrived back at the bungalow from school he would sit with his mother, and they would work together beside the single oil lamp as the Ranchi night gathered and closed outside their open windows.

Those were the memories, and they were with Robert for ever. He was too young to lose his parents, and too far away from them when they died. That night in Pontypool, when he returned from the chapel to his aunt's house by the coal tips, his melancholy had given way to a sudden, blinding rage of loss. She had heard, from her bedroom below, the window panes of his room smashing into the street, as one by one he punched them out with his bare knuckles.

Chapter Eight

Robert saw Colin Ewing's car already standing outside the Bavancore office building when he arrived for work, and he smiled to himself at the sight of it. There was no doubt that Sir Arthur Ewing's son was extremely keen to impress.

A member of the Bank's founding family, and the only son of the present Chairman, Colin Ewing was clearly en route through to preferment in the London Head Office. At the age of twenty-nine, he could hardly wait to get on with it.

Robert's guess of what Colin was planning for himself would not have been too far from the mark. These South India offices for perhaps fifteen months, Colin had calculated, certainly no more, then Bombay for twenty-four at most, in charge there of Funding and Treasury of course, though that dreadful old fart Sinna would have to be bustled out of the way to make room for that. Then Singapore for a year and a half as Deputy Managing Director, and Hong Kong for four or five, as perhaps Deputy Managing Director initially, then Managing Director. And finally back to London and Head Office, with just one more rung of the ladder to climb. And then, Colin would tell himself, he would run the whole boiling. As Chairman. Aged forty-five.

And if this was a blueprint for his career that Colin had not as yet shared with anyone else, least of all with his father, who was generally rumoured in the Bank to have limited confidence in his son's intelligence, it would not have surprised others to have known it was in place.

'Colin? You're up early. What can I do for you? You appear to be looking for something.'

Colin Ewing was sitting at Robert's desk, waving an unlit cigar in the air. Two of the drawers were open, and he had clearly been looking through the contents of them. He immediately leapt to his feet as Robert came in, and as the two men faced each other, their differences of dress and stature and presentation were in striking relief.

Robert was neatly but unemphatically dressed; of middle height, he stood there upright, slight, and with the classless competence of the classless professional man. His dark blue lightweight suit was worn, as almost always, with a button-down blue Brooks Brothers shirt and a striped tie, and the greying, short-cut hair was of a groomed but unfussily kempt man in his mid fifties. The piercing directness of the dark brown eyes was in sharp contrast to those of the plump, soft-looking, vacuously smiling young man before him. It was the strength and control of Robert that first impressed – and rightly so, for these were exactly the virtues on which Robert had built his strikingly successful career.

As Robert looked at the young man, his initial sense of mild amusement gave way to irritation. This was immediately apparent, though Robert himself didn't realise this; he never had. His was a face that carried his moods and reactions with a clarity that most found distinctly unsettling. He was intellectually dominant and he was articulate, and, in the self-confidence that his professional position and success had given him, he was inclined to an abruptness in his dealings with those around him that many found merciless and unyielding.

He wasn't a bully exactly, for no one would say that Robert was given to humiliating his inferiors, whether those of mind or of position. But his dismissive response to what he perceived as incompetence or inadequacy in others was all too clear, and his reputation in the Bank was that of a brilliant but remote and unmovable man. He carried with him respect and prestige, but there was fear of him as well, and jealousy too, though of this he was only dimly aware.

'It's not me you're supposed to be compliance and security auditing,' he said. 'And you won't find a lot in there anyway, I'm afraid. I'm only here for a week. And actually, I keep all the personally incriminating material under my bed, and the rest of it in a knocking shop I've discovered down in the port.'

As he said this, Robert felt a familiar prickle of self-dislike and discomfort at his assumption of the conventional vocabulary of philistine, locker-room badinage. He lacked facility in these ritualised exchanges, he felt clumsy in their articulation, and he despised ingratiation of this sort either in himself or in others.

'Ha ha. Very good, Robert.'

Robert reflected how plump young men who prided themselves on their bonhomie so frequently had laughs as cold as sin, and looked at him with a sudden shot of distaste. Colin was wiping the sweat from his brow, the regimental red braces under his grey linen suit making of him, for that moment in Robert's eyes, an absurd caricature of the Englishman in the tropics.

'Just looking for a match for the cigar. Here early because I couldn't sleep last night. The air conditioner made a noise like a diesel train. Better off at work.'

Difficult to blame him for being a member of the Ewing family, but he'll have to prove his competence to me, just as anyone else in the Bank of his age group has to do, Robert thought. He looks to me at this stage of our acquaintance to be an over-privileged, unintelligent and untalented young man. And I rather deduce his father feels much the same way about him.

As if on cue, Colin Ewing said, 'Father's always asking after you. Most warmly. Most warmly.'

Robert looked at him with renewed distaste. He feels nervous of me of course, he thought. That's why he's going through this nonsense of a conversation. Hanging on to his father's name like a handstrap on the bus. He'll hate himself for doing it, when he thinks back on it. Which will probably make him dangerous in any position of authority, however minor.

Robert's gaze on him and the attendant dismissal in his eyes brought a violent flush and sweat to Colin's face. He started to stutter something about realising that Robert and his father spoke to each other on the telephone at least several times a day, and that he knew how closely they worked together, and how much his father depended on him, and more on these lines, but was rescued from further discomfort by a knock on the door.

The region's Chief Clerk, Gupta, came in with some papers for Robert to sign, and Colin thankfully took this opportunity to escape, mopping himself as he went, and calling out an effusive greeting to the Manager of the Bavancore office, who had evidently just arrived. Before he disappeared, Colin put his head back into Robert's doorway.

'Robert – I wonder if I might have a talk with you a little later. Could you spare the time? Would that be all right? In private, if I may – say in half an hour?'

Robert nodded his agreement without looking up from his papers. He shuffled through the documents, scribbled his signature, half smiled his thanks to Gupta, got up from his chair, and walked across to the window to gaze out at the street below.

Amongst the throngs of people Robert saw an old man's corpse on its litter, held shoulder-high at each corner by four young men. They trotted along with it through the crowds, bound no doubt for the burning *ghats* at the far end of town.

Robert remembered the first dead body he had ever seen. Much like this, it had been an old man on a litter, being carried by his sons through the streets of Tollygunge. The palms of the old man's hands and the soles of his feet had been painted for the occasion a bright raspberry pink, and some flowers were thrown loosely across his supine body.

A passing car, perhaps a taxi, had caught the leg or the ankle of one of the young men as it drove by. He had fallen, and the old man's corpse had tipped to the ground after him. In what had seemed an instant, the crowds had gathered around the car and the driver and refused to let him move. They forced the doors open, dragged the driver out, and there was a savage cameo of fists and shouting and flailing of staves and kicking at his head as he lay fallen. The image of the affair most sharply branded on Robert's memory was that of a small child, a boy of perhaps two or three, gazing out from the back window, his face, and particularly his eyes, contorted with terror, and his mouth open in what seemed to be a silent, terminal scream.

India. The raw, bleeding, stark images of India. I've been coming here, on and off, for my entire working life, thought Robert, and whereas the colour and the passion and the sheer smell of the place used to intoxicate me, now they don't. The cruelties and the pain of it disgust me as I grow older.

I want order and peace in all that I touch. I just don't have the energy for India any more. I'm bored with corruption, and I'm bored with incompetence and with muddle. I've no patience left for the mess and failure and bungling ineptitude of it all. I want structure, and discipline, and I want things to work.

I used to love India as so many of my countrymen have before me. I remember where the love sprang from, but I can no longer rekindle it.

Chapter Nine

There were just the two of them in the dining room for lunch that day, and Robert was glad when he saw that he was to be alone with C.P. Nerappan, the Chairman of the Indian affiliate, and the oldest friend Robert had in the Bank.

'Colin Ewing, in my view, is a pain in the neck,' Nerappan was saying as they sat there together at the end of the meal, their coffee cups before them. 'An utter pain in the neck... and you can imagine my guilt at admitting that to you. Because of his father. Winchester together, and friends then, and all that followed that. I should have been more hospitable and charming to his son.

'But I'm longing to be rid of the fellow. It's not fair of me of course, but he irritates me considerably. Nepotism irritates me; it always has. Which coming from an Indian is rich, I grant you. But if he'd been any good, why didn't he make his life somewhere else, instead of tucking himself under his father's wing in his so-called Family Bank? He has to be a coward. I'm convinced I dislike him. Or would dislike him, if I was making the slightest effort to get to know him.'

He suddenly laughed, the inimitable wheezing, bronchial, fat man's quality of it terminating in the gasps and coughs that always made Robert laugh as well, even though he had no idea what the sudden source of C.P.'s amusement was.

'I tell you who that boy reminds me of...' Nerappan gasped,

and then the telephone rang, and Nerappan's voice as he got up to answer it, initially still chuckling, became crisp, irritable, and authoritative as he concentrated on what was being asked of him.

'Yes. Nerappan. No, I'm afraid we can't. No, we can't. I'm afraid the decision is firm. Absolutely firm. No – that's my final word on it. Absolutely my final word.'

As the telephone conversation continued, Robert listened and thought that he was not surprised that there were aspects of C.P. Nerappan's personality and style that grated very badly on some of those who worked with him. The facetiousness could have a cruel edge to those he considered his inferiors. His mockery of the accents and delivery of his less-educated countrymen was considered by many to be neither amusing nor gracious; his cleverness neither lightly borne, nor tactfully selective.

In all, there were rigours in friendship with C.P. Nerappan, and Robert felt them as much as anyone did. Not least in the need to heal and tidy up some of the carnage of damaged sensibilities that he tended to leave in his wake. But Robert, always tested and often infuriated by him, remained a friend to C.P. Nerappan as constant as only those who have a shortage of friendship in their lives will be. He had known him for twenty-five years; he felt a loyalty to him beyond that he felt for anyone else in the Bank. He might have doubted, on occasions, whether C.P. Nerappan held quite the same degree of loyalty to him but, whether so or not, it was of little consequence. Robert liked C.P. Nerappan very much indeed.

The receiver was dumped down on its rest, and Nerappan came back to the table, muttering an obscenity.

'C.P., C.P. – calm down! Ten minutes of inconsequential reminiscence before we both go back to work. Mine first. I was in a reverie driving to the office this morning about my past. Years before you and I met. The pimply grammar-school boy in box-wallah Calcutta. Twenty-one years old. Plain, uninteresting and socially maladroit. Very nearly turned down for the Tollygunge Club, until the Bank put up a fuss. Too rough for the ladies.'

'They would certainly have thought you looked like a wog, my dear fellow,' said Nerappan. 'Terrified you were one. I've sometimes wondered myself. Too sallow in the skin. Brown eyes. Dark hair. Most suspicious accent. You claim it to be Welsh, but who can be sure of that? I'm not in the least surprised they wanted to turn you down. They would have done entirely the right thing.'

Robert smiled, and raised his hand to thank one of the office messengers, who had brought in a note for him to read. He did so quickly, then pushed it to one side and continued, 'Not as bad as that, but almost. I was, of course, about the first non-gentleman that the Bank brought out to India as a graduate trainee. And they certainly went the whole hog with me. I was unmistakably working class, and quite hopelessly unsuited socially to what I thought the Bank expected from me when I arrived here. The Tollygunge Club business made me feel alienated and isolated. And severely underestimated. And, as a result, determined to be extremely successful. To end up on top.'

'My dear Robert, you have an astonishing capacity for self-pity. Rather pompous self-pity, to be frank with you, which transmutes into self-aggrandisement and rather unpleasantly aggressive business-school platitudes – from which I imagine we're all supposed to draw a salutary lesson. You even deliver that sort of statement in a declamatory, ornate style which sounds as if you were giving your Reith lecture.

'I know the Tollygunge Club. It's the most insufferable place. I was taken there for lunch with my father when I was home from Oxford one winter. And we had to sit there to witness a conversation between our English host and his friend discussing, most fearfully and portentously, the implications of the fact that the first Indian had just been admitted to the place as a member. What an idiot the Indian must have been, whoever he was. Allowing himself to be put up for membership in the first place.

'My father thought the most amusing way to react would be to profess a wonder and admiration for the Club's great liberal wisdom and generosity in making such a brave decision. I remember he risked a comment, most beautifully acted, as always with him, suggesting that a step such as the one they had taken was a gesture that might finally seal the permanence of friendship between our two nations. Not only did they agree, they insisted on drinking a toast to it.

'What pricks. What pricks. Oh dear, oh dear. What pricks!'

The gasps and the wheezing started all over again, to the point that Robert thought he should ask him if he was all right.

'Of course, of course. And I will say one thing for you English. Or you Welsh or whatever you are.' He went though a further period of expectoration and nose-blowing before he was restored.

'I'll say one thing. You do have the most marvellous vocabulary. I do love the word Prick. Pricks. Lingam. Lingam. We have no equivalent in the vernacular. Hindi lacks the capacity of the English language to provide an onomatopoeic emphasis and attack through the use of consonants. Pricks. Pricks. Very good.'

'C.P.. Look, I have a meeting to go to with the Bank's local lawyers, and God knows how many calls to make to London. And Colin Ewing has asked to talk with me in a moment – I assume about the compliance and security audit. Why don't we—'

'What does Colin Ewing want with you? Why isn't he dealing with this through me? What did he say he wanted?'

'These audits are purely automatic, C.P., you know that. He'll do all the ferreting under your wing. But my committee has the final responsibility, as you appreciate, and I assume that's what he wants to talk to me about. He's never done one of these things before. Wants to check the rules, I imagine.'

Nerappan muttered something under his breath as they both pushed back their chairs and set off together to leave the room.

'I don't want you to go back to London next week,' Nerappan turned to Robert. 'I shall miss you quite dreadfully. And you'll miss me. It's only when you're here that we ever have a chance to see each other properly. You have no other friend but me. Deny it if you wish, but it's true. Everyone else is too frightened of you; I'm not in the least. And who else am I going to talk to when you've gone? Who else will discuss the relative consonant structure of the phallic noun in English and Hindi? Who else . . .'

He shrugged, patted Robert on the arm, and turned to go into his office. Robert nodded and smiled at Nerappan's assistant, and went on down the passage.

'Don't romanticise me, my dear Robert.' He could remember the conversation now, one night perhaps six or seven years ago, in the garden of C.P.'s house up in the hills. 'Don't look to find in me something that isn't really there. You love me because you think of me as an idealised personification of your love affair for India. An India which is itself an idealised perception of what the country actually is.

'But the truth is that I have lost the essence of my own nation, whatever that essence is. Winchester, Oxford, a professional life as a banker in an English bank, the books I read, the movies I see, the theatre and the concerts that I flock to the moment I'm in London or New York, the language I speak most comfortably. All these things.

'I'm not English, but I've ceased to be an Indian. Particularly South Indian. I've become an observer of my own country. A satirist. A lampoonist. A poseur. I warn you, Robert, don't romanticise me. Give me the compliment of accepting me for what I am. You'll find me the more interesting if you do. And you'll find India the more interesting if you learn to love it as a serious man would. With knowledge and realism. And compassion if you want, but without sentimentality.'

Perhaps he's right, Robert thought as he pressed the bell for the Chief Clerk. Perhaps C.P., and to a lesser extent his wife, are no longer close to the essence of what India really is. Perhaps India is too prolix and mixed and vast to have an essence. Perhaps I haven't the first idea what I'm talking about. But there hasn't been enough friendship in my life, and I very badly feel the longing for it. And he's right – C.P.'s the closest friend I've got. Which is not, perhaps, saying a lot. And if I feel the need to romanticise him in consequence of that, then I shall certainly do so.

As Gupta came into the room in response to the bell he found

Robert, most unexpectedly, leaning back in his chair, his arms behind his head. It was the first time since Robert had arrived in Bavancore that Gupta had seen him smile, except for half-conscious gestures of thanks to him and to the other members of the staff. He was, if anything, somewhat disoriented and discomfited by it. Then Robert said: 'What's the most perfectly formed word in the English language, Gupta? A prize for you if you get it right.'

There was a moment's pause as Gupta rapidly adjusted his mode of thought to a day-time parlour game.

'I always like the word *whisper*, Mr Luscombe. Or *aspen*. As in *aspen leaves*, though I have no idea what an *aspen* looks like if I am honest. Or *window* is a very beautiful word. *Window*.'

'Good, but wrong. No prize. The correct answer is *prick*, Gupta. I have a definitive ruling today on the matter from your Chairman. Now – what is your position on the Poonjee Dam financing? Did our consortium do well, or could we have got a better deal? Or is it all water under the bridge?'

As Gupta laughed, Robert held up his hand to stop him, and smiled at him with affection. It was the first time in their years of acquaintance that Gupta had exchanged with him any conversation whatsoever but that of rigid formality, but Robert had always liked him.

'You're an extremely nice man, Gupta, and you've the most exquisite manners. No one, and I mean no one, would have attempted to pretend an amusement with that joke but you. You're an extremely nice man.'

As Gupta left the room, Robert watched him with a mixture of fondness and exasperation. I'm not at all sure that my envy for that sort of man is either intelligent or realistic, he thought. He's so thoroughly nice, or appears to be so thoroughly nice, that I probably ascribe to him all sorts of personal and familial happinesses and contentments that he very likely doesn't possess at all. He has a large family, I know that, and I position him in my mind, because of the gentleness of manner that he shows here in the office, as a man blessed with total and blissful domestic harmony.

And that both sentimentalises him, as C.P. would put it, and probably patronises and undersells him as well.

Because I myself have been an inadequate father, and quite certainly an indifferent husband, I tend to attribute quite unrealistic qualities of familial goodness and constancy to men of Gupta's type.

There's a falseness and a lack of perception in a judgement of that sort. And a sense of personal guilt. Most certainly that.

Chapter Ten

The door to Robert's office stood wide open, as he normally kept it, but there was now a rap on it despite that, and Robert looked up to find Colin Ewing standing there.

His body was bent forward in a bow, his hands pressed together in stage Indian sycophancy, his head tipped to one side, and his eyebrows raised in farcical comic enquiry.

'Free, Mr Luscombe, *sahib*? May a humble man enter?'

You're a better man than that, Robert thought. You perform all this nonsense of facetious voices and actorly over-familiarity when you're with me because you're frightened of me. But you must be better than that; you're more interesting than that.

'Colin. You'd better close the door,' Robert said, then hearing the coldness apparent in his voice, he made an effort to smile at the young man as he beckoned him into the room. 'You wanted me?'

Colin felt through his pockets for a match to light his cigar, and sat in the chair to which Robert pointed him. When he spoke it was, to Robert's relief, in his normal voice.

'Robert, I assume that my brief in this compliance and security audit is to report to you directly, as is usual? Or rather to you as head of the Deputy Chairman's committee – is that right? The Board will have the opportunity to see the report, but the responsibility for the audit's conduct, and the application and enforcement of the findings is yours, right? Usual rules? Nothing odd about this one, despite the fact that we operate here as a joint venture with Indian investors? I've never done one of these things before. I want to make sure I'm not going to make a cock-up of it.' He laughed, self-consciously.

'Yes,' Robert replied. 'That's how it's done. Each of our offices is compliance and security audited about once every four years. More often if we think there may be something amiss. We treat our joint ventures, such as this one in India, as if they were fully owned. You've seen the rules in the papers you were sent from my office. I suggest you look through those again. You'll note that you're free to enrol the services of any outside party you wish – including the local auditors, of course. Though you realise that much of the point of these exercises of ours is to audit the auditors ... ever since that Venezuela business in 1968, or whenever it was!'

'I've never really known that story. What exactly happened?'

'Oh – a major fraud. By our standards anyway. Bribes going in every direction possible, including to the auditors. It had been going on for years, apparently. We only realised what had happened when a member of staff reported it – probably because he was piqued at not being given a large enough share or something like that. It all happened before I was anywhere near being on the Board, I'm glad to say.'

'Why have I been asked to lead this one here?'

'All of the Bank's senior executives are responsible for at least two compliance and security audits over the course of their careers. We keep the process within the Bank, rather than have it done by outsiders. The theory is that we get more informed results that way. It's also felt to be good training for the person doing it. And the other way round too. It enables the Bank to get a feeling for the quality of the manager who leads the search. His or her real understanding of how the place works. How money flows through the system. How access to it can be controlled. How reliable the reporting processes are. How open the management is in divulging bad news. Those sorts of things.

All of which is reasonably straightforward.

'But there are more subtle issues too. For example, we can see the degree to which the compliance and security auditor can separate personal friendships and loyalties from his or her moral and professional duty. And – what always interests me – the reverse of that. How he or she can hold duty to friends, in the light of moral responsibilities. Or let's say again professional responsibilities. The two concepts sometimes get confused with each other.'

'But why this one for me?'

'It's time, or approaching it, that you did your first audit. And you happened to be here in South India, and we can't get you up to Bombay before next June. And . . .' Robert hesitated, remembering C.P.'s remark about nepotism, and at the same time finding himself oddly reluctant to hurt and insult the young man ' . . . and because your father said to me that he would like you to do it, when he knew that this office was the next one on the list. He thought it would be a good one for you to crack your teeth on, no doubt, with such a strong local Chairman in charge as C.P. Nerappan, who would stop you from making any too embarrassing errors.'

Robert looked across at Colin, and saw him for the first time as an overweight, vulnerable schoolboy, whose ego and boisterous humour and red braces and all the rest were statements of an adolescent's unease and lack of self-confidence.

So Robert said to him, almost affectionately, trying to reduce the customary curt articulacy of his voice to something a touch less formal and emphatic, 'And I will too, if you'll let me. Do remember that. I should get going right away, if I were you. You'll find you'll need every minute you've got if this report is to be in on time in three months. And it does have to be. Get going now, and let me know the moment you need help.'

Robert got to his feet, and Colin Ewing followed him.

'What do I do about C.P. Nerappan, Robert?'

'Follow the brief. Prepare for him a blueprint of your audit, and the people you wish to examine. You should give him written warning of the trail you intend to follow, of the documents you wish to examine, and the people you want to interview. All appointments have to be made through his office, and he can refuse to give you access to material if he thinks that would constitute a security risk in itself. But he must then get written permission from me or my immediate staff for that withholdment, countersigned by you.

'C.P. knows the ropes backwards, so don't worry about it. This must be the third or fourth compliance and security audit this office has had over the years. And he's done at least two for us of his own. One in Australia if I recall, and certainly one in Singapore. He found a rather pathetic little incident there of theft which we had to clean up. He saw it before he'd been in the place two days. Goodness knows what the locals thought they were doing.'

The two of them walked over to the door together.

'Sarah and I leave for England on Thursday of next week, as you know. Today is Tuesday. Why don't you and I have an hour or so together before I go? Say a week today. You can tell me how things are going. You won't have made much progress by then, so don't worry about that. But you might like me to mark your card a little.'

Colin turned to leave, then Robert added, 'Colin – tread just a little bit carefully. I don't mean that you shouldn't do the job properly. Heaven forbid. Just that you shouldn't throw your weight around too quickly at them all. Not until you've found your feet. You know what I mean.' He made a shrugging gesture, and smiled again.

'Of course, Robert. Of course, of course. I know exactly what you mean. And C.P. is such a living legend. Deservedly so. His office is run by very serious folk, which is more than one can say of the London office, in my opinion. Don't you agree? Spend their whole time at Ascot and Glyndebourne as far as I can see. Your lot excepted, of course. And Bermuda. And pinching their secretaries' bottoms.' He looked at Robert directly, his eyes screwed up as he drew heavily once more at his cigar.

Robert bit his lip to stop himself from being very forthright indeed to this young man. That remark, he thought, was straying towards the downright impertinent. How much Colin Ewing reminded him when he acted like this of a certain sort of back-bench politician; astute but philistine, compulsively ambitious, garrulous, eager to please, devious, plotting.

And as he looked at him now, he was for the first time uneasy about the audit, though for no defined reason. The Indian operation was well run and highly efficient, and it always had been. But it was a simple matter to find fault if one was trying hard enough to do so. And there was little doubt that Colin would be trying to find it. And the result of all that might be wholly unnecessary strife and turmoil for all sorts of people. More Brownie points for the young Turk, but a considerable nuisance for everyone else.

At that moment Gupta came around the corner clutching some files, and he pushed himself against the wall at the sight of Robert and Colin talking together in the passageway.

'Ah, Gupta,' said Robert. 'Hello. This is as good a moment as any to tell you that Mr Ewing is to lead the compliance and security audit here that we are due to carry out. We were going to announce it next week, but we thought we might as well get it under way now, while I'm still in India. So give him all the help he needs. As if you wouldn't.'

'Of course, Mr Luscombe. Of course. Is there anything particular I can help you with at this stage, Mr Ewing?'

'Oh, I'm just going to play around with the snippets to start with,' said Colin. 'Just ferret around in the trough for a few days to get the feel of it all. Just a good snoop. You know the sort of thing.'

He bellowed with laughter, Gupta giggled – rather oddly – in response, and Robert set off again for his own office, raising his hand as he went, as if in benediction. As he reached the door, he turned again and called after them.

'Colin – I'll call straight down to C.P.'s office to say that we've talked, and that you're to start right away. I should make an appointment to see him today.'

An Imperfect Marriage

He waved again, and this time shut his office door as he went into the room. The passage outside carried the smoke of Colin's cigar, and Robert was second to no man in his hatred of the smell of tobacco.

Chapter Eleven

Robert looked at his watch. Colin Ewing had arranged to see him at three o'clock, and it was almost that now. He rang down to his office.

'Could you come up to talk about things now, Colin? I've got quite a lot to get out of the way before I leave on Thursday evening, so I'd like to get on with it, if that suits you. Coming up?'

He was on his haunches checking files in the bottom drawer of the filing cabinet when Colin came in, having knocked formally on the door.

To Robert's relief he saw that Colin was not going to impose on him one of his music-hall Indian impersonations. He came in looking most purposeful and serious. Under his arm he was carrying a large leatherbound file box, and, as he sat down on the other side of Robert's desk, he put this in front of him, opened the lid, and laid before both Robert and himself two identical files, these marked, under their *Controlled Circulation Only* heading, as:

THE POONJEE RIVER DAM PROJECT FINANCING: DRAFT OVERVIEW BY COLON EWING.

Robert put a pencil line through the O and replaced it with an I.

'Colin, I always understood, not Colon,' he murmured. 'Makes you sound like a gambler off a Mississippi riverboat somehow. Or a man with notorious flatulence.'

'Damn!' said Colin, and gave his bellow of laughter. 'I told you this was a draft, Robert. Lucky it's just for you and me. I wanted you to look at this before you went. I've had to rush at it obviously but I'd be glad if you would point out any obvious gaps or mistakes in my understanding.'

'Yes, of course. But you've not been told just to look at the Poonjee River deal, as you know. It's obviously been at the top of everyone's minds in this office for the last year or so, but you've been detailed to do a compliance and security audit on all operations here, not just Poonjee.'

'I know, Robert. But it's been such an overwhelmingly important issue for everyone here – and in London too, of course, but much of the work was done here, so I do think it's necessary to start with this, work it through, and make sure that all is in order in the way that we handled the transaction before I move on to other issues. I think I've got to do it in that way, actually. I never really got to grips with Poonjee myself, as I arrived here when the deal was over and done with. Apart from anything else, I'd like to know how all you maestros pulled it off.'

He gave his great bellow of laughter, and took a cigar out of his pocket, before catching Robert's eye. He flushed and put it back, unlit.

'C.P. and the team here were the maestros, Colin,' Robert replied. 'Not us in London. We just applauded from the wings, and gave the odd nudge and push. But fine – do it as you wish, though we will expect you to have completed the entire audit within three or four months at the latest. So don't get so tied down on Poonjee that you don't have time for anything else. However, let me read this for a moment, and I'll tell you if the basic facts are correct and if you're starting off in the right direction.'

Robert put his hand over his eyes, and started to read the summary, making as he did so some quick pencilled notes in the margins. After a few minutes of this he pushed it aside, and said, 'Talk me through it for now, Colin, and we'll see what you've got. It looks fine, but you explain it to me.'

Colin reached across to retrieve his paper, and put it in front of him. He glanced through Robert's copy of it for a few moments then said, 'Well, what I've laid out here is this. Firstly, I explain something about the region overall. The Poonjee River is one of the dominant watercourses in South India, and should in theory be able to provide ample irrigation resources for whatever agricultural programmes there might be. But apart from the tea gardens in the Nilgiri Hills, nothing quite works in this part of the world. Poor irrigation and poor crop control, mostly. And mostly the former.

'There's plenty of rainfall, but it's concentrated almost entirely of course in the monsoon months. They get good reliable monsoons, but there's dramatically poor water conservation, made worse by severe deforestation. Only five per cent of the ground area has been left as it was. So we've got to the position, now that they've ripped away the forests, where eighty per cent of the monsoon rainfall simply runs away into the sea. The forests were there to act as natural reservoirs, but no one seemed to care. So now we're all set here to become a second Ethiopia.'

He looked up. 'With me so far? The plot unfolds?'

Robert waved him on, and tried not to show an irritation in the gesture. Colin looked back at his paper.

'Well, this is all the more galling, as in many ways this is one of the most promising areas of India. Possibly *the* most promising area of India. The population growth is well under control, there's good, stable, sophisticated local government, albeit Communist by persuasion, and educational standards are first-rate. Literacy in the English language is substantially higher here than anywhere in the country.

'So along comes the World Bank, in 1988, and writes a very interesting report. They tell the Indian Government that Maduram could be of crucial importance in India's development, if only this business of water storage and distribution could be sorted out. And the Government of India, who can smell a deal when there's one around, promptly asks them for two billion dollars, US, to do just that.'

He looked up to Robert once more and continued.

'So, after a good deal of chat, all is arranged. India gets its two billion, on the basis that the money is used only for the project proposed – the damming of the Poonjee, and the construction of a huge reservoir in the Trincampore Valley. And the World Bank is to get it all back in twenty years, including rolled-up interest of three per cent compound.

'And one thing more – and this is where we come in: the entire amount, roughly four billion dollars with the rolled-up interest, has to be underwritten by a consortium of international banks. Otherwise the World Bank won't do the deal. So – blah, blah, blah . . .' Colin read speedily on through the final sections of his paper again, to remind himself of the detail ' . . . blah, blah . . . four consortiums or consortia, or whatever they are, get in competition for this business. And the one we're in wins.

'The Indian Government has to pay our consortium a royalty of a very nice one and a half per cent per annum on the whole four billion dollars for twenty years, but they've got themselves underwritten on the back of the contract, so they're in the clear with the World Bank. And they choose our bid, because the other three consortia wanted a higher annual royalty: the deal with our consortium was the most attractive so far as the Indians were concerned.'

He made eye contact again with Robert. 'We have a twenty per cent share of the consortium's risk, so we get twenty per cent of the annual royalty income. That's worth over ten million dollars a year to us. Or enough to add seven or eight per cent to our profits before tax, as you know. A considerable deal.'

'Yes,' said Robert. 'A considerable deal. The news of it in London moved our market capitalisation substantially. Our shares went to a new high and we entered the FTSE 100 for the first time in our history. You're quite right. It mattered very much to us.'

He put his hands behind his head, and gazed at Colin for a few moments.

'But your paper then goes on to some very interesting areas. Some very uncomfortable areas. And, again, you're quite right. The

59

royalty income, stretching as it does over a period of fully twenty years, is a godsend to our earnings over that period. But, and here's the rub, if there's a default by the Indians at the end of the day, we're liable for a fifth of the underwriting exposure. Which would mean we would have to find seven hundred and fifty million dollars or more. On a forty-eight-hour call. Forty-eight hours . . . an unsettling prospect, for a bank of our size.'

'Yes,' said Colin, looking now at the final sheets of his paper. 'That's right. But that's not in itself the point of my audit.'

He paused, then said abruptly: 'This is what's the point of my audit, I think. Am I right?' He took one of the pages, and pushed it across to Robert. It read:

8. MAIN AREAS OF INTEREST FOR COLIN EWING'S SECURITY AUDIT

a) Conduct of the Consortium Negotiators

* How were the member banks for the consortium recruited?

* How were the proportionate % stakes of the member banks of the consortium fixed?

* Did the consortium apply illegal or unethical industrial or diplomatic intelligence to ensure that our tender was the one selected by the Government of India?

* Did the consortium apply illegal or unethical pressure or persuasion on the negotiators of the Government of India?

* Did the consortium negotiators secure any personal reward or gain from the success of the tender?

b) Conduct of the Bank's Officers

* Did any officer, employee, shareholder, trading partner,

professional advisor, or any other person or body connected with the Bank take any measure in the negotiation and/or conclusion of the Poonjee deal which led, directly or indirectly, to personal gain? If so, was this disclosed?

* Did any person or body, as above, conceal any vested interest in the success of the consortium's offer?

* Was the professional conduct of the Bank's negotiators in this transaction at all times within the Bank's traditions of honour and veracity?

Robert read this through twice, took off his glasses, and looked across at Colin.

'Yes,' said Robert. 'That's it, I suppose. It reads a little simplistically in some ways, but yes – that's it. Well done. A good summary.'

He was silent for a moment, then looked down again at the papers on his desk. He said, 'Somehow I hadn't anticipated that you would want to explore the Poonjee deal in such a way, Colin. But I can't say that you're wrong to do so, though an audit of this complexity, involving as it does some powerful outsiders, and some very big numbers indeed, is, I would have thought, outside your scale. Considerably outside your scale. Or let's say experience. Which is not to insult you. But we couldn't allow you to make a fool of yourself, or of course the Bank, in a thing of this magnitude. Also – I have to say that we have no reason whatsoever to believe that anything is untoward.'

'Isn't that rather the point of these compliance and security audits?' Colin said. 'That's what my father has always told me. To explore things that nobody would have ever thought needed exploring. To look into areas that no one would ever suspect needed looking into. That's why I've added that final clause, the one about the upholding of the Bank's traditions of honour and veracity. What the founding families always remind us about.'

He laughed, but with a slight hint of insecurity in his voice. 'Robert, I do think I should have a go at this, you know. I really do. I think it should be done. There'll be nothing there, I know that. But you have given me the responsibility for doing the audit here in this region, and it seems to me it would be very odd if we looked at everything else but the one deal that really mattered.'

Robert gazed at him steadily, his hands locked again behind his head. Then: 'It's difficult to say no. You're quite right. Go ahead then. But please don't make a single move that will get you or the Bank in trouble. Be sensitive enough to know what you're doing. Consult with me at all times. *At all times.* Please promise me that. Actually, I order you to do so. It's an order.'

'Oh, I absolutely promise you that, Robert. I absolutely do.'

Robert continued to study him, grimacing in a slow, oddly melancholic smile as he so often did. Then: 'It's good training for you, Colin, if nothing else. And who knows, perhaps someone *has* overstepped the mark somewhere, some place, some time. It can happen in the heat of the battle. Sometimes for the best of reasons. It's possible something of that sort may have happened here. I don't think so – but it's possible. Anyway do the research, get it done, but don't spend unnecessary time rushing up blind alleys.

'This is an important part of the world for us, quite apart from Poonjee. Deals are being done here all the time. Large amounts of money are being transacted by the hour. You've got quite a trail to follow, and we've given you only three months to do it in. That's not very long.

'So, Colin . . .' and although Robert smiled at him again, there was a note of unmistakable authority in his voice as he spoke, 'I should bustle a bit if I were you. Don't get tied down and diverted by chasing phantoms. And ask other people for help; don't just depend on me. Get as much help as you can, from as many people as you can.'

Colin peered across the desk, and made an elaborate show of trying to decipher the pencilled notes which Robert had scribbled into the margins of the pages he still held. Robert handed them across to him.

'Here, take them. They're just scribbles. I'm not going to add anything particularly helpful. You have the overall picture very well. Maybe I would have put the chronology a little differently, and made a little more in your introduction of the precision of the tendering, highlighting the importance of C.P.'s role in it all. How good he was at reading the minds of the Government of India people. We may only have a twenty per-cent share of the consortium, but all the other banks in it were dependent on C.P. by the end to get it right. I would think that his success in it all rather made his reputation. Not just here in the Bank, but internationally.'

Robert shrugged, then got to his feet and stretched. 'But then I know him very well,' he said. 'Quite probably I'm biased.'

Colin smiled, and also got to his feet. 'Many thanks, Robert. If I don't see you again before tomorrow, I'll be in touch with you when you're back in London. At least every seven days, if I may. I do hear what you say, and I won't do anything silly, I promise you that. Thank you, Robert.'

He gathered up the papers, and walked off towards the door, then looked back over his shoulder. 'Please thank your wife for the invitation to your party. I've replied direct, of course, but do thank her. I look forward to meeting her.'

Robert nodded and smiled and watched the young man as he went, again reflecting that his red braces and his striped Jermyn Street shirt were so absurd a statement of his Englishness and his social standing in this place and this climate.

Then he went back to his desk, took out a little leather-bound notepad from the pocket of his jacket, jotted a few words on it, and put it back again. He sat for some minutes longer, his face frowning in thought.

Perhaps this was one example of how the Bank's passion for self-regulation and policing was not in all cases entirely appropriate. To put it mildly. If the Poonjee affair was going to be investigated at all, it would necessarily mean talking to the other banks in the consortium. Certainly the lead bank. And possibly upsetting them, and running the risk of jeopardising future dealings together. All in the cause of internal policing. It seemed a little excessive. Not a good moment to be stirring the waters.

And yet . . . if Colin Ewing wanted to do it, then it was very difficult to stop him. Or to give him or anyone else in the Bank a credible explanation as to why he should be stopped. And he was right. The founding families had always made the most overwhelming fuss about veracity and honour and all the rest of it. There was that boy who was training in the Bank in the late 1920s or early 1930s, the younger son of the Chairman at the time, who was publicly dismissed and disinherited and turned over to the police in connection with some incident he had been involved in at the Bank, apparently of a very trivial nature. *Pour décourager les autres.*

Let the boy do it, Robert decided. Colin wouldn't be able to find an allsort in a licorice factory, so he's an ironic choice of man for the assignment. But let him do it. *In Veritate Virtus*, or whatever toe-curling motto it is the Bank proclaims to the world.

He was just in the process of making his way over to the filing cabinets again when the telephone rang, and he went back to his desk to answer it.

On the line was C.P. Nerappan, and, as Robert greeted him, C.P. cut him short, his voice sounding grave and heavy and rather hesitant, as if he was most uncharacteristically uneasy about what he had to say.

'Robert, are you alone? Robert, my dear, I have some rather difficult news for you. No, of a personal nature. I'd prefer to tell you to your face, quite frankly. I'll come on up. Straight away.'

Chapter Twelve

Sarah was still in bed when Robert had left for the office that morning. Although awake, she feigned sleep to avoid the need for conversation. She could hear Robert tiptoe out through the bedroom door, then give some hushed direction to one of the servants before the front door closed behind him, and he was gone.

Just two more days to go, she thought. It hasn't worked coming on this trip. I've absolutely hated it. I knew it wouldn't work, and I should never have persuaded Robert to let me come here. Why did I do it? Out of a sense of duty, probably for both of us. I've got so little to do here when he's at the office, and every evening seems to have been spent entertaining someone or other, or being entertained. I don't know anybody, and it's never really me that they want to talk to. It's only Robert they want to be with. Particularly that blessed C.P., and his superior, pseudo-intellectual Mohindra.

Such silly provincial people. They should see me back in London. They would find me a *very* different kettle of fish there, amongst my own friends, and in my own surroundings.

She got out of bed, put a light cotton dressing gown across her shoulders, and went to stand on the little balcony that faced on to the garden and out on to the beach beyond.

There they are, she thought. And as she watched the fishermen, their lithe, black, oily bodies bending and stretching as they pulled at the heavy nets, that tingle of excitement started again in her loins.

Oh dear God. How silly this all is. But it must be one of the things that happens as life goes on. When one gets on a bit. It must happen all the time. And Robert is so cold to me for so much of the time. All the problems I've had over the years have been because of that. Not that there's going to be any mistake or anything now. But it would be his fault if there was. Absolutely his fault.

He doesn't treat me as his wife. And certainly not as his equal. We never have anything to talk about now. He makes no attempt to communicate properly with me – except about the two girls, of course. And that's always a recipe for disaster.

He never says so, but he blames me for what happened to Rowena. He blames me for everything. He never says so, but I know he does: I can see it in his eyes. That look in his eyes of contempt for me, that's always been there. Secret contempt. Never expressed. Just there all the time.

Her eyes went searching for the fishermen again. There's no harm in a little walk along the beach as usual. Nothing wrong with that. Just a stroll to give the *mali*'s puppy a run, and get a breath of fresh air. I needn't behave stupidly or anything again. What's the harm in a little walk?

She went back into the bedroom again, and changed into a light cotton sarong, which she wrapped around her and knotted at the front. She washed her face, brushed her hair, tied it into a bun, then put just a hint of make-up on her mouth and eyes.

No need to wear any pants or anything. It's hot, and no one can see. So difficult to keep cool in this horrible country.

She opened the bedroom door, and started off down the stairs with as light a tread as possible, so that she could slip out without Mustafa making a fuss about breakfast or all the other things he would insist on going on about. But there he was in the hall, looking oddly suspicious and disapproving, though what right he had to be like that with her, goodness alone knows. She would have some papaya and a cup of tea or something like that, anything to keep him quiet, and then she would have her little walk on the beach. She wouldn't go far. Just along to the end, where the boats had been pulled up on to the sand, and she would throw a few sticks for the puppy, and maybe just have a breath of the sea air for a few moments. Sitting on the beach. Or perhaps under the banyan trees there at the end. Just for a moment. No harm in that.

She had her breakfast, then heard Mustafa in the kitchen, arguing with one of the other servants. Shouting away as usual, she thought. Now was the time to just slip out for a moment. She'd eaten his beastly papaya and drunk his nasty thick tea, and she'd be back in no time. And then she could talk with him and that stupid cook about what food they should serve at this awful party they were giving for the Bank's staff tonight. At which Robert would ignore her as usual, no doubt, while he talked with his C.P. and his Mohindra and his other friends. And left her completely alone, as usual.

Sarah put her napkin down on the tray, and went out through the French windows into the garden. There was no sign of the *mali*, nor the puppy, but she went on her way, leaving her shoes in the shade of the bushes by the gate as she always did, then picking up some leaves which she threaded between her fingers as she walked.

First she went straight down to the edge of the surf, and stood there for a minute or two, her hands behind her, her shoulders drawn back, her chin held up. All this so her body, in silhouette, looked young and firm and confident, the cotton sarong, damp a little now at its hem, blowing around her legs.

The fishermen were perhaps a hundred yards away, no more. She could hear them chanting their rhythmic liturgies as they pulled and heaved, then breaking into laughter and loud conversation as they mended the nets and sorted the catch.

Her hands still behind her back, she walked slowly along the wet sand on the water's edge, her head bent down, as if she was deep in thought. She passed where the fishermen were, continued in the same pose for another two or three hundred yards, then turned and walked back towards them. She was still going at no more than a snail's pace, her head bent and her eyes following the wet sand in front of her.

Her heart was thumping now with the excitement of it all, and as she passed the fishermen she turned up the beach beside them, lifting her head and smiling at them as she did so. The trunk of a fallen banyan tree lay on the beach a few yards behind them, and she sat down in its shade, the angle of it, and the curve of the bay, protecting her, she assumed, from the view of the houses dotted around in the trees at the beach's edge.

It was just at the aspect looking out at the sea that she was exposed, she thought. And there were only the fishermen at that angle who could see her. They were looking at her now, and she leant her body back. She let her legs, which were stretched out in the sand, open a few inches, and then a little more. She lay back on the sand and let her knees rise, and, as if snuggling herself into a comfortable position, she wiggled her buttocks a little.

Her heart was pounding now, pounding, and she knew she had no pants on, and she could feel the damp there. She remained still, then separated her knees a fraction wider. She opened her eyes, just a glimpse, no more, and the tall one, the tallest one, was standing right in front of her, looking at her between the legs. The others were behind him, and they were all looking, and now the tall one's loincloth had gone and he was kneeling down in front of her. He pulled up her sarong, and he entered into her, and she clung to him. He pushed, and she pushed, and she pushed with him again, and then she cried out and threw her head back, and it was finished.

She wanted to hold him to her, and to stroke him and to keep him, but he soon dropped out of her, and he separated himself from her and got to his feet. He pulled his loincloth around him again, and then all the fishermen turned and they went back to where they were, and it was over. She could feel his juice oozing from her now, and she lay as still as could be, her arm over her eyes. Her excitement had gone, and she felt unable to move for the shame of it, and in case they would mock her. But when in time she could hear no more voices she did look up, very cautiously and timorously, and she saw that they were walking away now, perhaps two hundred yards distant, in the direction of their shacks on the other side of the bay, and she was all alone.

She got to her feet, and walked, then ran, then walked again until she reached the garden gate. She steadied herself to walk through the garden, and soon she was safely in her bedroom again.

She threw herself down on the bed, her eyes screwed shut.

Dear God, she thought. There was no laughter, nor shouting, nor mocking of me. They never made fun of me. All those days I went on going there, and showing myself like that, but they didn't mock me. He just took me, that man, and then they went away. He took me, as I had been waiting for him to do.

It's over now. I'm going back to London on the day after tomorrow, and it'll never happen again. None of these sorts of things will happen again. They're just juvenile and irresponsible and I mustn't let them happen again. It's not my fault really. I must put this behind me now. Forget about it, and put it behind me. Lots of people do stupid things sometimes. I'm hardly alone in that. Goodness knows what people get up to. I must just put this behind me.

But as she turned over on the bed, she saw, to her shock, that Mustafa was standing in the doorway staring at her. His face was hard and unsmiling, and he grimaced angrily as he turned and shook his head and went off down the stairs.

Chapter Thirteen

Robert sat on the sofa in the corner of his office, sprawled at an angle against the cushions, his head tipped back and his arms crossed over his chest.

'I'm so sorry, Robert. So sorry.'

C.P. had said this, or something like it, every few minutes since he'd told Robert what had happened on the beach that morning, knowing of old that it would be some time before there was any meaningful response from him.

'Robert, I've spoken myself to the Police Superintendent. I know him well, and I can tell you that he is an unusually good man – intelligent, and sensible, and level-headed. He says there is no question of a rape charge. None whatsoever.

'Only the one man touched her, and there are numerous witnesses who will say that she provoked sexual contact with him. Over an extended period. And it's not only the fishermen who will say this. The Bank's bearer at the house – Mustafa, is it? – was watching it all through field-glasses.

'I'm afraid there's been a good deal of talk about Sarah in the bazaar and amongst the servants. I'm told those walks of hers on the beach have been rather odd occasions. They've been carrying on for the last week or so. In fact, since the day you arrived. The Superintendent simply wants no fuss about it, and no attempt to switch any element of the blame on to the fisherman. I'm sorry to be brutal with you, Robert, but we're old enough friends to be truthful with each other.'

There was a long pause while Robert stared first at Nerappan, then out of the window.

'A Passage to bloody India,' he muttered finally. 'Life Imitating Art. Who said anything about rape charges?'

'Well, to be honest with you, Sarah did, but I'm sure that was in panic, when she was cautioned by the police for gross indecency. As I mentioned, there was a complaint from the ICI Manager's wife in the house next door – who no doubt had been standing on a soap box to get a decent view. But she rang the police, and the Superintendent came round to the Bank's house to caution Sarah. But it's a caution only. The Superintendent told me that they weren't going to file charges, and he told Sarah that too – provided there was no nonsense from her, and specifically no attempt to stir up trouble for the fisherman.'

Robert leant forward now, and stuffed his two hands into his pockets. He stared at C.P. with an expression of intense concentration, but there was no pain in his face, nor the dazed, wounded look of the cuckolded husband.

'Christ. Some knee-jerk rape allegation. That's all we need.'

He stared at C.P. still, and was silent for some minutes, his brow creased, his eyes set in concentration. Then: 'Poor Sarah. More failure. More pain to come. More self-justification. More agony about what other people think of her.'

There was a silence again, then C.P. got up and went over to sit on the edge of Robert's desk.

'I'm concerned for you, Robert. I don't want to hurt you or insult you, but I think you must realise that Sarah has always been considered to be a slightly dotty woman by most of us who know you. Actually, an entirely dotty woman. I'm not sure anything she did would be considered damaging to you. Probably the reverse.

'So I don't want you to be ashamed of this, and hide yourself away, or rush off home without saying goodbye to people or any of that. It's imperative that one never shows wounds in this sort of place. The Bank is as competitive as any other male-dominated institution. Your position with us looks so powerful, and *is* so powerful, but you operate not just in the Bank, but in London at large.

'It's very important that you hold your status and your aura. You mustn't look as if you've been hurt. No one will care about what's happening in your family provided you appear privately undamaged by it. People will brush you off the track if they think that you have a fatal wound. It's easier said than done, but you've got to look completely untouched by this. Completely undamaged.'

'Yes, but that's not the point. I'm concerned for Sarah. Of course I'm concerned for her! You may think that she's a dotty woman . . .' C.P. started to protest and apologise, but Robert held up his hand, and cut him short. 'No – that's all right, C.P.. I don't accept that of course, in any way, though I agree that my wife is a troubled woman.

'Sarah finds life difficult. I'm a long way past the stage when I'm hurt personally about anything of this sort. Or when I've got any right to be hurt personally. My own conduct in this marriage has hardly been priestly. It's just that I find life a little easier than she does. For all the disasters of it, I seem to be able to cope. She can't. Of course I'm not going to run away – but she may want to. And it would be very much better for her if she could find the strength not to.'

C.P. smiled at him. 'You know, Robert, there's a morality tale that people tell in this part of the world. You find it in different versions and different guises, but it's a common thread in the Indian psyche. Perhaps it's familiar to you.

'It's the tale of the cobra and the mongoose. They fight, the mongoose has the cobra by the neck, and he's about to plunge his teeth into the snake when he stops and lets the cobra go. So the cobra says to the mongoose, "Why did you let me go?" And the mongoose says, "Because I've killed too many cobra. I kill cobra because I want to rid the jungle of all of you. I don't like the way you look, and I don't like the things you do. But as I was about to kill you, the Devil said to me, 'Let him go. Let him come to me in his own way. He'll come, you'll have what you want. But in coming to me in his own way, he'll let you live as well. The very characteristics in him that you so dislike are the very characteristics that enable you and him to live together. If you kill him, you'll lose your own reason to live' ".'

There was a pause, then Robert said, 'What the hell does all that mean? I've never understood parables. And anthropomorphy has always defeated me completely.'

'The parable means that you and Sarah are mutually interdependent, because of the way you both are. She is dependent on you because you're her only lifeline. She doesn't love you, of course. In fact, I suspect she thinks about you in any way but that. However, you're the only person who can release her from taking responsibility for her own actions – something she seems incapable of doing. And you in your turn are dependent on her just because of that.

'It's like a drug to you. You know that she can't cope without you to blame for everything in her life that goes wrong. And you can't bear to release yourself from the privilege of controlling another human being in that way. So you stay with her. And she stays with you.'

'Too prolix,' said Robert. 'Too prolix, too convoluted, and much too Indian. Balls. I don't know why I stay with her. I don't know why she stays with me. I think you underestimate the sheer inertia of a relationship such as ours. All I know is that I don't want her to be so humiliated by this episode that she is tipped into despair. I don't want to see that happen, for my sake as well as hers. I've been with her in her despair before, and it's a very draining process. I don't want her to go through all that again. Is that so strange? She'll be devastated by what has happened. She has an overwhelming need to be considered a good and decent woman. It's the persona that she's shown to the world all her life. It's her suit of clothes. She must be allowed to wear them. Pious sanctity is her shield. Unassuming piety.'

C.P. moved in his chair. 'I very much dislike religion being aped in that way, to be quite honest with you. I always have done. My exposure as a boy to your Church of England was not a happy one. Give me the noise and the chatter in a Mediterranean Catholic Cathedral, or indeed a Hindu temple, any day of the week. I have a dislike of that brand of reticence that is in itself a pose. Genteel English reticence. Church of England piety.'

Robert looked across at him, and folded his hands behind his head.

'If her reticence is a pose, then so be it. She needs it. We all of us shelter ourselves behind some sort of protective projection of a self-image. All of us. I do. I'm the working-class Welshman who has got through to be Deputy Chairman of a blue-chip English family bank, and has become well known in the City by judgement and intelligence and drive. That's the self-image that I need for myself, and that's the one I deliberately foster. And you do it too. You're the clever, detached, cerebrally maverick Indian who has also succeeded in the same place, despite your colour and race and your eccentric humour. That's the self-image that you need for yourself, and that's the one you foster – particularly the colour and race and humour bits. We both shelter behind these convenient caricatures of what we actually are. They're not true, of course, but they protect us.

'Well – we do it, and so does Sarah. That's all it is. Sarah shelters behind her own caricature and now that protection has disappeared. And she needs it. And I don't want her to break down on me.'

Neither said more for a moment or two, then Robert started to look as if he was about to move, though C.P. stayed motionless in his place.

'I must go, C.P.. I'd better go back to the house now to comfort her, and help her find her self-confidence again. Quickly. I just don't want her to break down. I know what happens when she does. It's very important to me that she doesn't.'

C.P. smiled at him, but remained motionless. 'You're a good

man, Robert. Your concern for her is remarkable.'

Robert's face showed a momentary, unmistakable flicker of irritation. He made a slight movement of his hand, as if in dismissal.

'No, C.P.. You misunderstand me completely. You have all that completely wrong, and I wish you wouldn't say it. I'm anything but remarkable; nor am I a good man, as you insist on putting it. It's not my concern for Sarah that we're talking about. She mustn't break down because I can't face her doing so. That's all I'm talking about – I can't face her doing so. Because I know what it brings. I know what it requires from me in terms of energy, and commitment and stamina.'

'Yes. The stamina, my dear, flows from love. You undersell yourself, Robert. You undersell yourself.'

Robert shrugged his shoulders and started to move from his seat, and as C.P. too got to his feet, he laid his hand on Robert's arm, and they walked together towards the door.

'You undersell yourself in this area, my dear, and I'm interested that you do. There's a good deal of the conventional, unromantic, professional, almost mechanistic banker about you. Of course there is, and it's this that has enabled you to build the career with us that you have. Many people in the Bank actually believe you to be quite alarmingly cold, or so I hear. I find that an extraordinary picture of you. You're a very good banker because you're without fear, and without prejudice, and you have that balance between high intelligence and shrewd judgement that is curiously rare. But you are underneath that, in a different compartment of you, a man who longs for love. And you've never found it.'

Robert raised his hand in farewell, and started off down the passage. 'You do talk in the most astonishing fairy tales, C.P., but you're important to me, and you know that. Thank you for telling me about Sarah. But let's leave it there. I must go.'

But C.P. called out to Robert again just as he was about to turn the corner. First he made to walk straight on, then he hesitated, and looked back at him.

'I assure you that what you are actually doing all the time, my dear, is looking for love,' C.P. said cheerfully. 'And you've never found it. You've never come anywhere near finding it. You've searched all your life, and all you've found is an illusion. It looks more than that, but it is in fact only that.

'What have you come up with? A demonstrable parental love for your troubled daughter perhaps; a rather remote if ineffective care of your wife; an exquisite regret for your parents – certainly those – but . . .' and now C.P. shrugged as well, throwing his arms open, a smile beaming across his face, then his hand too was raised in farewell.

How C.P. adores these games of conjecture and manipulation with other people's lives, Robert thought, hurrying down to his car. How dangerous he can be. Even to someone like me. After all these years.

Chapter Fourteen

The car in which Robert was being driven back to their house had been stationary for some time, trapped behind a rickshaw that had collapsed with a broken axle and strewn itself across the narrow lane. A little girl, dressed in an immaculate sari, stood at the side, up against the wall, rubbing occasionally and stoically at her knee. It seemed that she had been travelling in the rickshaw with her grandfather, who was now standing beside her, apoplectic and incandescent in his anger at what had happened.

It was the expression on her face that made Robert think of Rowena at much this age. There looked to be a calmness there, and a detachment from the raging around her that to many would have looked to be serenity. But that, Robert told himself, was where I went wrong with Rowena. That was how I lost her. I thought her composure and her physical courage and her control as a child was a quality in her of containment and peace. But that wasn't the case at all. It wasn't peace. It was unhappiness.

Rowena at fifteen. Solitary in her bedroom all day, writing her novel. Her second novel, as far as Robert knew. He'd seen the first. He had gone to her room one day when she was on an overnight trip from school, and, for one reason or another, had looked inside her desk. He found there the handwritten manuscript, and had sat on her bed for the following two hours or so to read it. The novel was named 'A Poem Called Absolutely Nothing', and in the preliminary pages was copied out a piece of verse that Robert had never seen previously. Written, Rowena had stated there, by a fifteen-year-old boy shortly before he committed suicide.

'This poem is dedicated to the poet's memory,' she wrote. 'He is unknown. But his poem deserves to live for ever.'

> *'Once . . . he wrote a poem.*
> *And he called it "Chops",*
> *Because that was the name of his dog, and*
>   *that's what it was all about.*
> *And the teacher gave him an "A".*
> *And a gold star.*
> *And his mother hung it on the kitchen door,*
>   *and read it to his aunts . . .*
>
> *Once . . . he wrote another poem.*
> *And he called it "Question Marked Innocence",*
> *Because that was the name of his grief, and*
>   *that's what it was all about.*
> *And the professor gave him an "A"*
> *And a strange and steady look.*
> *And his mother never hung it on the kitchen door*
>   *because he never let her see it . . .*
>
> *Once at 3 a.m. . . . he tried another poem . . .*
> *And he called it absolutely nothing, because*
>   *that's what it was all about.*
> *And he gave himself an "A"*
> *And a slash on each damp wrist,*
> *And hung it on the bathroom door because he*
>   *couldn't reach the kitchen.'*

Robert had put the manuscript down after a hundred pages or so, reread the poem several times more, then retied the handwritten sheets back with their ribbon and replaced them in the drawer of her desk.

Had Rowena been like this from her earliest years? Had there never been peace within her? Could he ascribe it all to her adolescence, or would that be cheating himself of the truth?

Those solitary rides on the underground she described, pointlessly out to the furthest suburbs and back again. The brittle, feverishly pro-active conversations sitting there with complete strangers – the only people that the narrator/Rowena said she felt able to communicate with. Was that really her? Was her isolation as deep as that? And from where did it spring?

Certainly there was little joy about her, and that he had always known. As a small child, she had never smiled, or so it now seemed in his memory. He had always had to coax her, force her almost to go to parties. She would be rigid with fear as he had dressed her for them, trembling sometimes in her stress, staring at him as if in plea as he gently brushed her hair and buttoned up her party shoes. But always silently. He could remember barely a single incident of conventional childhood naughtiness and tantrum. Just courage. And fortitude. And silent, uncomplaining control. What he had always thought was a form of serenity. But which he now knew for sure was something else.

But perhaps it was all just adolescence. Perhaps she would emerge from it unscathed. And he shouldn't read too much into a childish act of literary creation of this sort. She was a clever, sensitive girl at a difficult age. Perhaps that was all it was. And yet . . . he had reached to pick the manuscript out of her drawer again, and untied it to read once more the title poem.

> ' . . . he called it "Question Marked Innocence"
> Because that was the name of his grief . . .'

Now, years later, he was still trying to understand. Was that the point? Had he destroyed his daughter's childhood by the shortcomings of his marriage? Had he burnt out from her her chances of happiness? Could he still save her now?

Chapter Fifteen

Sarah was sitting on her bed when Robert found her, her bun poorly tied, wisps of hair hanging across her face. She was crying a little, and it was clear that there had been a great deal more of that, for there were tearstains down her cheeks, and her lower lip was red and sore where she had been biting on it.

Robert sat in the armchair on the other side of the room. Neither of them had said very much in the fifteen minutes or so that he had been there, but now he got to his feet, went over to the bed and sat down beside her, his hand placed tentatively on her shoulder.

'Be strong, Sarah. You'll feel better about this soon. It won't take long. You *will* feel better about it.'

At that, she started weeping violently, bending forward almost double as she did so, her head in her hands. It was several moments before she could speak, and even then she choked and sobbed as she did so, the tears and saliva from her mouth dropping down on to her lap.

'I'm sorry, Robert. I'm so sorry.' Then her voice rose and broke like that of a small child in distress, and she turned to face her husband, staring at him, her face distorted with her weeping. 'I'm sorry, Robert. The things I do. The things I do.'

She put her arms around him in an awkward, uncomfortable stance, and he held her too for a little, then gently disengaged. He

81

made himself smile at her, trying to use his eyes as well as the muscles of his mouth.

'There, old girl,' he said, softly stroking her back, using for once the phrase of familiarity that at times over the years he had adopted. 'There you are. All's well, old girl. All's well. Just one of those things. Calm down now, Sarah. Everything will be all right.' Gradually he could hear the sobbing quieten into little choking, whimpering noises as she began to settle.

'There we are. No harm done. No harm done,' he said, then immediately became acutely aware of the strangeness of the situation. More than strangeness, its total absurdity. Or so it would seem to any observer.

What had happened was that his wife had been discovered having enthusiastic intercourse with a fisherman on Bavancore beach, having, by all accounts, tried to seduce one of them all week. And she'd then been cautioned by the local police for gross indecency. The wife of the Deputy Chairman of a very grand English bank, out in India on an ambassadorial visit, cautioned by police for gross indecency.

And here he was, the injured husband, telling her that she would feel better in the morning. And – though only he would know this – feeling no emotion of any sort, apart from a certain sense of pity. Pity, not compassion. For someone he knew very well. Whom he didn't want to see hurt. Whom he wanted healthy, and strong, and in some level of control over her own life.

For at that moment he and Sarah were in the familiar context of another collapse of her life. Another defeat. Another confirmation of her inadequacy. This new failure would touch off in her another round of despair, and another inventory of all that had gone wrong in her life. To be followed by their rituals and repertoire of comfort and reassurance for her; favourable reassessment of incidents in the past, memories and discussion of little successes, then resolutions for a new start and a new life. In time all this would serve to calm her, he knew that, but it took so long to get there.

He stroked the back of her head while she clung to him, made vaguely uncomfortable by the feel of her and the texture of her hair. She felt physically unfamiliar to him now. There was no longer that edge of sexual anticipation and tension there had once been between them when they were in bodily contact in this way. He found it difficult to recall what it had felt like when there had been.

He held her away from him, and looked at her in as gentle a way as he could. She smiled at him, wistfully, and with her special look for these occasions, which Robert imagined was supposed to be that of a Disney baby animal. Suddenly he was anxious that he was going to lose control of the situation, and be pulled into statements of love and possession that he had no desire to make. Phrases of attachment, which, at that moment, and in her weakness, if he was forced to make, he would mean. Or think for a moment that he meant.

'You go through so much with me, my poor Robert,' she said.

And all he wanted to say in reply was that he didn't mind what he went through, as long as she was detached from him, and coping with her life, and leaving him free. But none of those things could be said now, and none of those things could ever be said, so he put his hand on the back of her hair again, and stroked her once more, and hoped that by putting into his eyes an actor's impression of warmth and compassion, she would let him escape.

'I expect you're jealous too. Jealous of that man. I'm sure you are. Poor Robert. What have I done to you?'

Thinking that jealousy was about the last emotion he was experiencing at that moment, and wondering if it was charity for an ageing, self-deceiving woman as much as anything else that had been in the fisherman's mind when he took her, he said, 'Yes, of course I'm jealous, my dear. I admit that. How could I not be?'

She broke away from his hold now, and tapped him almost playfully on the arm. 'Well, you do bring this sort of thing on yourself, you know you do. You know what I mean.'

She smiled at him, to his horror and to his shame for her, in the manner of a roguish ingénue. But then her mood switched quite immediately, and her face puckered like a child's in panic, and she put her head in her hands, and rocked in pain, backwards and forwards.

'Oh, Robert. What have I done? What's happened to me? What can I do? Please help me, Robert. Tell me what to do. Please help me.'

He got up from the bed, went across the room to the window and sat there on its sill, looking at her.

'Just let the hours pass, Sarah my love, and then the days will pass, and then the weeks. And before very long you'll find that this whole episode has sunk back in your mind into something merely disagreeable. Something that you would prefer hadn't happened, but that you can deal with.

'The great thing is not to let it defeat you. Kick yourself for it, hate yourself for it if you like, but accept it for what it is. A momentary, dangerous, undignified piece of sexual adventuring. Not more, not less. Get yourself to position it like that and you will be able to live with it. And remember that you're not the only person who gets into trouble with sex.'

He shrugged and she replied in a tone that sounded almost self-righteous.

'No, I'm certainly not that. That's quite true. It's a very common thing – in women of my age of course, but older too. Very common. And the fisherman was very determined, I can tell you that. Very determined . . . Let's leave it like that.'

Oh God, he thought, as she patted her bun, looking at herself in the mirror. Not that fantasy. *Please not that.* And although he tried to suppress it, a feeling now of positive distaste for her came over him.

'It's just that . . . it's just that I do hope people don't hear about it,' she continued. 'At home. At the church. People mustn't get to know.'

He watched her, impassively almost, as her face crumpled again, and, hugging her arms about her chest, she started to cry, 'Oh dear. Oh God. What will I do? What will I do?'

Robert leant forward, and looked at her as directly as he could.

'Sarah, there's no way forward for you except to tell yourself that it's happened, and there's nothing you can do about that. It would be nice if the world and his wife don't hear about it, but if they do, then to hell with them. Remember all those things about motes in eyes, or people in glass houses, or whatever it is? And the more courageous you are, and the more you look people straight in the face, and challenge them to judge you, then the better you'll feel about yourself. It's never the solution to run away. Never.'

She cried a little more, then stopped, and sat there on the bed for some moments staring at the floor in front of her.

'It's easy to say that, Robert, but I'll try. I just hope so desperately that no one at home hears about it. And the girls too, of course. I couldn't bear it if Sophie was involved in it all. It's been so difficult with her as it is in some ways, though she's such a good girl at heart. But she does show me respect, and I couldn't bear to lose that. Unlike Rowena, who has never shown me respect of any kind. As you know.'

She looked across at him, and he watched her with all the guilt that familiar remark of hers always put in him.

'Well, respect for us or for anybody else is a difficult attribute for Rowena at the moment. She needs to respect herself a little more before she can respect others – *genuinely* respect others. Perhaps the truth is that Sophie needs to as well.'

And the extraordinary thing, he thought, is that the bland, meaningless aphorism will content her. It did the last time we had this conversation, and it will do so again. As long as it does.

'That's quite true,' Sarah nodded. '*Quite* true! Neither of them has ever tried to make anything of themselves – particularly Rowena, of course. Until they do, they will never be happy. You may not think much of me . . .' Robert shook his head at her in mock exasperation, ' . . . but I went through a lot to please my father, and it took quite a bit of courage to go all that way out to India, and work in the sticks up in Darjeeling. I can assure you, it took a lot of courage for a young girl of my age.'

'Of course. It must have done. I'm sure it did,' murmured

Robert, and as he said the words he had a sudden vision of Rowena at the age of eight, trapped under her fallen pony, both her leg and her thigh broken, lying there with her face sheet-white, biting on her lip to stop herself from crying out with her pain. 'It's all right, Daddy,' she'd said. 'It's all right. I'll be all right.'

He put his hands over his face as the unexpected, brutally sharp image seared itself on to his mind. *Oh Christ, Rowena. Oh Christ. What happened to us all? What happened to you, Rowena? All your courage. All your containment and dignity. What happened to you? Why are you carrying the pain that you do?*

'Oh Robert, please don't be upset, my dear. I said I was sorry. You're quite right – it was just a silly episode. You mustn't let me upset you. I can see that I have. You're looking really sad now. It's all right, my dear. Don't be upset. It's all right.'

He took his hands away from his face and looked at her, making in doing so a deliberate effort of will to keep out of his eyes anything which she might construe as an absence of love or respect. Sarah has no sense at all of responsibility for her own actions, he thought. But whatever private hell Rowena is living in, she's never lost that. She's her own person. Or so I believe.

Aloud he said: 'I'll let you off one thing anyway, Sarah. I've cancelled the staff party here tonight. Tomorrow night's arrangements too. We'll take on our enemies back in England if we have to, but we'll let them have their run at it here, don't you think?'

She came over to him and kissed him softly on the mouth, pressing her body against his. 'Then we'll have two quiet evenings alone together getting ready for the journey. That's what we'll do. That'll be very nice.

'We need to be alone together much more,' she said. 'Then silly things like this would never happen. And you'd never need to get upset and jealous, you poor thing. Never at all.'

Chapter Sixteen

Robert, unable to sleep that night, got up just as dawn was beginning to break over the hills behind Bavancore.

Slipping a cotton dressing gown over his pyjamas, he crept down the stairs, and out through the French windows into the garden, then on to the beach beyond. He sat on a fallen branch, and gazed out at the sea, now silvering and pinking in the emerging light of the early tropical morning.

Two memories had been in his mind all the wakeful hours, and now that he was up, he was able to run them through once more. They were less sharp and painful now that the light was breaking, and he was out of his bed, as he knew from old they would be.

The first was of one afternoon twenty years ago almost to the month. He'd gone up to the bedroom in their London house to look for his driving licence, and despairing of finding it, opened a cupboard that he normally never used. In it, under a pile of sheets, he found a cardboard box and, mildly inquisitive, he looked inside it to see what was there.

A bunch of letters, all of recent date, showed at a most cursory glance that Sarah was in the middle of an affair with an acquaintance of Robert's, and that she had evidently been begging him to take her away from her marriage. The two children were barely one and three years old, and they had been home from India for less than six months, so Robert realised that the relationship must have started almost as soon as they had arrived in England.

They'd been failing in their marriage, and he knew that to be true, but even after all this time he could recall the acuteness of the shock when he saw what had been happening. And the pain of it too. Part of the pain, and he recognised this, was straightforward sexual jealousy, and nothing more important than that. But part of it was the affirmation of something that he knew perfectly well was the case, but was shocked to find confirmed.

They shouldn't have married. It was as simple as that. But they had, and here was the result. Whatever happened to this affair of hers, they were never now going to have a marriage. What had been before a point of indulgent self-analysis, and even perhaps the stuff of an exquisite melancholy, was now, abruptly, held up to him as the truth, and this in the harshest of lights. It was not that Sarah was being naughtily unfaithful. It was the fact that she too knew there was nothing for them in their marriage. The evidence for that was there in the cardboard box.

The second memory in Robert's mind that morning was of him and Rowena, together one day in his study on the day her school report arrived, just as she had passed her sixteenth birthday. He could recall at least an approximation of every word that had been said, though she had spoken so quietly that he could hardly hear what she was saying. He could see her trembling as she stared at him, as if she was once again a small child being dressed to go to her party.

'I can't do it,' she said. 'For whatever reason – I can't do it. There's something inside me . . .'

Robert had suddenly thought at that moment how very like him in her appearance she had become, and he was amused by that, and proud too, and wanted this scene to finish, so that he could say that to her. He got up from his chair at his desk, and made to cross the room to her. As he lifted his hands to take her by the shoulders and hold her, Rowena shouted, so suddenly and so out of character that he took a step backwards in his surprise.

'Leave me! Leave me alone! Don't you understand? I don't want any more of this. I can't take any more of this. I can't take any more of it—' And her voice broke, and her arm went across her eyes.

Robert stood there, still shaken, uncertain what to do or say. He shuffled his feet in an awkward gesture of unease, then said, 'I didn't mean to hurt you, Rowena. You know that. It's just that I'm anxious about you. You're sixteen, and very clever, and very creative and all of those things. All I want is for you to be happy and fulfilled. And you won't be happy and fulfilled unless you find some way of dealing now with school life. Mrs Harrison was saying to me that . . .'

Her arm was away from her eyes now, and she was gazing at him, but still quivering and shaking with her tears. She said, 'I can't do it. I can't do any more of it. I don't know why it is, but I can't. I'm going to leave school now. I'm not going back.'

Robert smiled at her, and went to her again to take both her hands, thinking that he would calm her and persuade her by a simple statement of love. But before he could say anything, she continued, 'Here's what I really mean. I want to be free. I can't pick up the burden for your life as well as mine. I can't cope with my own life, and I can't cope with yours as well. I can't take the burden of it. Your hopeless marriage, and your lack of compassion for Mum, and your hopeless . . . your hopeless . . . your . . .'

And now the weeping started as he had never heard it from her before, and she sank into the chair behind her, both her arms thrown across her face.

Robert left the room, thinking to allow her to quieten herself in privacy before going back to comfort her and to explain more of what he had meant to say. He sat on his bed to wait, but then he heard her running through the hall and the front door slam behind her.

He rushed to the window just in time to see her run up the street and away, her unbuttoned raincoat flying behind her as she went.

Chapter Seventeen

Rowena put her head in her hands as her thirteen-month-old son continued to howl his tears in his filthy playpen.

He'd thrown himself on to its floor now, and lay there, pounding his fists and writhing his body in anger, his mouth pressing against the mat. He'd wet himself, and his tiny blue romper jeans showed dark stains down their front. Outside the playpen, thrown on to the floor in the corner of the room, lay a second, identical pair, this one soiled with the child's excrement.

'Hold on, Jamie. Hold on. Rick will be here soon. He will. He'll be here soon.'

Gathering and willing herself to action, Rowena got up from her chair, went across to the playpen and reached inside to pick the child up. As she did so, he immediately stopped his crying, and sat there in his mother's arms, sobbing lightly, but gazing up at her, one arm up around her neck, his eyes narrowed in sharp concentration as they looked directly into hers.

'God, you look like your grandfather when you do that, my little one. You make me feel guilty about him every time you look at me in that way. It's quite uncanny the way you look so like him. The Luscombe ears, the eyes, the lot. You're a Luscombe, my Jamie. There's not much doubt about that.'

She looked round behind her to check whether the brown, bulging old armchair in the corner of the room had clutter on its seat, then lowered herself into it, still holding the child in her arms. He was too heavy for her to hold for long while standing. Small as she was in her full health, her weight now was down to not much more than ninety pounds, and she looked less than that, with her clothes hanging off her in loose folds, and her face chalk-white and drawn.

'You're a heavy boy these days, Jamie, that's for sure. You're a big boy for thirteen months.'

He cuddled up to her in the chair, and she looked with pride and love at him, as he smiled at her now with a beaming, open face, his dark hair standing up above it spiky and greasy. He was plump, but the plumpness had a bulky quality about it, evident of a gross and coarse diet, and his arms and legs were of painful thinness.

'I love you, Jamie. Love me too, my little one. Love me too.'

Jamie was staring at her again in his oddly focused and adult way, then he reached his free hand up and started to pull gently and affectionately at her hair, as he always did when he had the opportunity. She looked down at him and stroked the side of his head, her hand shaking, the fingernails uneven and bitten.

'Christ, Jamie. I wish he would come. I do wish Rick would come.'

She sat there rocking her child in her arms, every few moments moaning a little, the perspiration beading now on her forehead. On the cheap wooden table beside her was a tin box lid, overflowing with cigarette ends and ash, and beside that, quite bizarrely in these surroundings, a copy of her school magazine.

Jamie's playpen was against one wall, and a filthy sofa, torn in one arm, and bulging below with broken springs, was pushed back against another. A thin rug covered some of the floor, and an ancient, cracked, leather ottoman stood in front of the fireplace, which had in it some charred pieces of planking and packing-case wood and scrumpled, half-burnt balls of newspaper.

At the side of the rug remained the debris of some sort of meal. A cornflakes packet and an empty bottle of milk stood beside a china bowl, in which some dried matter was caked to the bottom, and a lump of yellow cheese, dry and cracked, sat there on a sheet of newspaper.

Rowena suddenly made a move, struggling to her feet with the weight of the child in her arms. Once successfully upright, she carried him unsteadily across the floor and put him back in the playpen, almost dropping him in her urgency to be free of him.

Jamie immediately pushed himself to his feet, and started to cry again, reaching his arms up to his mother in appeal for her attention. As his cries grew hysterical and persistent Rowena crossed to the sofa, and sat there with her legs drawn up, her back to the playpen, her arms wrapped around her knees. She was moaning almost continuously now, rocking her body backwards and forwards as she did so.

Some minutes later the door burst open, and a young man in a torn plaid jacket and jeans came into the room, half tripping over a plastic train lying just inside the doorway. Rowena immediately sprang into life, and was up and on her feet before he had regained his balance.

'Did you have any luck or not, Rick? What did you get? Did you get a rock? Where is it? Did you have any luck?'

Rick shrugged his thin arms, ran his fingers through his hair, and shook his head. His voice was hoarse and raw.

'No one about, Rowena. I looked all over for Sean and for Leroy but I couldn't find either of them, nor any other dealer I knew who would have some. I tried. We'll have a go at Donnie later this evening and hope he's back from wherever he's been. We'll be OK. Don't worry, Rowena.'

She started shouting at him now. 'You idiot. You fucking idiot. Of course I'm worried! How am I supposed to get through without crack? I've got to have it. Of course they're out there. They're always out there. Where else are they?'

Jamie had now fallen silent, and was gazing at his mother and Rick alternately, his eyes again wide open, as if in concern. He was standing, supporting himself by his grasp on the side bar of the playpen, his arms upstretched. Rick walked over to the child and smoothed his hair, squatting on his haunches so that his face and the child's were at the same level.

'Hi, Jamie. Christ, you're wet. And this playpen is filthy. I'll clean it up. Here, I'll change you first. Come on, Jamie. There's a boy.'

He picked Jamie up into his arms, and went to carry him through to the single bedroom beyond the sitting room. He stopped on the way to bend down to pick up the soiled jeans from the floor, and threw them into an open bin in the kitchen.

Rowena was sobbing now; her voice as she followed them through into the bedroom quietened a little, though there was in it still the undernote of fear.

'We'll have to get some more rocks you know, Rick. We'll never get through the night if we don't. At least, I know I won't. And there's tomorrow morning too. We'll have to get some more rocks.'

Rick had laid the child on his back on the unmade bed, and was putting on him a clean nappy from a supply he'd stolen from the local pharmacy the previous week, and which were now strewn all over the floor.

'Not many of these things left. I'll have to lift some more tomorrow. I can't bear him to be in a dirty one all day.' He turned and picked up a tube of baby cream, which he'd stolen from the same shop. 'He gets so sore too, poor little sod,' he said, now rubbing the cream around the folds of the child's groin. He smiled at him while he did so, and tickled and squeezed his stomach.

'This ointment seems to clear it up for him though. He needs it all the time.' He looked at the name on the tube. 'Dr Carruthers. I must get some more when this is finished. I meant to pinch the Johnson & Johnson stuff, but I couldn't reach it.'

He laughed, then immediately started an intense and desperate bronchial coughing fit, bent over double, his face puce with the effort. When it was over he straightened and wiped his face with a piece of crumpled Kleenex from his pocket. His face, as he turned to Rowena, was thin and gaunt, now ashen-white against his sparse fair beard, his dark eyes burning out from the paleness of it all.

'We haven't got enough money anyway, you know that. We'll have to get some more. You'll have to earn it working tonight. Are you working tonight?'

Rowena sat on the bed beside the child and started to stroke his stomach and his legs, her fingers trailing down him, her dark hair hanging over her eyes and face. When she spoke her voice was calmer and softer than before, but he could hear the edge of hysteria in it.

'Of course I'm working, Rick. Of course I'll work. There's thirty quid left from this morning – you've got that. That's enough for one rock, and a bit over. Ring Donnie again. We'll have to go on trying him until he turns up again. Reach Donnie and get him to bring four in all, and we'll give him the thirty now and I'll make enough working tonight to have another seventy for him in the morning. Easily. More if necessary. But he must come quickly. He must be here straight away. Try him again now.'

Jamie had now fallen asleep, both his hands brought up to rest on top of Rowena's, which lay on him almost still, just her fingers lightly tracing a soft pattern on him as he lay there motionless, his eyes closed, his mouth held open, his breathing soft and rhythmic. She watched him as he slept, her head tilted a little to one side, her elfin, delicate, pre-pubescent face frowning in concentration as she ran her eyes over him, her fingers gently stroking him all the while.

'Christ, he is lovely. He's so beautiful.' She stroked him some more, then smiled at him, and gently, softly, laid her hand on the top of his head. 'You're so lovely, my Jamie.'

Rick went through now into the sitting room, stopping as he passed the playpen to remove the mat floor from it. He took this into the kitchen to sponge, which he did with abrupt energy and urgency, leaving it tilted on the draining board to dry.

'Try Donnie again, Rick. Please. He must get home some time or other. Please try him again.'

Shaking the water off his hands, Rick walked across to the telephone and dialled the number from memory. His face started to contort in stress when there had been eight or ten rings without response.

'Jesus Christ. Jesus Christ, Donnie. Where the fuck are you? Are you ever coming back? Donnie? Donnie?' Then his face sank into relief, and he closed his eyes and wiped his brow. 'Thank God for that. I thought you'd gone or something. Why couldn't you answer? Where've you been all this time, man?

'It's Rick here. We need some rocks straight away, Donnie. Make it four. Straight away. Well, send someone. Please send someone. And Donnie – we've got just thirty quid. No, that's all we've got. Please, Donnie. It's all we've got at this moment, but Rowena is working tonight, and she's bound to earn at least a hundred. She always does. We'll have the money for you first thing in the morning.

'No, I know you don't give credit. I understand that. But you can trust, Donnie. You know you can trust us. Look – we'll make it eighty in the morning and thirty tonight. For four rocks. No, definitely tomorrow morning. Definitely. OK? All right then. OK. All right, we'll do that. Thanks. I agree. I told you, I agree. But make it quick. Get the rocks here quick. Quick.'

Rick put the telephone down and leaned forward for a moment, his forehead pressed against the cupboard in front of him. Rowena was standing behind him now, holding the sleeping child, and she smiled anxiously at him as he turned around.

'So he's sending it then? He's sending it now? What did he say?'

'Yes, he's sending it. He's sending a runner. But he wants us to take some heroin as well. Two bags. He wants a hundred and fifty for two bags of brown, and four rocks. The price is high because it's on credit. Thirty tonight, and a hundred and twenty tomorrow morning. A hundred and seventy if he has to wait a further day. And he wants another order from us tomorrow night.'

Rowena shrugged, then carried Jamie back through to the bedroom, calling as she went, 'He'll get that all right. There's no problem. I'll go out and work the street. I'll go to the café, or one of the regulars will ring. Norman, probably. He says he's in love with me. He seems quite well off as far as I can see. I'll get him to give me a present as well.'

'Norman – the cinema manager? If he's any money it will have come from out the till. What do you do to these mushes anyway? They all seem to fall in love with you.'

'I look about thirteen years old, that's why. I look like a schoolgirl, I've got the body of a child, and I'm nice to them. I'm never aggressive, and I let them do whatever they want. Anything they want.'

Rick smiled at her. 'So do we all. In our own way.'

There was a sound of muffled coughing from the bedroom, and then some desultory crying. Neither of them took any notice or action. Then Rowena sat down on the floor and started to knock her fists against her temples, her face now beginning to screw up in tension and stress. She crossed her arms about her body, and rocked slowly backwards and forwards.

'How long is he going to be, for Christ's sake? Did he say how long he was going to be? Where the hell is he? Why doesn't he come? Did Donnie say the runner was coming immediately? Why don't we call again and find out if he's on his way – find out if he has left? You call. Or I'll do it. Let me find out.'

She scrambled to her feet, reached for the telephone and was dialling the number when there was a knock on the door. She slammed the telephone back onto its hook, then rushed to the front door and flung it open.

Standing there was a youth with straggly long hair and a thin dark beard, dressed in a shirt, a black leather biker's jacket and torn blue jeans. He immediately stepped in through the door, and pushed it shut after him.

'Hi, Dermot,' said Rick. 'You took a hell of a long time. Where's the stuff?'

The young man felt inside his mouth, and brought out four little lumps covered in cling film, which he handed across to Rowena, who cupped them in her hands. He then bent down and reached inside the legs of his jeans, pulling out the two little bags of heroin that were secured there, suspended on a length of string from the waistband.

'Donnie told me to collect thirty quid off you straight away.'

Rowena gave him the money immediately, pulling the banknotes out from the pocket of her jeans, from which a condom packet fell at the same time. She picked this up, and went back into the kitchen, carrying the heroin and the crack with her. As she got there, the telephone rang and she shouted to Rick: 'Take this stuff and start making a bong. I'll see who this is. Yes? Rowena here. Hello, Doug. Yes, all right, you can come round later. No, not now. Later. All right, you can bring them too. But not more than three of you. No. And I'll want a hundred and fifty. No, a hundred and fifty. Oh, all right. A hundred then. But I will need that. Be here at nine. No, *not* before then. Nine. See you then.'

She looked at her watch, then went into the sitting room where Rick was squatting on the floor with a plastic beaker in front of him. Over this he was securing a lid of silver foil by circling over it the thick elastic neck of the condom, which he had cut away from its sheath. She took over from him, firmly stretched the foil down, then selected a needle from the box Rick had put beside him on the floor, and pricked a series of holes in a tight cluster close to the beaker's edge. This completed, she used the little scissors with which Rick had cut off the rubber condom ring, and made a slit in the silver foil, on the other side of the beaker, opposite the cluster of needle perforations.

Her face was calm with concentration now, and the two young men sprawled in the armchair and on the sofa, watching with intent, frowning interest at the familiar ritual being performed before them. Now she reached across, took the tin box lid down from the small side table, and from it scooped on a folded wafer of thin paper some cigarette ash, which she then used to cover the little holes she had made with her needle in the silver foil.

Rick had put the four little cling-film packages onto a plate; Rowena took one of the tiny parcels, and putting it on a rectangular dish of rigid green plastic, she unwrapped it with reverential, painful caution. There appeared a little knob of what looked like an irregular lump of schoolroom chalk, which Rowena then picked away at with her fingernails, pressing down with her fingers against the plastic in order to pick up the fragments as they broke off, these then being placed piece by piece on the bed of cigarette ash that covered the needle holes in the foil.

This done, Rowena carefully lifted the beaker so that she could place her lips over the slit she had cut in the foil; then the flame from a cigarette lighter was held over the crack rocks, which sizzled and popped as they ignited, the dense white smoke from them being drawn down into the beaker through the filter of the cigarette ash. Rowena sucked at her slit in the foil with a desperate, fevered strength. As her lungs filled as far as she could force them, her eyes and face gradually composed and settled, and in her stillness now, completely motionless as she held her breathing, her appearance had about it a quiet poise and serenity that gave her a lucent, childlike beauty. Then gradually she let go, her breathing was released, and she remained for some moments in what appeared to be a state of perfect calm and peace, staring before her as if in meditation.

As she sat there, Rick had taken the beaker from her and had himself inhaled the remnants of the white smoke from the first rock, clutching and dragging at it until it was finished and it would yield no more. Then a second rock was prepared for the bong in the same way, though there was more calmness in the preparation, and the beaker was shared between them in an almost stately ritual of partnership. Dermot had arrived at five o'clock. By a quarter past seven all the four rocks had been consumed, and only the heroin was left.

For at least the last hour, Jamie had cried intermittently and defeatedly, the pain of a child who was all too familiar with these periods of abandonment, and had learned the hopelessness of trying to press for attention that would never come. Dermot had sprawled half-asleep, half-watchful as the others finished their procedures, then, when all four of the rocks had been consumed, he sat more attentively and upright in his chair awaiting what was to happen next. His eyes followed Rowena as she went into the kitchen and came back with a large serving spoon and a box of alcohol wipes. Putting these down on the table, she returned again to the kitchen to take down the lid of a tin box from a shelf, then returned with this, a bottle of malt vinegar, and a packet of cigarettes.

Kneeling again on the floor of the sitting room, Rowena put the tin box lid down on the rug, and dropped into it one of the wipes. She opened the cigarette packet, took from it a cigarette, and broke the filter off it, separating the filter into two pieces. She poured some of the vinegar into the spoon, added the heroin, then lit an alcohol wipe in the tin lid with her lighter, and held the spoon above it. Almost immediately the mixture began to boil, and she dropped into it one of the fragments of cigarette filter.

Rick handed her a syringe, and Rowena, giving him the serving spoon with deliberate care, pulled up the plunger and drew through the sodden filter the dark brown sticky substance that the mixture had now become. Dropping her jeans and pulling aside her pants, revealing the bush of pubic hair, strikingly and shockingly mature in a body that looked in other ways so child-like, she stuck the needle into her left groin, and almost immediately her eyes turned up, she started to mumble incoherently, and slumped to the floor.

Rick grabbed the syringe, and having prepared a dose, was also now injecting himself; when he too collapsed, Dermot took the syringe and drew up into it the residue of the sticky brown mixture from the filters, and he then injected himself as well.

It was some minutes before Rick was sufficiently recovered to speak, and when he did so it was in a mumbled, thick tone.

'Dermot. You've got the thirty. Tell Donnie the rest of it will definitely be here in the morning. And that we'll need some more rocks tomorrow evening. This time, we'll try to have the money up front.'

As Dermot got to his feet to leave, Rowena looked at her watch, then sat up, and leaned forward, her elbows on her knees, her head resting in her hands.

'You'd better go out or something, Rick. These men will be here before long. You won't want to hear it all from the bedroom. Jamie's asleep now. Come back in an hour or so. It won't take longer than that. I'll make sure it bloody doesn't.'

She smiled at him, running the fingers of both her hands through her hair. 'Donnie will have his money.'

She got to her feet, and started to walk towards the bedroom. Rick went to the window, and stood there for a moment watching the rain falling and the leaves from the solitary tree in the street outside drop sodden to the ground. He shuddered with the chill of it all, and went to wrap himself in the old military greatcoat that was hanging on a hook in the dark little hallway. His arms hugged around himself, and the collar of the greatcoat pulled right up, he went back into the bedroom, and said, 'Look after yourself, Rowena.'

She looked back over her shoulder. 'Oh, you needn't worry about that. Doug's a pussy cat. A dirty old pussy cat, but a pussy cat.'

'Let's hope his friends are too,' said Rick, and went out of the front door, huddling himself deeper into the greatcoat as he went.

Chapter Eighteen

The Magazine Company offices were in King Street off Covent Garden market, in a pretty period building almost opposite the original site of Moss Bros, the famous man's clothing and dress-hire store.

The Covent Garden area and King Street itself had been the subject of extensive fashionable refurbishment in recent years, and it was a modish and chic location for a magazine publishing house to be. They were one of several in the neighbourhood, of greater or lesser size, but few were as pleasantly housed and situated as this. The quality of the offices was an indication of the success of the firm, now with five or six popular and established magazine titles on the newsstands, and a further two or three free glossy magazines on their lists.

Solly Lorenzo, previously a salesman with a rival firm, had founded The Magazine Company about ten years ago at the age of thirty-three. He had done this largely with money raised from the Venture Capital Division of the Moorgate & Mercantile Bank, one of a number of subsidiaries that Robert chaired.

But on top of this Lorenzo had himself put into the new firm his family's entire life savings, and after several near-terminal disasters in its early years, The Magazine Company had now emerged as one of the more successful magazine publishers in the market. Robert had seen the firm operate in both extremely bad times and rather good, and had developed a respect for Solly Lorenzo. He was tenacious and he was brave, and those were qualities that Robert admired.

It was almost two minutes to ten that morning before Sophie Luscombe arrived at The Magazine Company for work. The statutory office hours were from nine-fifteen to five-fifteen, but in the year and a half that Sophie had worked at the company as a secretary in the editorial department, she had only on a handful of occasions been on time. Usually she was at least fifteen minutes late.

She regarded half-past nine as being her accepted time for arrival, and would apologise only if later than that. And even then, only if the weather was clement. The least hint of rain, and she would aim for nine forty-five, arriving then with muttered curses about the London Transport bus system. Snow meant she would aim for ten-fifteen. Snow and ice together indicated ten forty-five. A flu epidemic, and she would be the first to be ravaged by it. Migraines allowed her perhaps three days off a month. Unspecified female conditions, occurring monthly, a further two.

This particular morning it was reported on breakfast radio that there had been a suicide on the underground railway tracks at Hyde Park Corner, and services temporarily suspended. Given the rain and the suicide, ten o'clock sounded to her about the right time to aim for, and she had almost a virtuous air about her as she came clattering through the entrance lobby shortly before that time.

She stood there opening and closing her umbrella so vigorously that showers of rain droplets were propelled out in front of her, most going over the legs of the telephonist/receptionist who sat there at an open desk, and who now sprang to her feet with a cry of rage.

'For Christ's sake, Sophie!' said Victoria, a Lady Diana clone, brushing herself down. 'Not only have I had to take messages all morning from your foul friends, but you now shake your foul umbrella over my one remaining decent pair of tights. Piss off.'

Sophie started to move away in the direction of the staircase, and

Victoria called after her: 'And Julian wants to know where you are. He sounds furious. He's going around muttering that you never sent his fax out last night. Or that you did, and shouldn't have done. Or something like that.'

Victoria resumed her study of *Hello!* magazine, a large pile of unopened office mail lying beside her on her desk. The telephone rang.

'The Magazine Company,' she drawled, continuing to flick over the pages of the magazine. 'I'll see if Mr Lorenzo is in. Whom shall I say is calling?'

Victoria always made a point of the *whom*. She had attended a fashionable girls' school in Berkshire, from which she had emerged with a single GCSE pass, a C grade in Home Economics. The *whom* she felt added a certain stamp of class to her performance at the switchboard. The mark of a decent education.

'Solly? It's Lord Whiteleys . . . Thank you, Lord Whiteleys. I have Mr Lorenzo. Putting you through.'

The *through* was her other contribution to the tone of the place. It was delivered in two notes, with the second on a rising curve, and the entire sequence in a style of deep confidentiality. She had copied the whole act from her mother, who had learnt it in her turn at her finishing school's commercial etiquette course.

Victoria took a mirror out of her drawer, propped it on her desk, and undertook in it a minute examination of her face. Eyebrows were plucked, cheek-blusher applied, lipstick painted on, and she was just prising wide her lips with her index finger and thumb of both hands, examining the condition of her teeth, when she realised that Solly Lorenzo was standing behind her.

'Lord Whitelaw,' he said. 'Not Lord Whiteleys, dear. There isn't a Lord Whiteleys, for God's sake. It's a department store. Lord Whitelaw.'

Victoria blushed a violent pink and grinned up at him in an awkward, coltish way. Solly started to say something more, seemed to change his mind, and picked up the pile of mail. He put it in front of her, and asked her to get it sorted right away.

'Of course, Solly. I'm so sorry, Solly. Can I get you a cup of coffee?'

Invariably cups of coffee, Solly thought to himself, refusing with a shake of the head and a grin. Whenever I'm furious with her. Which is most of the time. He heard her answer another call as he set off again, this time for the mail-room.

'The Magazine Company. Yes, Sophie Luscombe has come in now. Just come in – only a moment ago. Putting you through.'

The bitch, Solly thought happily, straightening and rearranging that day's choice from what was a prodigious collection of Hermès ties. The bitch. But they really would have to tighten up once more on office discipline. Except for his personal secretary, and one or two others, the staff were thoroughly unreliable about what time they arrived. They stayed late, but wandered in at all times. Particularly Sophie Luscombe . . . and she never stayed late.

Solly returned to his office, blowing a shadowy and dutiful kiss to a girl in the production office with whom he had had a momentary indiscretion after the staff summer party. Sophie, down in the editorial department, was now at her desk and answering the telephone call, her voice so loud that the entire staff in the open-plan office was forced to follow the conversation. It seemed that all Sophie's calls were in connection with her social life, which appeared to be of great complexity and considerable duplicity. Each friend in turn was invited to join Sophie in the intimate character assassination of the previous caller.

'Sophie! Sophie!' Julian Jardine, one of the two joint editorial directors, had now come into the room, and was gesturing and grimacing in histrionic dumbshow for her to finish her conversation.

'I've been trying to trace the fax you were supposed to send last night to Heinrich Günther at Frankfurt. Where is it, Sophie? Did it go? I think I probably made a mistake about some rights they're holding. I'm scared shitless about it.'

'I held it over actually, Julian. I wasn't happy that you had it right, so I decided not to type it in the end, and give you a chance of looking at it again this morning.'

Julian grinned at her, then closed his eyes, and wiped his brow with a scarlet silk handkerchief. He blew her an extravagantly enthusiastic kiss, having first moved as if with the intention of doing so, before a sharp change of mind.

'Thank God. Oh, Sophie – thank God. You're an angel, sweetie. An angel. It should have been three thousand pounds. I woke up in the middle of the night with the ghastly feeling that I said to you thirty thousand pounds by mistake. Did I, dear? Did I?'

Sophie looked in her shorthand notebook. She could decipher practically nothing at all of what she had written. Least of all that.

'Yes. Here we are – thirty thousand pounds. That's what I meant. That's what I was worried about.'

'Sophie, I love you. What intuition you have. Thank God. Let's get it out now. It might be better if I dictated the whole thing over again. Then we really must send it.'

Julian watched her as he dictated the letter, this time going at a deliberately slow pace so that she had some chance of getting it down correctly. Or at all.

God, she is a liar, he thought. We should really have got rid of her by now but somehow, a girl like that . . . One doesn't want to be unkind. Not unkind. We can't all be Little Miss Beautiful. Poor poppet, she's certainly not that. So one has to make allowances . . .

'There we are, dear. Thank you, Sophie darling. Let's get that on its way as soon as possible. It was supposed to have been there last night. I'll sign it straight away, and it might be as well if I call Frankfurt now to say the fax will be with them within a few minutes. They're waiting for it.'

As he turned away, Sophie's telephone started to ring again, and as she reached for it, Julian held up his hand. 'No more calls now, Sophie, if you don't mind. This letter really does have to go out.'

She should be better-looking than that, poor girl, he thought as he turned away. She's like a plump little porker. All little pink snout, and curly tail. Poor girl. One should make allowances really. There's a younger sister in the family somewhere, if I remember correctly from someone or other. Bad luck for Sophie if she's much better-looking. It does tend to leave a scar, that sort of thing.

By the time Sophie appeared at his desk with the fax to sign, Julian had worked himself into a state of deep contrition that he had been so critical about her recently to the others. He was a sentimental, kindly young man, who had known in his own life enough alienation and rejection to see in overweight, physically awkward girls like Sophie a fellow spirit.

Christ, she must find life hell sometimes. Absolute hell. The unkindnesses she must have to endure. People are such bitches. He smiled at her as she put the note in front of him.

'That's quite smashing, Sophie,' he said. 'Perfect, dear.'

Having signed the note with his flourish of a signature, he slipped a second *m* beside the first into the word commitment, and discreetly crossed out a second *c* from necessary.

'Marvellous. Quite perfect. Bless you, Sophie. Let's get it on its way.'

Julian watched her as she walked away, heavy-footed, her upper body wobbling slightly as she went. And what makes it more pathetic is that she's not particularly likeable either, if one is scrupulously honest about it, he thought. She attempts charm, the poor sweetie. She tries hard. But somehow . . . The telephone on his desk rang.

'Julian? Victoria here. I've a message for you from Barbara. She's at the auditors and would like you to ring her there. Shall I get her for you?'

Julian made a little *moue* of his mouth. 'I'll ring her later, dear. Keep the number, and I'll get back to her later. When I'm out of my meeting, poppet. Much, much later.'

Julian had never been comfortable with Barbara Thomson, whom he considered to be a wholly aggressive and disruptive element in the life of The Magazine Company. She had joined the firm about two years earlier as Finance Director, having worked previously as a senior accountant at the Ford Motor Company, and had become, in Julian's eyes, almost wholly impossible. Particularly since she had been shortlisted for the *Daily Mail*'s

Working Woman of the Year Award eight or nine months previously. She had now taken to writing papers of unfathomable numeracy on the relative profitability of the various magazine titles, and their consequent life expectancy, and brandishing these threateningly at the Monday management meetings. She power-breakfasted with potential investors. She made mysterious trips to the City of London. It had become understood in the office that she had unique access to Solly Lorenzo's ear. She allowed it to be understood that there were additional intimacies. She and Julian were not friends.

He rang through to Solly Lorenzo's personal secretary. 'Tracey? It's Julian, dear. Can I have a moment with Solly? Maybe now, poppet?'

Any attempt to see Solly Lorenzo without first going through Tracey Patterson was a tactless and fruitless act. She guarded his diary as if it was her last possession. Barbara, in her first, callow months, fresh from Dagenham and the Ford Motor Company, had seldom been granted entry by Tracey, except for the occasional five minutes when Solly was grooming himself in preparation for lunch at The Ivy. The fact that Barbara now walked straight into Solly's office without so much as a glance, poisonous or otherwise, at Tracey's desk, was the cause of outrage, and, on one occasion, a stormy and tearful scene in Solly's office late one Friday evening, during which he was reminded of certain little trysts and promises of the past. But Julian was the oldest of old friends.

'Of course, Julian. Anything for you. Come straight up. Will ten minutes be enough for you, pet?'

'Lovely, darling. I'm on my way.'

Julian found Solly on the telephone to a wholesaler, the knot of the Hermès tie now dropped an inch below the unbuttoned collar of the cream silk shirt, the cuffs each rolled up one meticulous fold, revealing on his left wrist a twenty-two carat gold Jaeger Le Coutre watch. He waved Julian to a seat, rolling his eyes in mock despair at his telephone conversation as he did so.

'Of course we're grateful for your support, Mr Potter,' he was saying. 'It's just that your returns this month give you a credit in excess of the entire value of your purchases, which is not exactly what we're in business to achieve. Yes, I know you took a heavy position on the new launch. Well – let's say I partly accept you did it as a favour to us. All right, so I called you personally at the time. All right. A favour to me. Yes – I've just told you, I accept that. A favour to me. Personally. But the fact does still remain that . . . No. No. Absolutely not.'

There was a pause. 'I'm afraid I rather resent that remark, Mr Potter. I said I rather resent what you've just said. Your remark. Look, Mr Potter, of course we appreciate your business. No we don't want the rest of your inventory back as well. No, we don't—' Solly held the telephone away from his ear as the bleeping noise indicated that the receiver had been slammed down at the other end. He put it back on the hook.

'Wanker,' he said. 'Couldn't sell a jock-strap to a bare-arsed Highlander. Hi, Julian. What can I do for you?'

'Barbara Thomson wants me to call her at the auditors. I thought I would have a word with you first, Solly. Do you know what she wants? I've never had anything to do with the auditors in my life.'

'Yes, I do. They warned me yesterday. It appears there's been a bit of naughtiness going on with some of the petty-cash dealings. In your department. These things need to be nipped in the bud as soon as one finds them, before they get out of hand. Call her, and see what they want to ask you. Here – do it now.'

Flicking through his address book, Solly found the number, and asked to be put through to the partner who conducted The Magazine Company audit.

'John? Solly Lorenzo. Do you have Barbara Thomson with you? She was trying to reach Julian Jardine, and I have him here with me at the moment. I'll put him through.'

Julian took the telephone. 'Barbara? It's Julian. I'm with Solly. You wanted me?'

Despite himself, his voice assumed a certain brittle acidity as he spoke, though he by no means wanted to alienate Solly. Now

Barbara was speaking, and Julian noticed again that she had in recent weeks assumed a certain mid-Atlantic drawl, deriving, he suspected, from Joan Collins and a diet of Hollywood soaps.

'Yes, I'm afraid we've come across something a little worrying. There've been quite a lot of very odd little invoices going through the petty-cash system. They don't amount to a great deal of money – barely one thousand five hundred pounds in total over the year. But it looks as if they've all been raised by the same person. They're manual invoices, which someone has made out on tacky little pads, then rubber-stamped with what's turned out to be a phoney company name and address. They're all for small amounts individually, and appear to relate to stationery items. They've been put in the cash box each time, and cash removed to their value. Do you know anything about them? Have you any idea who might have been putting them through?'

'No, I've never even seen them. I never go anywhere near the petty cash box.'

'Well, I've spoken to Solly, and he's keen that we move very fast to find the culprit, and get the whole thing stopped before it gets any worse. I'll bring some of these pieces of paper back to the office with me, and perhaps you'll recognise the markings on them or something. I'll be back in an hour or so. See you then.'

Julian put down the telephone, and looked across at Solly with a wry expression on his face.

'Sorry, Solly. I'm not at my best in this sort of thing. I always hope that someone else is watching the money box really. That makes me sound very unprofessional, but you know what it's like in this sort of world. We're all a bit chaotic about these things. We shouldn't be, of course, but we are. I always trust that Barbara or somebody is doing what has to be done.'

'Look at the invoices, Julian, and whatever else there turns out to be, and see if there are any clues as to who wrote them. I imagine there will be.'

'Of course I will, Solly. I just hope we can clear this up quickly. These witch-hunts are so bad for everybody's morale.'

'Good and bad, in my opinion,' said Solly. Julian watched him with affection. So much the cheerful, flamboyant young wide boy when the firm was launched, and now so formal and orthodox in his presentation, particularly at times like this. Julian's private joke, behind Solly's back, was that the board meetings were performed these days as if they were a gathering of the directors of General Motors; all polished board tables, and rigid formality, and heavy demeanour. Success had not so much gone to Solly Lorenzo's head, in Julian's view, as turned an amiable young maverick into a caricature of an Institute of Directors committee man. The main problem of the board meetings for Julian personally, he told his customary, devoted audience in the editorial department, was that he *never* had a *thing* to wear.

'The firm has a tendency to get sloppy,' Solly was saying. 'We won't have a witch-hunt over this, but we will use it as evidence to the staff of the fact that we want to run a properly disciplined operation. Everyone always thinks that they want anarchy, but then they go to pieces when they've got it. There's a much better atmosphere in the firm when people feel that it's being tightly run.'

Julian got up to go.

'Call me later, Julian. When you've had a chance to talk to Barbara.'

Julian wrinkled his nose and waved a hand at Tracey as he went by her desk, then passed through Reception to pick up some packages. He gathered them up, and was sitting at his desk an hour or so later, leafing through the page proofs that the packages contained, when Barbara Thomson came in and sat down heavily in the chair opposite him.

Julian saw that she was wearing the purple outfit with the enormous shoulder-pads that he particularly despised, and gazed across at her with venom.

'Barbara, darling. In my very favourite dress.'

Barbara Thomson looked at him with a glint of triumph in her eye, and took from her Asprey's executive case a large manila envelope. She drew from this a clutch of hand-stamped invoices, and pushed them across the desk.

'The invoices from your department. The fraudulent ones, darling.'

Julian looked through them. There were eight or ten in all, and each made out in the name of any one of three different suppliers. The standard invoice forms, as bought from any high street stationer, were identical, and the rubber-stamping looked as if it had been done by the same die, a defective capital T being the most obvious evidence of this. In one case, two invoices, made out in the name of two different suppliers, carried consecutive pre-printed serial numbers.

'And all three companies are phoney, darling, as I said to you on the telephone. We've checked them out. And what's as much of a bore as anything is that whoever raised them added so-called VAT charges on them as well. That's one of the things that the auditors are most fussed about, as they'll have to report it to the Customs and Excise. As you know, we'll have claimed the VAT amount back from the Customs in one of our periodic VAT returns. And the risk is that when the Customs are told about this they will insist on the most massive investigation of our records, going back for umpteen years. Or so I imagine. My experience of them is that they think of little else but protecting their backs. It really is a considerable nuisance. And a little embarrassing, to be frank, given the fact that it was the auditors who discovered it.'

Barbara's heavily painted face smiled pleasantly across at Julian. She let the moment linger, then said: 'They're from your department, darling. There's no doubt about that,' then settled back a little in her chair, a look of studied and histrionic enquiry on her face. 'Your department, dear, I'm afraid.'

Julian spread the invoices out in front of him on his desk. 'I realise that, Barbara, and I'm sorry about it. I tend to spend too much of my time publishing. I'll see if I can bring the villain to justice.'

Barbara decided that she had an opportunity to treat the last remark as indicative of a frivolous and professionally irresponsible attitude, and spoke now in a voice of grim rebuke.

'This is no joke, actually, Julian. These things matter. I'm rather surprised that you don't realise that. Solly was very angry when I told him about it. Very angry indeed.'

Julian held up his two hands, as if in mock surrender. 'You're right. Of course you're right. I'll be in touch later today.'

Barbara crossed the corridor, brushing her front against the buttocks of a particularly perky young male editorial assistant, who was bending over picking up some paper by the photocopy machine.

'Sorry, darling,' she said, and winked at the office odd-jobman, who was waiting to get past, wheeling some boxes on a little hand-barrow.

Julian watched her go, then took the invoices out of the file, and spread them out again on his desk. There it was . . . and there again. The little marks of green ink. Just tiny spots. But no one else used green ink in the office, he was almost sure of that, except for Sophie Luscombe. Dear God. Do we have to go through all this?

He looked across at Sophie's desk, just in sight beyond the filing cabinets on the other side of the room. She was sitting there talking on the telephone. Yet again.

This is awful, Julian thought. It isn't just a fiddled taxi receipt, or an attempt to charge up a coffee and Danish with her boyfriend, and all the attendant scruffiness of that sort of thing. The sums are not all that great, but the dummy invoices, and the VAT charge, and all the preparation of it . . . It's fraud. Petty fraud, but fraud. Maybe there's some sort of explanation – but it's difficult to see what it could be.

I'll go over to her, rather than drag her across here to me. If there's an explanation for it, and please God there is, it'll make the whole thing seem less bullying and heavy-handed.

Julian walked across to Sophie's desk, sat down opposite her, and, while she was talking, put the little pile of invoices in front of her. He saw her look down at them, colour very slightly, and then, rather abruptly, she brought her call to a close, and turned her eyes across to him.

'I'm sorry, Julian. Just a problem about some missing statements.' She spoke fast and edgily, then looked Julian directly in the eyes, in a manner which appeared to him to carry a hint of defiance.

'We seem to lose more than we can find in this department, sometimes,' she said. 'I'm thinking of coming in this Sunday all on my own to give the whole place a really good sort out and tidy. Completely go through all the filing, and get everything absolutely shipshape. Would you mind if I did that?'

Julian, as so often in his dealings with her, found his judgement wavering. She seemed to him to be either absurdly manipulative, or alternatively quite heartbreakingly inaccurate in her attempts to be part of the team. It wasn't her fault really that she didn't fit in. Some of the others could be pretty foul to her. Particularly the other women for some reason. And yet . . .

'Sophie – Barbara Thomson has brought me these invoices, that apparently someone has put through the petty cash box. They've only just come to light. The auditors came across them. It seems that the suppliers are all false names, and they're for so-called stationery and various items that we've never received. I don't know too much about it, but I'm responsible because they went through this department. I suppose you've no idea where they've come from, dear?'

That was an extremely silly way of putting it, he thought to himself. Much the best way of handling it would have been to ask her straight out if she'd done the thing herself. Quick and clean. And now I've made it prolix and difficult.

Sophie picked up the invoices and looked at them. She appeared completely composed, studying them one by one, then handing them back to Julian.

'I don't think I've ever seen them before,' she said. 'I don't go to the petty cash box at all. I so disapprove of the way people just help themselves out of it at the flimsiest excuse. Except . . . let me look at them again, Julian.'

She fanned the invoices out on the desk in front of her, then pursed her mouth and handed them back. 'It's just this tiny mark of green ink on the bottom of these two. Very few people use green ink here. I do for some sort of work.'

She opened her drawer, and took out a green-ink Pentel. 'The only other person who uses it, as far as I know, is Victoria Marsdon-Neil up in Reception. Perhaps you should ask her.'

She smiled in a dimpled, demure way, and passed the invoices back across the desk. 'Poor Julian,' she said. 'What a horrid job for you. Now, I must get back on the trail of those dreaded missing statements.' She picked up the telephone again, and dialled a number, smiling sweetly at him in dismissal.

Jesus Christ, thought Julian as he walked away. This is like *Daisy Pulls it Off* or something. All blackmail and revenge in the Upper Sixth, just before the annual hockey match against Hinckley Hall. The girl with the green ink. The innocent dupe expelled, and the wicked German spy's daughter momentarily triumphant. Until right and honour prevail.

Now what on earth happens? I suppose I'd better do as she suggests and go to have a word with that Victoria girl. Or whatever her name is.

Julian went down to Reception, this time much less hesitantly than when he'd first approached Sophie, and put the invoices down on her desk.

'Victoria, some dud invoices have been put through the petty-cash system. These ones. They've been put in the box, and money removed to their value. They've only just been spotted by the auditors. Do you know anything about them?'

Now that, he thought, breaking out into a sweat, was a little *too* abrupt.

'Do I know anything about them? Fraudulent invoices, going through the petty cash box? Someone pinching the money? Julian, that really pisses me off. Of course I don't know anything about them! Frankly, I'm really pissed off that you should ask me about them like that. Christ.'

She picked the invoices up, and looked at them more closely. 'Look. They're covered in green ink. Sophie Luscombe uses green ink. Ask her.'

And with that she pushed the invoices back to him, and, with pointed charm, took a call on one of the now several ringing lines.

'The Magazine Company,' she murmured. 'Yes, he's here. Whom shall I say is calling?'

Chapter Nineteen

Colin Ewing looked across the desk at the slight figure sitting behind it. The fan was turning in the ceiling of the office, but it did little more than blow on to the floor loose papers left unsecured by a paperweight. There was an air-conditioner unit framed into the window, but Colin had already been told that this was temporarily inoperative.

'Kaput, old boy,' announced the man behind the desk. 'Absolutely bloody typical. Damn nearly a hundred degrees in the shade, and the bloody air conditioner goes up the spout.'

Amarjeet Prasad was tall, youngish, bald and carried a quite magnificent caricature of an English military moustache above startlingly white teeth and a very weak chin. Colin had asked C.P. Nerappan about him, and had been told that he was a notoriously inadequate son of his effective and well-known father, all of which only served to engage Colin's sympathy for him.

Colonel Prasad, the head of the family civil engineering firm, was a Punjabi who had been trained by the British at Sandhurst, and had performed feats of quite startling gallantry and heroics in the 1964 war between India and Pakistan. In this he'd been in conflict with several Pakistani officers who'd been at Sandhurst with him, all of whom had been and were subsequently good friends of his. Colonel Prasad's war had been conducted by him as if it were a particularly robust game of rugby football. One or two of the chaps got hurt, of course, but the sportsmanship and team spirit were all one could have wished.

Amarjeet Prasad had inherited his father's dashing looks quite certainly, but, in C.P.'s version, absolutely none of either his heroism or his intelligence. He looked benign enough in Colin's eyes, as he sat there in his extremely untidy office, and he was certainly making great efforts to be agreeable.

'C.P. well? How is the old rogue? Eating his greens and all that sort of thing? Going easy with his grog?'

I wonder what on earth this man does when he is with any normal, self-respecting, straightforward Indian, Colin thought. I cannot believe he continues this act unless he's got an English audience, or the sort of quasi-English audience that C.P. would provide, were he in the right mood. Which I doubt he would often be, if presented with the prospect of having to give extended time to Amarjeet Prasad. I can't believe anyone could talk like this, without any apparent sense of concealed irony.

'In good form, I think, Mr Prasad,' raising his hand in acknowledgement of the latter's insistence that he should be called by his first name, 'Amarjeet. In fact, in good form I *know*, because I was talking to him about two hours ago in his office. He sends his best wishes to you, of course.'

'Mine to him, old boy. Mine to him. Now then – what's your poison?'

Colin looked at his watch, and saw that it was barely five-fifteen.

'Oh, a cup of tea, please. That would be marvellous. The Bank's rules, you know,' he added. 'No drinking in office hours. There are only two rules, actually. That, and the other one. For management trainees coming out to work in foreign branches: keep your mouth shut, and your bowels open.'

Amarjeet Prasad leant back in his chair and laughed with such enthusiasm that tears appeared in his eyes. Colin regarded him with fascination. If he was going to laugh at that, it might be amusing to try something on him that was actually funny. It would kill the bugger, more than likely. Well worth the experiment.

'Marvellous,' gasped Prasad. 'Marvellous. Oh dear, oh dear.' He wiped his cheeks, still laughing. 'Tea it is then,' he said and rang a bell for a servant. *'Chai lao. Jaldi lao.'* He smiled amiably at Colin. 'On its way, old boy. Now – what can I do for you? Build you a bridge? Knock up a road? Anything you say.'

'Just lend me a little hand with a survey I'm doing, if you would, Amarjeet. For the Bank. I'm talking to one or two of our bigger corporate clients in this part of the world to see how well we're doing our job. That sort of thing. A Head Office snoop on the far-flung empire, if you like. You know the two great lies of corporate life. Number one – Don't Worry, The Cheque's In The Post. And number two – I'm From Head Office And I'm Here To Help You.'

Amarjeet Prasad's delight with these, and the consequent renewed manic laughter, gave Colin the opportunity to glance at the tiny notes he had scribbled for himself in his pocket book, chuckling sufficiently to keep the momentum going until he had memorised again the sequence of events he wanted to track.

'So, I'm just going to ask a few questions for my survey – just for our own research. I do hope you won't mind. And I might take a few notes. Don't worry if the questions cover some very well-trodden areas. Just treat me like a complete moron. And throw me out the moment I become a bore.'

The tea arrived, there was a moment's fuss about where the ginger biscuits were, then Prasad waved Colin on.

'So, Amarjeet, perhaps I could start at the beginning. Prasad & Prasad is a privately held family company, started by your grandfather, and you and your father are the only two shareholders at this time, apart from a block of shares held in a family trust. Right?'

'That's it. Or rather that *was* it. We now have one extra shareholder, as I will explain in a minute. My father is Chairman, though he's not concerned on a day-to-day basis of course, and I'm Managing Director. My younger brother is also now in the firm, and we've just put him on to the board as Technical Director. I suppose we'll allocate him some shares in due course. Though between you and me he doesn't know his arse from his elbow. Never will.'

He smiled and shook his head in a theatrical gesture of dismissive affection, and Colin again felt a prick of jealousy as he saw the great swathe of white teeth, Colin's own being quite lamentably in need of cosmetic care and attention.

'Just family board members, then?' he prompted. 'No outsiders?'

'That's what I was going to explain. About two years ago we issued an invitation to one of Father's army colleagues to join the board as a non-executive, and to hold some shares. General Swami. You may know of him?'

Colin shook his head. 'Why him?' he asked curiously. 'And why now? And what will he be doing? Non-executive directors in family firms are not that common really. Not when all the shares have always been so closely held.'

'Oh, influence mainly. Contacts – that sort of thing. Military procurement. General Swami is a very popular man. Knows everybody.'

'And your father?'

'He does too. Between the pair of them they seem to have everybody covered who could be covered. You need to in India, as you know. Particularly in our sort of work. The Government like to be able to trust the contractors they employ on the big civil engineering projects. There are so many cowboys around. They need people who will do what they say they will do. On time, and reliably. This is not a very reliable country.'

Colin chuckled politely, and sipped at his tea.

'But if my father puts his name to a contract, then the other side knows that everything will be done that has to be done. General Swami too. We are the Eton of civil engineers here in India, my dear fellow. Blue chip.'

'Blue chip certainly, as I understand it, Amarjeet. And that reputation has brought your firm some very good contracts,

119

particularly in recent months. You were included amongst the main Poonjee Dam contractors, a very significant moment for a family firm such as this, I would have thought.

'And a little stressful too,' he went on. 'Some most appetising profits to be made, but plenty of cash-flow ups and downs on the way no doubt. Did you ever think it might be beyond a firm with quite a modest capital base? It must all give you some anxious moments, dealing with a contract as big as this.'

'Some anxious moments of course,' Amarjeet agreed. 'Some very anxious moments. But your Bank has been very helpful. We have a very good relationship with your people. We talk to them all the time, and we try to see trouble coming well before it actually arrives.'

'I'm glad to hear it. Delighted you came to us in the first place. We hadn't worked with you before, I think I'm right in saying? What brought you to us on this occasion?'

'Your reputation, my dear fellow. Your reputation in India is very high. You're not perhaps the most adventurous of banks . . .'

'God forbid,' murmured Colin, to show willing.

' . . . but you're very easy to deal with, and very straightforward. And you employ such top-grade people. C.P. Nerappan is quite simply the best. Tell him the truth, and he'll tell you the truth. Which is sometimes not very palatable. And he will not allow you to negotiate with him. He'll simply inform you of the terms on which he is prepared to deal with you, and that's that.'

'And the terms on which he was prepared to finance your Poonjee Dam contract are as summarised in the letter to you in June of that year? Was this the final letter? No alteration to these terms?' Colin opened his attaché case. 'Yes, here we are – June 23. This letter here, was that the final deal? Nothing superseded it? Nothing else on file?' He pushed the letter across to Prasad, and waited for his answer.

'Yes, that's the deal. As you can see, my father has countersigned it on behalf of this firm. That's what we agreed. Or rather, that's what we *had* to agree.'

He laughed, white teeth again gleaming at Colin, and pushed the piece of paper back across the desk.

'As you can see, the penalties on it if we miss an interest payment due date are most unpleasant. And we have had to give overriding personal guarantees in addition to the firm's security. C.P. was very tough on us. But we signed.'

He chuckled again. Colin did so too, but there was a concentration in his eyes that might have surprised some of his colleagues.

'Why did you sign? Wasn't it a tougher deal than you could have got from another bank?'

'It was tough. It was tough, but . . .' the young Indian shrugged, and pulled a mock wry face, ' . . . but it meant that the Moorgate & Mercantile Bank was behind us. And as I said, we felt that you were the most reliable people of all. So we signed.'

'And yet there is one aspect of the arrangement which does surprise me,' Colin said. 'The interest rate. You're paying only one and a half per cent over the Federal Base Rate. You say that C.P. won't allow you to negotiate with him, and yet you seem to have come out rather lightly on this count. Or very lightly, in my opinion.'

'Oh, that's easy to explain. We had an offer on the table from the Javed & National people. C.P. said he would match them, but only on interest rates. The security provisions and the default penalties he was immovable on.'

'So you *did* negotiate.'

'No. He merely said that he would match whatever offer the Javed & National made to us on the interest rates.'

'And you had an offer from them in writing?'

'Of course.'

'And you showed the letter to C.P.?'

'Of course. He looked at it, but didn't keep a copy for obvious reasons. We kept a copy here, naturally. Do you want me to find it?'

Colin smiled across the table at him, but more because he didn't know what to say than for any other reason. It was in some respects an unorthodox deal that C.P. had struck. Very punitive in some areas, but perhaps as much as one and a half per cent off the market in the interest rate he had levied. And that was significant money on lendings of this size. But it had been debated and discussed at the Loans Committee, and they had cleared it – Colin had read the minutes. And matching a competitor's offer was not such an unusual step to take. The odd thing really was that Javed & National had offered that rate themselves.

'Would that be convenient?' he said aloud. 'I'd love to glance at it if you wouldn't mind. Very good of you.'

A *babu* was despatched for the file, and Colin asked if he could also see their Poonjee civil engineering contract on which the Bank had lent. Whilst waiting for these to be found, Colin asked what progress on the Poonjee work there had been to that point.

'We're pretty well up to schedule. Our main job at this point is to build the feed roads up to the work-site, and those will be finished before the monsoon starts, unless we run up against something really untoward. We then get on with the widening of the trunk road up from Cape Comorin, and at the same time we have work to do on the new bridge that will take the trunk road across the Poonjee four or five miles downstream from the dam.'

The *babu* had arrived, and Colin looked first at the Javed & National letter. It had been signed directly in the Bank's name, Colin saw, and the interest rate quoted in it was clearly shown, exactly as Amarjeet Prasad had said. He gave it back to him.

'It must have been tough for C.P. to decide whether or not to follow that,' he said.

'Talk to him about it,' urged Amarjeet. 'Talk to him. It was very important to us that with borrowings of this size we did the keenest deal on our cash outflows as possible, and he realised that. The interest rate was more important to us than anything else. The Javed & National bid was there on the table. He knew we would have to go with it if your people couldn't match it.'

Colin picked up the Government contract, and started to leaf through it, then put it down again.

'I don't think I can face ploughing through all of that. I was just wondering what their payment terms to you are. Whether you have to wait for your money, that sort of thing.'

'No, we get paid very promptly. Every twenty-eight days by banker's draft. We have no problems at all.'

'Why not?'

Prasad looked at him, his face for once carrying an expression of irritation and suspicion.

'What do you mean – why not? Why shouldn't we be paid on time?'

Colin shrugged. 'I didn't think that was how it normally worked. My understanding was that waiting for money from the Government here was like waiting for the cows to come home. You wait.'

'Ah, that's because we're Prasad & Prasad.' All his good humour seemed to have returned. 'We've got a high reputation. People treat us well. That's what I was saying to you. We're blue-chip people. We're good people to do business with.'

Colin got up to go, brushing the crumbs of ginger biscuit off the front of his trousers, and mopping the sweat off his face with a blue handkerchief. After his statement of effusive gratitude for the tea, and the time he'd been given, and the helpfulness of what he'd been told, he turned to go, calling as he went, 'I do congratulate you on getting your money so promptly and reliably from the Government's procurement people. Gives them a nice warm feeling, does it, dealing with you? A nice warm feeling – like pissing down their trouser legs?'

And the abandonment of Amarjeet Prasad's delight at this saw Colin safely down the stairs and out into the street, with no need for any more to be done than a wave and a shouted goodbye at the door.

And the odd thing about all that, Colin thought, as he picked his way among the jostling, thrusting crowds – the odd thing about that is that it's so crassly obvious. So clearly fraudulent. Obviously where I'm being led is right.

Of course C.P. must be lining his pockets. I've never seen anything so blatant in my life.

Chapter Twenty

Rowena sat there on the floor, her hands shielding herself now as her partner got to her feet and picked up her clothes.

'That was lovely, dear. Both of you. Lovely.'

The middle-aged man looked around at the group of men with him, then back to Rowena.

'But we'd like a bit more, I think. We made a nice video of that, but you're a naughty girl you know, and you've got us all excited. Your friend too. Now we've already given you a hundred each for the little show. What about another fifty each, and we'll all have a nice time together?'

He took out his wallet, and she could again see the thick wad of notes tucked into it. He took three twenty-pound notes between his forefinger and thumb and showed them to her in a fan.

'There we are, dear. I'll make it a little more. We'll call it sixty. Sixty for you, and the same for your friend.'

Rowena gazed at him without answering at first, then she nodded slightly and looked up at Dixie, who was standing there waiting for Rowena to give the lead. Rowena shrugged her shoulders, in a dumbshow of weary compliance, and Dixie made to do the same, then looked across at the men and gave her ugly little smile, the crooked teeth discoloured and prominent.

This no longer means anything to me at all, Rowena thought. A hundred and sixty pounds earned in the evening. That's almost enough for us for two nights, if I turn one more trick tomorrow.

She lay back as the first man mounted her, and before she closed her eyes so that she wouldn't have to look at him, she could see that most of them were stripping off their clothes, and two of them were feeling at Dixie. The man was panting, and she was turned over on to her stomach and other hands were all over her.

No, I'm wrong, she thought. This does mean something to me. Thank God it does. I've never yet lost my disgust. Thank God I'm not so brutalised that I can't still feel disgust. And I won't act for them. They can do all this to me but I won't simulate anything at all.

She felt her body being pulled at, her legs held up and separated, people feeling at her, pulling at her, turning her, fingering her, entering her, ravishing her as an animal would be ravished.

This'll be over soon. Over soon. A hundred and sixty pounds. Plenty for the crack. Plenty for what we need. It'll be over soon.

I can still feel disgust. I haven't lost my soul. I can still feel disgust. I've got my baby. I'm still whole. I've got my baby.

Chapter Twenty-One

When the taxi drew up to the house Robert looked at it with loathing.

He and Sarah had lived there for five years, which was the longest they had ever been together anywhere. But neither of them had made any effort whatsoever to make of it a real home.

Robert could see this now with an outsider's eye as he looked at the house once more. The rose on the corner of the wall was shabby and lank. The paint on the windowsills was flaking and peeling, and the stucco too. The front doorstep was cracked and severed, and weeds grew up in between the flagstones in the little front space. Two rusty old dustbins, both without lids, stood outside the house, unconcealed and stark. Net curtains, grey with grime and dust, hung across the window of the dining room at the front. A window in the attic bedroom at the top of the house was cracked, and taped across with brown adhesive sealing.

In all, it was too obviously the house of a couple who had lost hope in their marriage, and no longer had the pride or the energy to make attempts to conceal it. As Robert looked up at the familiar place through the taxi windows he was both ashamed and resigned. And intensely, hopelessly tired. 'Home again, Sarah,' he said. And turning to her with what he hoped she could construe as a smile of love and encouragement, he added, 'I'm glad to be back, aren't you? It's good to be home.'

She turned to him, and she too tried to smile. 'Yes, of course it's good to be home. But at the moment I feel too tired for anything much. Look after me a bit, Robert. Just until I get my confidence back. You know how it is.'

He laid his hand on her arm, and patted her, then gently encouraged her out of the taxi, and into the house, the latest of so many they had lived in over the course of their married lives.

In their early years in India there had been a succession of places, wherever Robert had been sent to work. Then, when he was posted to the London Head Office in 1970, on his thirty-fourth birthday, they had bought the first of what had turned out to be several houses in varying parts of the town.

Initially there had been a pretty Regency house in Stockwell, but the street in which it stood obstinately refused to gentrify, as had been eagerly anticipated by the two middle-class families who had bought houses there. So both the Luscombes and the other family moved on, the immature wistarias struggling up the drainpipes, and the glossy front doors, and the shiny brass fittings upon them, left as a keepsake of their brief and unmemorable residency.

From there they moved to the bottom two storeys of a rambling villa in the wide, curving streets that lie at the northern fringes of Holland Park. But sharing a house and garden with a dowager lady with a small dog, both of whom detested and snapped at the children, proved a short-lived phase, and from Holland Park they moved barely a few hundred yards, to a little modern house tucked away off Lansdowne Road. But this house proved painfully lacking in space as the two girls grew up. It was anyway bought on a mortgage so large that Robert was in a continual state of anxiety as to how to deal with the cost of it as interest rates rose, despite the favourable terms of the mortgage through the Bank, and he was relieved after two or three years to sell it. They moved next to a mews cottage near Primrose Hill, but this proved dark and noisy, and finally they bought the freehold of where they now lived, a terraced house of no particular distinction, in a leafy road near St John's Wood High Street.

They lived there on their own of course, both Rowena and Sophie having left home, and there was talk of yet another move, as Sarah found the stairs too steep and too many, the drawing room too small and the basement too dark. But for Robert it had become something of a matter of indifference where he lived, though he would never have expressed that to anyone. Least of all to Sarah, for to fuel her dwindling self-esteem with any suggestion that she was failing to make anything of her family home would be one further statement of failure.

Their mutual courtesy remained, and they had their repertoire of comfortable rituals of simulated affection, but that was all. There had been too many houses, too many mortgages, too many false dawns, too many dark and disappointing kitchens, too many curtains that were never made and hung, too many rooms never finally bookshelved and decorated. Each time they moved it was the same of course, and the expectation died away. And if Robert had grown unconcerned about where he lived, his feelings now, just off the plane from India, had moved from indifference to defined dislike.

As he gathered the suitcases to take them into the house, he could sense that Sarah's mood had quite swung away from that strange euphoria of the last two nights they had spent together in Bavancore. Oddly flippant and skittish in India since her disaster with the fisherman, she now seemed to have declined once more into despair.

'Of course I know how it is, old girl. It's difficult to keep your confidence,' he said, but now there were the suitcases to take upstairs, and the letters to pick up from the hall mat, and the activity of that was enough to release the immediate tension of the occasion for her.

When Robert had shaved and had his shower, he found Sarah sitting at the kitchen table with a cup of tea in her hand, reading the parish magazine.

He went over to sit opposite her, then stretched out his hand and held hers for a moment. It was the sort of gesture that neither of them was accustomed to make with each other. He was trying to simulate love, or at least compassion, as if the pretence of it would absolve them both from their failure. But when she laid her own hand on top of his, he had to suppress an instinctive shudder.

Dear God, he thought. What can we bring to each other now? Sarah's own unhappiness has reached such a pitch that she makes a fool of herself with a fisherman. Then turns back to me for the reassurance that I can protect her from the damage done. And then I insult her by this affectation of attachment. Talking to her as one would a child, rather than to a fellow adult, in tones of parental concern and support, and confirmation that one will be there to pick up the pieces.

But he patted her hand, withdrew his own, then pulled towards him the pile of letters that had been awaiting them in the hall. He sorted them through, put the bills to one side, and took into his hand an envelope addressed to him in the familiar hand of Rowena.

As he looked at it, a clench of anxiety tugged at his stomach, and his fingers shook as he tore the envelope open. He saw that Sarah had returned to the parish magazine, so he let his eyes just flash through the letter, to see immediately how bad the news was. Then, steadying himself, he read it again, this time with proper care, and as he did so his fear gave way to the familiar, warm flow of love.

Dearest Daddy,

I don't think I've ever written to you since I was in that squat, after I had run away from school. Do you remember driving down to Camberwell to see me there? You sat outside in the car for hours, and I was too ashamed to come out to you. Eventually I did, and I got in with you, and we drove around South London. Initially in dead silence, and then we talked about our lives in a way we had never succeeded in doing before. And maybe nothing that we said changed anything very much, and maybe it was all too late, and maybe the damage had already been done to me. But I do want you to know that I often think of that day. I think it was the last time that I ever spoke to anyone in that sort of way.

I'm writing to you now because I am for a moment free of physical craving and fear, and my mind is clear, and it's so seldom like that. It won't last for long, but I wanted to take the chance while my mind is like it is, and I can concentrate on what I'm writing, and say to you some of the things that I want to say. And at this very minute there's enough crack for me for the whole weekend, and there's almost a thousand pounds sitting hidden in the kitchen, and I know I'll be all right for as long as I can imagine ahead, which is about a week at the outside. And Jamie is out with Rick, and everything is quiet, and I can think.

So I don't want anything from you. And that's why I can write to you. I don't want money from you, and I'm not in prison, and I'm not about to die, and nor is Jamie. By my standards, everything is fine. I wanted to use this moment to say to you something about love. And I wanted to try for the first time I can ever remember to say that I know what you have tried to bring to me in my life, and I wish it had worked. Except, when I was writing that, it didn't feel true. I'm actually past the point where I wish things had been different. I can only imagine my life as it is. But what I was trying to say was that you tried to give me love. And I do wish, even in my condition now, that I had known how to take it.

I can't love any more. I'm too ill now, if 'ill' is the right way to describe me. The only real love I can sometimes experience is what I feel for Jamie. Occasionally it feels like something that is real and mature and full of hope. But then I can't hold it. As soon as the hell starts again, I can think of nothing else but that. I even forget Jamie. Completely forget him. And that's not love. Not real love. Not the sort of love he deserves.

So that's all my letter is about. I hope the peace in me lasts long enough for me to get out into the street and post it. I even went to the Post Office and bought a stamp.

It's just that I can remember our ride together in your car around the South London streets that wet winter afternoon. And I remember watching you drive the car, and everything about you was so normal and straightforward and clean and unstressed. Your car was so tidy and ordered, and your shirt was buttoned at your wrists, and that lovely soft cashmere overcoat of yours was turned up at the neck. Just three apparently unconnected and random things. But when I looked at you I remember I thought you were so competent and so nice. I was proud to have you as my father. You make so little fuss about life. You never allow any situation to look too overwhelming or too full of danger. You can deal with everything. Or you seem to be able to deal with everything. Whatever life brings you, you just cope with it. The other three of us could never cope with anything. We still can't, I imagine. You coped for us all. God knows we didn't deserve it. We certainly never let you think that we appreciated it. Maybe we didn't appreciate it. I'm not sure I can remember.

You will see that there's no address on this letter, as you mustn't try to reach me. Perhaps I'll write again. Perhaps I never will. But look after yourself, Daddy.

Rowena.

Robert saw that Sarah was still immersed in her magazine, so he slipped Rowena's letter into his pocket, and slid his chair back to get to his feet.

Sarah looked up. 'Do you have to go to the office already?'

She picked up the pile of bills, leafed through them quickly and handed them to him, unopened. 'All for you. Horrid bills, I'm afraid. Please open the ones with my name on them and deal with them. Poor Robert. Always paying out money for us all.'

She smiled at him, looked down to continue reading, then said, without glancing up, 'Any other letters of interest? Nothing from Sophie?'

He turned round at the door, hesitated, then went on his way, calling out as he opened the front door, 'Nothing from Sophie. But I left a message that you would call her as soon as we got home. Don't forget. Give her my love, my dear. Give her my love.'

Chapter Twenty-Two

Robert sat in Solly Lorenzo's private office and looked at him with a face that was shaken with dismay.

'I am so sorry, Mr Lorenzo. I'm so sorry.'

'It's hardly your fault, Mr Luscombe.' Solly smiled at him, and there was considerable warmth in his eyes as he did so.

'Kids.' And he opened his arms wide in an expressive gesture of helplessness, shrugging his shoulders, palms upwards. 'My daughter Hannah was like having a crazed juvenile delinquent around the place at one stage,' he said, then cursed himself inwardly for the tactlessness and banality of the remark. His daughter, a University College, London graduate, clever and attractive and competent, and now at twenty-three just launched on a career as a television researcher, was hardly a sensitive choice of comparison for Sophie Luscombe. Overweight, ill-adjusted Sophie Luscombe, with a history of trouble and disturbance behind her.

Damn, thought Solly. Damn. How can I mend that one?

'Now I'm sorry, Mr Luscombe. That was a particularly stupid thing to say. Most insensitive of me.'

And as Robert heard him say this, his mind went back to their conversation together eighteen months or so before, when he had asked Solly Lorenzo, as a personal favour to him, to give Sophie a job at The Magazine Company, she having fallen foul yet again of her current employers. That had been the last of many occasions when he had broken for her his instinctive rule that his children should succeed in standing on their own two feet, but somehow with Sophie . . .

Robert grimaced, then looked directly across at Solly Lorenzo as he spoke, but there was a note of defeat in his voice. 'It's hardly fair of me to put it this way, but . . . do you have to make a charge, Mr Lorenzo? I'm very embarrassed to put it like that, but Sophie is my daughter, and of course I feel I have to do all I can to protect her. Though she hardly deserves it in this case, if I understand correctly what she appears to have done.'

'We do have a problem over this, Mr Luscombe, and you can understand what it is. It was theft of the most painstakingly fraudulent variety. She falsified those invoices, which was a very stupid thing to do. One of the minor irritations of it was that it got us into trouble with the Customs and Excise over the fact that we had been reimbursed by them for the false VAT that we had paid her. That in itself put the accounting department through a lot of work and trouble – although the sum of money involved was in itself fairly trivial, of course.

'Then, by far the worst of all, she went to great lengths to try to implicate another member of the staff, Victoria Marsdon-Neil, the girl at Reception you saw as you came in. To the extent that she made out another false invoice, hid it in the poor girl's desk and tricked Julian, her boss, into finding it there. He, thank God, had the sense to realise what had happened. All the staff knew about it, and as you can imagine there was complete uproar over the whole thing.'

'Yes.'

Robert gazed across the desk at Solly Lorenzo, and there was such disappointment in his face that Solly tried desperately to find something else to say. Then Robert shifted slightly in his chair, and attempted to smile at him.

'Yes, it really is rather a grotesque story. As I say, I am most desperately sorry. And . . . very ashamed.'

'You mustn't say that,' said Solly. 'There's no need for you to say that.'

'Well. I can understand it if you feel you have to proceed on a formal charge. She's behaved in an appalling way. I don't like her letting you down, after you've been so very good to her. Or letting everybody else down either.'

'Or you.'

'No. Not me. I'm not the point. It's not a question of letting me down. I'm her father. That's a very different thing.'

God, I do agree with you, Solly thought. Poor sod. But then he said, 'To be practical about it, Mr Luscombe, she's been sent home and dismissed, as you know. That's obviously inevitable. The problem about deciding formally not to charge her additionally for theft is that we've made an enormous song and dance about dishonesty here in the last few months. We think it's good for the firm, and good for morale. Two people here have been sacked for playing around with their expenses, and one of them was very near retirement, which made it particularly painful for everybody. The directors have been read the riot act. A senior manager was given a formal, posted warning for putting some of his private mail through the office franking machine. That sounds like self-righteous trivia, I know. But we do think you can't have two sets of rules. And this offence of Sophie's is so serious that we would be softening our whole stance if we let it go too easily. Particularly as she has admitted what she did.'

Solly put his elbows on the desk and joined his hands in front of his chin, looking directly at Robert, and trying to show in his face the concern and sympathy he had for him.

'So it's a bit of a bugger, as you can see.'

Robert got to his feet, and put his coffee cup back on the tray on Solly's desk. 'Yes, it's certainly that. Let's leave it there for now, shall we? Thank you, Mr Lorenzo. Thank you for seeing me.'

'Mr Luscombe – look, I don't think we can do anything, but I will think about it over the next day or so, and I will take soundings from Julian and the others to see what the mood of everybody is.

And I think you should anyway see a lawyer, or Sophie should. Except I rather think you will yourself somehow.'

'Yes, I will. Thank you, Mr Lorenzo. Thank you again.'

As he passed through Reception, Robert made a particular point of smiling at Victoria, with an expression that was designed to indicate to her that he was apologising for what had happened. She smiled back, colouring abruptly as she did so, and Robert lifted his hand in a small gesture of farewell.

He returned to his office at the Bank, and the moment he got there put a call through to his personal lawyers. He found, to his dismay, that Peter Rutherford, the partner who normally looked after his affairs and a friend of many years' standing, had just left for Switzerland on holiday. So he spoke to the senior partner, explaining the help he needed, and it was arranged that Robert would come into the office the following morning to meet a lawyer by the name of Alice Livingstone, who was a new recruit to the firm, and highly recommended to Robert.

That evening he made several attempts to reach Sophie, but her telephone remained unanswered. Sometime after eleven o'clock he got out his car to drive around to the flat in Battersea she shared with some friends, but he found the door locked when he arrived, and there was no answer to his repeated ringing of the bell. He tore a page out of his pocketbook, and pushed a note under her door, explaining that he had arranged to see his lawyers the next day, and asking that she should be there as well, if she saw the note in time.

His meeting was at nine o'clock, and it was with no great surprise that he found himself alone in the waiting room at their offices when the time was come. Exactly on the hour the door burst open, and Robert found himself looking at a young woman of perhaps twenty-eight or twenty-nine, who promptly dropped a great bundle of files on to the floor. Robert went down on his haunches to help her pick them up, noticing that each of them had his name printed on the front.

'God, I am sorry, Mr Luscombe,' she said. 'I was in such a panic to get here in time to look through your files before we met. As it turned out I've hardly done so, and here I am dropping them all over you anyway.'

She grinned at him, brushing her auburn hair back from her eyes as she did so with the palm of her hand. Her complexion had a special bloom, Robert thought, and he noted, with amusement, that her sparse make-up was erratically applied and distributed on her mouth and eyes.

But for all that, she was a girl of quite emphatic attraction; self-confident, pretty, and with a most agreeable smile. One of those smiles that was so open and unassumed and full of good humour that it almost demanded a response in kind, and Robert found himself smiling back at her, and with a warmth that he normally found very difficult to extend to anyone on early acquaintance.

'Really sorry,' she said. 'How do you do. I'm Alice Livingstone. We haven't met. As Jonathan explained, Peter is away for a couple of weeks, so you've got me.'

He found himself staring at her, then, realising what he was doing, he searched for something to say. But, before he could speak, she rescued him with an invitation to follow her to her room, where she sat him down and put the files in a stack on the desk in front of her.

'I've really not got very much further than establishing your family details, Mr Luscombe. I see there has been quite an amount of work for us to deal with one way or another over the years.' She flushed, and shrugged her hands in a gesture of apology.

Robert said in a tone designed to ease her embarrassment. 'Yes, there has, I'm afraid. Peter has always been very helpful. I have one of those families that has never run very smoothly.'

'I can see that.' She flicked through the files in front of her, as if to demonstrate their volume, then gave her open, artless smile to him again, pulling the slightest of grimaces to indicate sympathy and acknowledgement.

'I see that you had lunch with Peter last Friday – the day you returned from India – and he made a file note after that about the incident with your wife. I think we've got all the facts we need for our record. The case is closed as I understand it, and the police have decided to take no further action. I think Peter just wants to tidy that bit of it up with our associate office there, but after that we can put it behind us. But now, I believe . . .?'

'Yes. Now I'm afraid I have another problem to deal with. It's over my daughter, Sophie.'

'So Jonathan told me, though I haven't a full brief of exactly what happened. Can we start again with it?'

As Robert told her the story, he found himself watching her with a curious feeling of intensity and heightened awareness. She scribbled a note or two as he spoke, asked the occasional question, and followed what he said with an intermittent frown of concentration on her face. He was half-aware of what he was saying, and half-aware of the tension that was building in him. As she wrote her notes he looked at her arms, and her shoulders, and the way her neck was angled, and although his eyes ran over her thighs and her breasts it was not lasciviousness that he was feeling, but the totally unexpected, unlooked-for instincts of love, and he recognised that, and marvelled at what was happening.

Robert was by some distance not a purist in his admiration of women. He found a large proportion of them attractive, and the girl before him quite remarkably so, but he had been conventionally faithful in his married life, and he was not a man who went out of his way to envy other men their wives, or waste himself in carnal speculation. He had an extreme embarrassment and distaste for the exotic, the flagrant, the pornographic. The prudishness, however, was by no means evidence of a lack of erotic interest or drive, for Robert had plenty of that.

There was some aspect of her smile, her good humour, her intelligent self-confidence – the straightforward pleasingness of her physically that made her the more perfect for him. He thought she was, at that moment, the most attractive girl he had ever seen, and the *coup de foudre* of sudden, immediate love was upon him.

When Alice turned around to bring his coffee to him she saw him gazing at her, and she coloured a little at this. She was prone to blushing, and this always irritated her, so she tried to disguise it now, as she often did, by immediately assuming an air of professional energy and bustle.

'Well, that's a very clear brief of where we are. Thank you. My immediate reaction is that we would be very foolish to attempt a defence of any vigour if Sophie is charged and prosecuted. I don't want to be offensive, and suggest to you that your daughter would mislead us, but we would have to be one hundred per cent certain that she was genuinely innocent before we did anything else but advise her to plead guilty and depend on a good presentation of the case thereafter. We would play it entirely differently, of course, if she is genuinely innocent of it all. But from what you say, that doesn't seem to be very likely. Though you haven't spoken to her as I understand it?'

'No. I've been calling her flat but she doesn't seem to be there, and I have no idea where she could be.'

'So I think all we can do at this stage is to wait and see what happens. Mr Lorenzo is to call you later today as you said, and if they're going to get the police to make a charge, then the sooner we can find Sophie the better. Just assuming for a moment that we are not going to attempt a Not Guilty plea and an active, combative defence, though obviously that depends on Sophie, then it will be a question of doing what we can in Court to make the sentence as easy for her as possible. And for that we'll need a really strong barrister.

'That can be sorted out when Peter gets back from his holiday. So – why don't you telephone me as soon as you have any news from The Magazine Company? And I'm sure you'll do all you can to find Sophie in the meantime.'

She smiled at him, and he smiled at her in return, and he knew at that moment, with what felt like a total certainty, where this unlikely connection would lead. For them both. Not him alone – for them both. How and when, he had no idea . . . but it was a moment of complete conviction.

I love her, he thought. It's the most unexpected thing that has ever happened to me. There's been no preparation for this, no period of adjustment, no history of us getting to know each other. I've been with her for five minutes, and I love her.

I'm going to have her in my life. We're going to be lovers. She's going to be mine.

Chapter Twenty-Three

Solly Lorenzo called Robert later that morning, and told him that the directors had decided that they would have to tell the police of Sophie's fraud, and proceed to a charge against her. Robert had guessed this would be the case, and was prepared for it in his mind.

'Mr Lorenzo, you are absolutely certain that she's done what she's alleged to have done? I've been trying desperately to reach her to ask her the question myself. I should be most grateful for your reassurance that you know what you're doing.'

'We made her sign a statement for us when she left. I wanted to be certain there weren't going to be any diversions about unfair dismissal or anything of that sort. The statement was absolutely clear. I just don't think we have any choice, for the reasons we mentioned yesterday. The police have got to be involved. I hate doing this to you, Mr Luscombe. I hope you realise that.'

'Of course I understand. Let's hope we're lucky and she gets away with a considerable fright but not too harsh a punishment. I'm all for the fright. It might have been better if she'd been frightened more severely in the past.' Robert paused. 'As soon as I've found her, I'll get my lawyers to call yours and we can arrange for her to go to the police to be charged. As you can imagine, I would like to do it in an orderly fashion, and for us to go to them, rather than have them pounding on the door of her flat in front of her friends.'

Solly nodded his head. 'I hope she's lucky too. I really do. She's a girl who needs some sort of psychiatric care and possibly some other counselling as well in my opinion. She's a very nice girl at the bottom of her. Just needs some help.'

And that I mean not at all, if I'm sincere about it, thought Solly. I wouldn't dream of hurting Luscombe with a hint of what I really believe, which is that I have an instinct that his daughter's got a rare quality of manipulative evil about her. She's a nasty piece of work actually, and poor old Luscombe is going to have to face up to that one of these days. He's not going to have much choice, if she continues as she is now. None at all.

But Robert was speaking again, and as Solly listened to him he could hear the resignation in his voice.

'Maybe she does,' said Robert. 'Perhaps you're right.'

There was a silence for a moment or two, and then Robert said, 'Please don't be embarrassed about all this, Mr Lorenzo. I do completely understand. You've been very kind to me, and you've been very good to Sophie. I do understand.'

Dear God, Sophie, Robert thought as he put the telephone down. And his mind roved over her childhood and his instinctive lack of affection for her, even to the extent that when she was a baby he'd found it difficult to undertake any physical contact with her. Always concealed from Sarah of course, and never discussed with anyone, but it had been there, and he was ashamed that it was so.

It was so different with Rowena. Why should that be? The same blood, the same flesh . . . but so different. What a failure that was. What a failure of natural instinct and affection . . . And then Robert's heart gave a lurch of pleasure and anticipation. He could call Alice now to tell her what Solly had said.

Alice. Alice. He sat at his desk, his elbows resting on its surface, his face now in his hands as he thought of her, and tried to recall as much of her face and her body and her voice as he could. He remembered most of all her white arms, paler-skinned than he had seen in anybody, and the soft down on them, and the square hands, with the neat rounded fingernails and their colourless, unfussy

varnish. Over her shoulders she had thrown a cardigan and the
sleeves of it had hung down beside her arms. The plain cotton shirt
underneath had shown the curve of her breasts, and the white,
white skin of her neck. On her Robert thought that he recalled a
simple necklace of some sort, perhaps a rope of garnets and little
seed pearls, and the plainness of this, the unfussy country
Englishness of it, had moved him.

He telephoned her office, and then at last it was her voice on the
line.

'Robert? Is that you? What's the news? Have you heard from The
Magazine Company?'

And as Alice was telling him the steps they would now take with
The Magazine Company solicitors, and what he was to do next, and
how he should redouble his efforts to find Sophie, and what Alice
would impress on her when she could meet her, and all the rest of
what had to be arranged, Robert imagined her face and her mouth
and the way her hair was brushed back from her forehead.

'Robert? Are you there? Did you understand that? Was I clear?'

'Yes. I'm so sorry. I did understand – thank you. Well, the next
thing for me to do is to find Sophie, which I will, somehow or other.
And Alice – please can I see you?'

'Yes.' She laughed, and it was the first time he had ever heard
her laugh. He had no idea whether it was a pretty laugh or not by
any objective standards. He was past the point where he could
measure any aspect of her by objective standards.

'Yes, of course you can. Though why anyone should want to see
me at a charge of one hundred and seventy-five pounds an hour
has always mystified me. Shall it be before you've located Sophie?
Or shall we leave it until you have, and I can see you both
together?'

He felt himself becoming absurdly reckless and indifferent to
any sort of caution. He just wanted to see her.

'No. I really would like to see you tomorrow anyway, about
something else. Privately. There's something else I have to deal
with. Please can I see you?'

And suddenly he was struck by fear, a knife-thrust of jealousy and possessiveness. She had worn no wedding ring this morning; he had searched for it, and there was no ring. But she would have a boyfriend, of course. Someone her own age. She probably lives with someone, he thought in a panic. It's certain that she does!

But he forced the fear and physical imagery of that from his mind, and said, 'So could we make it sometime tomorrow?'

'Of course. Why don't you come here at eleven? Would that be convenient?'

'I'll be there. And Alice,' in saying her name he felt again a jolt of happiness, 'Alice, don't sound puzzled like that. Don't worry. It's just something I want to talk to you about. Just something personal. That's all.'

Chapter Twenty-Four

Colin sat at his desk perspiring liberally, despite the fact that the air-conditioner unit in the window was chugging away, and doing as much as it could to make the place habitable. Bavancore in April is a hot place to be, and an overweight young Englishman in a tie, smoking a cigar, red braces over a Jermyn Street shirt, is not in his natural milieu.

There was a message for him to telephone Amarjeet Prasad, but he wanted to complete a line of thought before he did so. On the desk before him was a yellow legal pad, and on the top sheet of this he had scribbled in his tiny handwriting a series of balloons. These contained a phrase or two within the balloon; some stood on their own, and others were connected together with arrows, some of these crossed out, and others reinstated or redirected.

With C.P. Nerappan now in Delhi on business, Colin was in charge of the Bavancore office until he returned, and he had been there since shortly after seven o'clock that morning. Now at four o'clock in the afternoon, Colin was hot, tired and longing for some air.

'Fuck it,' he muttered to himself. 'Fuck it.'

He got up from his chair, and attempted some elaborate stretching and bending procedures, which succeeded only in giving him a slight rick in the neck and a pain in his side. He sat down again, put his hands in his pockets, and gazed out of his window across the harbour and towards the bumpy little hills beyond.

One thing is absolutely clear anyway, he thought, and that is that C.P. is in some way making some money out of the Prasads. Or maybe *with* the Prasads. It was all very lacking in corroboration at this stage, but he was convinced that the anonymous letter was correct. To him, it had the ring of probability about it. It was written in such a self-assured manner; unhysterical and certain of its grounds.

He reached into his jacket, slung across the back of his chair, took out his wallet, and extracted from it a folded single sheet of paper. It had been typed on a word processor, was unsigned and lacked a letterhead or any other form of identification. The note had arrived one day that week at Colin's house. He'd first opened it on the morning that he'd been to see Amarjeet Prasad. He unfolded the letter, and read it again.

Dear Mr Ewing,

I am told that you are currently investigating the circumstances of the Poonjee Dam project financing, and the conduct of the Moorgate & Mercantile Bank in the transaction.

I am very well briefed as to what happened, and I may decide to assist you in your investigations by writing to you from time to time with a hint or two, although always, and I regret the need for this, anonymously.

Let me start you on your way. You must have wondered about the relationship between the Prasad family and the Bank. If I were in your place I would consider what encouraged the Prasads to approach Hindustan-Moorgate & Mercantile in the first place. It was the impression of most people that Colonel Prasad had particularly strong connections with the Javed & National Bank. Certainly Javed appear to have done most of the banking for Prasad & Prasad in the past. Why did Colonel Prasad now decide to approach Hindustan-Moorgate & Mercantile?

Some more clues for you. If you were to look at the Bank accounts of all the people in the South India Head Office, I think you will find that only one of them is considerably fatter now than it was before the Poonjee project came about. That of C.P. Nerappan. He has made money from it, I can assure you. Consider how that was done.

Consider too that it would have been impossible for him to have taken any step which would not have been obvious to the Chief Clerk, Mr Gupta. My information is that Gupta is no better off than he has ever been. Reason out why not. And finally, for this letter anyway, two more hints. Why was General Puri brought on to the Prasad & Prasad Board? And who really did negotiate the Prasad & Prasad civil engineering contract for Poonjee with the Government of India? If negotiation is the right term for what occurred.

Good Luck!

Colin folded the letter again, and replaced it in his wallet. I could do without this compliance and security audit being treated like a treasure hunt at the vicarage house party, he thought. The curate's glasses steaming over with the excitement of it all, little clues from him, then tea and lemonade on the lawn. Or in my case a cigarette and a feel behind the toolshed with Glenys whatever her name was.

He put his arms behind his head, gazed out of the window, and brooded for some moments about Glenys. Then, collecting himself, he placed the yellow legal pad in front of him again and sat there frowning at it, propelling pencil in his hand, occasionally making some notes on the page or crossing others out.

He had talked to Gupta on Wednesday, and he certainly appeared to be sanguine enough. Colin had asked him why the Prasads should have brought this business to the Bank, and he seemed puzzled by the question. He said that his impression was that they wanted a more substantial bank than the Javed & National for this because of the large borrowings they required. And that the Bank's offer was as keen as Javed's on the interest requirement, and tough but acceptable in other respects. So why on earth shouldn't they give the Bank the business, or words to that effect. And Colin thought he saw what he meant.

Oh fuck, Colin mouthed silently to himself once more. Why should I be dragged into this anyway? If C.P. has made a naughty fiver, well so be it. Who hasn't in this country? Everyone's doing it. And I could do without helpful telephone calls from my father saying how pleased he was that Robert Luscombe had given me this audit to do and that if I screwed it up he'd have my balls for breakfast. Or in his language: 'I must have at all times a sense of the family traditions of the Bank's honour and veracity.' And that he looked forward in due course to reading my report in the light of these. Christ. Like the day my prep-school headmaster caught me with a copy of *Ladies of the Night*, and called my mother down from London especially to do her worst. Which turned out to be a lecture on the family's moral traditions. Later encapsulated by my great-uncle being caught in bed with the Colonel's wife next door at the age of seventy-five. Him, not her. She was seventy-six . . .

There was a knock on the door, and Gupta came in, carrying, in C.P.'s absence in Delhi, the daily printout of the Bank's cash balances and interbank lendings, which he handed to Colin.

'Hello, Gupta. You bring me these things and I never know what to do with them, except to nod wisely and make a whistling sound. You've probably noticed – I've been doing it all week. For heaven's sake tell me what I'm supposed to be looking for.'

Gupta laughed, and pointed with his finger at a set of figures at the bottom of the sheet.

'Just keep an eye on the liquidity ratios, Mr Ewing. Though I assure you we would never breach any of our internal rules or regulations, let alone the mandatory provisions of the Reserve Bank of India. But just keep an eye on the ratio summaries.'

149

Colin looked at the sheet, scribbled his initials on the bottom of it, and handed it back to Gupta.

'Thanks, Gupta. Now help me about something else. Talk to me a little more about our arrangements with Prasad & Prasad. You explained to me the other day that they came to us because we had the scale to cope more easily with the ups and downs of their cash flow in the Poonjee business than a smaller bank such as Javed & National. I can see that, and I'm sure you're right, but the interest rate point does still confuse me. We contracted at the rate we did because we felt we had to match the Javed offer. And yet Javed seemed to have quoted certainly a point and perhaps as much as a point and a half *less* than the rate at which one would have thought the market would have placed this one. Why should that be? Why did they do that? Tell me again.'

'You would have to ask Javed & National, and I'm not sure that they would tell you. I very much doubt that they would tell you. But I would assume that they were concerned not to lose Prasad & Prasad as clients after having done so much with them over the years, that they felt there was no real risk of default, and offered what they thought would be an offer which would give them the contract without threat of a competitor improving on it.'

'Do you think they realised that we'd offered to match them, whatever they quoted?'

'I would very much doubt it. They would have had genuine grounds for official complaint if they had known they were being used in that way. I've never heard that they had made an issue of it after the event. I'm sure it would have come to our ears if there had been a fuss, or if they had made any kind of formal objection.'

'All very odd, Gupta. Very odd – or maybe simply as straightforward as you suggest. God knows. Thanks anyway.'

So the only way to handle this, Colin thought, is to ask Javed & National why they quoted such an unnecessarily silly rate. And I don't think I can do that without asking Luscombe's permission. Which he'll refuse to give for the very good reason that I'm stepping into an area which could injure the Bank's reputation in the financial community. I shall be talking with a small competitor, with whom we have only the most insignificant and cursory dealings in the normal way of things, about a most confidential contract of the Bank's. So Luscombe would be right. Except I'm going to do it anyway.

But in order to defer the moment, Colin walked off down the passage, cigar in his mouth, and stood in the urinal in the washroom at the end, facing as he did so directly at the No Smoking sign on the wall. He shook himself down, washed his hands, and wandered back to his own room, a growing feeling of nervousness coming over him.

Well, the only way to do this is to go for it, he thought. Head on. Directly to old Mohammed Javed himself. *Now*. Before discretion and caution change my mind. And while I still feel like it. Into the breach, etc. Here goes.

He dialled the number himself, asked to be put through to the Chairman, gave his name, and that of the Moorgate & Mercantile Bank, and waited to be connected, his nervousness increasing as he did so. When the old man's weak and quavering voice came on the line, his English laboured and the accent pronounced, Colin had an abrupt moment of panic. He retreated in his fright to the sort of conversational opening that would have been more suited to an encounter between two slight acquaintances at a St James's club.

'Mr Javed? Colin Ewing. How are you? Marvellous to hear you. Family well? You well? Everything well?'

The sweat was now beginning to pour down Colin's back and brow, and he was conscious that there was another stream of inanity forming in his mind for delivery. He was just beginning to release this, when he was saved by Javed's response, which was delivered in a tone of withering iciness, and cut in on Colin in mid-sentence.

'Mr Ewing. How can I help you?'

Colin pressed the sleeve of his shirt against his forehead to stop the sweat running down his face, and found himself suddenly, by his standards, quite alarmingly direct. Particularly as he had no notes in front of him as to how to frame the questions he wanted to ask, and his mind had now gone almost completely dead.

'I'm calling about Prasad & Prasad, Mr Javed. About how you decided on the interest rate for the Poonjee borrowings.'

There was a dead silence for a minute. Then: 'That, if I may say so, is a little abrupt of you. And I am by no means clear about what you are saying. There *are* no Poonjee borrowings, as far as we're concerned. You lent them the money. I'm in the middle of a meeting, Mr Ewing.'

Colin almost shouted the next statement, thinking the telephone was about to be put down on him.

'But you quoted them! You made them an offer! I saw the paperwork!'

'Mr Ewing, I know your father, of course.' There was an extended coughing fit, and then he resumed: 'I know your father. I'm surprised that you're telephoning me in this way. It's not how things are normally done. But because of my respect for your father I'll answer your question.

'We never quoted the Prasads on this transaction. We refused to quote them. If you ask me why, I would say that it was because we were unhappy with some of the arrangements they wanted to make. Let's leave it like that. We advised them to take the business elsewhere. I can assure you that we never wrote to them, and we never quoted them. I can assure you of that. And that really is all I want to say on the matter. My best wishes to your father, Mr Ewing, and now I must go.'

Colin replaced the receiver when he heard the line go dead. He claims there was no letter from Javed to the Prasads, although I saw one. So that was a forgery, or perhaps a dummy letter done for a fee by one of the Javed people, or else the old man is for some reason lying to me. But if it *was* a dummy letter done for a fee . . . why? For whom? For the Prasads, I suppose, so that they could get a better interest rate from us. And C.P. went along with it. Perhaps unwittingly; perhaps not.

I really must talk to Robert Luscombe. This is becoming difficult.

Either he or I must speak to C.P. now, and hear his reaction. Preferably Luscombe.

Colin called the London office from his house shortly after two o'clock in the morning, hoping that with the time difference he would catch Robert as soon as he arrived at the office for work. It was two hours before his call was returned however, and Colin was half-befuddled with sleep when he reached across the bed to pick up the receiver.

'Sorry, Colin. It's a bad time to ring, I know, but I've just got your message. I'm going to be out for the rest of the day, and I gather that you need to speak to me urgently.'

Colin explained what had happened, and asked if Robert would be in contact with C.P. about the Javed issue, or whether Robert wanted him to do it.

'No. Neither of us will at this stage. You obviously haven't heard. C.P. has had a heart attack in Delhi. About five or six hours ago. He's very unwell.'

Chapter Twenty-Five

There is a certain sense of inevitability in the bearing and conduct of a man who at the beginning of a love affair is about to declare himself to the other person.

Robert knew what he was going to do, and longed to do it. He had known Alice for barely a month, and had met her about ten times. On four of those occasions he had been in the company of a somewhat surly and uncooperative Sophie, whom he had reached, after three days of searching, when she had eventually returned to her flat. On two further meetings Peter Rutherford had been there as well, and it was therefore only four times at most that he had been alone with her.

On all these occasions the conversation had dealt with the professional issues on which Alice and her firm were advising Robert. There had been a growing confidence in the way in which they had spoken to each other, but no intimacy, or personal indiscretions, or revelations of any sort. But it had reached the stage that when Robert invited Alice to lunch with him, he was confident that she would do so. And do so without a self-protective attempt to pretend that the invitation had a professional connotation to it.

So they met one Friday at a small Italian restaurant in a Chelsea mews, and Robert's heart gave a leap when he saw Alice walk along the cobblestones towards him, turning her wrist as she did so to see from her watch whether she was late. He had asked her to be there at half-past twelve; absurdly early as he knew, but he wanted her to be with him for every minute that he could claim. He himself had arrived fifteen minutes before that, so that he could ensure they were given the secluded table in the corner that he had marked out when eating there alone with a book one evening in the previous week.

He was now intensely nervous, and sat there with his hands on the table, fiddling with his glass and his napkin, breaking and crumbling the little sticks of bread that had been put in front of him.

As she came into the restaurant, which was still empty of any customers apart from them, Robert got to his feet and waited for her to come across, then put out his two hands to her waist while he kissed her on the cheek. Now he had touched her with a degree of intimacy for the first time, and there was a feeling of something like panic in him as he knew that he had done so.

There was a little awkwardness over what she wanted to drink and eat, and what he would have, and in truth he wanted nothing whatsoever. But soon the business of it was over, and he looked at her, and she smiled at him. His hands were on the table before him, and they were shaking now in his nervousness, and his heartbeat felt feathery and erratic. Then he reached across and put his hand on top of hers, and he found himself saying what he had been wanting to say ever since he had first met her.

'I have to say this, though I'm very frightened to do so. But I do have to say it. I've fallen in love with you, Alice. I'm completely in love with you. I've never fallen in love with anyone like this before. It's . . . well, it's the truth.'

Alice said nothing, and he said no more, but there was a lightness and relief in him now. He had a certainty that it was going to work. The difficulties in front of them were too great even to bear contemplation; but, somehow, it was going to work. He knew it was going to work. He could see it in her eyes. They were going to be together.

The waiter arrived, their food was put in front of them, wine was poured, and it was a frustrating and prolonged business for him before they were alone again, and he could touch her, and now it was with both hands, as he held hers in his.

'I'm in love with you, Alice.'

And this time she said, 'I wondered if you were. You did seem as though you were. I've been having some very muddled thoughts about you too. I'm glad you've told me. You're very brave to do so. I'm very pleased you have.'

But no talk of love, Robert thought. Muddled thoughts, she says, but does that mean love? Please God make her love me. Make her love me. Don't play with me. Don't let me fall in love with her like this, then take her away.

Alice looked across at the waiter, who was standing leaning against the wall, gazing at them. 'We must eat the fish, or pretend to or something. Though right now I feel incapable of eating anything whatsoever.'

They both picked up their knives and forks and pushed around with the food in a languid, desultory sort of way, but they ate little, drank nothing, and eventually their food was cleared away. Then they ordered coffee, though neither wanted it, and for Robert it was only as a means of being able to stay in the restaurant together for some moments more. He held her hands all the time now, and told her again and again that he loved her.

'There is such a limited vocabulary in these things, Alice. I wish I could say it to you in a different way, so that it sounded less trite. But it's the only thing I can think of saying. I can't find another way of saying it. But don't let the triteness of it make you think it isn't real. It's very real.'

Alice sat at the table with Robert's hands resting on hers, staring at them. She looked at her watch, grimaced, and said, 'I have to go now, Robert. Back to the office. There's a meeting. We must see each other very soon.'

As he looked at her he thought that he had never wanted anything or anybody in his life as much as he wanted her. He had no previous experience of a physical and emotional attachment of anything approaching this. He wanted to say to her what he felt in a language that would get away from the clichés and aphorisms of conventional romantic vocabulary, but he could find no words but the same.

So he said them again, and he knew that she could hear in his voice, however banal the language, the unmistakable focus and force of something real.

'I love you, Alice. I've never been in love before. I love you.'

He saw her into a taxi, and before clambering in, she turned to him, put her arms for a moment around him, then kissed him very gently and softly on the mouth. The cab drew away with her, and Robert stood watching it until it had turned the corner and was gone.

' *The birthday of my life is come,*' he thought, still staring at where the taxi had last been in his view. And then, again, '*The birthday of my life is come, my love is come to me.*'

Chapter Twenty-Six

My heart is like a singing bird
Whose nest is in a watered shoot;
My heart is like an apple tree
Whose boughs are bent with thickset fruit;
My heart is like a rainbow shell
That paddles in a halcyon sea;
My heart is gladder than all these
Because my love is come to me.

Raise me a dais of silk and down;
Hang it with vair and purple dyes;
Carve it in doves and pomegranates,
And peacocks with a hundred eyes;
Work it in gold and silver grapes,
In leaves and silver fleur-de-lys;
Because the birthday of my life
Is come, my love is come to me.

Robert read the Christina Rossetti poem three or four times through, mouthing it quietly to himself as he did so in his rhythmic voice of the Welsh valleys, which he still carried after so many years away from Pontypool, and his aunt, and the tiny terraced house in the grimy, defeated little street.

He closed the book, and laid it on his lap, then stared out at the rain, and the wind blowing the blossom off the cherry tree in the street outside his study window.

Upstairs, Sarah was still in bed, genuinely asleep, Robert thought, and in a moment he would leave for the office, and all the accustomed, satisfying order of his life there. But it was still barely a quarter past seven, and he placed his coffee cup back on its saucer, and walked across to his Victorian mahogany writing table underneath the window. On it were lying the three or four pages of foolscap on which he had been drafting the final few paragraphs of a speech that he was to make in Geneva the following week.

He sat for a moment with them in his hands, his mind five thousand miles away, with C.P. Nerappan and a Delhi hospital. Then, pulling himself together, he read the pages again, still and hunched in his concentration for almost twenty minutes. He made some alterations and additions in his neat, small hand, before laying his Mont Blanc propelling pencil down on the table and putting the pages away with the others in the drawer.

He had been up since five o'clock that morning after a night of very little sleep. And although he had dreamt only very briefly, it had been a disturbing, bizarre affair of India, and violent quarrelling, and the shouting in the night of angry men. It was a dream which Robert had experienced quite frequently, and he knew its roots in his childhood.

Robert remembered the actual incident again, precisely as it had happened. His mother was sitting in the corner of the room under the single table lamp, intent on her embroidery, sewing silently and calmly in the dull, ineffectual light under which she was working. His father was standing in his shirtsleeves by the open windows, gazing out at the night of provincial India, silent, pensive and, it seemed to the tiny child, strangely melancholy. And then, suddenly, there had been a shouting, and a noise of men quarrelling, and the door of the sitting room had burst open. The cook rushed in, crying out, clutching at his arm and the blood-covered sleeve of his white shirt. There had been an argument over some domestic issue, it transpired, and nothing more than that – a quarrel over the constancy of the affections of the cook's wife, perhaps – but there had been a fight, and knives, and a stabbing, and a certain concern for a moment or two about the extent of the wound.

But it was slight, and the following day the cook was back at work at the brick and stone stove out in the open yard. The incident was, by the standards of India, a trivial affair. But the memory the child carried with him was that of his father softly sponging the blood from the man's arm with a bowl of disinfected warm water, whilst his mother prepared a bandage from a length of clean white linen, crooning for him as she did so, as if to lull him to sleep with some gentle melody.

What is the metaphor that constantly pursues me in that story? he thought. Is it just the gentleness of it, and the competence of it? Or the healing of pain and disorder? Why does it linger with me? Why are my childhood memories of my parents always in this form? The railway journey on the footplate of the Howrah Express, the correspondence-class afternoons, the bloodied arm of the cook. What am I trying to find?

He pushed the drawers of the writing table shut, and thought of locking them when he remembered that they held the only copy he had of his now nearly finished speech, but he didn't do so in the vague thought that it would insult Sarah with the suspicion that she might tamper with it. Then, before leaving for the underground station, he again picked up the book, and read once more the same poem, this time silently and quickly. *Silk and down; doves and pomegranates; leaves and silver fleur-de-lys*. On the one hand all the tumbled, integrated, heightened imagery of the poetry of romantic love and what he knew to be his idealised, obsessive vision of Alice. And, on the other, Sarah asleep upstairs, ageing now, and unloved.

Christina Rossetti, on the one hand, and Stevie Smith on the other. He went to his bookshelves, ran his fingers along them until he turned up what he was looking for, then, still standing there, he thumbed through its pages until he found the poem.

> *Nobody heard him, the dead man,*
> *But still he lay moaning:*
> *I was much further out than you thought*
> *And not waving but drowning.*
>
> *Poor chap, he always loved larking*
> *And now he's dead*
> *It must have been too cold for him his heart gave way,*
> *They said.*
>
> *Oh, no no no, it was too cold always*
> *(Still the dead one lay moaning)*
> *I was much too far out all my life*
> *And not waving but drowning.*

Too far out all her life, thought Robert. Too far out, and drowning. Drowning all her life. Without, poor Sarah, the saving graces of intelligence and wit and perspicacity, and the consequent dignity of Stevie Smith. All these years she's been trapped in her lack of self-confidence and achievement. With only me to realise that she's drowning and not waving. And I do realise it. But I can't help her.

And now that I suddenly see the chance for love, I'm rushing after it. I don't want C.P. playing this absurd game of misrepresentation with me. My wife is drowning, and I'm no longer trying to reach her in the water. I'm walking away from her across the beach because I see the chance for myself of love. That is the truth of it. That's what's happening.

Robert picked up his briefcase in the cramped little front hall, and unlocked the front door. When he had pulled it shut behind him he realised that he had forgotten his hat and his umbrella, but he was reluctant to go back indoors in case he disturbed Sarah, so he turned up the collar of his coat and went off through the rain without them.

It was a ten-minute walk to the station, timed to the minute, so much preferred to the nonsenses and pretensions of the Bank's Jaguars and chauffeurs. So familiar and programmed was the whole affair to him that Robert found himself on the platform and into the train without a conscious recollection of the details of purchasing his ticket or finding his way to the platform.

He found a seat, initially ignoring the indignant stare of the middle-aged woman who had been approaching it fractionally later than him, then almost immediately he rose again to give it up to her. Now, reaching to hold on to a handstrap, as always in discomfort as he did so from the shoulder he had injured in a fall some years before, he saw on the platform a man who, until he turned more full-faced towards him, he thought was Solly Lorenzo. But the incident had switched his mind back again to Sophie.

How many of her troubles, he thought, had been caused by the failures of Sarah and himself to put a proper marriage together, for her to draw strength from? How much of Robert's own success stemmed from the fact that his own parents were so obviously fulfilled with each other? Sarah's life, Rowena's life, Sophie's – how much damage, he thought, had he wreaked in other people by those days of sexual passion in Darjeeling all those years ago?

He was out of his train now, and out of the station, and walking, as he did almost every working day of his life, along the south side of Cannon Street, up the little ridge of hill, and on towards King William Street. There, in a grey, unpretentious building along by London Bridge, the Moorgate & Mercantile Bank had their headquarters.

The rain was falling even more heavily, and Robert held the collar of his coat together over his chin, huddling his head down and staring at the pavement as he went.

Sarah, and Alice, and his parents, and his aunt in Pontypool, and Rowena, and Sophie. C.P. Nerappan too. C.P. in his Delhi hospital, so nearly struck out from his life but, thank God, still there. Loyalties, friendships, failures, compromises, defeats and, sometimes, like a sudden shaft of light on a darkened field, some moments of exhilarating happiness.

The lights were against him at the wide junction by St Clements Church, and he stood there in the rain gazing unseeingly across at Eastcheap, and the red buses and the taxis in line to swing across the river to Bermondsey.

R.S. Thomas, he thought. Wales, and R.S. Thomas and the imagery of light, and perception, and the transcendent. And as he started to walk forward, staring down at the glistening street, carried along by the impetus of those around him, he muttered:

> *I have seen the sun break through*
> *to illuminate a small field*
> *for a while, and gone my way*
> *and forgotten it. But that was the pearl*
> *of great price, the one field that had*
> *the treasure in it. I realize now*
> *that I must give all that I have*
> *to possess it. Life is not hurrying*
>
> *on to a receding future, nor hankering after*
> *an imagined past. It is the turning*
> *aside like Moses to the miracle*
> *of the lit bush, to a brightness*
> *that seemed as transitory as your youth*
> *once, but is the eternity that awaits you.*

I do both, Robert reflected, looking up from the pavement before him, and down to the river, grey and dank in the gloomy light of the early spring morning. Here am I hurrying through to a future that recedes before me, as it always does, hankering after a past to which I ascribe a purity and gentleness that was probably never there. But I do know about the sudden shafts of light, and the miracle of the lit bush, and a glimpse of the transcendent. I do know how to turn aside and gaze at it, and acknowledge the moment. I do understand the pearl of great price. I've seen it.

Such happiness, he thought, as he turned into the narrow courtyard, and up the steps towards the vast, heavy doors of the Bank. There have been moments of such happiness. Happiness that easily surmounts the periods of pain and failure. And now, through Alice, perhaps a new kind of joy.

'Good morning, Mr Luscombe,' called the commissionaire as Robert passed through the cavernous, resonating reception hall, all gloom, and Gothic statement, and mighty columns, and curving staircases.

'Good morning, sir. Fine weather for ducks. Sir Arthur asked me to catch you as you came in, and would you call through to his office, please, sir. First thing, sir, the Chairman said, if you would, sir. Thank you, sir.'

Robert raised his hand and smiled in response, and made an effort to adjust his mind to the practical needs of the day, and what was to be done, and the meetings ahead in his diary. The creaking, groaning 1930s lift was hidden away at the back, tucked out of sight behind a false, grandiose folly of a marble screen, and as he stepped into it, calculating what time he could ring the Delhi hospital to hear more news of C.P. Nerappan, he found to his dismay that he was going to be imprisoned there alone with a member of the junior management whom Robert wanted very much to avoid.

He had recently directed his department to investigate the young man for probable insider trading. The scale of the misdemeanour was inconsequential, though the Bank's rules and guidelines on the subject were uncompromisingly lacking in ambiguity. But Robert had learnt of the young man's personal circumstances – the Down's Syndrome child, the depressive, anorexic young wife, the widowed mother whom he was entirely supporting – and he knew that he would only be able to supervise the completion of the investigation if he was kept free from any personal involvement and the inevitable consequent tug of loyalty to the boy. Otherwise Robert could never do it. And he was smiling at Robert now, as if – and Robert's stomach lurched at the suspicion of it – he was appealing to him for clemency and understanding and forgiveness.

'Good morning, Mr Luscombe. All well?' Thankfully, thankfully, Robert had recently moved his office down to the second floor, so the lift stopped almost immediately. As he escaped from it there was a muddle as he entangled with the office mailman and his trolley, who was trying to get in at the same time as Robert was getting out, and this enabled him to scurry away with no more than a half-greeting and a wave of the hand before the lift door closed again, and the young man was gone.

How I loathe the parading of moral certainties in life, Robert thought to himself. How I dislike being put in a position where I am judging other people for their apparent failures. Particularly people like him. I like intelligence, and I like meritocracy. I have a prejudice against the bully, and the manipulator and the moral coward, and I delight in their downfall. But for that boy, and others like him, I feel none of that. I've no pleasure whatsoever at the prospect of seeing him destroyed.

Now Robert was at his office door, and he hung his sodden raincoat in the cupboard out in the passage. He paused at his assistant's desk to see what messages she had left there for him the previous day, then went into his room, and looked with a certain wry satisfaction at the order and the discipline of his life there. The current files neatly stacked on the table by the window, the day's *Financial Times* waiting folded for him at his desk, beside it the fax detailing the market closing prices from New York. The computer and the printer stood on the little side table, and there also, as always, was the printed list of his day's engagements.

There was control in Robert's professional life, and there was competence, and no one who saw him at work could ever doubt his efficient and effective hold on his affairs.

But that's what there was, he reflected. Efficiency and effectiveness. What there was not was the smallest glimpse into the recesses of his internal life. He looked around at his office. In here, he thought, is not a photograph, nor a memento, nor a keepsake, nor a single article of private, familial connection. How is it that I've spent my life in this way?

And that, he thought, was what gave such irony to C.P. Nerappan's great speech about love being the governing passion of his life. To those whose only experience of him was to see him at work, it would be a natural assumption that he was without passion of any description, bar perhaps an inordinate punctiliousness for the proper discharge of his professional duties. That's what they would think. And they would be right in a way. Too much in him had been sublimated. Too much had been rationalised and controlled.

And yet – that was only partially right. It had been his work that had given him the greater part of his satisfaction and absorption in recent years. He'd been very fortunate to have it. As his emotional life had become less adequate, the more satisfaction he had drawn from all the rituals of his professional life. He was good at it, and enjoyed his success. Failure in his career would have hurt him very deeply. Too deeply to contemplate.

At that moment the telephone rang on his desk, and it was Sir Arthur Ewing on the line.

'Robert? The porter rang through to say that you'd just arrived. Are you alone? Have you a moment? Can we speak freely?'

'Good morning, Arthur. Yes, I'm alone.'

'I only returned from Germany late last evening, as you know, and your message about C.P. Nerappan was waiting for me when I got home. I am of course deeply shocked and concerned. Deeply concerned. Do you know his condition? Do you know how he is?'

'As far as I can gather from the doctors over five thousand miles of crackling telephone line, he's rallying and comparatively strong. But it was an unpleasantly severe heart attack, as it's been described to me.'

'Is he out of danger? Will he pull through all right?'

'Yes. As I understand it – yes. Certainly he'll pull through.'

There was a moment or two of silence before Arthur Ewing spoke again. Then, 'Good. Excellent. I'm very relieved, of course.

Very relieved and pleased. Could you do everything that needs to be done? Flowers to the hospital? Flowers to his wife – all that sort of thing? My name on them, of course. With yours as well, perhaps. As personal as possible, I think. Can I leave all that in your hands?'

There were one or two further unrelated comments from him, and then he was gone, and Robert remained sitting on the edge of his desk, his arms folded, gazing blindly out at the leaden grey skies above the rooftops of the City of London.

How odd that was, he thought. How offensive that was, in its coldness and cynicism and lack of interest. Me to arrange flowers, in his name only, though mine as well if I really insisted.

And how patent that all he was really interested in was whether C.P. was going to pull through all right. And how dead his voice when he was told that he would.

Suddenly, and with certainty, Robert knew why.

Chapter Twenty-Seven

Alice sat hunched in her seat as the taxi swung into the curve of Sloane Square, then straightened to head for Cliveden Place and Eaton Square beyond. She gazed out at the bright tubs of daffodils standing on the doorsteps of the pale cream stucco houses either side of the wide street, then the wallflowers and the tulips in the neat beds of the communal gardens.

Like school, she thought. Like the High School in Long Road on the first day of Summer term, with the undergraduates all back at Cambridge. The whole town packed with their bicycles, and the hordes of them in King's Parade and Trinity Street. And her father's rooms up on the top floor of Old Court in Corpus Christi, looking down on the oval courtyard below.

Nowhere in the world is as beautiful as Cambridge, she thought. I was always at peace there. With my father, and with the colleges all around us, and that English calm and gentleness and tolerance about it all. Adult life had never been like that for her. Not yet. Not in her twenties. The professional part of it had been fine, but the rest of it . . . too much of it hadn't worked. Too much hassle with love affairs, and break ups, and partings. Too many overstressed and painful attachments. And now Robert, and the opportunity for the whole thing all over again. If that's what she wanted.

Do I really want it to happen? she thought. His declaration of love had been no great shock. Something of the sort had been in the air, and it was not really a surprise when he said it. She liked him well enough for the possibility of love to be there.

But I don't want to get hurt, she thought. Nor cluttered up in a situation with wives and children and guilt and all the rest of it. I don't want to get involved in anything that's going to end in hurt and pain and loss all over again. There's been too much of that. And yet . . . maybe it's possible. Maybe it is.

The taxi was stuck now in a traffic jam on the south side of Trafalgar Square, and she gazed across at the National Gallery opposite.

'God, what a family,' she muttered, then glanced up to check whether the cab-driver had heard her. I can't face getting involved with all that. I don't want any of that at all. There's going to be no mess in my life of that sort *whatsoever*.

Other people's families. Wives. Guilt. Pain. Other people's daughters. Getting involved emotionally to a degree where she was not controlling the situation. And then finding all the love tarnished by the guilt and the difficulty of it all. Allowing it to get to that. And if she did, the inevitable horror of what happened in the end. The mess, and the guilt, and the pain of the parting.

That's not how this was going to be. Whatever the excitement of it initially, she mustn't let that happen. She must keep this under control.

The taxi drew up at her offices in Chancery Lane, and she fumbled around with her wallet, in no haste whatsoever to go back inside and join meetings and concentrate on other things. When she heard from Peter Rutherford, who spotted her passing through Reception, that their clients had asked if they could meet instead on the following day, she took the opportunity to tell him that she was going to take the afternoon off. This was most unlike her, and Peter looked momentarily surprised, but she left immediately, before he had time to pry, and then set off back along the route the taxi had brought her. She sat for some minutes on a bench in St James's Park, then wandered along the path which runs beside the lake on the north side, holding her attaché case in one hand, and staring down at the ground as she walked.

Is it wise to let this even start? she thought. I tell myself that I can control it, but is it sensible to let it start? If I'm going to stop it, then now's the time to do it. Otherwise I'll have to be so careful as it gathers momentum. I'm attracted by him, certainly. His family life is in tatters, so I'm hardly treading on hallowed ground there. Probably he needs me. Perhaps through me he can find some sort of fulfilment and happiness. As long as I can ensure that I keep the relationship under control. Keep it at a level and a temperature at which it can be a source of pleasure and friendship and happiness for him, and for me – rather than anything that threatens the stability of either of us too much. I can do that. I do have the capacity for constancy. I'm good at holding friendships and relationships intact, and building them, and growing them. At all sorts of levels. As I have, in a different way, with my father.

And a jolt of pain went through her as she remembered how he had looked when she had seen him last, sitting in the garden on that bench he and she had made together in one of her school holidays fifteen or more years before. He had lost so much weight since he had had the stroke. His face was grey and drained with tiredness, and he seemed all the time to be so cold and shivering. And squeezing and kneading at that squash ball in his right hand, to try to get some better movement back in his arm and shoulder on that side. Though I think that's not going to come very easily, if at all, from what the doctor told me. But he needs to feel that he's fighting it. Thank God his speech is not too drastically impaired. I must go to Cambridge to see him again this weekend. I can't bear the thought of him dying. Far too young. Far too young at sixty.

'Hang on, Tom. Hang on,' Alice said aloud, then looked up and smiled at an old lady who was planting some flowers in a window box, amused that she should be heard talking to herself. She waved down a taxi to take her the rest of the way home to Shepherd's Bush, suddenly decided now to take Robert into her life, but perhaps only for a short period, and with care and control, and sensible understanding of what was possible, and limited expectation.

And we can be lovers, she thought. There's no reason why that can't happen. We can be physical lovers – I hope we are. There can be that, but only that. Because it's not there. Nothing more is there. I like him very much indeed. But it's not there. And it never will be there.

Chapter Twenty-Eight

Colin had put the receiver down when Robert rang off, and stared for some minutes into space.

C.P. had had a heart attack? No wonder poor old Luscombe sounded so upset. Those two were like brothers – or rather lovers. He'd never seen anything like it. Poor little Fielding in the Corporate Finance Division and that smart-arsed report he wrote off his own bat. Highly unpleasant about the Hindustan-Moorgate & Mercantile results on some grounds or another. Sent it to everybody. Proud as punch. Copy to the Chairman, and all that stuff. Straight down from Oxford, Keble or wherever it was, wet behind the ears, didn't know the form. Luscombe takes umbrage on behalf of C.P. and all hell's let loose. Deputy Chairman's executive committee wheeled into action. Formally minuted. Naive and childlike representation of complex issues. Speak when you're spoken to. Into the doghouse. Damn funny. Serves him right, the little prick.

Colin grinned happily at the memory of it, and lit himself another cigar, then laughed out loud as he thought of it again. Still, this Poonjee affair was somewhat doghouse territory itself. In fact, most decidedly so. That was the problem with these so-called compliance and security audits. No other bank would touch them with a bargepole. Anyone remotely sensible would consider it to be absurdly dangerous to allow these internal reviews to be held with these terms of reference. Too much power in a rival's hand, in the endless game of office politics. Too much licence of interrogation. Too good an opportunity to pay off old scores. Too prone to upset people doing a perfectly good job.

They could be right. It's all because of the founding families' smug appreciation of their personal virtue. A gentleman's honour. Leave it to the regiment. Give the erring officer a revolver, shut the door behind him, and know that he will do the right thing. In Veritate Virtus. Who but us would dare these days to have that all over their letterhead?

So what do I do now? Carry on. I have to carry on. I have no choice. All I can do is to establish whether or not C.P. has been naughty, and whether anyone else here has been naughty as well. Preferably, Robert Luscombe will do it himself, and I can keep out of it. If he won't, I'll do it, but as unaggressively and carefully as possible.

And that should wrap things up on Poonjee, and I can find something in the Bank's affairs elsewhere that will tactfully finger someone unpopular and insignificant, and then I can file the thing and be rid of it. Covered in glory for my perception and maturity. Blushingly denying the rare sharpness of my intelligence. Shyly bending to the insistence of the Board that I should return immediately to London and become Managing Director . . .

He was in the process of exhaling a large volume of smoke, cigar in his right hand, his left tucked into his red braces, when the telephone rang.

'Is that Colin Ewing? We haven't met, I'm afraid, but I know your father very well, of course.'

As always, Colin's initial reaction to this introduction was one of irritation, and he took the handset of the telephone away from his ear and grimaced at it in fury.

'I'm Mohindra Nerappan, C.P. Nerappan's wife. First of all, I'm not sure if the news has filtered through to you that my husband has been taken unwell in Delhi. He's had a heart attack, but he's resting now, and much better I'm glad to say, and I shall be travelling up to see him this weekend.'

Colin was a little taken aback by this conversation. She's very cool about it, he thought. Or maybe she and C.P. are not particularly close. Maybe it's one of those Indian marriages of the professional classes where both sides keep their distance but are painstakingly courteous about each other in public.

'Yes, I've just heard the news. I'm extremely sorry, I really am. And very shocked. Is he really on the mend? Is there anything I can do?'

'He's recovering well, but it'll be a day or so before we know the whole position, and as I say I'm going up there to be with him. But before that I would like to see you, if you could spare the time. There are one or two things I would like to go over with you if I might.'

Much of Colin's distrust of women of Mohindra's type surfaced on hearing this. Not only did he know that she was some sort of academic – and academic women always rather frightened Colin – but she had that particularly self-confident presentation of herself that suggested that she was going to be assertive and arrogant with him. He suspected that he was going to be given a detailed instruction from her on how to run the Bank while her husband was away, and he was irritated by the prospect of it.

'Could I ask you to drive up to the house, Colin – if I may call you that? Why not come up for dinner tonight? Just the two of us.'

The arrangements were made, and Colin arrived there punctually at eight o'clock, after a drive up from Bavancore of almost an hour. The house was tucked away in some hills immediately to the east of the town, and looked down on villages and fields of the valley below. The final approach was on a rough dirt road, and then one turned the corner to find unexpectedly formal high wrought-iron gates and fencing, and beyond these a gravel driveway leading up to a large white house, fronted with formal pillars and porch, and standing in immaculately tended gardens.

Colin was shown to a drawing room at the rear of the house, and as he came through the door a tall, strikingly good-looking woman in a crimson silk sari got to her feet and held out her hand to him.

Colin was settled down with a drink, and they talked away about inconsequential things for a time as a means of introducing themselves to each other. As they went through for dinner, Mohindra paused, then addressed Colin with an air of sudden, intense sincerity.

'I'm concerned on behalf of my husband, Colin. I don't want you to misunderstand anything that I'm about to say to you, but I have to be frank with you, particularly because of C.P.'s illness.'

Colin made a movement of his hands, indicating in mime that he was anxious to hear what she had to say.

'I've had two telephone calls over the course of the day that have worried me. One was from Colonel Prasad, and the second was from General Swami. Colonel Prasad is concerned that you're conducting an investigation that could seriously embarrass Prasad & Prasad, and you know what important employers they have become in this part of the world. But that's not all. He's also concerned that what you're doing is embarrassing the Bank. General Swami said much the same thing.

'And there are some other issues as well. There's a suggestion that there's a breach not just of ethics but of contract in the fact that Amarjeet Prasad showed you some confidential papers without the formal permission of Javed & National.'

Colin made an attempt to adjust his expression to register a suitable concern, but inside of him there was the beginning of resentment. Rather too much of his life had been spent being lectured, mostly by his family, on how his behaviour was upsetting other people. He was no longer a child, and he was increasingly unwilling to be bullied. Particularly by someone like this rather grand wife of C.P. Nerappan.

'I'm very sorry to hear that,' he said. 'Most concerned to hear that. But I am a little confused about why they have spoken to you about it. C.P. is out of action, of course. But with him away, I would have thought that they might wish to have spoken to me direct.'

'General Swami at least I know very well indeed. He's a major benefactor of my university, and we have been on a number of committees together. Colonel Prasad I know less well, though we have met each other through charities which we both have an interest in. They turned to me because they thought that you and I might be able to have a private word together. Informally, and off the record. It would be difficult for them to do that directly with you themselves, for obvious reasons. Or C.P.. And anyway, C.P. is now ill.'

The bearer, dressed in an immaculate starched white uniform, was standing now beside Colin's elbow. He was holding out to him a large silver platter on which various foods were arranged in neat segments, and Colin took a generous helping of most of them.

'I'm glad you're hungry. Your father loves South Indian food, of course. We always prepare for him a very special Maduram prawn dish whenever he comes here for dinner. I'm so glad to see you like our cooking as well.'

'Delicious, delicious,' Colin said, rubbing his hands and beaming at her, at the same time curling his toes as hard as he could force them, as a means of dissipating his rage at this recurrent dropping on him of his father's name.

'Well, perhaps the Prasad people don't quite understand exactly what I'm doing,' he said. 'It sounds to me as if there's a misunderstanding. I'm not undertaking some sort of wildcat review off my own bat. I'm doing a compliance and security audit of this office because I've been instructed to do so. By Robert Luscombe, as Deputy Chairman and on behalf of the Board. You know that, Mohindra. C.P. has done these audits himself. They're part of the tradition of the Bank. They're unique to us. They're said to train the person who is doing them, and they're a check from within the Bank itself that our so-called exemplary ethical standards are being upheld. Or that's what we tell ourselves.'

'Of course, of course. I know that. I know how wedded your father is to the whole ideal behind them.'

'Dear God,' muttered Colin to himself, his lips closed. 'Dear God, dear God.'

'But it is a little difficult to explain it all to outsiders,' she continued, 'who may think we're simply trying to make trouble where none exists. Particularly difficult to explain to people here in India.' Mohindra picked delicately at her food, then called the bearer over to her to give him some instruction or another.

Now what in God's heaven does that mean? Colin thought. Why the rider about India? What is she trying to say to me? And why the bullying of me by these *leitmotif* references to my father . . . Why is she so uneasy?

'Difficult to explain to people in India?' he prompted, dabbing at his mouth with his napkin, then crinkling his eyes at her in what he always considered to be an exact impersonation of his father at his most painstakingly and insincerely charming. It was an act that had been much practised from the time when Colin was a small boy, and he was very proud of it.

'Life in India is not always conducted as if in replica of the ways of the West,' she continued. 'I'm glad that it's not. We have our own sense of how life is most pleasantly led, and of what is significant and what is not – and what makes our own society, with all its idiosyncrasies and traditions, work most effectively. And sometimes, those things are not exactly how you would conduct your affairs in England. And – as I say – I'm very glad that is so.'

Colin had a second run at the crinkly smile, wondering if he had set the angle of his head at quite the optimum angle on the first occasion. He did so now with an added gesture of the hands, also copied from his father, used on occasions when it was politic to indicate quite overwhelming fascination and absorption in what was being said to him, and a longing for it to continue.

'My father has always reminded me of that. Constantly. You know his admiration for India.' Naughty but fun, Colin thought to himself. It might be better if she doesn't realise that I'm attempting to take the piss out of her.

'I'm sure he has.'

Mohindra Nerappan leant forward, and fixed him with an intent, almost wistful stare. No, she doesn't, Colin saw with relief. She hasn't got sufficient sense of humour.

'That's rather what I'm trying to hint to you, Colin. Things are different here. If you had more experience of India, I know you would be perhaps a little more sensitive to the way we conduct our affairs.' She smiled at him now, which Colin took to be a hint that the little interview with the Headmistress was drawing towards its close.

I'm not at all clear where this is taking us, he reflected. 'A little more sensitive to the way we conduct our affairs.' What on earth does that mean? She can't be suggesting that a touch of bribery and corruption amongst the Bank's officers is to be looked on as a harmless little tradition? Or perhaps she is.

'Let's go through, and we'll have some coffee in the drawing room.' She smiled again as she rose, and settled the sari on her shoulder. 'Come,' and as she led Colin away, she slipped her hand through his arm, and held him almost with a hint of intimacy.

Colin reverted to his repertoire of imitations of his father, pleased to have a chance of performing them once more in public, and there was a little scene of mannered delight and appreciation as coffee was poured into delicate porcelain cups and they both settled down again in their chairs. But Colin was beginning to feel within him a real distaste and anger, and suddenly he was tired of the game, and of his mimicry of his father, and the way that this woman had underrated him, and patronised him in doing so.

'But you must explain to me a little more of what you mean, Mohindra,' and as he said these words his irritation began to grow in him to the point where he knew, from of old, that he was shortly going to be very rude and very direct. Colin, when angry, was an unexpectedly formidable foe, to the point when he surprised even himself.

'If you're suggesting that it's acceptable to the Bank that its officers in India should take bribes, then I can assure you that it's not. If you're suggesting that ... look, Mohindra, it's not very difficult to deduce that C.P. has been very close to the Prasads. I'm going to be very direct with you, because I think that would be more helpful to both of us than polite prevarication.

'I'm told that C.P. and General Swami made approaches to certain members of the Government of India, and that these succeeded in winning some of the civil engineering contracts in the Poonjee Dam project for Prasad & Prasad. I understand that C.P. and the General have had certain other dealings together in matters of army procurement and supply, and that Swami was the man who made the original introduction and negotiated the initial arrangements between the Bank and the Prasads. And, finally, I believe that money passed hands between Swami, on behalf of the Prasads, and these Government officials in the securing of these Poonjee contracts. And the way that the Government arranged to settle their bills: to put it bluntly, they were bribed.'

Mohindra Nerappan gazed at him for some moments, her face cold and set.

'Is that all? Have you finished? I'm amazed that you should speak to me like this. You call that being direct? I would say that you have been more insulting than I would have believed possible in a member of your father's family. I intend to make it quite clear to Arthur that you have been extraordinarily rude to me. I very much resent it.'

Colin shrugged. 'You must do as you wish. If you want to speak to my father, then you must do so. I didn't intend to be rude, but there are aspects of the dealings in this affair that I believe contravene the ethical guidelines of the Bank, let alone the law. I'm not sure that complaining to my father that I've failed to show you sufficient homage is exactly facing the point.'

'Facing what point? And who talked about homage? But putting your rudeness aside for one moment I think the problem is that you simply do not understand India. We do not necessarily regard the giving of tokens of appreciation for kindnesses shown to one as being a crime. Of course General Swami is well connected with the Government. Of course my husband is as well. Of course the

Prasads would have ensured that they were not put into the embarrassing position of being . . .' She hesitated.

'Outbribed? Caught? Exposed? Outmanoeuvred?' he said, pulling on his cigar.

As Mohindra looked across at Colin, and observed his flushed, angry face, she tried to calm down and restore herself. It occurred to her that she had been very stupid. She had called this young man here because Swami had wanted her to. And he had looked such a weak, flabby caricature of his father on her first sight of him, when he walked into the drawing room, that she had bullied him. Patronised him. He looked to her to be all that she disliked in a certain type of young Englishman. Over-privileged, over-dressed and over-indulged. Soft at the centre and lacking in any sort of moral texture and courage.

The Prasad people had clearly told her a very limited story of what had happened. They simply wanted her to warn him off, and when she looked at him she had thought that would be extremely easy to do. She thought from what the Prasads said that he was in some way trying to injure C.P.. Out of dislike, or envy, or career ambition, or something of the sort, and she wanted C.P. to be left alone.

But she didn't take him seriously enough a moment or so ago when he suddenly produced those accusations about C.P.. He flustered her by them, and she had behaved very stupidly in consequence. This Ewing boy had got a misleading appearance of weakness. C.P. could be cynical about money, and there was a secretiveness and obliqueness about him that she had never entirely broken through. If he had done something morally careless, then he and she must deal with that themselves. She should never have become involved in this way with the Prasads. By doing so, she had allowed herself to be put in an absurdly unpleasant position.

She tried to look at Colin now in a way that would indicate that she wanted them to cool down from the heat of anger. They should start the conversation again. It was her fault. They needed to start again. Much of what she had said was perfectly sensible, she reminded herself. The standards of India *were* different from those of England. Or were they? She recalled all the City of London scandals in recent years. The English had a very fine line on rectitude and fiscal virtue. Their performance, however, particularly in these years of the nation's decline, did not exactly coincide with that. There was just as much greed and graft there as anywhere else. In its own way, perhaps more. It was just that the greed and graft tended to come in an Old Boy tie, so in some respects it was less easy for a foreigner to spot.

'I was going to say that the Prasads would not have allowed themselves to be put in the position of looking ungrateful for the Government's confidence in them. But I think you would have told me that that was rather a pompous remark. And on reflection, if you had done, I would have agreed with you.'

She gave him a half-smile, got up, turned the air conditioner off, and opened the French windows that led into the garden. She checked that the mosquito netting door was securely in place, then stood there looking up at the stars, and listening to the raucous taps and calls and the twittering, clattering, cheeping noises of the tropical night.

'Do you mind if we have some fresh air? It's a lovely evening, and there's a full moon, so the whole garden looks silvery and still.' She stood there for some moments, then turned again, and came back into the room, though this time she sat in a different chair, much nearer to him, and when she spoke her voice was much more gentle, and the edge of anger had gone from it.

'I hate quarrelling. C.P. will tell you anything you need to know as soon as he's well enough. I'm sure he will. In honesty I don't know quite what has gone on between C.P. and the Prasads and the Government of India. You'll have to ask him. I'm sure there will be some very straightforward explanation to it all.'

'Of course. Yes, of course I will.'

She poured more coffee into his cup, then sat again, smoothing out her sari in a pensive, reflective manner before she turned to him and spoke again.

'Colin – I was angry with you, and I'm sorry that I was. It was undignified, and ungenerous. I partly misjudged you personally, I'm clear about that. And there is a certain anger in me about the English that always tends to surface in certain circumstances. Perhaps because I'm of the generation that I am, and I've never quite forgotten some of your countrymen's arrogant sense of superiority over men as distinguished as my father.

'And I didn't very much relish the idea of a young man like you playing that role with my husband. C.P. has his faults, and I know them better than anyone, but he has been a very considerable servant and colleague of your English Bank for his whole career. And remarkably loyal to your people. C.P. is mine, and always will be. And I don't like this sort of chatter about him.'

They sat there silently for some moments, then Colin moved his position in his chair so that he was facing her directly, and when he spoke, he too took care to do so in a voice in which the anger had all been dissipated away.

'Mohindra, I'd like to be shot of all this just as soon as I can, believe me. I'm going to ask Robert Luscombe to handle all this direct with C.P.. It really is beyond me, and it would be a great relief to me to be taken off it. But the trouble is that the dealings between the Prasads and the Government of India over the civil engineering contracts were not ... let's say not entirely orthodox.

'Now – that's the Prasads' business, and the Government's business, and it's nothing to do with the Bank, unless C.P. has in some way introduced the Bank into the affair. It's been suggested to me that he did. Perhaps that's true and perhaps it isn't. It's possible that it's true, and that C.P. had perfectly straightforward pragmatic reasons for doing so in the Bank's interests. Perhaps that's the most probable thing of all. As you say – C.P. understands India, and I don't. And nor incidentally does my father.

'But now all this is being said it can't simply be ignored. So I'm quite certain that when C.P. is well enough, he'll be the most anxious of all to put the whole matter on formal record. And preferably to Robert Luscombe, and not to me.'

He gave his great bellow of laughter, and there was a parting ten minutes between them full of attempts now from both of them at humour and warmth and pleasantness. But as Colin had paid his last compliment about the house and the garden and the food and the room and anything else he could think of, and he had waved to her for the final time as the car went off down the drive, his face lost its smile.

If only that were all, he thought, how much easier that would be. It was rather exhilarating initially being asked to be the dormitory sneak. Ewing in power, suddenly. The man to watch. But it had now become considerably less amusing. He didn't actually want to expose C.P.. And by doing that, hurt poor old Luscombe as well.

Because he couldn't bear telling Mohindra tonight that it was more than just a little cosy naughty with the Government. He didn't know who was sending him these anonymous letters, but the second one was as specific as could be.

It seemed that C.P. personally took a quarterly payment from the Prasads, representing half the difference between what they paid to the Bank in interest and what they would have had to pay had someone not forged that letter from the Javed & National.

The arrangement, as Colin had worked out for himself, was worth twenty *lakhs* a year to C.P.. The proof of it, according to the letters, was sitting waiting with the Delhi law firm the Bank sometimes used.

And this, beyond any doubt, meant the end of C.P.'s career.

Chapter Twenty-Nine

Sarah and Sophie sat in the kitchen together, a pot of tea on the table. Beside it was a chocolate cake, a large slice of which Sophie was putting into her mouth. Her head was tipped back, and her other hand cupped under her chin to catch any crumbs that fell.

'You mustn't say that, Sophie. You had some happy times at The Magazine Company. You did very well there. Everyone was so pleased with you. You told us so when you were here to dinner only the night before your father and I set off for India. And I know Solly Lorenzo or whatever his name is said nice things about you to your father many times. Many times. You mustn't say that now.'

Sophie looked across at her mother, and shook her head.

'I was simply trying to please you both when I was here before. You know how upset Daddy gets if he thinks any of us are not enjoying something that he thinks we should be enjoying. Not living life exactly in the way that Daddy wants us to live it. We're never really allowed to be ourselves really, are we? We always have to be like little Robert Luscombes. It's a shock to him when we're not. When we're ourselves; adults with our own minds. When we express our own personalities. He never likes that, does he?'

'I know, darling, I know. But you must be fair. He did get the job for you at The Magazine Company, didn't he, when you left that estate agents' firm. And you know how much you hated it there. And you were a little naughty there too, weren't you? There was a bit of trouble with them too as you well remember. So Daddy was helpful, the way he got you the interview with Solly Lorenzo. You must remember that.'

Sophie made a snorting noise and cut herself another piece of cake, then sucked the chocolate off the end of her fingers, flicking them dry and clean in a peculiarly delicate, genteel gesture.

'It's always help on *his* terms, isn't it? Always the way he wants it, never what we think or want for ourselves. And we always have to go to his people. First of all I'm made to work at the estate agents that do all the work for the Moorgate & Mercantile Bank. Then I'm sent off to a magazine publishers that Daddy has got an investment in or whatever it is. Whether I liked it or not. It's what I was saying. We're none of us ever allowed to be ourselves. To do what we want to do. To use our own talents. We all have to do what Daddy thinks would be good for us. No wonder Rowena ran away. It's little wonder really, is it?'

Sarah sighed, and started to clear away the tea things.

'And anyway, Daddy may have got me that interview at The Magazine Company, but it was me that got the job, wasn't it? It's a really competitive firm to get into, I can assure you of that. Solly Lorenzo made it clear when he saw me that I was one of many candidates being interviewed for the position in the editorial department. And that I would have to win the job on merit, not because of being Daddy's daughter. And I did. It was nothing to do with Daddy in the end. They were competitive interviews, and I won them.'

'I'm sure they were, darling. I'm sure you got the job on your own account. And that's what I was saying. You did so well at The Magazine Company. That's why it's so disappointing that you've left. We're disappointed for you. Not disappointed *at* you, mind, but *for* you. At least, that's the way I think about it. And I'm sure your father does too. Sometimes he's not very good at saying that sort of thing. You know what men are like. But I'm sure he's as disappointed for you as I am. I don't mind for myself a bit. Not one scrap. It's you I mind for. Only you. You know how much I've always cared for you.'

Sophie got up from the table and went across to kiss her. 'Thanks, Mum. That's a really nice thing to say. You're such a brick. You always have been. You never let me down, do you? You've always shown me that you love me, and you're always there for me, and you're so unselfish. You're such a lovely Mum. And you've not had an easy life, have you? Your mother dying when you were a baby. Being brought up by your father all on your own. That must have been so difficult for you. Then India, and marrying Daddy and everything. It's been such a hard life for you. I think you're a remarkable woman, I really do. You always think of others, and never of yourself. You're too selfless for your own good sometimes. And I wish you were appreciated more, and treated better. By Daddy. You put up with too much. Allow him to take too much. Use you too much. In every way, I shouldn't wonder. Every way. You know what I mean.'

Sarah made a little face and frowned at Sophie. 'Now then, Sophie. You mustn't say that sort of thing. He's been a very good father to you, and a good husband too. We've been together many years. We've learnt to respect each other. Give and take a little. All men have their little ways. And their little needs,' she turned away demurely as she said this, patting her bun. 'Men are not like women in that sort of way. You must understand that. If I've been good to him over the years, then it has been my duty to be so. And we all have to learn about duty, Sophie. You have your duty too. I have mine, and you have yours. We all have our duty.'

'That's what I mean, Mum. You always know your duty. You always think of others. You're too good for him. No, I mean it. He doesn't know how lucky he is.'

'Now, Sophie. That's enough of that. He's your father – you must respect him. You have your duty to him too, you know, not just me. And so does Rowena, of course. But then Rowena . . .'

'Oh, Rowena. Darling Rowena – *Daddy's* Rowena. She's certainly done her duty to the family, hasn't she? She's never let anyone down, has she? Pretty little Rowena. Daddy's darling Rowena. And where did that get her? Or him? You talk about duty, Mum! It wasn't me that ran away from school to a squat at the age of sixteen, was it? What about Rowena and her duty? He spoilt her all the time. She had to get away from him in the end. I expect she could hardly breathe for it all. He never thought about anyone else but her.'

'I know, darling, I know. Some of it was Daddy's fault, maybe. He was a little possessive of her; tried to own her too much. Smothered her in some ways, I think. Too much on top of her when she was growing up.'

Sophie made a surreptitious snorting noise and turned her face away, making a little show of suppressing a sarcastic smile.

'You can say that again,' she said, then repeated the business of the suppression of her mirth, and looked out of the window with an expression of elaborately contrived innocence.

'What on earth do you mean by that, Sophie? What can you mean?'

'Nothing, Mum. Don't worry. Nothing at all. I must be going. Before anything else is said,' and she got to her feet, 'which we might regret. Thanks for the chocolate cake, Mum. Just like the old days. That stupid policeman this morning certainly gave me an appetite if nothing else. All that silly fuss about nothing. If they want to take me to Court, then let them. They'll be sorry if they do, I can tell you that. I'm not exactly the only one, you know. I could tell you a thing or two about The Magazine Company. And I certainly will if it gets that far, and it won't be just to you. I'm going to tell the whole story publicly, about some of the directors and their expense accounts, and the other things that go on. You'd be really shocked.'

'Now, you must be careful. Sophie. We don't want to make things worse. Throwing out those sort of threats won't get us anywhere at all. And I think your father hopes that he may eventually be able to persuade them to drop the charges. He's already repaid Solly Lorenzo the money, you know. He did so yesterday. Did you know that?'

'Yes. He told me he had this morning. I think I was supposed to fall down on the ground and clutch the hem of his garment in gratitude or something. He made it sound like that, anyway. I was grateful, of course, but I do wish he hadn't made all that song and dance out of it. It was such a piffling sum. That business with the invoices was more of a joke than anything else really. Just a bit of fun. It was meant to be like an April Fool really. Nothing to get excited about. Not in comparison with everything else that goes on in that place, as I said to you a moment ago. He was wasting his time and money giving them the money in my view. They won't thank him for it.'

Sophie went out into the hall, and retrieved her bright yellow plastic raincoat and rain hat and matching Wellington boots, then sat on the stairs and put them on. Sarah stood there watching her, leaning back against the wall for support, her arms folded across her bosom.

She does look so sweet, she thought, as Sophie pulled the plastic rain hat down over her head, and drew its strings under her chin. Like a plump little schoolgirl. But the plumpness is just puppy fat, and I'm sure she'll grow out of it. She's a very pretty girl really. Very pretty in her own way. She looks just as she used to when she was tiny. Everyone so loved her. They still do, I'm sure. She's never really grown up. Still my cuddly little Sophie, with her naughty little face, and her dimpled little smile.

'Goodbye, Mum.' Sophie pressed her lips on Sarah's cheek, and made a loud kissing noise. 'Look after yourself, and I mean that. Be selfish for a change. It's time you did things for yourself. Don't let yourself be so used by everybody. Stand up for yourself.'

Sarah laughed. 'I will, darling. Perhaps you're right. I'll be more selfish, as you put it.'

She put her arms around Sophie, and hugged her to her. 'We've always been such friends, haven't we? You look after yourself too, Sophie. You're very precious. And Daddy will have another talk with The Magazine Company, I know he will. He'll sort everything out.'

Sarah watched proudly from the front door as Sophie clumped off down the street. Such a good girl really, she thought. So affectionate. She's just a little naughty sometimes, that's all it is. I'm sure Robert will be able to sort out this business over The Magazine Company. Sophie is probably right. They're making a lot of fuss over not very much. They sound like rather nasty people when all's said and done. Really rather vindictive. Robert will have to deal with it.

She turned to go back into the house, bending down to pick up the milk bottles from the step. Then she looked down the street again, watching Sophie as she turned the corner at the end, and departed from view.

What a funny remark Sophie made, Sarah thought, when I was mentioning that Robert had spoilt Rowena by being too possessive with her. It gave me quite a shock.

I wonder what on earth she meant by it. What could she have meant?

Chapter Thirty

Colin Ewing's flight from Bombay arrived at Heathrow at seven-thirty in the morning. He felt overweight, crumpled, unshaven and with an unpleasantly incipient hangover as he stood in the arrivals hall, waiting for his luggage to appear on the carousel.

His appointment with Robert Luscombe was at eleven-thirty, so he calculated that he had just sufficient time to breakfast first at Brooks's, his club in St James's, before changing, as long as the traffic into the West End was not too thick.

But there was a tedious delay before his final bag was found, and then a further hold-up in the Customs Green Channel for his luggage to be examined, Colin having chosen an unfortunate moment to test the theory of a friend of his, that you are only stopped by customs officers if you attempt eye-contact with one of them when passing.

With all of this it was nearly ten o'clock when at last he arrived at Brooks's, too late for breakfast, and he could do no more than shave and change before catching a taxi down to the City. Robert Luscombe was himself a most precisely punctual man, notoriously impatient of tardiness in others, and Colin was sufficiently uneasy about the meeting ahead of him not to risk his irritation unnecessarily.

He was there safely on time however, and waited in the office of a contemporary of his for a few moments before Robert appeared.

In time he came in, shook his hand, and sat down opposite him.

'Hello, Colin. Thank you for coming. Good flight? Is Peter Phillips away? We may as well talk in here if he is. I would prefer it if we could, so that I can be safely away from my telephone. Let me start straight away by confirming to you that I've read your first report, and that I'm obviously very concerned about it. And that I sincerely hope you haven't shared it with anyone else at this stage.'

'No, I haven't. With no one.'

'Not even with your father?'

'Not as yet. But I'm staying with my parents tonight, and that was one thing I hoped you would give me guidance on. I don't want to say anything I shouldn't.'

'Well, your father *is* the Chairman. It's clearly his right to know where we are in this. And in due time I'll ensure that he's properly briefed, of course. But let's come back to that when we have finished together this morning. I think the best way for us to start is for me to tell you what I think of your findings so far. And when I do that, I want you to take my word for it that I have put my personal relationship with C.P. Nerappan quite to one side.'

Colin nodded, and half smiled, as if Robert had stated the obvious, trying to show in doing this his trust in his detachment.

'I've been in contact with the Delhi lawyers, and I've now seen the evidence, as your letter-writer described it. I know you haven't seen what they were holding there. I can tell you that it's very persuasive, but not, I think, watertight. Not until some experts have had a look at certain details of handwriting and copying procedures and that sort of thing, though I sincerely hope that we never have to get down to that level.

'I'll tell you what there is. There are copies of an exchange of letters between three firms of Bombay lawyers; one of them representing C.P., the second the firm of Prasad & Prasad, and the third General Swami. These letters confirm that the Prasads will pay C.P. a sum of money each month in return for services rendered to them in the form of general consultancy, as they put it. The arrangement persists as long as the Prasads hold their debt with the Bank, and as long as the rate of interest they pay to the Bank remains at no higher than one and half per cent over Indian Federal base rate. Swami gets what's called an introducer's royalty from the Prasads, for as long as C.P. qualifies for his payment.

'So . . .' and Robert grimaced, and shrugged '. . . so I have to say it does look as though C.P. has let us all down very badly. On this, if nothing else. He's given the Prasads an artificially low rate of interest on their debt, and he's being personally rewarded by them for it. There are peripheral points in this on which we have no information really, and perhaps in due course we'll have to find out more. Most importantly, I would say, the question of that letter from the Javed & National people, which persuaded our Loans Committee to rubber-stamp the deal. And it does seem beyond question that the letter was a forgery. Beyond question.'

He suddenly shot a broad grin across the desk. 'I tell you something, Colin – you're going to get a severe dressing-down from your father some time for having telephoned old Javed himself in the way that you did. The old man rang your father that night in absolute apoplexy over it. Much talk about the insolence of youth, and the arrogance of privileged children, or so I'm told. They both seem to think you're still a schoolboy.'

Robert burst out laughing, and looked at Colin with what seemed like genuine affection. 'You can be such an idiot, Colin. But I must say I thought that telephone call to Javed was extremely bright of you. It cut all the corners. We would have been fumbling around with this interminably otherwise.'

'I'm afraid it rather put the final finger on C.P. though,' Colin said. 'And I didn't at all like having to do that. Partly for your sake, Robert. But also because of C.P.. I know he detests me, but I don't in the least detest him. I didn't like doing it. I don't like finding him so badly exposed as this.'

Robert studied him, and the laughter had all gone now. Then he said, 'Don't misunderstand me on this. Mohindra Nerappan is right. India does have its own set of rules. We're going to talk in due course about the relationship between the Prasads, Swami and

C.P. on one side, and the Government of India people on the other, over the civil engineering contract. That's a classic area for bribery. And it's possible that we'll decide that a certain amount of oiling of the wheels was the only way that anything could ever have been brought into life. And it was of course in the Bank's interests that the whole thing should be brought into life. We'll come back to that at another time.

'But the business of the interest-rate transaction is in a different category. If it's what it appears to be, it's an unforgivable fraud on us, by one of our most senior colleagues. When I say unforgivable though, I mean unforgivable by the Bank. As far as I'm concerned, if C.P. has had an aberration of judgement over this affair, then I'm his friend and I'm there to . . .there to . . .'

Robert hesitated, and turned away, and Colin watched him, wondering if he should say anything in response. What a very odd little speech, he thought. He was delivering it as if he was reciting from a prepared text, but then he lost his nerve with it. He doesn't know how to handle this at all.

'Of course I understand,' said Colin. 'Personal friendships are very precious things. They matter more to all of us than anything else in the world.'

And what that statement of the blindingly obvious is supposed to do for us all, I have no idea, Colin thought. But the poor old boy needed rescuing and perhaps after that deathless exchange of the profound we can move on a bit.

'I don't know if you can take this part of the exercise very much further, Colin. After we've finished today, you'll have to write up your report more formally, but my recommendation to the Board will probably be that I personally fly back to India as soon as possible, and confront C.P. with the evidence we hold. Though I would like to think about that. Certainly the ideal would be for him to resign, and go quietly, provided of course that he doesn't have another version of the events that would turn your conclusions upside down.'

'They're not my conclusions actually,' said Colin. 'They're my initial responses to the prompts I received from an apparently very well-informed anonymous letter-writer. No more than that. The evidence on the interest-payment issue has been seen by you, but not by me. On the question of the bribery of Indian Government officials all I have done is repeat to you some hearsay. If you want me to find proof of this I shall have to go back to India and return to work on it.'

'My feeling at the moment is that that would be unnecessary. If C.P. wants to resign because he has been detected taking money off the Prasads as a reward for defrauding the Bank, then he'll do so, and the matter will be closed.'

Colin shifted in his chair. 'No action for fraud? No criminal proceedings? Nothing in Court?'

Robert grimaced, and as he did so his mind turned to Sophie, and her conduct at The Magazine Company, and the double standards of most of the world when it came to wanting the law to reserve judgement on the lives of people near to them.

'Yes. I know. It's a very uncomfortable area. That will have to be thought through. Your father will decide in the end, I suppose. It will turn, I imagine, on a matter of judgement as to whether the bad publicity that will inevitably come from it is an acceptable consequence of taking the affair to law or not. But I know what you're saying. It's an uncomfortable area.'

There was a pause while both men looked at each other. Then Robert spoke again.

'Do you think that wraps Poonjee up for you, Colin? You've done a very good job. Is it time now to look at all the other things in the region that you are supposed to be dealing with?'

Colin bent down to his briefcase, and took from it the initial briefing document that he had prepared for Robert when he was in India. He pushed it across the table to him.

'I don't think we can stop there actually, Robert. I'm not sure there is much more I can do in India until you or I have our talk with C.P.. But we still have to deal with the whole area of the relationship between the Bank and the consortium. And the conduct of the negotiations between the consortium and the Government of India. At the moment we haven't done much more than look at one of the most inconsequential areas of the whole affair – what happened between us and a civil engineering contractor. And I must say we've not got off to a very encouraging start, as far as our own probity is concerned.'

He laughed, but Robert did no more than smile vaguely at him, whilst tapping the table with his pencil. Then he shrugged, and said, 'All right. But it's a very big subject. Perhaps we should think more carefully as to how it should be undertaken. Perhaps we should put someone of more experience to run with you on it. Otherwise, how will you start? Given the fact that we absolutely don't want to run the risk of upsetting all our other colleague institutions on this. Old Javed is one thing, but . . .' he raised his eyebrows in mock horror, then looked back at Colin's paper, and turned the pages over until he found what he was looking for. Then he read out:

'How were the member banks for the consortium recruited? How were the proportionate percentage stakes of the member banks of the consortium fixed? Did the consortium employ illegal or unethical industrial or diplomatic intelligence to ensure that our tender was the one selected by the Government of India? Did the consortium apply illegal or unethical pressure or persuasion on the negotiators of the Government of India?'

He flicked the page over, read on silently, then looked up at Colin again.

'Etcetera, etcetera, etcetera. Extremely heavyweight stuff by any standards. Under the spirit of our self-imposed self-damaging compliance and security audits, which are, as I'm sure you know, the wonder of the entire banking world, I would agree all this is a prime area in which our conduct should be monitored. But looking at it again, it seems to me like at least a year's job. For a large, expert, experienced, specialist team. No offence, Colin, but . . .'

Colin gazed across at him, and if Robert had known him better, he might have noticed in his eyes a sign of that sudden wash of irritation and determination and tenacity that had so surprised Mohindra Nerappan.

'Ah, but I have a secret weapon, you see. So secret I haven't the slightest idea where it emanates from.'

He bent down again to his briefcase, and after some rummaging in it, his head emerged again above the desk, flushed and pink with the exertion. In his hand was a letter, word-processed, and with neither a heading identification and address, nor a signature. He handed it across to Robert.

'Whoever is writing these things,' he said, 'seems to have a remarkable access to information. It may all be nonsense of course, but you read it yourself, and it's difficult not to feel that there's a sense of reality about what's being said. Also, the trail that's being laid down for me to follow is so clearly specified. I don't believe I have any choice but to follow it.'

Robert was reading the letter for the second or third time, and it was a minute or two before he had finished. Then he looked across at Colin, and with his elbow on the table began to nibble at his thumbnail, a habit of his when he was deep in thought that Colin had noticed before, and of which he made a note now to add to his collection of office impersonations.

Eventually Robert spoke.

'There is something extraordinarily dispiriting about anonymous letters. I got one myself once. Someone had cut a whole collection of words out of newspapers, assembled them together into a sequence that made up a note of quite astonishing unpleasantness, and sent it to me in the office, having smeared it with what was clearly human excrement. It was the act of a lunatic, of course. But it upset me far more than I would have ever imagined.'

He looked down again at the desk, picked up the letter, read it once more, and handed it back to Colin.

'And now these things. If they were as insane as anonymous

letters normally are we could throw them in the bin. But they're not. They're totally lucid and articulate, and they're written by someone who knows exactly what they're at. So I don't think they can be ignored.

'You've been given some very precise information as to the dealings between the consortium negotiators and the Government of India. You're told why our bid won. And you're told to go to a New York law firm personally, to contact a specific partner there and ask him a specific question. An extremely specific question. And you're told to do so to his face. Yourself. Together with its supplementary.'

Robert leant back in the swivel chair, thrust his legs straight out in front of him, and locked the fingers of his hands together behind his head. He stared at Colin for some moments.

'I don't know entirely what's going on, and you don't know either. I'm Deputy Chairman of the Bank, and I haven't missed a board meeting in ten years, and I have no idea whatsoever whether all this stuff has a line on the truth or not. None whatsoever. The whole thing is a complete mystery to me. If there's anything in it at all, I can tell you it's never been discussed at the Board, or anywhere else in my hearing or knowledge. So I think you'd better go and find out. I think you should fly out to New York and see what all this is about. I assume you've got a visa? You'd better fly tomorrow.

'I'll let you have your dinner with your father tonight. But I wouldn't advise you to discuss with him this business of C.P.. You'd better leave that to me – *and* the anonymous letters and the way the consortium negotiated with the Government of India. Leave the whole thing to me.'

He smiled at Colin, then got to his feet. Colin rose as well, and shook Robert's hand as it was held out to him.

'Goodbye for now, Colin. All very jet-set – our very own gumshoe. Call me as soon as you've seen the New York lawyer, Colin. And before, I repeat *before*, you telephone anyone else. No Mohammed Javeds, Colin. Stay in line. Stay absolutely in line.'

He raised his hand and left the room. Colin sat again at the desk, stuffed away in his briefcase the letter and the Poonjee summary brief, closed the lid, and, most unusually for him, set the two combination locks on it. He then wrote a limerick on a memo sheet, tore it off and tucked it into the in-tray that stood on the little side table beside Peter Phillips' desk.

He looked at his watch. Back to Brooks's for lunch perhaps, then a sleep, and over to Eaton Place at about six-thirty. Looking harassed, but full of *gravitas* and measured responsibility from the day's exertions in the service of the founding families. Whose word is their bond.

Chapter Thirty-One

As Sophie trudged away from her mother's house in her plastic mackintosh and her Wellington boots and her Paddington Bear rain hat, she was trying to decide where to go next.

She was not too sure that it would be wise to go back to the Battersea flat quite yet. It might be better to let that Annie woman have time to calm down a bit more. What an unbelievable scene that had been. How could she have known that that brooch of hers was made with real emeralds? And Annie should have made sure herself that the clasp bit worked. It wasn't Sophie's fault it had dropped off: the thing was bloody broken in the first place. It would turn up somewhere. Stupid fuss about nothing. Of course she would have asked before she'd borrowed it, if the silly cow had been there to ask.

And anyway it wasn't fair. My parents never gave me anything like that, Sophie brooded. Some chance. No one has ever given me things like that. Not like other parents did. Rowena was always being given things, but never me. Always darling little Rowena. I'd only wanted to borrow the rotten brooch for the evening. Just for that one evening. Miserable cow.

Sophie wiped a raindrop off the end of her nose, looked at her watch, and made a sudden decision. She'd go to see Rowena. That would give her a surprise. Rowena didn't even know she had her address.

Sophie grinned to herself, blew her nose on a sodden tissue she found in her raincoat pocket, and remembered the meeting the previous week in the office of that lawyer woman that her father was gazing at with such rapture. Alice Livingstone, or whatever her name was. She could see the letter from the private investigator sitting in the file in front of the Livingstone woman on the other side of the desk, and read it upside down. Daddy had obviously traced Rowena so that he could give her more money. And cuddles and love and all that sickening performance. A fat lot of good that would do him. God, he did spoil her. And God, did she manipulate him.

She dug around in the pocket of her jeans, and found the torn-off piece of newspaper on which she had scribbled down the address as soon as the meeting had been over, so that she wouldn't forget it. Here it was. *33b Plender Terrace, NW1.* She pushed the piece of newspaper back into her pocket, and turned into a branch of Waterwell's, the booksellers, that she was passing at that moment. When inside, she went over to the map section, picked up an *A to Z*, bent it over double to break its spine, and looked up the page that would show where Plender Terrace was. On glancing over to the counter she saw that the booksellers there were talking to a customer, so she slipped the book into the pocket of her raincoat, and set off again to the door.

They make far too much money anyway these people, she thought to herself. Bloody immoral. Taking books was nothing like normal shoplifting. Books should be there for everyone, without people profiteering over them. It's disgusting, the price of books. And the money they all make. People are far too greedy, and that's the truth, thought Sophie, wiping away another drop from the end of her nose. And they've no idea about the importance of literature, and how it should be available to everyone. Free. It's not just there for the rich. Greedy bastards.

She caught a bus in St John's Wood, changed to another, and forty or so minutes later she was stumping up Plender Terrace, the rain by this time falling in a thick drizzle. The houses in the terraces either side were ill kempt and shoddy, made to appear the more dispiriting by the litter of old newspapers and paper bags that lay there sodden on the pavements and in the gutters. Rusting and battered dustbins stood outside the houses on the doorsteps and in the street, and dog excreta lay trodden and slimy on the pavement. Cars in various states of age and disrepair stood on either side of the street, and a skip, at the junction at the end, was piled high with broken furniture and cardboard boxes and stacked sheets of corrugated iron, sticking out at all angles from the sides.

Few of the houses were numbered, but Sophie calculated what she thought must be number thirty-three, saw that the front door was ajar, pushed it open and walked inside. There was a bicycle or two standing there, and a pushchair, missing a wheel, propped up against the wall. Cigarette ends, old milk bottles, unopened envelopes and various pieces of dirty paper were littered over the torn linoleum on the floor.

Looking around, Sophie saw that the door on the right of the little hallway was unmarked, but the one at the end of the passage had the letter B crudely inscribed on it, the red paint running down in rivulets below it. She was beginning to feel greatly cheered by what she was seeing. Daddy would be horrified if he were to be here, she thought. So much for teacher's pet. The prettiest girl in the class. Daddy's darling Rowena. The light of his life.

She knocked eagerly on the door, and after a pause she did so several times more. There was no answer, so she gave it several bangs with the side of her fist, followed finally by a kick with the bottom of her foot. At this, the door she had first passed shot open, and Sophie turned around to see a youth standing there behind her, unshaven, and dressed only in a vest and pyjama bottoms, with a can of lager held in his hand.

'What the fuck do you want?' he said. 'Can't you see that there's no one fucking there? Making all this fucking noise. Fuck off, will you.'

Sophie gave her best smile, and stood facing him, her little girl's coat and hat and boots looking demure in these surroundings.

'Sorry to disturb you. So sorry to make the noise. Do you know where Rowena is? I'm her sister.'

The young man took a pull at the can of lager, and looked at her with a gaze that had marginally softened. 'No. How the fuck should I know? But you've woken the fucking kid with all that fucking noise. Listen.'

Sophie turned again, and she could now hear the sound of a child crying, evidently in a room somewhere at the back of the building. She tried the handle of the door, but the Yale lock above held the door secured.

'Here. Hold on.'

He turned to go back into his own room, and came out again holding a plastic credit card. Going over to the door of Rowena's flat he put the edge of the card into the jamb of the door above the Yale lock, then drew it slowly down so that it slid the tongue of the lock back. He pushed the door open.

'There you are. All yours,' he said and went back to his own room.

Sophie walked in the door, and left it open behind her as she went through into the sitting room. From the bedroom beyond there was now the sound of the child's voice raised to a full scream, but Sophie took no notice of it, and indeed was barely aware of it, as she started on her exploration of everything she could find in the sitting room and the kitchen beyond.

The first thing she saw was an orange plastic beaker lying on its side in the middle of the sitting-room floor, silver foil stretched tight across its mouth, secured by a rubber band. There beside it was a cigarette lighter, the lid from a biscuit tin, and a wooden crayon box, containing hypodermic syringes and two packeted condoms.

The unexpected sight of the technical implements and equipment of drug-taking gave Sophie a shot of sudden, vicarious excitement, and for a moment her breath shortened and shallowed, and she stood there staring at them.

When she turned away she saw some used nappies and a pair of soiled dungarees lying on the floor beside the playpen in the corner, and Sophie turned them over with her foot as she moved towards the kitchen, her pink, snoutish nose curling with disgust. She looked through the fridge and the cupboards to see what else she could find, and whilst in the process of opening up various tin lids and boxes the telephone rang. She hesitated but left it unanswered, and after a prolonged period it stopped ringing, but then started again almost immediately.

This time she picked it up, and straight away a man's voice came on the line. 'Rowena? Rowena? Is that you?'

'Yes. Hello,' she said, a prickle of excitement and intrigue in her.

'It's Alec, Rowena. You certainly took your time picking up the phone. Hello? Rowena?'

Sophie had remained silent, unsure of how to proceed, but she tried now to keep the conversation going. 'Sorry. I was doing something else.'

'You don't sound like you normally do, Rowena. Are you OK? I wondered if you were free to see me. I'd like to come round. I'll give you fifty this time. You told me to call whenever I wanted to, after last Friday. Can I come now?'

'Er, not just at the moment. Give me fifty for what?'

There was the sound of raucous laughter at the other end of the telephone, followed by a bout of coughing.

'What do you think? For the same as last week, that's what. What's the matter with you? You got your mother with you or something? Why are you pulling my leg? I've got the fifty with me now. When can I come?'

Sophie looked at her watch, and saw that it was now almost twenty-past six.

'Come here at nine o'clock,' she said desperately, giving herself as much time as she could need to finish her search and be safely away, then put the telephone down.

She sat down on the kitchen stool, still in her plastic raincoat and hat, and thrust her hands into her pockets.

'Christ,' she said aloud. 'Christ. The dirty bitch.'

She was aware of a slight but definable sensation of sexual titillation. Sophie was still a virgin, though there had been the occasional incidents of fevered activity with various men, that for differing reasons had remained unconsummated. These had left her with a most heightened speculation about the sexual act, and for the briefest of moments she wondered if she should stay until nine o'clock and meet the man herself.

But she put the thought aside, and renewed her search through the kitchen cupboard. Finding an opened tin of baby milk powder, she took off its plastic lid to discover tea bags inside. Then, pushing her finger under the tea bags, she found some folded twenty-pound notes which she drew up and counted. Taking from these one of the ten notes that were there, she pushed this into the pocket of her jeans, replaced the tin in the cupboard, and went through at last into the bedroom, where Jamie's cries had now subsided into a sobbing whimper.

Sophie looked at the child as he lay there in his cot, and wondered, with no enthusiasm at all, whether she was obliged to do anything for him. He looked up at her with wide eyes, sucking at his thumb now, his cheeks and chin wet with tears and dribble. Sophie stood beside the cot and gazed down at him, then turned away and started to look through the drawers of the cupboard in the corner, for no very good reason taking a new packet of contraceptives she found there and putting it in her pocket.

The child was now standing at the bars of the cot, and as she turned around, he held out his arms and whimpered to her to pick him up. She went over with the half-intention of doing so, then, when about to stretch her arms out to him, she realised that he had soiled himself, and moved away from him again, pulling a face of disgust. She went back into the kitchen, where she remembered she had seen a bottle of milk in the fridge. She took it out, poured some directly into a baby's bottle that was standing unwashed in the sink, and went back into the bedroom to give it to him.

Initially she turned away to leave him there sucking at it, but then she hesitated, turned back, and put her finger in his as he reached up for her. She stared at him for a time, then, in an unaccustomed gesture of gentleness and care, she smoothed and stroked his hair with her other hand, before freeing herself and turning away.

When she was back in the sitting room she took a pencil from the mantelpiece and, sitting down on the sofa, left a message on the back of a large unopened envelope which she found on the floor beside the front door. She wrote,

Dear Rowena

I've come here hoping to give you a nice (!) surprise and to see if I could help with Jamie, or do anything else for you. The young chap across the passage let me in. Jamie's really sweet, and I gave him a good cuddle and a nice play and a hug and a lovely bottle of milk. He really went for it!

I like the flat! See you soon, I hope. Lots and lots of love, from your gorgeous sister,
Sophie. xxxooxxx

PS A friend of yours called Alec telephoned and said he would drop in for a chat at nine. He sounds nice!

PPS If you have a spare boyfriend, do let me know!!!

Leaving the note propped up on the mantelpiece, she went out again through the kitchen, and took one more twenty-pound note from the tea-bag tin, stuffing it in her pocket with the one she had taken earlier.

Then, pulling her Paddington Bear rain hat over her eyes, Sophie went back into the wet street, and trudged off to find the underground station.

Chapter Thirty-Two

'I'm afraid your condition is as you suspected yourself, Sir Arthur. You have a classic disorder of the central nervous system, in which the neurones of the basal ganglia are specifically affected. Parkinson's Disease, in other words.'

Arthur Ewing gazed across at the Swiss doctor, and felt no emotion of any sort.

He knew quite well what was the matter with him, and had done so ever since he had gone into Hatchard's bookshop in Piccadilly three or four months before, and looked up his symptoms in a popular medical encyclopedia. The technical confirmation of it from this man merely made him wish, in irritation, that he had not wasted the time in coming to Zurich. It was a day which he could perfectly well have spent at the office.

He had first realised that there was a problem when he was playing tennis in Cadogan Place, and felt unable to put any semblance of power into his normally combative game. Hardly having been to a doctor in his adult life, and having no idea whose opinion he would trust, he had done nothing about it for over six months, but he was aware of a growing weakness and slowness in his movements, and a developing tremor in his hands. The latter he concealed the best he could, but he knew that his slowness, and the lack of vigour and spring in his movements and walk, must be growing obvious to others. Though the more obvious it was, and the less he was able to dissemble and conceal it, the more Arthur's stare challenged those with him to comment, and particularly to sympathise.

His wife had made appointments for him to see doctors, but these he then broke, saying that he was contemptuous of the entire profession, and anyway in perfectly good health. But it was fear, of course, that stopped him. It was the first time for many years that Arthur had felt fear about anything, and, having no idea what was the matter with him, he was very frightened indeed.

But five minutes with the Hatchard's encyclopedia and he knew what his condition was. And at home that night at Eaton Place he had stared into the mirror in Virginia's bathroom, and he knew quite well what he saw. The beginnings, just the beginnings of the disorder certainly, but unmistakably, the evidence was there. The first glimpse of a rigid, mask-like quality in his face; the hint that the expressive quality of it, normally so animated, was deadening away. And his hands, until then the hands of a strong, youthful man, physically and mentally powerful, now those of a compulsively shaking, fading invalid.

He looked at his watch now, and rose immediately to his feet. If he hurried he could be at Kloten airport in time to catch the earlier plane back to London. The doctor's comments, and he was still droning on about palliative drugs and the like, had brought Arthur, perversely, the first glimmering of returned strength.

'These neurones secrete dopamine as their neurotransmitter, and it is the lack of the dopamine that has affected your ability to control and regulate your muscle movement and tone. But we can give you relief from the worst excesses of these symptoms, and that's by prescribing dopamine for you as a drug. And I can say this,' the specialist added. 'Your intellect will, I assure you, be completely untouched by the illness. Completely preserved. I'm sure that must be a considerable reassurance to you.'

But it wasn't particularly. Arthur already knew all that from the Hatchard's encyclopedia. As too what the man was now referring to – that disgusting nonsense about introducing dopamine-secreting brain tissue removed from aborted foetuses, which he had no intention of subjecting himself to under any circumstances – and he was now in his overcoat and on his way, the doctor still talking as he got up to go to the door to see him off.

As Arthur sat in the plane and stared down at the clouds below him, he resolved from that moment to live week by week; perhaps even day by day. He was not to be cowed by looking too far forward. He knew that however strong he remained in his intellect, his strength and movements were declining on him so quickly that he could not stay in command at the Bank for long. But for the present, he was in control. And he was determined that not a single minute of what was left would be wasted. Not a single hour would pass him by. There was still too much to be done.

He looked at his watch once more, and saw that there were at least forty-five minutes of flight left before they arrived at Heathrow. He had already finished the day's newspapers on the flight out to Zurich that morning, and wished now that he had put into his bag the various files on which he was currently engaged. But, seeing from the window what he took to be the Vosges Mountains, his mind turned back to his youth, and particularly a holiday there as a boy with his father's brother when they had together climbed the Ballon de Guebwiller.

He had been fond of the man, as all who knew him were, but he smiled to himself now in memory of what had occurred. For Arthur had taken over as Chairman of the Bank at the relatively early age of forty-three, propelled there by a coup against his father and his uncle that was of short and brutal precision.

The pair of them had been holidaying one summer in their mother's ancient house outside Positano. As had become their custom, they spent not only the whole of August there, but the final two weeks of July as well, and it was the early days of September before they returned to the Bank. If they had but known it, they would have returned in haste, for Arthur had been busy in their absence. He had spent the time touring all the Bank's principal institutional shareholders and making special presentations to them; the focal point of these was an exposé of the mountains of cash that had been wasted in a series of amateurish initiatives that his father and his uncle had dallied with in their gentlemanly decade together at the helm.

When they entered their offices on their return, they looked bewildered at the disappearance of their own furniture and pictures and the unexpected presence of Arthur's. Then Arthur came in, bearing with him a copy of the report he had prepared, together with the correspondence he had received back from the shareholders confirming their dismay. The two of them were then presented with individual letters of resignation to sign, together with a copy of the Press statement that, they were informed, had already been publicly released, ten minutes earlier.

They went quietly, or relatively quietly, as Arthur knew they would. Their revenge on him was limited in its scope by the fact that the family's assets, including the Positano house and the shares in the Bank, were tied up in an impenetrable trust. Neither of them ever spoke to Arthur again, which was entirely to his relief. In due time, however, he was summoned to his father's deathbed where, rendered speechless by a stroke, he could do no more than mouth silently his final reproaches to his son, and attempt, and fail in the effort, to write a parting, and no doubt unpleasant message to him on a scrap of paper.

Most of the research for the coup had been done for Arthur by C.P. Nerappan, who stayed with him that summer at his house in Cheyne Row. Enthralled by it all, Nerappan also planned the tactics of the operation, right down to the securement, in case they proved to need it, of the address of a certain pair of sisters in Maida Vale, Edwardian man as Arthur's father was.

But the deed was done without any need for the more exotic strategies that C.P. had prepared, and with the father and the uncle, muttering their curses, back on the train to Italy and away from the Press, Arthur's executive control of his family Bank was secured. And, in his view, and that of an increasing number of others, not a moment too soon. For the kindly, paternalistic, indolent reign of

Edward Ewing had served to deplete and depress the Bank's standing and finances at a time when several other banks were making swift and energetic progress, driven in most cases by the immigrant refugee members of ancient German-Jewish families.

Arthur was not then a popular man – certainly not in the way that his father and uncle had been so easily accessible and liked – and, in truth, he had never become so, even now as an older man. Knowing now that his days at the helm of the Bank were drawing to a close, he wondered whether his physical decline, once it became too obvious to camouflage, would lead to a sentimental rapprochement with those from whom he was distanced. He doubted it.

For his brusqueness with his inferiors, and his extreme energy, and his wickedly apt articulacy and expression, had never been of a sort that encouraged others to feel comfortable with him. And nor had he tried to any great extent to help them do so; certainly not men, whom Arthur regarded as universally his enemies, unless they very clearly identified themselves as members of his team, and strictly subordinate members at that.

With perhaps one exception; Robert Luscombe. And although now Robert himself was a man of powerful office, when Arthur had first pulled him out of the pack of the Bank's middle managers to be at or near his side on his succession to the chair it was to many people's complete astonishment. Particularly as there were some more senior than Robert who were expecting that preferment. And amongst the surprised, no doubt, was C.P. Nerappan, who was Robert's immediate contemporary, but to all appearances closer to Arthur than anyone.

Robert appeared at that time to fail so many of the usual tests. His tastes and mode of life, for example, were out of the conventional mould. He would be found in his leisure moments at the Wigmore Hall or the London Library, rather than the Sandown Park or Portland Club milieu of Arthur's normal circle. But above all, it was clear to everybody that Robert was of an independent and unsycophantic mind. Sharply, uncomfortably intellectual, and by no means to be counted on as an automatic supporter of anything, unless he was entirely persuaded that it was correct. This was not the stamp of subordinate that Arthur usually took to. At thirty-three, Robert was an uncompromising and autonomous young man. Some would say that he was arrogant. All would say that he was potentially a disruptive team-player.

Close colleagues as they became, the two of them were never equals of course, and decidedly not in the social sense, for Arthur, with his Earl's younger daughter of a wife, moved in circles as aristocratic as Robert's were classless – if Robert could be described as moving in circles at all, given the restraints and circumspection of his familial life.

And it was the thought of his wife that brought Arthur back from his reverie and into the present. He felt in his pocket for the little wrapped box and the diamond brooch that he had bought for her in Zurich two hours or so before, on the way to his plane. She would be there at the airport with his chauffeur to meet him, and he wanted something to put into her hand.

It was a tradition between them in their long, eccentric marriage. Good times were simply enjoyed. Bad times were marked by the exchange of gifts. As a statement, were any needed, of their mutual dependence.

Chapter Thirty-Three

Colin arrived at the front doorstep of his parents' house in Eaton Place precisely on time, at half-past six. As he had done since he was a small boy, he straightened his tie and looked down to make sure his shoes were clean, his socks pulled up, and his jacket and trousers clean and presentable before he rang the bell.

It was his mother who came to the door. 'Darling! So lovely to see you.'

She took him gingerly in her arms, and holding his face a full inch away from hers, their cheeks parallel, she made some loud kissing noises in the air, first one side and then the other. She held him out before her and studied him, her head at an angle, and her eyebrows raised quizzically, this designed, by old tradition between them, to indicate an amused, cynical, worldly observation of her playboy son.

'Hello, Mother. Lovely to see you too,' said Colin, and looked at her with an attempt at affection, and with the thought that she was nothing like so stupid as she made herself out to be.

She was prone to these ludicrous caricatures of the upper-class brainless Englishwoman, and it was curious that she did it. On the few occasions in Colin's life when she had allowed him to talk to her with any seriousness he had found her to be thoughtful and sensible. But most of the time she appeared as an irritatingly vacuous and ornamental woman of her class. She actively and deliberately presented herself in that way. As a mannered simpleton. It was a curiously English affectation, and most odd, Colin thought. And in some ways it had overtaken her whole personality.

She had married Arthur at an absurdly young age; only just a week past her eighteenth birthday, and for all intents and purposes still at school. Arthur himself was barely nineteen, and straight back from the Australian sheep property to which he had been banished with his final year at Winchester still uncompleted. They had met three years before, when Arthur was sixteen, and Lady Virginia Ulverton fifteen, and there had been two separate attempts at elopement thereafter. The second and more successful of these had got as far as Paris, and was given exuberant coverage in the tabloid newspapers. The Ewings were brought to the point where to banish Arthur immediately to Australia seemed the only way to avoid any more trouble.

So off he went to New South Wales; a long way from Mount Street but, as Lord Ulverton had feared, by no means far enough. For soon he was told by Arthur's embarrassed father that the boy had absconded from the little town of Rankin's Springs with the equivalent of about eight hundred pounds, acquired in a single night of cards in the back room of the only pub in the town, and that he was headed for Sydney and, it was feared, the next boat home.

At that point Virginia's parents decided to make the best of things before anything more disastrous occurred, such as pregnancy and Gretna Green. So the service at St Margaret's, Westminster was set for the Saturday immediately following Arthur's return, and the tabloids declared it to be the wedding of the year.

The Ewings and the Ulvertons made between them the best of what could have been something very much worse. And, as matters turned out, they were right to do so, for there was little doubt at any stage of Arthur and Virginia's happiness together. They were still with each other forty-five years later, and if it was an unconventional marriage in many of the more obvious ways –

Arthur was continually unfaithful to Virginia throughout, starting, it was rumoured, with one of the bridesmaids at their wedding reception – none doubted its affection, nor its rooting, which, as the years went on, seemed to strengthen each day that passed.

Virginia was initially baffled by her husband's infidelities, but in latter years barely so much as irritated by them. He was so obviously devoted to her in every way that in her view actually mattered. Superficially a strong, almost stridently powerful woman, she was in fact dogged throughout her life by long periods of ill-health, and Arthur proved at these times to be a slavishly devoted companion. Most clearly of all when she contracted diphtheria in her late twenties, and nearly died. Had she ever previously been doubtful about his underlying love for her, then she never was again. He barely left her side for ten days; barely shaved, barely slept, barely moved. She never forgot it.

Colin was their only child, most unexpectedly conceived and born when the marriage was already some sixteen years old. Virginia had by this time assumed that either she or Arthur was infertile, and was delighted with her pregnancy. As was Arthur too, in his fashion, and emphatically the more so when the baby was born, and he was a son, and an heir to the family Bank when the time for that had come.

But, the first euphoria of the child's arrival in their lives having worn away, it was by no means an entirely successful parenthood. Arthur found Colin, overweight and unathletic from the start, to be a disappointment. Too easily emotional, too lacking in male vigour, too attached and clinging to the various nannies who passed through the household, too whimsical and theatrical in his tastes and his games. And for Virginia too there was a disappointment in the child, for reasons that she knew were neither generous, nor parental, and were never revealed or discussed with anyone, including Arthur. For herself, a quite startlingly pretty woman, the plainness of the little boy was an unmentionable but specific blow. And although Virginia bustled around to conceal that, in his pretty clothes from Harrods, and expensive haircuts, and the teddy bears

214

and rocking horses, and modish uniforms of fashionable nursery and pre-preparatory schools, it was clear, by the age of six or so, that Colin was neither physically attractive, nor very much talented, nor precociously charming, nor anything very much at all. A pleasing enough child, of course, and so very affectionate. But Virginia, and her famously photogenic family, were used to rather more than that. Looking at her siblings' children – very *much* more than that.

So she put Colin to one side, as her husband had, and concentrated on the important aspects of her life; the Season, the grouse moors and country-house parties of Scotland and Yorkshire, the summer sailing in the Mediterranean, the charity committees and the balls, the dinner parties at Cheyne Row, and the month's wintering in the pretty chalet Arthur had bought in Gstaad.

Colin was never neglected precisely, for care of one sort or another was always there for him if he needed it. It was just that, in the bustle of their lives, Arthur and Virginia saw almost nothing of him. And he, more relevantly, almost nothing of them. Virginia, whenever actually with Colin, was kind, concerned, and generous. All of those things. It was just that she was very seldom there. And then, at the age of seven, it was time for Colin to go to boarding school, and it was anyway too late.

The life that Arthur and Virginia led was in many ways one of absolute orthodoxy for people of their sort and time, despite the extravagantly colourful start to it. In Virginia's case that was certainly so, for her intelligence and wit were largely wasted and dispersed in a busy life of inconsequentiality and philistinism. But for Arthur that construction of it would not quite suffice. Much of his life was conventional enough; his profession, the membership of White's, the grouse shooting, the carefree adultery, the Chelsea and subsequently the Mayfair houses, the society-hostess profile of his wife, the gambling at the Claremont and the Portland. But there was an element of him, some thought the heart of him, that was more unorthodox and interesting than this.

From the time that a young newspaper financial journalist, on a walking holiday in the Black Forest, happened by chance to recognise both Arthur and the head of MI5 sitting together talking in a village café, the Press would hint every so often at his involvement in this world. A Sunday newspaper went so far as to investigate a rumour that his frequent travelling in the Middle East, and, most unusually for English bankers in those times, behind the Iron Curtain, was linked to some intelligence initiatives in which Britain was found subsequently to have been involved. The paper never published the report, but even the fact of that carried, at least for those journalists who had so painstakingly researched it, a sense of mystery and complicity in shadowy places. For the cancellation was only at the last minute, and there were rumours as to who had been seen descending in the proprietor's personal lift in the early hours of the morning only a day or so previously.

It was the maverick, heedlessly courageous, pirate adventurer aspect of Arthur's character that gave the rumours a certain smack of truth. Born in 1928, he was of a generation that missed one world war, and barely came in on the very terminal stages of the second. Born ten years earlier, or thirty years earlier, he would have been the archetypal English war hero. Patriotic to the point of jingoism, intensely aggressive, impossibly brave, oblivious to personal danger.

But, in the absence of that, all the drive and thrust was worked out in a business life that was cavalier and adventurist. Even with this, however, there was a level of physical energy left unburnt. Until his late twenties he still sparred at least once a week in a gym in the Whitechapel Road, demonstrating, to himself perhaps rather than the world at large, his ability to compete with younger men, and his aggression, and his contempt for pain.

Colin – poor Colin, as he knew his aunts called him – was not of this stamp. Indeed, apart from his appearance, he seemed to his relatives to have nothing in him of his father at all. Eaton Place, and everything about it, bore down on him throughout his life like a burden too heavy to carry. From his earliest memories, it had always been so.

But now he laughed, and patted his mother on the arm, and threw his coat down on the chair in the hall. He rubbed his hands together in mock vigour, and grinned at her again, pulling a schoolboy face ritually intended in their relationship to indicate a voracious appetite.

'Bit of home cooking, eh, Mother? Couldn't be better. Been looking forward to it for days. Father home yet?'

At that moment Arthur Ewing's legs appeared at the top of the stairs, and as he came down to greet him, moving with unfamiliar caution, Colin stepped forward, smiling nervously.

'Colin. Good to see you. Good flight? How are you?'

There was a robust exchange of handshakes, and Colin was led up to the first-floor drawing room where, drink in hand, he was sat down in the chair by the window, which for some reason was always assumed by his parents to be the one where he should be placed.

Colin watched his father as he turned to speak to his mother about some matter or another and, not for the first time in his life, reflected on the irony of their relative appearances. For although Colin knew that he had grown in adulthood to be superficially very like his father indeed, particularly in his eyes and his facial conformation, he felt in his presence to be like a larger, coarsened edition of the original. In fact, Colin had developed the impression that he could actually feel himself go through the processes of changing shape and appearance when with his father. There were times when away from him that he felt positively svelte. The moment he was with him, however, he had the bizarre sensation that his stomach was at that very moment growing increasingly bulbous, and his posture more lumbering, and his movements gauche. He was never in any way at ease.

For Arthur, even as the unmentioned pall of Parkinson's Disease began to take its grip, was without doubt still a man of most formidable presence. He was by no means tall – perhaps no more than five foot eight or nine – but he held himself rigidly upright, he dressed formally and stiffly, and his grey hair was expensively and immaculately tended. His conversation, famous for its deliberate and studied pauses and silences, was still capable of being offset by sudden flurries of charm and persuasion, and could be an art form of personal magnetism. His physique, lithe and athletic in his youth, was now reduced and slender, and his face, once so strikingly handsome, had now an uncomfortably staring, haunted quality about it. But women, in the main, continued to find him attractive. The more so, in some eyes, as the years had gone by, and he had aged in the abrupt and courageous way that he had, and his personal fame, and position in the land, and, in some senses, his notoriety had grown.

There were those who thought that a certain side of his character was most clearly displayed in his card-playing exploits with others of his kind – brutal occasions of high stakes and the destruction of the weak. Colin's fear of him was no more than that of most who had crossed his path. And crossing his father's path was about all that Colin felt he had ever succeeded in doing with him.

As the three of them sat down to dinner there was the usual little farce with the electric bell, which was left positioned on the table beside Colin's mother, and seldom worked. But after much pushing on this, the latest of what had been in Colin's memory a long line of Portuguese servants appeared with the big silver tureen of game soup, and Colin made his effort to drink it without the sucking noises which he had never managed to learn the secret of avoiding, and which always irritated his father.

They went through their accustomed repertoire of conversation. First of all Colin's first cousins, his immediate contemporaries, were praised for their initiative and intelligence and prospects in the world; the comparison with Colin left unstated but unmistakably there, hanging over them as a melancholy cautionary tale. Then Arthur spoke at length of his personal workload and the indolence of most of his fellow directors. This having been absorbed in reverential silence, Colin's mother asked after a girl whom she still, even after a disastrous engagement, had hopes of Colin marrying. Colin himself grinned and perspired and mopped himself throughout the meal in a parody of the vacuous son having an occasional meal with his disappointed and distinguished parents.

It was a great relief to him when it was over, except that before he could escape to the drawing room and then his bedroom he would have to endure the agonised and traditional ten minutes alone with his father, when his mother had risen from the table and left them alone with their port.

As she went, smiling on the Portuguese servant with that characteristic expression of sweet, uncomplaining charity and devout forgiveness that, in Colin's memory, presaged the unfortunate woman's certain dismissal, Colin obeyed his father's wave of the hand that he should again sit, and took a cigar when Arthur, with an air of hesitancy, as if wondering if the boy was old enough, passed the box to him.

'And your first compliance and security audit, Colin? How's it going? When will we see it? Everything going well?'

Colin grinned again and mopped his brow while fumbling with the cigar cutter, trying to make it look as if he was charmingly unaccustomed to handling one. Why can't I get this asinine expression off my face? he thought. A man of twenty-nine. Every time he addresses a word to me I smirk like the village idiot and wipe my shoes on the back of my trouser leg. No wonder the pair of them think I'm a simpleton.

'Quite well, Father, thank you. Yes – as well as can be expected. Yes . . . quite well.' He smirked again and reddened. That's what's called a considered response in the banking world, he thought. Not a syllable wasted. Crisp and manly. Precise and to the point. Doesn't beat about the bush. Gives it to them straight.

Arthur looked at him pensively through a cloud of cigar smoke and poured himself some more port, passing the decanter on to Colin, his hands shaking a little as he did so. He glanced at him, as if challenging him to comment on what he had seen, paused, then spoke.

'I hear from Robert Luscombe that you're looking at the Poonjee arrangements as well. That surprised me, quite frankly. I would have thought you would have had enough on your plate looking into the overall dealings in India and learning from the management there, if you would listen. There's no one more competent in the entire Bank than C.P. Nerappan. He could teach you more than you would believe about how banking really works.'

Colin nodded and smiled. You can say that again, he thought. He nodded again and drew on his cigar, now in a manner which must have appeared to his father to be surprisingly self-assured.

'I certainly believe you,' he said. 'I can see that C.P. has a lot to teach. The only thing is that the Poonjee business was so important that one can't really do an audit on the region without starting off with that. It's by far the biggest thing they've ever been involved in. One of the biggest things *we've* been involved in anywhere.'

Arthur shrugged his shoulders, and gazed at his son coldly. He made a sort of hrrmphing sound, then said, 'Well, don't get out of your depth. There are complex issues here, well beyond your experience. And I'm not at all sure that . . . Well, let's just say that Poonjee was a most major business, with international implications, and of great significance to the Bank. Still . . .' and as his father looked at him again, his eyes hooded and cool, Colin felt the familiar prickle of fear.

'Still . . . you will at least get a sense of the quality of the Bank's officers, and learn something from that. Particularly Nerappan, in this instance. And realise how privileged you are to be part of it, and what that privilege means in terms of your responsibility . . . your responsibility as a member of the family.'

They got up from their chairs, Colin greatly relieved the subject of Mohammed Javed had not been brought up, and felt his father's arm on his shoulder as he went through the door, and they made their way towards the drawing room. He reflected how fortunate it was that Robert Luscombe had decided to tell his father himself what had been going on in India. He would never have believed him if he had to tell the story himself. Never.

'You must realise now that I would have preferred you not to have taken on anything as difficult as the Poonjee deal at this stage of things, Colin. I'll be completely frank with you. You are who you are, and as a member of the family you can't afford to make any mistakes. And you've got a lot to learn. A very great deal to learn indeed. People will be reading your report with additional interest because it'll be the first time they'll have had the chance to see what you're made of.

'So don't attempt any rash judgements or conclusions. If you've doubts about anything, just remember that I'm here. On thinking about it, it might be better if you kept me closely in touch before you commit anything to paper. In fact, I ask you to do that. Robert Luscombe is in charge of you, of course, but . . . you're a member of the family, Colin. And the family has quite a tradition. Quite a history. Quite a position in the world. You must never forget that, Colin. We have a great responsibility.'

'In Veritate Virtus, Father,' said Colin, and hoped that his face carried the requisite and seemly expression of solemn demeanour and manly responsibility.

'That's it, Colin. Exactly. You're quite right, old boy. Quite right. Well done.'

Chapter Thirty-Four

Colin rang the law firm of Rosenbaum Siegel Schneider & Schwab as soon as he arrived at his New York hotel.

Marty Schwab's personal office returned his call about an hour and a half later, when Colin was in the bath. He leapt out to the telephone, and stood there on the carpet, naked and dripping with soapy water, whilst he was passed through several different assistants, with numerous instructions to hold the line, before he was connected.

'Mr Ewing? Colin Ewing? It's a pleasure to speak with you, sir. It certainly is. I know your father of course; Sir Arthur. We had some very fine conversations together a while back over the Poonjee consortium arrangement. He's a very warm and sincere gentleman.'

'Absolutely. Isn't he just? Most sincere. And warm. I'll say he is.' Any more of this and he'll find me completely inseparable in his mind from Bertie Wooster, Colin thought, shivering a little now as he stood there in the direct blast of the icy air conditioner, the telephone held firmly to his ear.

Marty Schwab's voice purred on discreetly down the telephone.

'I'm so pleased that you called me, sir. I imagine you're here on your father's business – the Bank's business?'

'Absolutely. The Bank's business. My father's business. Yes, absolutely.'

Not only was Colin without clothes or towel, but he suddenly realised that he was carrying a fulsome grin on his face. He'd only been to New York once before in his life, and the Marty Schwabs of this world were still a little outside his range of experience. The grin reflected his nervousness.

There was a short silence. Then, 'Well, Colin. That sounds very fine. Would you care for me to meet with you? How's your calendar?'

Colin's face, still carrying the grin, assumed a sudden expression of panic, until he recalled that calendar meant diary.

'Good. Good. Yours good? Mine's good.' For a man on the treadmill of professional success, Colin thought, I suspect that I don't always deliver myself to my best advantage. No more than that – just a suspicion. May well be wrong.

Marty Schwab, however, seemed entirely unconcerned, and after much muttering between him and what Colin imagined must be his assistant, it was arranged that Colin would see him the following morning.

Colin wrapped himself in a towelling bathrobe, rang room service for two rounds of drinks for both himself and a phantom guest, and settled down on his bed.

Beside him was a file. In this he had placed the three anonymous letters, and also a message, apparently from the same source, that was awaiting him when he had arrived that afternoon at his hotel. With the file was the brief he had himself written on the Poonjee deal, from which Robert Luscombe had read aloud to him the previous day in London, and a yellow legal pad, on which he now started to make notes under three columns, one marked WE KNOW, the second HOW DO WE KNOW? and the third WE ARE TOLD.

Under WE KNOW, he listed the following two items:

* that C.P. Nerappan defrauded the Bank of interest received from Prasad & Prasad, to his personal gain.
* that C.P. Nerappan was involved with the Prasads in bribing

Government of India officials to secure civil engineering contracts, again to his personal gain.

HOW DO WE KNOW?
* Because our original information from the anonymous letters was upheld by the documentary evidence now in the hands of our Delhi lawyers.

Then, under WE ARE TOLD, checking the two points off individually on the anonymous letters and the fax:

* that the Bank knew that the Chicago and Illinois Trust (CIT), the consortium leaders, had traded illegally with Iran, and by possession of this information, and threatening to disclose it, secured from CIT a 20% position in the consortium.
*that the consortium negotiators bribed Government of India officials to doctor the consortium's sealed bid, after the opening of the bids from the rival consortia, to ensure that ours was the most attractive. And that, consequentially, we won the contract.

Colin re-read the letters and the message through once more, put them back in the file, then leant over and dropped it into the attaché case that lay open on the floor beside his bed.

The doorbell rang for the arrival of the waiter with the tray of drinks, and Colin went through a flurry of anxiety first over where his money was, and then, when it was found, how much he should tip. This was followed by an extensive explanation to the incurious man as to where his imaginary friend had gone, and it was several stressful minutes before Colin was back on the bed, the yellow legal pad on his knee, and the two glasses and the four little carafes of Jack Daniel's standing on the tray beside him on the bedside table.

How odd those anonymous letters are, he thought. They read to me as if they are very well informed indeed. Not only that, the person writing them seems to know exactly where I am, and where

I'm going all the time. Including the fact that I was arriving at this particular hotel this afternoon.

He looked at the message again, then rang through to Reception to ask how it had been communicated to the hotel, but the telephonist could remember only writing it down on the instruction of some unidentified caller earlier in the day, whose voice, accent and sex she could no longer recall.

Colin spent some moments writing down on the legal pad the names of all those who knew of his movements in this detail, gazed at the list, then scrumpled it up and threw it into the waste-paper bin. The names were so absurdly unlikely as the source of anonymous letters that they were distracting him from the task of preparing himself for the meeting with Marty Schwab the following day, but having thrown the list away he couldn't get it out of his mind.

He went to the bin, smoothed the piece of paper out and read it again.

Robert Luscombe

Robert Luscombe's secretary (Celia?) – that one who looks like Woody Allen and booked my flight and hotel

Peter Phillips – did I put it in the limerick?

C.P. Nerappan – because I had to play it as if nothing had happened, and report all my movements confidentially to him

Father

Mother

The Portuguese maid?

Me

Gupta – he knew I was flying on to New York, I think

Gupta may have scribbled a note about my movements and left it on his desk?

The porter at Brooks's

He stared at the list for some minutes, then again threw it into the bin.

God knows, Colin thought. And anyway I'm not sure it matters that much at this moment. It depends on how I get on with Schwab tomorrow. We might be near the end of the story after that, and the report can be written and the whole thing closed off. But then . . . why am I being led by the nose like this? Who has the motive to expose all these things? What on earth is going on?

'Too difficult for me,' he said aloud, as he poured himself the third of the little Jack Daniel's carafes into his glass, then went across to the window to gaze down at the lights of Manhattan.

Just a country lad on the make, he thought. Surprised by the wickedness of the world. And being treated like a pawn by someone with what appeared to be a grudge to repay – not only on C.P., but against the whole Bank as well.

All too difficult for Colin. Poor old Colin. The family dumb-dumb.

Chapter Thirty-Five

The offices of Rosenbaum Siegel Schneider & Schwab were on the top two floors of a very grand office building on Madison Avenue in mid-town Manhattan.

Colin arrived precisely on time, having spent the previous fifteen minutes pacing around nervously in the street outside the building, and was shown through to a meeting room at the back.

The room was dominated by a vast mahogany board table, around which stood sixteen matching armchairs, all furnished in highly polished crimson leather, with gold crests embossed on the backs of the seats. The walls were lined entirely with dark wooden bookcases, which were crammed with rows of matching volumes of legal texts. In a corner of the room, lit by a thin beam of light from the ceiling, was a bronze bust on a pedestal, with an inscription mounted underneath the bronze on a brass plate.

Colin went over to look at it. *Leonard Rosenbaum, 1905–1986. The beloved founder and senior partner of Rosenbaum Siegel Schneider and Schwab* he read, then turned as the door opened beside him, and the small, immaculately dressed figure of an elderly, grey-haired man came in, treading noiselessly and cautiously on the thick fitted carpet in his brightly polished black brogues.

'Mr Ewing, sir. Colin. I'm so happy to meet with you. I'm Marty Schwab.'

He held out his hand and shook Colin's, holding it for a moment longer than Colin was expecting. As he released it he gave it the slightest of squeezes, as if in delicious anticipation of future confidences and conspiratorial friendship.

'And how is your father, Colin? You must give him my most sincere greetings. We had some fine meetings together. It was a privilege to have our dealings with him.'

When Colin had been pacing about in the street outside he had resolved to speak only in the voice of the clipped, glacial banker, a man of few words but decisive action. Now he bit his lip to stop himself from responding in his usual style, and limited himself to a manly, pensive nod, and an expression which he managed to convert from an incipiently inane grin to an acceptably gracious and mature smile. He held it for a moment longer than strictly necessary, rather pleased with the effect.

'He sends his very best regards to you and your firm, Marty.'

Colin was beginning to get quite carried away with the fineness and sincerity of it all, adding, tempting Providence but unable to resist it: 'And to Mrs Schwab, of course. His warmest regards.'

Cool, thoughtful, melancholy brown eyes were watching him from across the table. 'Mrs Schwab passed over twenty-five years ago, I'm afraid to say.'

He smiled, showing a row of capped teeth of a startling whiteness and brilliance, and laid his tiny, manicured hands side by side on the table in front of him, then held them up palms forward, as if in surrender.

'What the hell. He's confused, and who wouldn't be? Women here, women there. Too damn confusing for anybody. Eh? Eh?'

He broke into what Colin took to be a chuckle of a fraternal nature, a hint of locker-room coarseness and conspiracy in it, then placed in front of him a stiff, crisp manila folder, and laid his hands back on the table, either side of the file.

'Now you must tell me the purpose of our talk, Colin. I'm just a little surprised that Sir Arthur didn't warn me of this in advance. I would have liked to have consulted my clients in Chicago if there are any points your father wishes to introduce on which I would need instructions. But . . .' and here the quite riveting show of bleached, capped teeth again came into display ' . . . that's not what one would say between friends. And we're certainly friends. And anyway . . .' he pointed to the telephone ' . . . if I don't know the answers, we can pick that up and get them. Right? Right?'

Colin had been up since five o'clock that morning working out his line of questioning, finally reducing it to the six points which he had written on a little sheet of paper and tucked into his trouser pocket. He was hoping to be able to talk without these notes in front of him, in order to give the impression of casual informality and disinterest. But now he found that his mind had gone completely blank, and he was forced to feel in his pockets for the paper, which he found eventually after an increasingly fevered search.

Marty Schwab sat there smiling pleasantly while all this was going on, and continued to sit there silently while Colin, now pink in the face and perspiring freely, gazed desperately at his notes, trying to decipher what he had earlier written.

He turned finally to Schwab, mopping his brow.

'Here we go!' he said, then took out his handkerchief and blew his nose loudly and repeatedly, trying to give himself a few moments to calm down and gather his thoughts. Schwab by this time was glancing down at his watch, which he tapped, pulling a wry little face, and told Colin that he was due at another meeting before long. He then left the room for a moment, apparently to warn his secretary that he might be delayed.

'It's over the way the consortium was first put together,' Colin said on Schwab's return, deciding in his panic to go straight in with the main question. He had earlier prepared a tortuous and subtle route, the passage of which he had now entirely forgotten.

'The consortium,' he repeated. 'How it was all carved up. If that's the way to put it.'

He bellowed with laughter, and Schwab, his eyes flickering with concentration, showed the teeth amiably enough, but said nothing in response, and gazed now at Colin again with his expression of melancholy, alert directness.

'The way the consortium was put together,' Colin said again, returning Schwab's gaze and beginning to feel a stillness and calm within himself at the prospect of the hunt ahead.

At last Schwab replied.

'Well now, my confusion grows. I'm not clear why the question is being asked. Your father approached my clients, the Chicago and Illinois Trust, on behalf of your Bank. You must know that, of course. My clients had clearance from the World Bank to head the consortium themselves, but you'll recall also that one of the conditions of the process was that banks from all the major industrial powers had to be represented as consortium members. Your father was kind enough to make the suggestion that the Moorgate & Mercantile Bank should be the consortium member from the United Kingdom. My clients thought that was a very good idea. A most helpful solution.'

Schwab's hands remained still and calm on the table, either side of the manila file, which was still unopened. His voice remained soft and courteous, and his dark, sombre eyes held their gaze so directly that it appeared that he hardly so much as blinked.

Time to throw a rock in the pool, Colin thought. He thinks I'm here specifically on an errand from my father. That's useful. He laughed, rubbed his hands together, and leant forward, as if in conspiracy, his eyes twinkling. Now for the supplementary.

'I don't blame them. Some little secrets to share with us, I gather. Little Middle Eastern secrets.'

He laughed again, then realised to his horror that he was tapping his nose with his forefinger, in the manner of the stage wag. Not just Bertie Wooster but Lupin Pooter, he thought. The Holloway Comedians. He turned the tapping into a scratching motion, then dropped his hand again.

There was a pause while Marty Schwab opened and glanced at a folded note that his secretary had just slipped in front of him, before he crumpled it, put it in his pocket, looked up again and studied him. Then his teeth were again exposed, and he gave a mirthless chuckle.

'Your father told you the story? He told you? Let's just say that we found that we both had certain things to share with each other. In confidence. We had some fine discussions, and we could see in the end that it would be a sensible thing to be on the same side together. And my clients felt so comfortable with your father, and it seemed he with all of us, that we decided to allocate Moorgate & Mercantile a larger stake than we originally had in mind. It seemed sensible. We all got on together so well. Had so much in common. Knew each other from old. The Special Relationship. Brits and Yanks together. Is that how your father put it all to you? Much on those lines?'

So that's that, thought Colin. Like taking sweets from a blind baby. We blackmailed our way in.

'Much on those lines, yes,' he said. 'Much on those lines. It all sounds very reasonable to me. Nice to do business with people you're fond of. People you feel good about. People you can trust. People you've worked with before. Friends.' Colin was on the point of adding further to this list, when he was rescued by Schwab.

'Now – is there something I can do for you, Colin? Or for Sir Arthur?'

Colin was so pleased with himself for unearthing the acknowledgement of how the Chicago and Illinois people had succumbed to the Bank, and so surprised and fascinated to discover, and so immediately, that the principal instigator of it all appeared to be his father, that he forgot, yet again, what other ground there was to cover.

And then he remembered. There was the issue of how the consortium negotiators had taken steps to ensure that they won the contract from the Government of India. The next stage was going to be a little tricky.

'Well, I'm really moving into a sensitive area here, Marty. Something a little delicate for the normal channels. There's a little bit of a problem, and my father thought . . .' He shrugged and smiled, his expression carrying a hint of mutual connivance and self-interest. 'He thought perhaps . . .'

'Colin. You can trust me. With anything you can trust me. We're partners, remember? Old friends of Sir Arthur. What seems to be the problem?' He raised his hands, and opened them outwards in a gesture of care and concern. 'If it's delicate, then it's for me. If it's sensitive, you can trust me to do what's right. That's what I'm here for. That's what I do.'

'I know how much my father would appreciate that, Marty. He spoke so very affectionately of you to me before I left. Most affectionately.'

Schwab creased his eyes and nodded in melancholy acknowledgement at the compliment, then shook his head slowly from side to side as if in wonder at the sincerity and the fineness of it all.

'To speak frankly, Marty, there's a problem with an official of the Government of India. A minor official. One who may have felt that he had not received quite the level of courtesy and respect from the consortium's negotiators as one or two of his colleagues did, when they helped us with the processing of our bid. And he wants the gap closed – if you take my meaning.'

Damn, thought Colin. Too crude and too fast. I should have come to it much more obliquely than that. I'll put him off unless I'm careful. All I want by using that story is confirmation that they bribed these people. I don't want to frighten him off the scent.

Marty Schwab opened the file that had been lying in front of him, tilted it at sufficient angle to prevent Colin from seeing what papers were in it, leafed quickly through it until he found whatever he was looking for, studied it for a moment or two, then closed the file and laid it back on the table in front of him.

He smiled humourlessly at Colin, and stared at him for a moment longer than was comfortable. Then he said: 'Your people led those negotiations, of course. We had a member of the team certainly, but the Moorgate & Mercantile people had the field expertise. And we were grateful for that, of course, most grateful. But the bottom line was that your Mr Nerappan was the guy who called the shots on it all. With Sir Arthur's guidance and help, of course, on some of the more delicate ethical issues. The more intricate ones. We were glad to leave it in your people's hands. We could see that Sir Arthur and Nerappan knew what they were doing. You know how it is in that part of the world. You have to get it right.'

He paused, staring at Colin again. Then he continued: 'You say one of those people felt slighted that your people didn't show him quite the same courtesy and consideration as they did to some of the others. Between friends, what does he intend to do about it? What's his problem?'

Colin stuck his hands in his pockets, and gazed back at Marty Schwab. 'He threatens to tell a friend of his in the Indian Prime Minister's office.'

'Tell him what?'

Colin paused before answering. He was beginning to enjoy this. I should slow it down, he thought. Not show him too many cards at once. Or pretend cards at once. But I can't resist it.

'Tell him that our consortium won the tender by tampering with the official processes.'

'By tampering with the official processes. I see. That's a big deal in India. A big deal. And what could the Prime Minister care? It was a great result for him. India merely has to pay less royalty to the underwriters. By ensuring that we came in with a lower deal than the other three groups.'

'By having a peep at what the others were bidding – is that what you're saying?' said Colin.

'It was achieved, as I understand it, by arranging for the Government officials to ensure that our consortium was the one that gave India the best deal – in the interests of both parties. That's all it was. But that's not something my clients would wish to have public embarrassment over. Nor your father. Nor our other partners in the consortium. But we've nothing to be ashamed of. Your Bank did a fine job for the team, no doubt about that. No one could have done it better. All sides should be content. The Government of India got one hell of a keen deal, which is good for their taxpayers – if there are any – and our people got the contract, to the benefit of all our shareholders. And we've got plenty of them.'

There was a long pause while the two men looked at each other. Marty Schwab brought his hands up under his chin, and his gaze on Colin was still unremittingly direct.

Then Colin said, 'And the other three consortia? The ones that lost out?'

Marty Schwab shrugged, and there was a hint, for the first time, of a genuine smile of amusement in his eyes. 'They lost out.'

'And the man who threatens to reveal the story, unless we bribe him some more?' The word 'bribe', Colin thought. I've used it. Let's see how he reacts.

There was a pause, then Schwab turned his full gaze on to him again.

'I don't believe we should do anything about anything, though your people will be the best judge of that. Whoever this man of yours is, if we were to give him more now, then he will simply come back for more later. It will never end. We should say no. And assume he's bluffing. Whatever we gave him the first time around, or didn't give him the first time around – it's enough.'

So there we are, thought Colin. It couldn't be much clearer than that. We blackmailed our way into the consortium. And when we got there, we led the troops into a nice piece of rewarding bribery and corruption with the Government of India. The family Bank. *In Veritate Virtus*.

'I think my father's concern is for the reputation of your clients and ourselves. He was so closely involved, you tell me, in all the negotiations themselves. He feels anxious to protect the reputation of all who were concerned in the deal.'

'Yes, of course he is. It's never good to be caught with one's pants down. Particularly at your father's age.'

Colin joined obligingly in Marty's chuckles, continuing with them absentmindedly and rather too long, as his mind raced on to what else he could get out of him. But then Marty Schwab had gathered up his file and was getting to his feet, looking at the gold watch on his tanned, hairy wrist.

'It's been a pleasure to talk with you, Colin. I have another meeting. I will, of course, brief my clients very thoroughly about this development. I'm glad your father used you as the . . .'

'Messenger?' said Colin, so pleased with what he had succeeded in unearthing in the previous half hour that he was in a mood to encourage an insult that he could enjoy afterwards.

' . . . as the man to handle this little matter. It does need discretion. And common sense. It's good your father can have someone in his family to turn to. He must really depend on you. He must indeed. I know how I feel about my own son.'

They were walking up the corridor now, Marty Schwab's hand under his arm, his brown, manicured hand squeezing at his elbow.

'Oh, absolutely. Father and I are like peas in a pod. Inseparable. Quite devoted to each other. Never apart. Proud to serve him. Proud to be his son. What a man!' he called out, as the doors of the elevator closed on him, and he was left with a parting image of Marty Schwab, his hand held high in farewell, and his gleaming, bared, impossibly white capped teeth.

Chapter Thirty-Six

Robert sat in his car outside the café. The rain was drumming now on the roof, and the water ran down the windscreen in such a stream that he turned the wipers on so that he could be sure to see Rowena when she came out again. He had been there now for almost an hour. Soon after he had arrived, he had seen her emerge with a middle-aged man in a hat and mackintosh, her overcoat wrapped around her. They had gone together into the covered alley that ran down the side and back of the building, then five minutes later they both came back into the street. The man hurried away immediately towards the underground station, and Rowena turned back again into the café.

Robert looked at his watch, and saw that it was almost eleven o'clock. He would wait until she left the café to return to her flat. It was usually about half-past eleven that she went back, when the café was emptying and there was no one else to pick up. Or so the private investigator had informed him in the report.

Robert reached into the inside pocket of his jacket and took the long envelope out again. He pulled out the typed sheets, and read them once more.

Miss Luscombe resides at 33b Plender Terrace London NW1. She occupies a rear apartment on the ground floor, consisting of a sitting room, a bathroom, a kitchen and bedroom. She shares the apartment with a Mr Richard Hornbey, aged twenty-five, and her baby son, aged thirteen months.

The owner of the building is a Mr Silvio Moraes, and the rent of seventy pounds is paid to his messenger in cash, weekly and in advance. Our sources suggest that Mr Moraes will occasionally accept personal services from Miss Luscombe in lieu of rent.

She and Mr Hornbey have lived together at this address for a period of twenty-five months (but see paragraph below). Their previous place or places of abode are not known.

Mr Hornbey worked for a period of eight months for a local removal firm EUROTRANS as an assistant book-keeper. He was dismissed nine months ago for stealing money. He was given a suspended sentence for the offence in the High Court after almost three months held on remand in Pentonville Prison. He has held no employment since that time.

Miss Luscombe is also unemployed. There is no record of her having held employment since she left school eight years ago, aged sixteen. During that period there have been three judgements against her for prostitution, and she served six months in a juvenile remand centre three years ago on a drugs possession and dealing charge. I can confirm that she is currently active in prostitution, and she and Mr Hornbey are known to be frequent and heavy consumers of illicit substances, including heroin and crack.

The undersigned had the opportunity of observing Miss Luscombe with her child on following them on a walk. From evidence to date it would appear that the child spends almost all his time at the house, frequently alone, but he looked quite bonny, and was adequately clothed.

'Bonny,' thought Robert, gazing out of the car window at the rain, now easing back again into a steady, persistent drizzle. What an odd word for the man to choose. Like a Scottish nanny. Rather what he looks like, actually.

He turned once more to the second page of the report.

The undersigned has observed Miss Luscombe's movements in some detail since being instructed by the interested party last month. She appears to have a number of regular clients, whom she services at her house, where she is also visited by persons whom the undersigned has reason to believe are dealers in illicit substances. Miss Luscombe's other clients are solicited on the street, or at one or two favoured places, most frequently the Coronation Café in Holloway Road. Her usual pattern is to arrive at this premises at about . . .

Robert folded the papers again, and stuffed them away in the envelope. My daughter. And amongst the tragedy of it all there is this farce of me reading a report on her written in this absurd quasi-legalistic babble. *The undersigned. The interested party. Reason to believe. Illicit substances.* Christ.

He wiped the steam off the side window beside him with his hand. A gang of youths swaggered and shouted as they passed up the street, then went into a dingy-looking pub on the corner.

It is strange how these disasters happen and somehow one survives them, he thought. This is me. Sitting here in a side street in the toughest part of Camden, hidden in a car, witnessing my daughter's acts of prostitution. Whose childhood brought to me more happiness than anything else in my life has ever yet done.

He was staring at the door of the café, and saw another man go in, similarly dressed to the one he had seen with Rowena earlier. The shabby, fashionless gentility of his clothes was in odd contrast to the leather and exuberant show of a young West Indian who burst out through the door as the middle-aged man was about to step inside.

I have no idea what I can do for her. I don't know where to start. All this is simply beyond my experience and my competence. If I knew how to approach her, I would. But I don't know how to relate to her, or what I can say to Rowena that could actually help her. I don't want to be the figure from another generation, too out of touch to have anything relevant to say or contribute. I don't want to feel alienated, and awkward, and a creature from a different world and different culture. I want to help her. I want to say something to her that she can grasp and understand and find connected to her life. I want to be more than the sentimentally affectionate and loyal father. I want to be real to her. But I've no idea how to do it.

A girl approached him as he sat in the car. She was dressed in a tiny skirt, tight blouse, and a plastic, sheeny coat, and her childish, garishly painted face peered and pouted at him through the window in a nightmare parody of the coquette.

Robert smiled at her and shook his head, and she veered away, her face now distorted with whatever obscenity she was cursing him with, jagging her fingers abruptly up into a Vee sign as she went. And, as it always did, the coarseness and raw violence and anarchy of the act shook Robert, and he sat there huddled and discomfited, his overcoat collar pulled up high at his neck.

Then the door of the café opened and it was Rowena again who stood there in the stark, crude light, gathering her coat around her. With her was the man who had gone into the café a few minutes before, and as they turned together down the covered alley, Robert found that without realising what he was doing he had sprung from his seat and was out of the car and running across the road after them as they disappeared from view, shouting as he went.

Rowena turned and put her hands to her face as he rushed across the road to them, his overcoat open and flapping around him as he jumped and swerved to avoid a hooting, cursing taxi cab.

'Rowena! Rowena!'

He was standing beside her now, panting, dishevelled, reaching towards her shoulders. The man with her turned and, half running, went back up the alley, around the wall and back into the street.

'Rowena.' He was still panting as he stood there, his eyes fixed on hers, his arms now on her waist. Then he stood back from her, and dropped his arms to his sides.

'Come home, Rowena. I want to look after you. Please let me look after you. Please come home. Please come home.'

She was staring at him still, her eyes narrowed and creased in an expression Robert recognised as one she had carried in moments of concentration ever since she was a baby. As he watched her, he thought how little she seemed to bother with the orthodoxies of the prostitute's life. There was virtually no make-up on her face, her hair was brushed simply and unaffectedly, and her clothes – jeans, sweatshirt, trainers, her blue overcoat thrown casually over the top – were those of a conventional young girl. She was far thinner than Robert had ever seen her, and there was a bleached, ill pallor about her face. The effect was that of a fourteen-year-old child in need of nourishment and care, and Robert recognised at that moment what the nature of her sexual allure was for her customers, and a disgust for them came over him.

For some moments she said nothing. Then, edging and backing away from him a little, she said, 'You shouldn't have done this. You shouldn't have come like this. I didn't want you to find me. I told you not to find me. I want to be alone.'

'I wanted so much to see you. Rowena . . .' He shrugged again, then wrapped his overcoat around his chest, and gazed at her, shivering. 'Rowena . . . I couldn't just leave you unfound. There are ways back from all this. We can get you to a clinic and make you well again, and free of all these drugs and all the other things that are ruining your life. Let me help you, Rowena. Please let me help you.'

There was again a pause of some moments before she replied. 'Leave me alone, Daddy. You mustn't follow me like this. I'm doing the things I have to do. That sounds absurd. What I mean is that . . . Daddy, leave me now. It's too late. I don't want to hurt you. Thank you for coming to help. But please leave me alone.'

Robert stood there, his hands thrust deep into his pockets, looking down at his daughter.

'You wrote,' he said. 'You wrote. I know we love each other. We always have. We've always been special to each other. You wrote because you love me. You still love me, despite . . .'

'Yes. Of course. Of course I do. But . . . it's too late now. I don't want to go to a clinic. I've tried before. Perhaps in the future I will again, but at the moment I've lost the will to try. I need the drugs. I have Jamie, and I have Rick. I can't see further than that now. Maybe soon? Maybe.'

She shrugged, then gave him that half-smile that he remembered so well. She stepped forward and, for a brief moment, put her arms around him. He immediately tried to put his own arms around her in response, but as he did so she broke away, and walked back up the alley towards the lights of the café.

Robert watched her as she went, but she never turned back, and he was left there until she was out of sight, standing alone in the dank, littered alleyway. Then he too went back the way he had come, back to his car, numbed and deadened by what he had seen.

He was always waiting for her, he thought. Ever since her life had started its collapse, he had been reduced to the helpless role of an observer. Sitting in a car, standing on a street; waiting. Outside her prison, outside her squat, outside her hospital, outside this café in the Holloway Road; waiting. There for her if she wanted him, of course, but it wouldn't be that. At least not in the coarsened, melodramatic sense that there was in prospect a great, lachrymose remorse and reconciliation scene between the faithful, undyingly loyal father and the defeated, homesick daughter. Not that. Never that. There was too much tenacity and strength and pride in Rowena for that. But he was there for her. And on most of these occasions she knew that he was there for her. And possibly, he thought, that was a point of comfort and reassurance and familial protection for her.

And whether it was or not, for him it was what he wanted to do. He had to be near her; for himself. He needed it; for himself. Not in the proof or demonstration of anything to or for anybody. He needed her. He had no idea whatsoever whether she needed him. And it was not a point that he ever spent time these days considering.

He had waited for her in the rain then as well. Eight o'clock in the morning outside the remand centre, and the grey, dingy light and the filthy, unswept streets of the winter day. Everywhere empty of people or activity or noise; the sodden newspapers and

241

the crushed cigarette packets and beer cans there in the gutters; the brambles and wild buddleia shrubs in the wasteland of the old bombsite behind him heavy and dripping in the incessant drizzle. He had waited there since six o'clock, just in case there was some change to their timing, and she was released earlier than Peter Rutherford had been told.

But precisely on schedule the gates had been pushed open, and there was Rowena. Slight, thin, pale, her hair unbrushed and unsecured, she stood there in a dirty plum-coloured anorak, her blue jeans stained and torn, her shoulders hunched and bowed in the wet chill of the day. A limp, almost empty plastic carrier bag was held in her right hand, containing, he guessed, the very few clothes she might have retained from the ones that Robert had sent in after her arrest.

Robert had got out of his car and stood there gazing at her. His well-pressed suit, his black lace-up shoes gleaming and polished, the air of the senior banker en route to a day at board meetings; all of this in such ludicrous juxtaposition to his daughter, standing there in the rain like a homeless, dishevelled waif.

'Rowena,' he had said. 'Rowena.' And they had stood there staring at each other for some moments, one on either side of the street, and neither moved. She made a slight shrugging movement with her shoulders and hands, and half smiled at him, but still stood there, staring.

Then, 'Hello,' she said very softly, as if withdrawn from emotion. 'Hello,' she said again, but still she didn't move, or make any step towards him.

'Hello, my darling. I'm glad you're safe. I'm so glad you're safe. I just came to see if you were all right. I'm very relieved to see you. I'm very . . .'

The sentence trailed away. He wanted so much to walk across to her, and hold her in his arms, and feel her wrapped there, and part of him, and part of what he possessed, and secure, and protected, and in his care. But they just stood there and watched each other, and he had known that the offer he made then to drive her away in his grand, gleaming, flatulently assertive office car was a mistake, and he cursed himself for it.

And so it was, for she had raised her hand to him, and then she was gone, off along the street and across the main road at the end of it, her head down, her hair wet and straggling, the anorak dark and stained with the fall of the rain, the plastic bag trailing down listlessly from her hand.

She had said nothing more, but before she turned away she looked at him with an expression of gentleness that, for a moment, and forever in his memory thereafter, he construed as one of love, and he had never forgotten it.

Prisons, squats, cafés in the Holloway Road, and hospitals. These were the stark, dark points of reference in Rowena's teenage and young adult life. And, for Robert, the waiting there, and the longing for the sight and the touch of her, and the hope, too painful to lose, that one day he would again be able to reach her, and influence her life.

Two o'clock in the morning; the message from the police, and the frantic, frenzied drive to St Thomas's Hospital across the empty streets of London; jumping the lights, heart pounding, shouting prayers and entreaties and exhortations for his child to the God he didn't believe in, for the grace and mercy and protection in which he had no faith.

Arriving at the hospital, and pausing there in the car park, hunched at the wheel, hands to his face, too frightened to go to her in case it was too late, muttering now, slowly, slowly, the suddenly recollected fragment that came to his terrified consciousness.

'*Remember not, Lord, our iniquities, nor the iniquities of our forefathers: Spare us, good Lord, spare Thy people, whom Thou has redeemed with Thy most precious blood, and be not angry with us for ever. Look down from heaven, behold, visit, and relieve this Thy servant. Look upon her with the eyes of Thy mercy, give her comfort and sure confidence in Thee, defend her from the danger of the enemy, and keep her in perpetual peace and safety. Amen.*'

He had recited the words twice through, deliberately, calming himself, soothing himself as he did so, controlling his breathing, drawing strength from the rhythm and the beat and the flow of the ancient prayer.

'Be not angry with us for ever,' he said one more time, then found his way to the casualty ward, and there was Rowena, and the drips and the oxygen containers and the nursing-care paraphernalia of near death surrounding her and covering her, and the struggled ugliness of her comatose breathing coming in guttural, harsh gasps from her throat.

And now he was being forced to drive away without her once again. He was nearly there now, only a minute or so away from home; the terraced house of no particular distinction, with the shabby and lank rose on the corner of the wall, and the flaking and peeling paint on the windowsills and stucco, and the cracked and severed front doorstep, and the two rusty dustbins unconcealed and stark amongst the weeds in the little front space.

God knows, Rowena, he thought. God knows why it's all worked through like this. But you've put a stamp on my life that is yours alone. And I love you, Rowena. I love you. And I pray for your peace.

Chapter Thirty-Seven

Sarah sat opposite the Reverend Derrick Hilden-Parker, her hands clasped in her lap, her cheeks still damp from her tears. She was dressed plainly but well. She wore a soft cream blouse, buttoned severely high, and a grey cashmere cardigan and skirt, this with no adornment apart from an enamel dove of peace brooch. It was simplicity and understatement itself, and served to show her affecting beauty to the most clear advantage.

The vicar sat behind his desk, his eyes, as so often, looking at her with an expression of nervous, defensive response to the ardent, overt devotion for him that she displayed in hers.

'I feel I've failed so badly as a woman,' she said. 'Perhaps I could have helped Robert more. I could have tried harder. We should have talked about things. We've never talked about anything very much, and that's been most of the problem. But whatever it is, I feel I've failed the whole family, somehow. I haven't been helpful to any of them. I've failed with all of them, in their different ways. I've failed with them all.'

'You mustn't distress yourself, my dear,' he said. 'You've nothing to blame yourself for, nothing at all. You're a very selfless woman – and a very innocent woman. You mustn't say that you've failed. What your husband has done is quite unforgivable, if what you tell me is true. By any standards whatsoever. You must leave it to me to consider whether to advise you to institute proceedings.

No, my dear, no.' He held up his hand, and shook his head as Sarah tried to interrupt. 'Unpleasant as it is, I doubt that you've very much choice in the matter, if he's behaved as you describe. But that, Sarah, is the point. *If.* If he's done the things you say. That's what you must be absolutely certain about.'

'Sophie's quite adamant on the matter, Derrick,' Sarah said. 'She really is. She was reluctant to tell me, but I managed to force it out of her in the end. She said that she's been trying to sublimate it all these years, and that she feels it's damaged her development as a whole woman. But in the end she let go and told me. She said it was a great relief to her to do so at last. And then she said . . . Oh dear . . . Oh dear . . .'

'Now, Sarah. Now then.' Derrick Hilden-Parker stretched his hand across the desk, patted her on the forearm, then gave it a little squeeze before withdrawing it. She was crying now, noisily enough to be heard in the rest of the house, and he knew that his wife would be home any moment from shopping. The pat on the forearm only seemed to encourage more weeping however, and Sarah now reached across the desk to take his hand, which he allowed, but only for a moment, and nervously.

It did sound such an appalling story, of course, but he'd never actually met Robert Luscombe, and it was difficult to know what to think. Rather like that last time, two or three years ago, when Sarah's daughter came with that extraordinary story she was so upset over. And which caused so much trouble. She was certainly uncomfortably over-emotional and excitable. Sarah too. He recalled with horror a letter of love he had received from her two or three months ago, which he had opened innocently at the breakfast table, and had only narrowly managed to conceal from Vera before smuggling it away and throwing it into the dustbin.

'Now then, Sarah. Now then, my dear.' He patted her hand with his free one, then gently slid the other away from under her hold. He immediately got to his feet to establish a distance between them, and stood over at the window, facing down at her. He smiled in what he hoped was a reassuring, but not physically inviting or encouraging manner.

'I don't know what to think,' she said, still the catch of her sobbing in her throat, then blew her nose several times, and wiped her eyes with the back of her hand. 'It's not a very nice thing to hear about your husband. You've never met him I know, but I can assure you it's not something one would have thought of him at all.

'But I suppose it never is. One does read of such dreadful cases with children nowadays. All the time one seems to read about it. And the men involved always do look so conventional and inoffensive when one sees the pictures of them. So straightforward, and so unlikely. I suppose it's always like that.

'And Sophie is adamant about it. She told me that ever since she was a child she hasn't felt safe spending a single night in the same house as him. It had got to that point. Not even if I was there as well.'

She blew her nose once more, then tucked her handkerchief back into her handbag, gave a sniff, and smiled up at Hilden-Parker. He smiled back, while thinking that she was making a more than usually irritating display of the brave little woman bearing up to life's travails. But he must help her if he could.

He said, 'Well – perhaps we should go over what Sophie told you, and then see what should be done. What exactly did she say? Or would you rather not repeat it? Look – only tell me if you want to, my dear. I really don't want to pry into your affairs or anything like that. On second thoughts, it might be better if you had a word with an expert in these things, rather than me. A counsellor of some sort. A medical man, perhaps. A . . .'

'He made them . . . rub him, that's what Sophie told me. You know. Rub him.' She buried her face in her hands, and was quite silent for some time. Then, taking her hands away, 'When they were both very small. And then, when they were a little older, she said he . . . you know. Mostly to Rowena, but once to Sophie too. He made her watch while he had his way with Rowena, then did it to Sophie too. That's what Sophie told me.'

They stared at each other, then Sarah shrugged and said, 'I don't know whether it's true. How do I know whether it's true? But that's what Sophie told me. I had to drag it out from her, but that's what she told me. She thinks that what Robert did ruined the lives of both of them. Rowena and her. She may be right. How do I know?'

Sarah's eyes now filled with tears again, and the next sentence emerged almost as a shout, as the sobbing started once more.

'How do I know? But I'll tell you this. If he did the things to them that Sophie says he did then he's ruined my life as well. All three of us have had our lives ruined by him. That's what will have happened. That's the extent of it. That's . . . that's why I'm here. I need help, Derrick. Please help me.'

Hilden-Parker winced, then tried to turn it into an expression of proper sympathy and concern.

'I do want to help you, Sarah,' he said, 'of course I do. But one does have to be careful in these things not to . . . well, one must take care that there's no question of faulty memory, or a trick of the mind, or – well, it does happen, my dear – *fantasy*. I'm not for a moment suggesting that Sophie's account of the matter is deliberately false. Not at all. I don't know her very well, of course, though I have to say that we did have a little talk a couple of years ago which would suggest . . . well, let's say that I'm sure that she would *try* to tell the truth. Of course she would. Naturally. Any daughter of yours . . .'

But Hilden-Parker could hear the laboured, hypocritical compliment and flattery pan out before him interminably, and he tired at the thought of it. So he did no more now than smile weakly at Sarah, and shrug his shoulders, and hope that enough of the sense of it would be carried that way.

Sarah's head was in her hands, however, so she missed the gesture, but after a moment she looked up and said, 'I depend on you, Derrick. I trust you. I'll do whatever you say, whatever you advise. I'm muddled, and I'm frightened. If Robert has done what Sophie says then he's ruined all our lives. I do feel that. I'm not a very worldly woman, and I don't know very much about these things. Perhaps I'm *too* innocent – I don't know. I've led such a sheltered life. My father a clergyman, and we lived very quietly . . . Well, I'm not somebody who is accustomed to these things, or has seen very much of the darker aspects of life. I depend on a friend like you to tell me . . . Not that I'm suggesting that *you're* an expert in these things.' And she laughed, and Hilden-Parker too, and the tension was broken a little.

Taking the opportunity, he said, 'Of course I'll help, my dear. Of course I will. And I'll help in this way. I'll tell you what I think you should do, and I'm going to ask you to promise me that you'll do it. And this is it! I want you to talk to your husband direct. I don't want you to talk to anyone else at all. *No one else at all*. You must sit down with your husband, and tell him what's happened, and what Sophie has said, and ask him to tell you the truth. And then you'll know. You'll know by his response what the truth of it is.

'Let me say it again; I'm not for a moment suggesting that Sophie's deliberately telling a lie, but sometimes memories, misunderstandings, dreams – it was all a very long time ago, and there are often confusions in these things. So I want you to talk to Robert. Will you promise me you'll do that?'

She pulled a little face, and nodded her head, and smiled up at him once more, letting the expression linger there in her eyes. Then she said, 'I do love you, Derrick. I know you told me that I shouldn't say these things to you, but I can't help it. I'm so much in love with you. And sometimes I so . . . so . . .'

Then she started to cry again, and at first he left her sobbing there with her hands over her eyes while he said consoling words from his position at the window. But she cried the more, and after a few minutes he went to her, and squatting in front of her chair he put his hand for a moment on her hair.

The door opened, and Vera Hilden-Parker walked into the room. She made to leave, then paused, turned again and stood there watching them, a look of gathering thunder on her face.

'Ah, Vera. Vera.'

There was a gentle disengagement, whilst Sarah reached for her handbag to find a fresh tissue and Derrick Hilden-Parker got to his feet and brushed down the front of his clerical grey suit, smiling a little pinkly at his wife.

'There you are, my dear. Poor Mrs Luscombe has had a shock, Vera. A most unpleasant shock. She's so upset. Her marriage, you know. Something very unfortunate and disagreeable. We were just—'

Vera Hilden-Parker, a stout, opinionated woman with a loud voice and a notoriously worldly cynicism, stood there, hands on her hips, pursing her mouth in the familiar expression that her husband had long since learned to dread.

'Yes, I can see. One-to-one counselling. Pastoral work. Caring for the flock. What you're good at. What you like best.'

Sarah was now on her feet and making for the door. For a moment Vera stood there, but then moved out of the way and Sarah hurried across the hall to the front door, Derrick Hilden-Parker following a pace or two behind, now tugging at his shirt-cuffs and smoothing down his shirt.

'Don't rush, Mrs Luscombe,' Vera called after her, in a girlish, cooing, prettily sarcastic voice. 'Do stay, my dear. Don't mind *me*.'

Sarah turned and smiled a little uncertainly at her. She started to say something, then stopped, turned again, and went out into the street.

And as she hurried away from the house she was certain in her mind of one thing at least. Under no circumstances would she speak to Robert. Absolutely none whatsoever, despite her promise to Derrick. It didn't feel true, all that business, even while she was saying it to him. She could tell now there was nothing in it.

What a little tyke Sophie is, she thought. She'd get up to anything, that child. She lets her imagination run away with her, making those naughty stories up like that. But she's such a sweetie at the heart of her. What a pity it is that Robert never tried harder with her. She's such a poppet, and he'd have found that out for himself if he'd tried more to get through to her. And been a better father.

She's a naughty little tyke with all her funny stories, but there's so much good there. If you look for it.

Chapter Thirty-Eight

There is a drabness about Elm Park Gardens that many who pass by there mildly dislike.

The mansion blocks stand shoulder to shoulder on either side of the street for its whole length, and the grey brick in which they are faced is certainly less suited to ameliorate the English climate than the warm terracotta of the Dutch gabled buildings grouped together a mile or less to the east, in Knightsbridge and Chelsea. On wet days there is unquestionably a certain dingy chill to the place but, once inside, the visitor would find the apartments in the buildings to be cheery and pleasant, and the residents of a particular and rather agreeable sort; predominantly professional people, often bachelor men or single women, but couples too, most frequently childless, amiable, middle-aged people, a number of whom have lived there for many years.

Alice Livingstone's flat was at the top of one of the blocks. It was previously lived in by Alice's godmother, a broadcaster and novelist who had died suddenly the previous spring. Alice had stayed with her as a child on theatre and sightseeing holidays, invited to come when her father was away lecturing or at conferences. She had always enjoyed herself, despite the incessant homesickness for her father, and she was greatly surprised, and delighted, when she found that her godmother had left her the flat in her Will. She had been living for some time in Shepherd's Bush in

An Imperfect Marriage

a house owned by two friends of hers from Cambridge, and in truth, despite the amusement of it all, she was relieved to have an excuse to move out. She was beginning to tire not only of the lack of physical comfort of such a place, but also its unremitting, undergraduate camaraderie and the absence of personal privacy and solitude.

She moved to Elm Park Gardens one Saturday morning in June, hiring for herself a self-drive van in which to carry her few pieces of furniture and the two tin trunks she had brought down for the occasion from her father's house in Cambridge. The trunks held all the bed-linen and clothes that she possessed; her collection of books and records she carried separately in heavy plastic skips that she hired for the day.

A boyfriend had volunteered to help her carry all this load out of the van and up the stairs of the liftless building but, little to her surprise, he had failed to arrive. So she managed it all herself, refusing the assistance that was offered with a great show of gallantry by her new neighbour on the top floor, a frail bent widower aged, at the least, in his late seventies. It took several trips and a good deal of unpacking to lighten the loads, but finally she had everything safely stacked on the floor of this, the first home of her own.

She sat down amongst it all, a mug of tea in her hands, crosslegged on the carpet which looked so much more threadbare than she had remembered it, but delightfully congenial for all that. She looked around at the furniture and ornaments that remained from the disposal of her godmother's estate, and decided that while she had there the skips and the tin trunks and, most important of all, the van, she would use them to remove those things she didn't want to keep. So, for the rest of the day, she sorted and loaded and delivered and scrapped until, almost at midnight, she was through with it all, and again sitting on the carpet of the drawing room, with a glass of red wine in one hand, and a cheese sandwich in the other.

The boyfriend had not called, either in explanation or apology, and that, she thought, was a relief more than anything else. She was

0

used to these things ending in this casual, unstructured way. Better that by far than the business of them dragging on in mutual, growing disaffection, with the trips to bed the only genuine moments of straightforward, unaffected contact. And better that by a very long way than the guilt and pain of the split with attached men, going back to their wives.

Alice got up and walked around all the rooms, still holding the glass of wine in her hand as she went. This is so lovely, she thought. If I never do marry and have children I shall stay here for the rest of my life on my own. And be very content and grateful that I do so.

She stood at the door of the main bedroom, and looked at the comfortable, plum-coloured carpet, and the big double bed, and the thick curtains, frayed a little she now noticed, but well made and substantial. And, like the carpet, reminiscent of home life at Grange Road. The bathroom too, with its elderly, chipped tub, so like the ones she had grown up with. The kitchen, with its rather inadequate attempts at modernisation, but for all that clean, and comfortably worn and practical. And the spare bedroom, with the same intricately patterned floral wallpaper that had been there ever since she had first stayed with her godmother as a child.

She pushed the bed to one side, and could see then the tear she had made at the edge of the paper in the crude shape of a horse, beside which she had drawn in pencil a groom in leather breeches and cloth cap. She remembered how guilty she had felt when she had done it, and how she had pushed the bed right up against the mark on the wall before she had left, in the hope that it would never be found.

Earlier in the day she had made up her bed in the main bedroom, and she went to it now, lying there for some time with the light still on, gazing around her, at the shelves full of books, and the T. B. Hardy water colours on the wall, all of which, so unexpectedly, were now hers. At last she fell asleep, and when she awoke it was Sunday, and she walked down in the early summer sunlight to the little shops on the King's Road to buy her newspaper and some milk and a croissant. She returned to her flat, and sat on the floor, the newspaper spread out around her, rejoicing in the privacy and security of her new life.

Then the call to Cambridge, and Tom's delight, chuckling in his thickened and fumbled voice, disguised for Alice as best he might, but carrying, unmistakably, the desolate evidence of his recent stroke.

She told her father of all that had happened the previous day, and promised that she would go up to Cambridge the following Saturday. Then she went through into the kitchen, and continued the task of sorting through all the china and glass and cooking equipment to see what she wanted to keep and what she would give or throw away.

As she squatted on the floor with all this around her, she looked at her watch and calculated how many hours and minutes were left before Robert would come. Eleven-fifteen now. Seven hours or so to go. She would have a sandwich for her lunch while she did some more sorting and clearing out, then she'd go out this afternoon and buy something to cook for their supper. She would make a risotto maybe, about the only thing that never seemed to go wrong. It was Tom's favourite meal, so much so that he would happily eat it seven nights in a row.

God – I must do something to improve my standard of cooking, she thought. The main problem is that I have a total personal indifference to what I eat. But there is just a touch of arrogance in there as well, and affectation: the successful career woman, who is too busy to bother with what keeps the second-grade, suburban members of her sex busy and occupied. A statement of contempt for the housewife, from the high flier of a West End lawyer.

And not only is that an affectation, it also doesn't deliver what I actually am. What dominated my life for so long was my domestic existence with Tom. When I was a child I used to look after him so well, and it wasn't merely a childhood game. I enjoyed the domesticity, and I wouldn't in the least mind experiencing it again.

She sipped her coffee, and leant back against the sofa, and thought more about where she was and where she'd been. And although she had no knowledge of it, it was an irony that the childhood she was recalling now was in one sense a replica of Sarah Luscombe's, for Alice too had lost her mother at a very early age, Hodgkin's Disease killing her when she was twenty-five, within eighteen months of the initial diagnosis being confirmed.

But unlike Sarah, Alice had known her mother just long enough to have memories of her, though very few. Throughout her early and middle childhood Alice would rehearse them, in the same way as another child would put aside a set time each evening to say her prayers. She had held them in her mind laid out and sorted into what she calculated was sequential order, and she would sit on her bed or wherever she might be, and screw her eyes tight shut, and she would force through her mind each of the images in her memory one by one, until the final one was reached, and the ritual was over.

There were some photographs to help her, and Alice had all these stored together away in a big cardboard box in her father's study. And when her father was working there, Alice would take them all out of the box, and spread them on the carpet, and make Tom tell her where each one had been taken, and who took the picture, and how old her mother was, and whether she had been happy that day. In the later photographs Alice was sometimes there in the picture as well, and these were her favourites. One was best of all, and that had been taken just a few days before her mother died. It showed Alice sitting on her mother's lap, her back to the camera, both arms locked around her mother's neck, as if in parting.

But although the photographs were important, the memories were of a different category. They were in themselves of simple, familial occasions, but in that lay their significance. Her mother moving, and walking, and reaching into cupboards, and picking things up, and talking to her father, and smiling; no more and no less than that. Apart from one with a poignancy in it so acute and so sharp that Alice would work and force to get it into her mind but, when successful, would flinch away from its immediacy; her mother one night putting Alice to bed, and smoothing her forehead, and straightening her sheets, and singing to her a soft lullaby.

The house in Grange Road was her childhood home throughout; ludicrously too large really for a family that had been reduced to just her father and herself. But her father preferred doing much of his teaching there to his rooms at Corpus Christi, and the house in term-time was always full of undergraduates and fellow dons. It was always quite prodigiously untidy, for on his wife's death Tom Livingstone abandoned any attempt at domestic order, beyond that provided by a cleaner who was supposed to come twice weekly but very seldom did. And, from the age of only eight or nine, by Alice.

Tom organised his life so that he was at home with her as much as it was possible for him to be. Although he was obliged to take part in college life, he particularly kept the occasions that he dined in Hall to the minimum. When he had to be there he would leave as early as possible to get back to her, and when Alice heard his bicycle crunching on the gravel and the slam of the front door, she would rush down from her bedroom, where she hid away from the babysitter, and where all her books and toys were kept and her homework done, and leap up into his arms.

And then, in the mornings, there were the rituals with Tom's morning tea, and getting Alice dressed for school, and the last-minute bowls of cornflakes rushed down at the kitchen table. And until she was too big to do it, she would each morning, in all but the worst winter weather, ride to school behind him on the pillion seat of his bicycle, her school hat crammed over her ears, her blazer buttoned tight, her arms hugging him, her satchel and his bag stuffed together into the large basket attached to the bicycle's front handlebars.

Alice was aware from an early age that she was an object of pity and gossip amongst Tom's friends and, more particularly, the legion of her friends' mothers in her playschool and primary-school years. But she never felt herself to be unduly deprived. There were her memories of her mother, and the photograph box, and the familiar old house in Grange Road. And there was Tom. And Tom she regarded as being the most perfect father in the world. No one else had a father like hers. No one else had a father who was always there for her, with his arms around her if that was what she wanted, always funny, ready to sing their special songs and play their special games, so untidy and hopeless and needing her care, and her tidying, and her presence in his life.

There was the occasional incident arising from Tom's own private life that caused trouble. Once Alice, aged thirteen, came downstairs at three o'clock in the morning for a glass of cold milk from the fridge, and a naked woman came out of the lavatory opposite Tom's bedroom as Alice passed by. They had stood there gazing at each other in mutual horror, Alice clutching an empty glass, and the young woman her breasts and her groin, before Alice pushed past and went on down to the kitchen, coughing loudly and indignantly outside her father's bedroom door as she came upstairs again a few minutes later. Another time, she had found him in someone's arms in his rooms at Corpus Christi, when one afternoon she had burst in there without knocking. There was a desperate flurry of limbs disentwining and clothes being pulled down and straightened before a blushing Alice stuttered an apology and rushed out again, puce in her embarrassment, Tom calling out after her some inconsequential, embarrassed remark or another.

Both these incidents caused an awkwardness between them for a day or so, but no great damage was done, and soon all was passed over, and never mentioned again. And Alice realised, even at that age, that to be hurt by this sort of incident would be unrealistic and immature. For Tom was cheerfully masculine, and there was, and Alice felt this herself as much as anyone could, a pleasingly physical and uncomplicated aspect to his personality.

Indeed in many ways she grew torn in her mind as to whether a stepmother in her life would necessarily be an unwelcome development. It would depend very much on who she was, but there were one or two people in his life whom she thought she would have been happy to have with them at Grange Road, and one young post-graduate English student in particular. She could see that women clearly liked Tom, and he them, and in her adulthood Alice grew to wonder how he had been able to combine his most dutiful single parenthood of her with what she realised must have been a normally active physical life. It was only on those two occasions that she had caught him unawares, and her embarrassment both times was such that she was very relieved it hadn't been more often.

For it would be wrong to say that Alice had no physical awareness of her father. He was the only person she had ever, in her conscious years, lived with, and perhaps it was inevitable in a relationship so totally compressed as theirs was, without a break or separation of any length for the whole period of Alice's childhood, that there were aspects of it that were of unusually complex texture. There was no immodesty of any sort, but there was a focus to it beyond the conventional.

Which does suggest an at least partial explanation of what later happened in Alice's life. For although there had been numerous sexual escapades with boys of her own generation, the only occasions when she had fallen in love had been with men older than herself. There had been two or three of those, each as ultimately unhappy in their conclusion as the last.

The first time had been when she went to Spain at the age of eighteen, for her bridge year before going up to Newnham College, Cambridge as an undergraduate. Tom had arranged a job for her as a trainee assistant at the Prado in Madrid, working for a friend of his who was running a department there at that time. He had been recently divorced and was living there alone, and Alice, before barely a week was through, was in love with him. She was determined to sleep with him, and in time she did so. But the affection was unrequited, there was a guilt and consequent self-anger in the man for allowing himself to have an affair with his friend's teenage daughter, and Alice in the end came home to

England weeks earlier than scheduled, unhappy and listless with the failure of it all.

Tom wondered for a time whether he should ask the college to postpone her place, in order to give her time to gather her spirits together again. But she mended of course, and apart from a most unfortunate term, when she got entangled with one of the dons, her University years passed without too much emotional damage done. Alice, still bruised from the summer in Madrid, and finding in her undergraduate life a certain, almost guilty sense of release in her first real weaning from Tom and Grange Road, was not anyway wholly in the mood at that time for romance. Moreover she surprised herself, if not Tom, by showing herself now to be distinctly clever, and there was the very good degree that followed from that, and the pride in her achievement, and then London and the grindingly hard work, if considerable professional satisfaction, of her introductory years as a lawyer at Freshfields.

She was a pleasingly attractive and intelligent girl, by no means reticent or fearful of love. And at least every eighteen months or two years there would be an attachment with someone or other; usually older, often married, always in her bed within a week or so, always in love as he had never been in love in his life before, and always gone from her, in a final, bleak moment of parting, no more than three or four months after he had first arrived.

And now there was Robert Luscombe. But this time it was going to be different. This time she would control it properly, and pace it properly. If they were going to be lovers, then so be it. She wanted to be his lover. She hoped that would happen. But she would be under control. The relationship would develop at the pace she wanted. And what she would work for in the relationship was happiness and constancy, and friendship. No abruptness in the parting. No fantasy as to what was possible. No pain, no guilt, no excesses of emotion. The long-term future would be whatever it would be. In all probability there wouldn't *be* a long-term future. But for now, it was one careful, controlled step at a time.

Oh Christ, Alice thought. She got up from her cramped position on the floor, and went to the window and looked down on the well-kept communal gardens at the rear of the buildings. Earlier that morning some children had been running around the flowerbeds, shouting with laughter, a puppy snapping and gambolling at their heels. Their mother had stood watching them, her hands in the pockets of her thick cardigan, smiling and calling out some word or other to them.

Oh Christ. Go carefully. I try to think all the time of control, and care, and low expectation, and then I let myself slip into a fantasy about children, and making a comfortable, conventional home, and all the rest of it. I've got to do as I say. I've got to go carefully. I'm at an age and moment in my life when there's a risk that I'm going to chase marriage, where the prospect of marriage does not at all exist. And then get hurt.

Alice turned away from the window, and bent down to pick up some plates and store them again in the cupboard. But I don't want to move away from him at this stage of things; not until it's clearer what's going to happen. At the moment I want to go on with him. That's all I need to think about for now.

She went to her handbag, and took from it a passport photograph that she had removed surreptitiously from his file at the office, and at which she had recently been looking continually. She sat on the sofa and spent some moments studying it, then got up and propped it on the mantelpiece.

Chapter Thirty-Nine

Three or four miles away in St John's Wood, Robert was at that moment sitting at the kitchen table.

He was gazing at the letter that he had found lying on the doormat when he had got back from Geneva that morning. Words, part-words and single letters had been cut from newspapers, then glued carefully on to a single foolscap sheet. This was smeared with what he assumed to be dried human excrement, from the experience of the previous letter of this sort he had received two years ago.

He read it again.

Dear Mr Luscombe,

I am informed, by impeccable sources, that you ruined your two daughters by what you did to them when they were children. They both had their lives spoilt by the sexual practices you forced upon them when they were little girls. You taught them to do perverse and unnatural acts with you. You degraded them with your filth and your animal appetites. You defiled their pure and lovely bodies.

You are a monster. Your behaviour, however ill and disturbed you may be, is depraved and evil. You are a disgusting pervert and you must be punished for what you have done. I have decided therefore that my duty is to inform the proper authorities. The police will be told of this, as will your colleagues at the Moorgate & Mercantile Bank. I may consider separate notification of the media.

Your daughters need care and help. Your innocent and selfless wife needs protection. You will be hearing from me again, after I have taken the steps that are required to expose you for what you are. You must first be punished. Then you must turn to God to forgive you. You must fall on Him for His mercy. You must prostrate yourself at the mercy seat. No man is so vile that God, in His blessedness, will not forgive him.

The letter terminated at that point, with no form of identification or marking. The envelope had been typed, the postmark showing that it had been mailed from West London.

It seemed quite obvious to Robert that this letter was from the same source as the earlier one. On that occasion, the letter had accused Robert of forcing certain explicit and demanding sexual practices upon his unwilling wife, which the composer of the letter had claimed to have witnessed through the crack of the curtains in the Luscombes' bedroom. Robert had thrown the letter away, and he now recalled this with some annoyance, as it would have been helpful at this moment to have been able to take to the police both of them together.

He read the letter again, made to put it in the envelope, then, grimacing with distaste, he noticed again the smear of excrement on the page he was holding. He carefully folded it, slid it into the envelope, and went into his study with it to find a plastic file in which to place it. He then went back into the kitchen, washed his hands most thoroughly under the tap, and thought about the letter again.

There was something about the language, he thought – *pure and lovely bodies*, *filth* and *animal appetites*, and all that toe-curling stuff at the end about God and the mercy seat – that sounded stagey and contrived. And quite particularly sinister.

He would talk to his lawyers first. And there was a shot of pleasure in him when he remembered that talking to his lawyers meant talking to Alice. But . . . what a dreadful thing to have to bring to her. What a humiliation to have to so much as discuss the abominable accusation that he had ever molested Sophie or Rowena. Or – even worse – to talk about the contents of the original letter he had received, which speculated on his physical life with Sarah.

So perhaps it would be better to do exactly what he had done with the first letter all those months and years ago. Just throw it away and forget about it. These people who send anonymous letters are always insane. Five minutes later they probably have no idea what they've said or written. If he ignored it, the whole nonsense would probably just disappear.

Like it did the last time. At that time too there were all these grotesque threats of exposure to the Bank and everyone else that one could think of, never actually carried out of course. To react to this drivel, and go to talk about the whole thing with the police and Arthur Ewing and all the rest of it, was just to play into this man's hands. Or woman's hands. It was evil, and untrue, and written by a lunatic; best ignored and forgotten. Completely ignored and forgotten.

Yet, who *is* it? he thought. Who could be writing these things? There are matters that people could be unpleasant about and write anonymous letters about – there are in everybody's life – but this stuff is so completely wild it has no resonance or hurt to it. I've been, at best, an indifferent husband to a difficult wife; that's certainly true. And a father who has failed to provide a good domestic environment for his children. That's true too.

But sexual perversity, or evil of that sort is completely outside my experience or range. The accusation gives me no unease, because I know it has no ring of anything in me that I can recognise. It's not me. Whoever is writing these things either doesn't know me very well, or thinks that other people are acquainted with me so little that they will believe the story. Or he or she is simply blackmailing me, on the basis that once the rumour is planted then its mere existence will give it veracity and status.

No smoke without fire, as they say. God – how I hate that expression, with its spurious logic and neatness. It's wrong, of course. And it can lead to such astonishing cruelty and barbarity.

Robert got up from the table, and went into the hall, picking up his suitcase to take to his bedroom. The house was empty, and would be so for at least another seven days, as long as Sarah actually stayed at Folkestone that long. But Sophie was with her, so she probably would.

A whole week for me to be alone, private and undisturbed, Robert thought. To catch up with correspondence, to think, to walk, to work, to do whatever I want. And to be with Alice. To be with her all the time in my mind, and for some time at least actually physically so.

He sat on the bed, then looked at his watch. Just seven hours more, he thought. Less than seven hours more, than I'll be with Alice. With the expectation of it there was a clench of anxiety as well, however. He hadn't previously seen her alone in her own surroundings. They had until now only met in contrived circumstances at her offices, or on three or four occasions in restaurants for lunch. Once they had walked back together across Hyde Park, and had stopped for a few minutes to sit on a bench overlooking the Serpentine. But tonight would be the first time they had been alone, in privacy, and without the pressures of time and work. The anticipation of it quite sickened and winded him, and he crossed his arms for a moment across his chest, and rocked forward at the waist.

'God – I do love her,' Robert said aloud. 'I love you, Alice. Alice. Alice.'

The speaking and the repetition of her name gave him a surge and release of elation. He looked again at his watch. Less than seven hours to go, he thought. Six and a half hours, then I'll be with Alice.

And then his stomach felt void again, and suddenly acute,

immediate desire was once more upon him, and he could see her naked, and her body was white, and she was on the bed, and she was looking up at him, and her eyes were on him, and he was coming to her.

Christ, I want her, he thought, his hands brought now up to his face, and covering his eyes.

The anonymous letter, now in its plastic file, lay beside him on the bed, and as he looked down and saw it, he picked it up and threw it on top of a chest of drawers, out of his sight. He'd show it to Alice because they shouldn't have secrets of that sort between them. But he didn't want to have to look at it again.

Chapter Forty

'Robert – I'm going to keep the letter here if you agree, and take it in to show Peter tomorrow. I think we should talk about it with him just to see if he feels there are any steps we should be taking now. Possibly bringing the police in, or ourselves trying to trace who sent it. It's all lunatic, but I'd prefer it if you weren't just sitting there waiting for another to arrive, or for something to be sent to the Bank. I would much prefer us to have the initiative. I don't believe this is the moment to take a passive stance and wait for the whole thing to blow away. That was not a very pleasant letter. We must deal with it. Peter is very good on these sorts of issues. Would you mind if we did that?'

Alice smiled then, to signal that the conversation was over, and ran her finger down his face. She willed herself now to put to one side for the present all the complications and problems that there were between them, and simply deal with the moment.

And as Robert looked down at her, he noticed, for the first time since they were unclothed together, the age and looseness of his skin and body in comparison with hers. He almost wanted to hide his arms again so that she too would not think what he had thought, but she was stroking his hands now, holding his palms out with fingers outstretched so that she could look at his skin and run her touch over the joints and the little veins.

'Don't leave me, Alice. Never leave me.'

And if I sound like an indifferent lyricist of an indifferent popular song, then so be it, Robert thought. I can't find in me the sort of heightened language and imagery that I wish I could. I'm simply numbed by love for her. I just want to repeat these phrases because they are the best I can do. And they bring me peace. I'm saying to her what is true.

Her face seemed to Robert the most perfect he had ever seen. Her long auburn hair, damp with the sweat of their love-making, her full, smiling mouth, her skin white and lucent and unblemished. He couldn't imagine a woman more lovely.

'Never go away. Stay with me, Alice.'

She smiled again, now bending her arm and putting her hand behind her head, her white, naked breasts exposed and open to him. Then she reached up, and pulled him down to lie beside her again, her mouth locked on to his, her body pressed hard up to him. He could feel her breasts pushing against his chest, and he closed his eyes, trying to hold locked in him the memory of the moment so securely and in such definition that it would never be lost.

Chapter Forty-One

Douglas Tilton could hear the car draw up outside the house, and as he got up to go and greet them, Sarah and Sophie clambered out, and his heart leapt at the sight of them. It had been more than six months since he had seen either his daughter or his granddaughter, and he had been excited about their arrival for days.

Though now past his seventy-sixth birthday, he still lived on his own. He had retired from the vicarage when he was seventy-four, having been bequeathed a most pleasing sum of money by a lady parishioner who had been devoted to him for decades. At that point he had moved to a large bungalow, newly built and standing in a cul de sac amongst a cluster of others, in a pleasant part of Folkestone well away from the traffic and the noise of the port.

For all his supposed retirement, he still occupied himself with the affairs of the parish, this wholly to the chagrin of the new incumbent, who was allowed little doubt by the older members of the congregation that he was a very poor substitute and successor for dear Father Douglas, as Sarah's father liked to be known by all. Actually, it was not so much the official duties and functions of the parish that Father Douglas still busied himself with, for he rather groused at any suggestion of these, but rather the social and chattering side of it all, which in that parish had always been very much a full-time business. It was a large congregation, and it was a busy congregation, largely made up of retired or late-middle-aged

269

people with time and appetite for gossip and tittle-tattle, which they were accustomed to find most adequately provided from amongst their number.

The new vicar, who let it be known on his very first day that he would like to be called Teddie, and not Father anything at all, had not made a good start. He was given to guitars and folk songs and the recruitment of the young men and women of the town to attendance at occasions he called 'monthly ceilidhs'. Father Douglas was an incense and bells man, and regarded the town youth with distaste. In both these things he was entirely in line with the opinion of the pews. The only youth that the members of the parish of St Jude's, Canterbury Hill embraced with any enthusiasm were some but by no means all of their own children – devout, pious young people who knew their place.

Very like dear Sarah, of course. Or rather very like what Sarah was in her childhood when she and Father Douglas were together. What a sweet, lovely little thing she was. Too good for this world really. Motherless, but so brave about it. Not a vice in her, the poor little scrap. An angel. And she still was. Such a joy to see her when she came down to Folkestone. Such a pity it wasn't more often, but one heard that she had so much on her plate, poor lamb. She worked so hard.

Sarah's arrival this week had coincided with the preparations for the summer flower festival, and no sooner had she arrived, and had tea with her father, than the three of them, despite the weather, went off in the car down to the church to join all the ladies busy there with the decorations.

There were cries of delight when they arrived, and everyone came down from their stepladders and the organ loft and the pulpit to kiss Sarah, and Sophie too. She looked just a little plumper than before perhaps, but so sweet and friendly and pink-cheeked and nice in her Paddington Bear plastic raincoat and her Wellington boots and her rain hat. Just like she was when Sarah brought her down when she was little. With her sister, Rowena – the younger daughter that poor Sarah had had so much trouble with, and had done everything for. Absolutely everything for . . . with not a jot of help or sympathy from her husband, according to the rumours.

But wasn't Sophie a poppet? She'd grow out of this puppy fat, of course. Those lovely bright eyes, and that friendly smile . . . not pretty exactly, but such a sweet little face. She remembered them all, didn't she? She never forgot them. And she was so sweet with her grandfather – and he with her too, dear Father Douglas. He doted on her. You could see it in the way he looked at her. He absolutely doted on the girl.

Teddie arrived to see how the decorating was going and winced perceptibly when he saw the Tilton family. But he came over immediately, his hand outstretched, and Sarah and Sophie allowed themselves to be introduced, if perhaps a little glacially. On seeing Teddie the ladies melted away again to their ladders and their organ lofts, as if to emphasise their detachment from him, and soon Sophie was busy making a charming decoration of Queen Anne's lace, Regale lilies and Pascale roses around the font, and Sarah a bold display of red hot pokers and blue delphiniums on the steps of the high altar.

Then the three of them were on their way again to the bungalow on the hill, shouting their acceptance to join the others at the little parties and groups and meetings that the parish thrived on. All this in Teddie's hearing, though there were few of these functions to which he had himself been invited.

'Stay longer than a week this time, Sarah. You have such fun when you get here. And I'm a poor old man now, who needs his daughter with him. And his little granddaughter,' Father Douglas said, turning round to give Sophie a poke and tickle in the ribs. 'His naughty granddaughter, who's always up to her games and pranks,' tickling her harder as he said this, and wrinkling up his nose in imitation of a walrus or some other mammal whose exact specification had rather got lost over the years in the repetition of it.

Sophie made the gasping shrieks and screams and wriggles that were traditionally demanded of her on these occasions, and she was still writhing and giggling under her grandfather's increasingly explorative hands as Sarah turned the car into the kerb outside his house.

'Now then, you two,' she said. 'Now then. You'll make her sick, Grandpa. Stop it, Grandpa. Stop it, do.'

And so they went inside, the three of them laughing at the fun of it all, and if her grandfather's gentle smack on her bottom as she went in ahead of him and bent down to take off her Wellington boots was lingering and reflective, more so really than Sophie was expecting, well then no harm was done, and he was only being affectionate and cuddly. And he lived alone so much it was no surprise that he got over-excited when Sarah and Sophie came to stay. They were the only family the poor old man had. Not counting Rowena. But a fat lot of interest she'd ever shown in him.

So they had a nice cosy evening together at home. Just the three of them; Sarah, Sophie and Grandpa. Exactly as they used to have when Sophie was tiny, when they had played blind man's buff and musical chairs and grandmother's footsteps. Just the three of them at Grandpa's house. All at home and loving together. Best of all in the summer, when Sophie would be on the beach with her bucket and spade the whole afternoon through when the weather was nice. And she would get her little back and tummy and thighs quite pink with sunburn sometimes, and Grandpa would rub his special soothing ointment in before she went to bed, pulling her pyjama bottoms down so that he could be sure to get it spread all over.

They talked that evening about Robert, as they usually did, and Sarah's father told her that in his opinion she was far too good for the man, and had too much pluck and spirit to be married to a desiccated businessman like that. A dried-up sort of chap. A worldly, calculating career man. Successful now, of course, or so one gathered, but tight and mean with Sarah. Earning what he must do, you would have thought he would have put her in a better house by now. Just a working-class Welshman really, who had happened to get on in the world. No sense of family. No fun in him of any sort, let alone any sense of religion. Never went inside a church unless he was made to, or showed any interest in the things that had made Sarah the woman she was. It would be different if he took care of her properly as his wife, or appreciated all that she had done for him. Or was generous and giving with his money. But, as far as Father Douglas could make out, the fellow never thought about anybody but himself. Himself and Rowena. And look where that had got them both.

'You could have had whomsoever you wanted, my dear,' he had said. 'I can assure you of that, Sophie. Your Mum could have had the pick of the lot. But all she wanted when she was a girl was to help me and be with me. And to say her prayers, and develop as a handmaid of God. A wonderful daughter, that's what your mum is. And a wonderful woman. I thought she might take the veil at one time. She would have graced it if she had – graced it. But there we are, my dear. She could see that father of yours needed her, and she gave her life to him. She's been as good a wife to him as he could have had. Much too good for him. She deserved better. Very much better.'

'I've always said she's too selfless, Grandpa,' nodded Sophie. 'Too selfless for her own good. Look at her – nearly sound asleep in her chair, quite tired out after her journey here and making sure the house was nice for Daddy to come back to from Switzerland or wherever he's been to, and she won't go to bed until you're ready, Grandpa. Come on, Mum. Come on, Grandpa. Bed-time.'

And so they all went off to their rooms, but the bungalow had just the one bathroom, so there were the usual little giggles and fun between them all as to who would go first and who was taking too long in there. And Sophie was half expecting it after the last time she had been at Grandpa's, so she was not really surprised when an hour or less later she heard the creak of floorboards outside her room, and then the door-handle slowly, slowly turning, and Grandpa creeping in with his pyjamas on.

She lay there pretending to sleep while he gently, cautiously pulled down the duvet, and there she was with her nightie tucked up around her waist, just as she had arranged it when she heard his footsteps, and she watched him through her eyelashes as she opened her thighs, as if settling in her sleep, then turned on to her front, hugging the teddy bear she always brought with her, her legs now wide, wide apart.

Chapter Forty-Two

The immigration line at Delhi airport can be of unendurable slowness, particularly when an occupant of it gives way to every person, male or female, who edges in front of him.

Colin's manners on these occasions, as even he recognised, were in their courtliness and zeal a parody of one sort of Englishman abroad; leaping backwards, and sweeping off his panama hat to usher ahead of him a pregnant woman in a sari, then offering to carry the bags of an ancient, bent *babu* figure, to the latter's surprise and irritation, who assumed the florid young *sahib* must be in some way taking the *pipi* out of him.

Thus it was that, having initially been in the first fifteen or twenty passengers in the line, Colin eventually went to the immigration desk the very last one of all. By the time he had bent down and squatted on the floor to look in his travelling case for his passport, which took him several increasingly stressful minutes before it was at last found, he straightened again to find a white cardboard disk being slotted into a frame behind what was now a closed Perspex screen.

Colin rapped politely on the screen, grinning amiably, his face dripping with the sweat that had come from his exertions of a moment before.

The young man behind the counter shook his head, and put his hand over the top of the frame to point at the notice, tapping it meaningfully.

CLOSED UNTIL FURTHER NOTICE it said. And below, in smaller letters:

Enquiries In Triplicate On Official Forms To The Chief Superintendent Ports And Entry Points. Office Hours Only. Closed Weekends And Public Holidays. Have A Good Day.

Colin held up his passport, the grin beginning to assume a maniacal appearance. He shouted at full volume through a tiny grille in the Perspex screen, bending his head sideways to get his mouth right up against it, and now waving the passport, as if it was a little Union Jack on a stick.

'Old sport. Old sport! I was in the queue. Couldn't find my passport. Took me some minutes. Got it now. Here we go.'

A beggar in the corner, who a moment ago, while there were tourists around, had been cowering and moaning, his eyes turned up and only the whites showing, was now on his feet. He reached for a newspaper and a pair of spectacles from under his rags, and chuckled at the little scene being played out before him.

The young official was sipping at a tiny terracotta jar, full to the brim with milky, orange-coloured tea. There was a pause while he sipped at it again, gazing at Colin the while, and then he replied, to Colin's surprise, in a voice of normal volume, which was perfectly audible as there was no top or ceiling to the Perspex screen.

'You're too late. I am closing for the day. Too late, I am saying. Read the notice. The bureau is now closed. Closed absolutely.'

At that he threw the terracotta jar into a waste-paper basket behind him, then blew his nose, individually by nostril, by an exquisite process of bending daintily over the waste-paper basket and pinching it between thumb and forefinger, the elbow held high. He spat, and set off for the door behind him.

'Old sport . . .' called Colin, but the door had now slammed shut, and Colin was alone with the beggar and several scuttling, bowed, barefoot figures in cotton saris, who were sweeping the floor with ancient brooms. He pushed at the gate in front of him, but it was locked.

'He's gone, *sahib*,' said the beggar, removing his spectacles and laying down the newspaper, which was open at the financial pages. 'Gone for his tiffin. Very bad man. A disgrace absolutely. Most corrupt and idle.' He shook his head, replaced his spectacles, and resumed his study of the market's closing prices.

'The thing is, I need to get through to my luggage,' said Colin. 'Can't stay here. Lose the lot, and that sort of thing. Office driver waiting. Affairs of state. Ha ha.'

He patted and wiped his head and face with his vast white handkerchief, then made a sudden and most vigorous attempt to attract the attention of another official, who had come out of one door in the recessed area behind the enclosed Perspex screens, and had immediately gone into another.

A few moments later the man stuck his head out again, as if noticing Colin for the first time.

'Yes?' he said. 'The bureau is closed. Come back another time. We are not open.'

'I'm trying to get through, old sport. Got myself trapped. Silly of me. I need to get through.'

The official came across to the window, and tapped on the white card notice, as his predecessor had done.

'We are closed. You should have been here when the bureau was open. If you want to come through we will have to make special arrangements,' he said. 'Most inconvenient. Highly irregular. Against the regulations absolutely. Special charge will be needed. For the Widows and Orphans of India Fund.'

Colin pushed his passport through the hatch, which had now been slid open. He included with it a folded 100-rupee note, which disappeared up the sleeve of the immigration officer's jacket in one imperceptible motion, as the passport was studied from several different angles, then elaborately and painstakingly stamped. Finally, it was pushed back through the grille, and the little gate in front of him clicked open.

'Welcome to India,' said the officer. Colin thanked him and passed through to find his luggage, rummaging in his pocket for another note to tip the beggar, who was now standing at the gate at the salute, his back and quivering hand and arm in a ramrod parody of a British Tommy.

The two suitcases were circling forlornly and alone on the carousel, all others having by this point been claimed and cleared. But they were safe, and he took them off and bore them away with the assistance of a magnificently turbaned and moustachioed baggage-*wallah*, who organised Colin's passage through Customs with practised expertise, his instructions on the correct bribes to be given en route all delivered in a hoarse whisper, redolent with garlic.

The office driver was there, and the air-conditioned car cool and welcoming. After a tip to the baggage-*wallah* of the first bank note which, in his longing to escape, he could find – a hundred rupees, or the equivalent to the man of about four weeks' wages – they were on their way to the hotel and the large gin and tonic about which Colin had been dreaming from the moment he had found himself marooned in the immigration hall.

A drink, he thought, as the car swerved from the path of an oncoming bus, on which gesticulating hordes hung all over the sides and roof. A drink, a bath, another drink, another drink, and then I suppose the call to the hospital. To check whether C.P. is well enough to see me tonight as scheduled, or if we should leave it until the morning. Please God, the morning.

Chapter Forty-Three

C.P. sat up in his bed, pillows piled behind his back, his face so haggard and lined that Colin was shocked to see it.

He had been shaved that morning, but the barber had left little patches of stubble in the cleft of his chin and in the fold of his neck, and these showed white against the brown of his skin. His eyes were watery, and from the corner of his mouth there ran a tiny mark of spittle. His hair was neatly brushed and combed, but his appearance overall was unkempt and debilitated, and when Colin heard him speak, the voice thickened and coarsened, he realised how ill C.P. had been. And still was.

As C.P. talked, Colin watched him for the signs of exhaustion that he was not prepared to subject him to. He honoured him in his way, and the prospect of grilling and bullying a man in this condition was not to Colin's taste. Why couldn't Robert have done this? Why did he change his mind? Make it clean and quick, he thought. Make it courteous and defined and decisive and then let the unfortunate man be.

'C.P.. I've already explained. I don't believe that the Javed letter to the Prasads was genuine. I think it was forged. And I think it was forged so that the Loans Committee would approve an interest rate on their deal as much as a point and a half under what they should have paid.'

C.P. was now silent, and although Colin had paused, as if in

279

invitation for him to respond, he simply lay there watching him, his handsome, intelligent face now, strangely, looking to Colin almost amused and mocking.

Colin was sitting in a chair beside C.P.'s bed. He was leaning forward a little from the waist, trying to put himself in such a posture that C.P. would not find in him an impression of languor or insolent aggression, now that the normal weighting of their relationship was reversed. If there was going to be interrogation, it was going to be done respectfully and seriously.

Colin repeated what he had said, dropping his voice almost to a whisper as he did so. 'I think it's clear that the Javed letter was not a genuine one, C.P.. I don't want you to think that I enjoy saying things of that sort, because I do understand the implications of what I'm saying. But I have to tell you that I'm certain I'm right. The letter was forged.'

At last C.P. responded, and as he did so, again Colin thought he saw mockery and dispassion in his eyes. 'How can you be certain that you're right?'

'Because I spoke to Mr Javed. I spoke to him myself and asked him about the letter. He denied that it had come from his office. He denied any knowledge of it. He said that Javed & National didn't want to do business with the Prasads – didn't want to get involved with something they didn't like the look of. He was absolutely firm on the point. Categorical on it.'

C.P.'s eyes creased into a smile, then he started to laugh, and the coughing fit that followed was sufficiently protracted for Colin to wonder if he should call a nurse to check on him. But he settled in due course, waved away Colin's attempts to give him more water, then lay there for a few moments, wiping at his mouth and eyes with his folded white linen handkerchief. Then, when he spoke, he appeared to have gained strength and animation. The conflict had apparently enlivened him, and he pushed himself more upright in the bed as he spoke.

'My dear boy. My dear Colin. My dear old chump, as I believe you English like to address each other. When you're throwing bread rolls across the room at Drone's. I don't want to be rude, my dear, but pitting you against Mohammed Javed is like tossing a lily-white Christian boy into a pitful of Persian pederasts. He had you for breakfast – isn't that the expression? Or is it luncheon?'

Colin reflected that for someone who had been educated at Winchester and Oxford, C.P.'s affectation of unfamiliarity with the English vernacular tended to be irritating, but he put the thought aside.

'Yes – breakfast. And I'm flattered to be thought of as a Persian's catamite. But actually, C.P., I think he was telling me the truth. I'm convinced of it.'

C.P. laughed again, but carefully this time, and to Colin's relief there was no repetition of the previous coughing fit. He put his hand out, and patted Colin on the arm, the vitality and humour in him appearing to increase by the minute.

'I can't think why I so took against you, dear boy, when you were first landed on me. On reflection, I find you're actually very naughty, and rather interesting and amusing. You affect your Wooster act or whatever it is because you enjoy the joke. You like us all to underrate you. Either that, or you have a strong line in self-mockery. Which is something I much enjoy in people. Whatever it is, it works, for in fact you're distinctly bright. And quite formidable. And most persistent. And brave. But . . . you've been outwitted by Javed. I can assure you of that. Or bullied by him, perhaps more accurately.

'Mohammed has never set much store by literal truth. He finds it a rather vulgar, restrictive notion. He would have enjoyed his conversation with you. It's exactly what amuses him. He's a very competent actor himself. I imagine he played the strait-laced, upright, man-of-conscience banker to you? One of the old school – his word his bond? As canny a man as the next fellow, but could never bring himself to trust the natives? Your father and him like twins? That sort of thing?'

Colin grinned. He started to speak. 'But C.P., there is—'

C.P. held up his hand, like the schoolmaster who would brook no interruption.

'The point, my dear, is that Javed & National have dealt with the Prasads since Doomsday. And they always will. They're as thick as thieves together. Can you imagine them *not* being involved and knowing all the detail the moment the Prasads hit the jackpot?

'This Poonjee construction contract is by far the biggest thing the Prasads have ever been involved with. Providing the debt for that would appear to be excellent banking by any standards. We thought so. Why shouldn't Javed & National think so as well? It would look to anybody, I would have thought, like a classic case of lending against guaranteed cash flow – on a very large scale, and all underwritten by the Government of India. If the Prasads have slipped a little something into the hands of some underpaid, overworked middle manager somewhere, to make sure the contract money is flowed to them nice and promptly and reliably, what about it? What's that to Mohammed Javed or anyone else? Actually, what's it to you? Have you never given a tiny token of your esteem, in the insufferably genteel phrase of the subordinate classes in your country, to anyone who has done you a service? Never? *Never?* I don't mean a tip. I mean more than a tip – a bribe.'

Colin thought back uneasily to the events of the previous day at the airport, shifted his weight in the chair, and shrugged.

'It's a matter of scale really, don't you think? These things are like apples and oranges. There's bribery and there's . . . there's . . .' he hesitated.

'Bribery,' said C.P.. 'Large-scale, small-scale, it's still bribery. Javed & National live by it; they always have. Mohammed Javed wouldn't recognise life without it. As a matter of fact, he couldn't abide life without it. He couldn't control what happened. He pays for everything he wants, and then he knows where he is.

'We're different, my dear. We're British. Even me, God forbid. I've become British. We'll bribe in the little ways, but not the big ones. The little bribes – the twenty rupees to the traffic policeman who lets us off a traffic offence, or the man with the bootleg Scotch, or the controller who puts us at the head of the taxi queue – those little bribes make us feel rather grand and worldly and superior and amusing. We offer them with enthusiasm. But the big bribes, the sensible ones, the buying of major services from others who have them in their ownership, the services that would ensure that our lives and companies and our institutions are made stressless and successful and useful – those are the ones we throw our hands in the air with moral outrage over.

'We amuse Mohammed Javed a good deal, I should think. We amuse me rather. We're like children in an adults' world. Not innocents, children. We're certainly not innocents, because it's us – the British, us – who are the first into the petty financial improprieties of life. Extravagant personal habits. Extravagant corporate habits. Sloppy, arrogant, high-handed giving of small bribes, which we decide are really tips, and thus allow us to patronise and assume superiority over the other party. Children. Because we don't have the courage to examine our so-called standards in the light of how we actually behave. The repugnant quality of exuding and proclaiming moral stature for ourselves where none actually exists. None at all. *In Veritate Virtus.* Christ.'

Colin started to try to say something in response but was again immediately interrupted.

'We're certainly no better than Mohammed Javed. Certainly not. But nor am I suggesting that he is our moral superior either. We're probably all going to the devil in our own way. Remind me to tell you the parable about a mongoose and a cobra some day. But where he's more attractive than us is that he has no posturing about him. He would love to have our motto for the Javed & National Bank. He's no doubt furious that we thought of it first. And why? Because he can laugh at himself. Because he has that quality of self-mockery I was congratulating you on earlier, and in which, in my experience, you are most untypical of most of your countrymen. It would strike him as a very good joke. It strikes us as a precisely accurate statement of our values. We deceive ourselves. Utterly. Self-deceit would be considered a grave moral weakness by

Mohammed Javed. Failure. And damaging and silly.'

C.P. smiled at Colin, and poured himself a glass of water. 'Heavens, you've made me feel better, my dear boy. I feel quite like my old self. There's nothing like a little rhetoric. You must come more often. Stay the night. Stay the week. You're the best tonic I've ever had.'

He settled himself back amongst the pillows, then turned to plump them up a little more, drank another sip from the water, and looked at Colin, the smile again on his face.

'Colin, my dear. I think you came here to tell me that you'd caught me out being bribed by the Prasads. Wasn't that it? That I let them have a cheap loan from the Bank in return for a nice little sweetener. And that I arranged it by forging a letter from the saintly Javed people. That's it in a nutshell, isn't it?'

He chuckled happily, then wiped his eyes with his handkerchief, which he then used to blow his nose; loudly, and with a vigour and gusto that Colin, half an hour earlier, would have thought an impossibility.

'Your evidence for this, Colin, you sleuth, you?'

Colin smiled back at him, though he was beginning to feel a distinct sense of unease and disorientation. This wasn't turning out at all as he had expected. He was looking forward to getting back to his hotel and his yellow legal pad, on which to doodle his charts and arrows and get his mind straight again.

'The evidence? I'd put it differently and say that there are two lines here which have to be looked at, C.P.. The first is that the lawyers here in Delhi say that they hold documentation which demonstrates that you have been receiving payments from the Prasads. The sweetener, as you put it, for having organised a cheap loan for them. And the—'

C.P. put up his hand to halt him. 'What do you mean – the lawyers say they're holding documentation? Have you seen it?'

'No, I haven't yet. I thought I would have a look at it this afternoon. I was going to call the lawyers immediately after this to arrange a meeting with them.'

'Well, make sure you do so, Colin. I'm dying to see this documentation myself. What do they say they have?'

Colin looked at him, wondering if he was wise in feeding C.P. with so much material, or if he would be better to dissemble a little. But there was something in C.P.'s self-confidence and lack of alarm over it all that was compelling. And this was hardly a police enquiry. Actually, under the rules of these absurd compliance and security audits, he was probably bound to allow C.P. access to the same facts as everybody else. To hell with it.

'Rather a lot, C.P., to be perfectly honest with you. First of all there are some letters between three firms of Bombay lawyers; one supposed to be acting for you, another for Prasad & Prasad, and the third for General Swami. These letters say, apparently, that the Prasads will pay you a fee each month as long as the Prasads continue to have their Poonjee debt in place with us at this very low interest rate. And General Swami gets a fee from the Prasads for as long as you qualify for this payment.'

C.P. chuckled and sipped at his water. 'How delightful. What an opportunity I've missed. With all this English-gentleman nonsense washing around inside me and confusing me, I missed a trick. I see that now. I could have been rich, instead of an impoverished bank official with a nasty case of displaced national identity. We'll come back to that one in a moment, but before we move on; if you haven't seen these letters yet, who has? Only the lawyers? You haven't had the documents faxed or couriered to you? How odd that is. Why on earth not?'

'Robert Luscombe has been shown the material, C.P.. He's seen it. He felt it was genuine.'

Colin shrugged, embarrassed that he had drawn so crudely into the conversation the name of the man whom he knew C.P. was closer to than anyone. He looked at C.P. and waited before he continued, wincing to himself. Not only had he lost all touch with the brief he had set himself before coming to the hospital, but now he was beginning to feel a marked sense of self-dislike.

This is the most unpleasant exercise, he thought. How typical of the Bank that we go through these charades. I'm beginning to detest the whole affair. Why should I have to insult and hurt this man, who is more than twenty years older than me, considerably more intelligent, and a very nice man. And who has been an extraordinarily effective servant of the Bank for his whole career.

C.P. was looking crestfallen and puzzled. The humour had left his eyes, and he was frowning now, biting his lip.

'Robert has seen it? And he believes this poppycock?'

They looked at each other for a few moments, then C.P. repeated, 'Robert has seen it? He's seen it and he thinks it's genuine? I can't believe that you're telling me the truth. I just can't believe it. Robert thinks it is true?'

There was a pause. Then he said, 'Let's have it all, now we've started. You said there were two lines of enquiry or evidence or whatever we call this vicious nonsense. We've had one. What's the other?'

Colin shifted again in his chair. I wish to God this was over, he thought. Rot the Bank, and this asinine, damaging, absurd system. It's not me that should be here with C.P. today. Why wouldn't Robert come over and talk to C.P. himself? If there's a fraud or a professional-misconduct issue, or whatever it is, it should be dealt with at the highest level. By the Deputy Chairman, with police and legal representation. I'm just a young middle manager of limited experience, who has been landed with something of considerable unpleasantness. And the fact that I'm my father's son makes it much the more disagreeable. But let's get it over with now, and then I'm going to go back to the hotel, get on the telephone, and insist that I'm taken off this thing immediately. Tonight.

Nevertheless he said, 'Well, the other is something rather different. There's no suggestion here of personal benefit in an underhand way. The second strand of enquiry is over how the consortium won the contract. I went to New York, as you know, because I posted my schedule with you before I left. I met there Marty Schwab, of Rosenbaum Siegel Schneider & Schwab, the lawyers for the Chicago and Illinois Trust people, as I expect you remember. He confirmed to me what I had already been told was the case, that the consortium won the contract by bribing officials of the Government of India to show us the other bids so that we could offer something better. Which we then did, and won. And the people on our side who led the negotiations were all paid bonuses for doing so. Including you.'

C.P. turned his head to the window, and lay there gazing at the blue sky outside, and the crows swooping and cawing in the great trees in the hospital gardens. As Colin watched him, he saw that he was tiring. The vitality that he had shown throughout their conversation had left his face again, and for a moment Colin wondered if he should slip away, and call a nurse.

But then C.P. turned back to Colin, and said, his voice now more blurred and flat, 'If I didn't feel so damned tired suddenly I would laugh, but I can't raise the energy. Tell me one thing, Colin, before you leave. You never would have gone off all over the place like this without someone helping you or pointing the way for you. Who did? What happened?'

Colin hesitated, as he had earlier, but admitted, 'There were letters, C.P.. Someone kept on writing to me, anonymously, telling me where to go and what to look for. I just had to sit there, and another one would come. Since I had nothing else to go on, I tried following the trail. And the trail I was led on did turn out to be very well informed. Quite extraordinarily well informed.'

C.P. was staring at him, and Colin was undecided if it was irony he saw there in his eyes now, or weary detachment. And the more he looked back at him, the more he thought it was the first.

'Did Robert know about these letters? Did you show them to him?'

'Yes. Of course I did.'

There was a long pause, and then C.P. said: 'Is that it? Is there anything else?'

'No. No, that's it. There's nothing else.'

C.P. held his gaze on Colin's eyes, and the two men studied each other. There was neither animosity nor aggression in the air, but neither was there any more of the jocularity and energy that C.P. had shown for so long. When C.P. spoke again, the clumsy unfocused blurring to his voice made him at times difficult to follow, and Colin leant forward in his seat to catch as much as he could.

'Colin. On the second point I would say that there is no case to answer. There's no doubt that the consortium ensured that ours should be the winning bid. Certainly I received a very generous bonus for being a member of the successful negotiating team. Not from the Bank, but from the consortium itself. As did the others. It was in our original letters of appointment.

'But the question, the real question, is who actually arranged that we should win? Who organised the arrangements that your sources suggest were made with the Government of India people? Do you know the answer to that? You think it was me. It wasn't me. I found it happening, but I had nothing to do with it. Who was it who actually made the arrangements? That's the question you should certainly be asking yourself. I repeat – it wasn't me.

'But on the other issue, I have to tell you that Mohammed Javed did indeed have you for his breakfast. Let's say for a moment that we don't know for certain why he led you the dance that he did. But let's try one thesis. You can try one thesis: it's your compliance and security audit. Let's say that Javed had a little joke. Not just with you, but with the Moorgate & Mercantile Bank as a body. That he's not all that comfortable that Prasad & Prasad is going to survive, despite the value of the Poonjee contract. Perhaps he's seen the real set of books, and thinks that they are in more difficulty than we ever imagined they could be. More hopelessly in debt. More dishonest in the valuation of their assets, whatever the situation may be with Poonjee. Perhaps old man Prasad and old man Swami have been helping themselves to the family silver. I wouldn't be in the least surprised if they had, particularly old Swami. Perhaps the young Prasad has, too. No one could genuinely be as stupid as that young man pretends to be.

'So what does Mohammed do? I tell you exactly what he does. Having seen the accounts, the last thing he wants to do is to lend them any more money. The Prasads owe him an uncomfortable amount as it is. So he does a very clever thing. He knows that the Prasads have given us an agreement that allows us to match the best offer from Javed & National and get the business. He wants us to do the business. He wouldn't touch it himself, because he's got too much money in there already, and the first thing he's interested in is getting that repaid. And the lower the rate of interest, the more likely the Prasads' survival. And I imagine, if you check the share register with enough creative imagination, you'll find that he is also a personal shareholder. And because of that he wants them to survive and prosper, of course.

'So – he bids low, we match, we win, our money goes in, and the first thing that happens to it, I would wager, is that the Javed & National get their debt back with accrued interest. In full. With our money. That's what it was there for. That's why old Javed wanted it in there. Now he's out, and we're in. God save us.'

Tired as he was, and the longer he spoke the more drawled his voice and the more slurred the words, C.P. gave Colin a wide smile, his eyes again full of humour.

'Try that one, my dear boy. Try that one for size.' He yawned, and wiped his forearm across his forehead, then smiled at Colin again. 'I have myself, some time ago. It's what happened. It's what I found actually happened. You're not the only one Mohammed Javed had for breakfast . . . But now I'm going to sleep. Come back tomorrow, when you've had a look at the documentation the lawyers are holding. It's forged, of course. It's all balls. And bring the anonymous letters too. They're all balls as well, in their own way. They're balls as well.'

As C.P.'s eyes began to close in sleep, Colin got up from his chair and began to tiptoe away to the door. He was halfway there, treading his way in tiny, exquisitely delicate steps, his tongue stuck out in his efforts to get there silently, his arms stuck out either side to give him balance, when he heard C.P.'s chuckle behind him.

'You're such a prick, Colin. My favourite English expression. You're such a buffoon. You're such a prick.'

Chapter Forty-Four

Peter Rutherford sat at the head of the table with Alice on his right, smiling amiably down at the gathering, his plump, pleasant, earthy face heavily coloured from the sun of his holiday. It was the first time Robert had seen him since their lunch together on his return from India, and he looked at him with affection.

It was not because of Peter's professional ability and competence that Robert used him now for all his private work, for in truth there had been rather too many occasions in their dealings together when documents had been mislaid, briefs only superficially read and mastered, and indifferent advice given. Peter's lack of genuine professional weight was on occasions a matter of irritation and embarrassment to Robert, and sometimes he showed it. But there was too little friendship in Robert's life, and too little casually amiable communication and contact, and whatever Peter was not, he was certainly a friend. And as the years went by, and Peter coarsened and thickened in his physical appearance as the claret of a thousand lunchtimes took its toll, and the intellectual and perhaps moral focus in him slipped day by day a little further away, then the more Robert was loyal to him in return. He no longer believed in a single professional word that Peter said, and would certainly never use him in the affairs of the Bank. But Robert longed for friendship. And he knew that Peter, in his decline, had need of him too.

As always he had been making a great fuss over the ordering of trays of coffee to be brought and files to be found before they could settle down. But at last he was ready, and he pushed across to Robert his copy of a report that had arrived that morning from the private investigator.

'The affairs of your family are keeping this man in a way of life he can never have been expecting, Robert.' He smiled his florid, generous, conspiratorial smile, and Robert glanced across at Alice, who had flushed a little, as he knew she would, at the mention of the word 'affairs'.

'Before you read that, Robert, you must be aware that we'll have to tread carefully. Jenkins, or whatever his name is...' Peter glanced at the foot of the past page '... Jenkins is giving an opinion, based only on circumstantial evidence. I suspect he's right in his conclusions, but circumstantial evidence is all he has had to go on. So before we start pulling the police in, or any of that, we'll have to decide the best way of approaching it. All right?'

Robert picked up the document. *The undersigned has examined the letter received by the interested party...*

Robert put his head in his hands, and groaned. He looked up and saw Alice smiling at him.

'Yes, I thought the opening sentence would have a macabre appeal to you. Mr Jenkins has a certain reliability in his vocabulary.'

She laughed, and as Peter looked at them both there was a flicker of speculation and conspiracy in his expression. There was nothing Peter liked better than a prickle of sexual intrigue in the air.

... and fingerprint tests are now being performed upon it by appropriate specialists. The excrement sample is also under examination for its DNA specification. Results from both these tests will be available by the end of this week.

The briefing of the undersigned by Ms Livingstone, representing the interested party's solicitors, included a confidential summary of the interested party's family situation. This firm has already prepared

*and distributed a report on Ms Rowena Luscombe's circumstances,
but we were now informed by Ms Livingstone about the background
of both Mrs Sarah Luscombe and the older daughter of the marriage,
Ms Sophie Luscombe. In the first instance the undersigned was given
detail of the situation appertaining to Mrs Luscombe's adultery on a
recent visit with her husband to Bavancore, in South India . . .*

Robert glanced across at Alice, whose head was bowed as she read
the paper on the table before her.

'Adultery', he thought. What an odd term for that strange
incident of Sarah's. I wouldn't accuse the unfortunate woman of
that. Adultery is what I committed last week with Alice. It was the
most affecting experience of my life. But it's adultery. It was an
important, conscious, significant act of love, and consequent
betrayal. Sarah's was a bizarre momentary act of sexual desire. It
signified nothing whatsoever. The adultery was mine.

He was still staring at Alice when he caught Peter Rutherford's
eye, and he looked quickly down again, and continued reading Mr
Jenkins's report.

*. . . and in the second instance Ms Sophie Luscombe's recent dismissal
from the publishers The Magazine Company for a case of admitted
theft, this following previous similar occurrences at earlier periods
of Ms Luscombe's life.*

*Given the pious and devout sentiments expressed in the letter, the
undersigned explored the movements of Mrs Sarah Luscombe in recent
weeks, following Ms Livingstone's informal comment that Mrs
Luscombe's social interests and activities were dominated by her
connection with various church circles, particularly those
surrounding the parish church of St Matthew's, Wetherby Gardens,
and the vicar there, the Reverend Derrick Hilden-Parker.*

*Following this lead, the undersigned has taken pains to achieve a
certain intimacy and understanding over these last few days with
the cook-housekeeper at the vicarage.*

As a result of this, the undersigned can confirm that ten days ago

Mrs Luscombe paid an evening visit to Mr Hilden-Parker, ostensibly for pastoral counselling. Mrs Hilden-Parker, however, inadvertently interrupted them at a moment when Mrs Luscombe is reported to have been weeping with her head on Mr Hilden-Parker's chest, and her arm about his person, while he was engaged in patting her hair. The housekeeper was told by Mrs Hilden-Parker, after an altercation between her and Mr Hilden-Parker immediately following Mrs Luscombe's departure that, and I quote, 'It's always the same with him, wherever he goes. Always the same.'

This comment prompted the undersigned to make enquiries of certain parties within the Diocese of London with whom the undersigned is connected, and it has been confirmed that there was an incident of some sort in Mr Hilden-Parker's previous parish of St Michael-And-All-Angels, Bethnal Green.

He and his wife left this parish some nine years ago, following which he spent a period of almost two years under professional therapy and rest at a religious centre near Doncaster. I have insufficient data at this time about the nature of the incident in question, but I believe there was talk of Mr Hilden-Parker indulging in an emotional and physical attachment with a lady of the parish, and that anonymous letters, of a threatening and abusive nature were examined by the police.

This area of my research has yet to be resolved, but the view of the undersigned is that, given the history as drafted above, he is the probable and likely sender of the anonymous letter to the interested party. The expectation is that the fingerprint and DNA tests, when available, will confirm these findings.

Beneath was the name *Albert Jenkins, IPSI AERD* through which a neat, spidery signature was scrawled.

'Institute of Private Security Investigators, and Association of Enquiry and Research Directors,' said Alice. 'I asked him. I was wasting too much time trying to work them out. Robert – there we are. We should wait until the tests, I suppose, but you're never going to want to prosecute the unfortunate man, I would have thought. What we want to do is to stop him before he sends you something or does something that we really will have to take action about.

'So, Peter, with your agreement, my recommendation is that Robert goes to talk to Hilden-Parker. Even shows him Mr Jenkins's report. Warns him off – frightens him, if you like. Possibly insists he has some more therapy or other professional help. But, however foul that letter was, I think Robert's instinct will not be to destroy him. Is that right?'

They both looked at Robert, who was doodling on the notepad in front of him.

'Yes, I suppose so. I can't see that setting the police on to him is necessarily the answer to anything very much – which is not to say I'm very enamoured by his conduct. Not about his conduct to my wife . . .' He leant back in his chair and burst into laughter, in which both Peter Rutherford and Alice joined, though again there was in Peter's eye a certain watchfulness and conjecture ' . . . not about my wife, but I certainly object to the letter, which was a very unpleasant communication indeed. Though the odd thing . . .' he broke off and, with his hands locked behind his neck, his eyes had wandered away from both Peter and Alice, and were staring at the wall opposite.

The odd thing, he thought to himself, is that clearly he sent that other letter too. But if he's as obsessed by Sarah as all that, you would have thought that there wouldn't have been so long an interval between the sending of the two letters. Particularly as he'd got away with the first without any danger, or apparent reaction from me. But . . . who knows.

He turned back towards the two others, who were both waiting for him to continue, and he smiled at them. 'I'm going to telephone him now,' he said. 'Strike while the iron's hot. Arrange to go straight around there.'

The number was found, the call made to a rather startled-sounding Derrick Hilden-Parker, and it was arranged that Robert would go to the vicarage immediately.

Chapter Forty-Five

By the time the taxi drew up in Wetherby Gardens, all Robert's feelings of resigned indifference to the anonymous letter had given way to anger.

It was the re-reading of a typed copy of it as he sat in a traffic jam in Pall Mall that changed his mood. And the increasing fury in him was not so much towards Hilden-Parker, whom Robert, although he had never met him, suspected was a pathetic inadequate, but towards Sarah.

How *dare* she spread this sort of malicious evil around her acquaintances, for obviously that was what the scene at the vicarage was about. Suggesting that I had taught my two daughters to do perverse and unnatural sexual acts with me. Degrading them with my filth and my animal appetites. Christ. Is the woman a lunatic? A deranged imbecile? After her own ludicrous, ridiculous behaviour in India, as well. God – to be rid of her. And her sanctimony and her piety and that ghastly old humbug of a father of hers as well. How *can* she do this to me?

He bundled banknotes into the hand of the taxi-driver and ran up the steps of the vicarage, ringing vigorously and continually on the front doorbell as soon as he got there. A smiling, if anxious-looking Derrick Hilden-Parker opened the door in due course and showed him into his study. He shut the door and turned to Robert, beginning some hesitant, ritualistic comment about the weather, but Robert cut him short, throwing the letter down on to the table in front of him.

His voice was hard and curt, and he noticed that his finger was shaking when he pointed down at the table. He found himself to be now genuinely angry.

'This version here has been typed while the fingerprint and DNA people check the disgusting original out. Is it yours? Is this evil garbage yours? Did you write this thing?'

Hilden-Parker went to the table and picked up the letter. He turned to Robert, his face now red and beginning to bead with perspiration. He brushed the sleeve of his jacket across his brow, then said, 'May I read it?'

'Of course you can bloody read it. Are you mad? Read it, for Christ's sake. Read it.'

As Robert watched him, much of the edge of his anger, which had flared up so suddenly, began to dull. Hilden-Parker's face looked so loose and weak and incompetent in profile. Too much so to make him an enemy fit for that sort of attack and aggression. He saw that the sweat was now running freely down the man's face, and he was licking at his lips, and feeling at his collar.

Robert sat down heavily in the armchair behind him, and watched him now almost with amusement. It's not him I want to attack, the poor man. It's my wife, who has fed him with this awful, depraved lie. I've never seen anything so pitiable in my life as this man's guilt and panic.

Then Hilden-Parker turned, and looked down at Robert. When he spoke, his voice was so shrill and taut that Robert thought he was about to break down on him completely.

'Would you excuse me for a moment? I need to . . . I need to . . . would you excuse me?'

He went out of the room almost at a run, slamming the door behind him. When he came back, over five minutes later, presumably having had time to settle himself down in the bathroom, or wherever he'd been, he seemed at first glance to be marginally more composed, but his voice still had a strangled quality about it when he spoke.

'No. I didn't send the letter. I didn't send this. Why do you think I sent this? How dare you say that—'

Robert interrupted, his hand held up to make Hilden-Parker halt, speaking coldly and so quietly that Hilden-Parker stretched his head forward to hear him. Rather like a frightened giraffe, Robert thought.

'Because you seem to make a habit of it, don't you? It's what you do, as I understand it. As I've been informed. It's what you did in your previous parish. Your nasty little penchant. Like an old lady. The poison pen from behind the twitching lace curtains.'

There was a silence for several moments, and Robert and Hilden-Parker stared at each other. Robert saw that the puceness in his face had now faded to an extreme pallor, and he waited for him to speak.

'So . . . so because there was a mistake once, then I'm the one who is assumed to be guilty every time that same offence is committed again. Is that it? Is that what you're saying? Why won't you believe me? A mistake was made, I was ill, actually I was very ill, I went through treatment and now I'm cured. I didn't send this letter you've brought. I've never seen it before. I've nothing to do with it. Nothing to do with it!'

'So what were you talking about with my wife when she came around here last week or whenever it was? The Flower Festival? The Young Wives' Prayer Group? The Methodist Missionary Society? Come on, man! What were you talking about?'

'I don't entirely remember. There are so many . . .'

'Oh, yes you do. She had a nice weep and you patted her comfortingly on the bottom. She was . . .' He held up his hand to halt Derrick Hilden-Parker's interruption, and continued ' . . . she was feeding you with this nonsense, wasn't she? Those are your "impeccable sources", aren't they? She gave you all this stuff because . . . God knows. I don't know why she gave it to you. Probably because she wants to bed you. Perhaps she thinks you want to bed *her*. From what I hear, that is exactly the position. You'd like nothing better.'

The coarseness of the remark hit Robert, as if it was not him that had said it but another man, and he immediately felt the shame of it. This isn't me, he thought, reflecting that he was good at neither the bullying nor the crudeness, and hated both. He knew nothing about the unfortunate man's life, except in hearsay, and he was disgusted at himself for talking about his own wife in that way to a stranger. Whatever the circumstances. However he felt about her at that moment. Whatever he felt about her own betrayal of him.

He stared at Hilden-Parker, who was now sitting in a chair across from Robert at the other side of the room, leaning forward in it, hugging himself in misery.

'Look . . . let's try to bring this conversation to an end,' Robert said. 'It's not very much fun for either of us. You're a very stupid man to do what you've done. You know the evil of it. And you've done it to me twice. *Twice!* I haven't raised that with you before, but I'm doing so now. I've had from you two of these disgusting poison letters in three years, or whatever it is. Most people would say that twice—'

'No. No. Not twice. Once.'

Hilden-Parker's face now was haggard. His voice had gradually lost all its shrill quality of panicked indignation and self-protection, and had become quiet, withdrawn, and composed.

'I did it once. I admit the first one, but only that. Only once. Two years or so ago. And I'm very sorry.'

'What are you talking about? What do you mean – you're sorry? What's being sorry got to do with these disgusting accusations about my relationship with my children? Accusations of—'

'I've never made any accusations about you and your children. I wouldn't dream of doing so. I've never seen this letter before. I'm telling you the truth. The letter I wrote was the first one. That was the one and only letter I wrote.'

Robert held up his hand to stop him, shaking his head. 'You sent the first letter, you admit that. But they're both yours. You sent them *both*.'

'No,' Hilden-Parker replied. 'The second letter isn't mine. I sent the first. Only that one. You have my absolute and solemn word for it. Only the first. In the name of God – I accept the blame for that. But only that. Only the first.'

Chapter Forty-Six

Alice watched her father as he sat opposite her on the garden bench. Both his hands were held around his cup of tea to stop it spilling as he lifted it to his mouth.

He sipped it a little, just enough, Alice thought, so that he could demonstrate to her that he was capable of it, then, as carefully and slowly as before, he got the cup back to its saucer, rattling it there as he withdrew his hands.

Alice got up, went to him, tucked his scarf more closely around his neck, stroked his hair for a moment, then suddenly leant forward and held him in her arms.

'I love you, Tom. I ought to be dissembling with you, and encouraging you along, and telling you that you look marvellous. And how much you've improved since I saw you last week. But I can't.'

She was crying now, silently, but the tears were rolling down her face and chin, and she held him the more tightly to her, so that he would not see.

'I can't do that to you. Treat you like a child. Lie to you. I'm so devastated to see you like this, Tom.'

She made then a great effort of will to pull herself together. She drew back from him and smiled, and he as well.

'You were always there for me, Tom,' she said. 'Your rooms at Corpus, and here at Grange Road . . . it was such a wonderful, confined little world of just you and me together. I'll never forget it, Tom. And my own children will grow up to think of you as some sort of God, I can promise you that.'

Tom took hold of his right forearm with his left hand, and lifted it, dead and inert, so that both hands now lay together on his lap. The squash ball was there, and he slowly gathered it into his right palm, then frowned and closed his eyes as he tried to gather his strength together to make the hand perform the kneading motion with which he was attempting to recall life to it. Ponderously, heavily, the fingers began to move.

'Children, Alice? Your children?'

He was looking at her as he dragged, dragged the words out of himself, and she could see in his eyes, glinting a little, a hint of the mocking, teasing Tom style of him in his good health.

'Children? Is that how you tell me? Are you going to marry him then? I thought nobody married these days.'

Alice sat back, and as she looked at him she was for a moment wholly taken aback that she had so dropped her guard and control in this way. Laying herself open to that sort of response from Tom. She couldn't understand why she had done that. She had encouraged him to say the one word that she had deliberately and entirely excluded from her own thoughts. She knew that it was an indulgent, dangerous fantasy. Marriage. Children with Robert. That wasn't something she'd allowed herself to believe possible. And it wasn't possible. This relationship with Robert was not going to end in marriage. She was a mature, sensible woman. So why had she made that slip? Why had she said that about children?

'Divorce, Alice? His wife, his first children, all of that . . . and his age? He's so much older than you. His health, his death. The father of small children. Your children. You a widow. All of those things.'

And he knows, of course, that there's no possibility of marriage, she thought. He's seen this before, and he knows me so well. He's convinced that it can only come to an end in due course, and that it'll be an unhappy parting. He's trying to warn me of that, in his own way. He's doing what he can to make me face up to what he believes are the facts. And he's tiring already. He's beginning to talk in shorthand, so that he doesn't have to get through a long sentence.

'I don't believe Robert's ever had happiness,' she said, and in doing so looked for a statement, a half-truth, a cliché, anything that would enable her to deny the fact of what they both knew was there.

'His children and his wife have devoured him in their different ways. He's grown used to it. He's lost the drive to expect anything else. He's lost all his expectation of contentment in that part of his life. And hope of anything different.'

She shrugged, and tried to smile at Tom in a way that would break the spell and change the subject, but he was still staring at her, and his eyes carried now that sombre, penetrative quality, despite the fatigue of his illness, that Alice knew so well.

'I want him to have a real life ahead of him, Tom,' she said, and the attempt to smile him out of his warnings was gone from her now. 'He's in love with me. Perhaps something's possible between us. Perhaps. I wish it could be. But probably there can be nothing. I don't know. I don't really want to know at the moment.'

Tom looked down at his hand, now still and twisted in his lap, the squash ball lying in the fold of his thighs. When he looked up there was a smile in his eyes again, but his face, still so immobile, and dropped – grotesquely dropped down its right side –was drawn and pale with the effort of the conversation.

'Alice. Good luck, Alice.' There was a long pause while they looked at each other, then: 'Is it because of me? Did that childhood of yours do you harm? Did we live in too close a world together?'

He attempted a shrug, but the gesture, performed in laborious motion by him, looked clumsy and inarticulate. He struggled on, the sentence interminable in its fatigue.

'We were together, that's all. We were alone, and we both made the most of what we had left. We did pretty well. It didn't seem so difficult. We liked each other. Let alone loved each other.'

She looked at him in deepening sadness. I ought to want him to go soon, she thought. To let him die soon. I could tell myself that he'll always live in my heart, and that I'll never forget him. And of course I couldn't forget him. But however ill he is, I want him to live. I can't contemplate the idea of life without him. We've been each other's entire family for so long. Owning only each other. I so want him to live.

She dragged up her wooden garden chair so that it was immediately in front of him, then leant forward and took his hands in hers. 'We did fine, Tom. We did fine. You were a lousy housekeeper, but we did fine.'

They smiled at each other, and Alice could see now in his eyes a glint of life. For a moment she thought that he was going to banter with her, but he appeared to abandon the effort of it, and she smiled at him again, as if to encourage and reassure him.

'Pollyanna and the widower father,' he said at last. 'That's what. All very Disney. Spreading rays of sunshine all over the neighbourhood like a couple of angels of light. Too good to be true, we were. A quite sickening couple, I wouldn't be surprised. All we needed was a fluffy sheep dog and we'd have been complete.'

He attempted to smile once more, and as he started to try to struggle from his position, Alice helped him to his feet, and walked arm in arm with him as they made their way back into the house.

As she drove away, Tom stood there in the shabby, peeling portico, leaning on his stick, unable, despite an attempt at it, to raise his other hand in his customary dismissive, emphatic wave. She paused at the road and looked back to watch him in her car mirror, then turned, and waved to him herself, immediately fearing that it might be for the last time.

I'll never see him again, she thought. And as the sense of panic and certainty of that washed over her, she felt for a moment nauseous and dazed, before there was an ebbing again, and she was calm. Not that. Please let him live. Please live, Tom.

She drove now so slowly, so lost in thought, that a lorry behind her hooted angrily, the driver gesticulating, and she shook herself together to gather her concentration, and accelerated a little up the slipway and on to the main road.

I found myself wanting to present all the business about Robert to him with such definition and certainty, she thought, wondering why it had emerged in the way that it did. She was not at all sure what she was trying to do. That mention of children – it was as if she was defying him to challenge her over the relationship, and whether or not it had any future. But they both knew the same thing. They both knew what was ahead.

And as Alice was driving away, Tom turned and went slowly back into the house. His face grimaced with dismay at the privacy of his home being breached by the pop music and shouted laughter emerging from the bedroom – Alice's old bedroom – in which the young nurse he now had with him in the house all the time was staying.

He hobbled his way into his study, shut the door on the noise and sat, heavily, in the cracked old leather chair that was drawn up to his desk. In front of him was a photograph of Alice, aged eight or nine, sitting on the garden wall, grinning at the camera, the neighbour's cat in her arms. He gazed at this for some moments, then, more laboriously now that he was on his own, and did not have to pretend to have facility and movement that he no longer possessed, he pushed his hand forward across the desk to the silver frame, and traced the shape of her face with a single, shaking finger.

And the strange thing about her is that she never will marry, he thought. It has nothing to do with the fact that she seems to prefer older men. Except in this way – she seems able to go into a relationship only if she knows it can prove to be nothing more than an affair. Even now. Even with this. For all her competence and cleverness and all her other strengths she shies away from any relationship which could actually have a resolution to it. This one with Robert Luscombe will break up as they all break up, and she knows that's what will happen.

Maybe it was because of him. Maybe she turned to men whom

life had hurt. Maybe they had been so close when she was a child that he had destroyed in her the capability of breaking away. He didn't know, and anyway it was too late.

But it was worth it. So often when she was a child he had considered marrying again, once or twice he had very much wanted to marry again, but for one reason or another it had never worked out. Mostly because of Alice. Because of the intensity and concentration of their relationship together; too difficult for someone else to enter and compete with. Or so it had seemed at the time.

He lifted his dead, still hand with the other, and laid them both side by side on the desk top. It was worth it. But . . . there had been so much time in recent years when he'd been alone. And now it was too late.

Too late for anything else but simply willing himself to live for one more day at a time. One more day at a time. Too late now for anything but that.

Chapter Forty-Seven

Derrick Hilden-Parker sat there in the café fingering his cup and saucer, looking, in his baggy khaki trousers and his high-necked sweater, both younger and better-looking than when in his habitual clerical suits and dog collar. But his face was tired and furrowed, and there was a listless, passive quality about him.

'Cheer up, Mr Hilden-Parker! You look quite miserable. I've never seen you so out of sorts.'

He looked up at Sophie Luscombe, and attempted a smile, but it ended up more like a grimace of pain. He shrugged.

'Just a bit blue, Sophie. A little worried.'

He made another attempt to smile, this time rather more convincingly. Sophie grinned back at him, her pink cheeks and her cheeky little eyes and the blue jeans-dungarees and white T-shirt with the Donald Duck motif on the front making her look, were it not for the fullness of her breasts, just like a plump little twelve year old.

'You mustn't worry about anything, Mr Hilden-Parker. Nothing at all. Things always work out for the best, that's what Grandpa tells me – when you trust in the Lord. Pray to the Lamb and everything turns out sunny and nice. That's what Grandpa always says.' She sucked at her straw, then wiped her nose.

'I'm so glad you were free to come today,' she said. 'I found it was your day off, so I thought it was worth ringing up to ask. I

306

thought you might find time when I said I had a message from Mummy.'

'Well . . . it wasn't only that, Sophie. I like to keep in touch with the young of the parish, you know. Young things like you.'

But his heart wasn't in it somehow, and his voice sounded drab and heavy, and he turned back to his cup and saucer, his face again lost in thought. They sat there for a minute or so without speaking, then he appeared to try once more to pull himself together.

'And your grandfather, Sophie. He must have been glad to have you both down to stay last week. How was he keeping? He's retired from the parish now, hasn't he?'

'Oh, he's still just the same,' said Sophie, picking up in her fingers the last of her chips, and dipping them in the ketchup. 'Just the same. As loving and affectionate as always. The same old Grandpa, with his funny little ways.'

She sucked busily once more at her strawberry milk shake, making a loud bubbling noise as she chased the last few drops of it around the bottom of her glass. When she looked up there was a little rim of it left on her upper lip, and she wiped this off by twice drawing the back of her sleeve across her mouth.

'And he so loves Mummy, it's lovely to see it. She does need lots of love, you know, Mr Hilden-Parker. She needs lots of hugs and looking after. She doesn't get enough of it. She needs it from you, I'm sure. In a pastoral, caring way.'

'Well, well, there we are, Sophie. She's a wonderful woman, of course. I admire her very much. She's a saint. You're lucky to have her as your mother.'

'Oh I am, I am, Mr Hilden-Parker. She *is* a saint. She's like a handmaid of the Lord, as Grandpa has often said. That's why I hate to see her treated badly. Or defiled. That's why I was so upset that time when I came to see you and your wife and told you what she was being made to do by Daddy. That I happened to see one day by mistake. I think you very kindly wrote to him afterwards, didn't you? And told him that he shouldn't do those sort of horrid things to Mummy. Do you remember?'

She smiled at him again, and started now on her chocolate ice, which she stirred round to make nice and creamy and smooth, just as she liked it. She drew the spoon out of her mouth slowly and luxuriantly, then turned it upside down and did it again, licking it carefully before plunging it in the glass bowl again for more.

He gazed at her with great unease. It was only the previous day that he had been put through that meeting with Robert Luscombe, and the shock of all that had been said was still very much with him. Another complaint to the Bishop would certainly mean the end of his career. And not only that . . . the tabloids no doubt, and the parish gossips. It was some moments before he spoke, and when he did so he had to make the effort to lift his head from his hands, and attempt to get some animation into his voice. Sophie was looking at him encouragingly, her most winning little dimpled smile on her face.

'Letter? Did I write? I hardly remember it all now. Perhaps I scribbled a note of advice. I can't recall really. It was quite a long time ago, you know.'

'Yes – you did write, Mr Hilden-Parker. I expect you've forgotten. Actually I kept the letter, the one you wrote. Daddy seemed very angry and I saw him throw this letter away in the dustbin, though I didn't know what it was, and I took it out afterwards to read it. In case he was in some sort of trouble, or something like that. Something I might be able to help him with.'

She went back to her ice cream, tipping the glass bowl to one side and scraping busily and noisily at the remains around the sides. Then, after one final lick at her spoon, she pushed her plate to one side, wiped her mouth once more on the back of her sleeve, and sighed.

'Gosh, that was good. Thank you so much, Mr Hilden-Parker. That was really nice. Delicious. I must rush now, or I will be late for my evening classes. Tonight's the first one. I'm so looking forward to it. The course is called *Deprivation and Family Counselling Today* –

The Caring Woman's Responsibility in a Material World. It should be really interesting.'

She got up from the bench and pulled on her anorak. 'Goodbye, Mr Hilden-Parker. Thank you again for a lovely tea.'

She smiled and waved as she started to walk away, then turned, her hand to her mouth. 'What an idiot, I nearly forgot. Mummy said will you telephone her? She didn't want to ring the vicarage herself. I think perhaps she thought Mrs Hilden-Parker . . .'

Sophie shrugged, waved again and set off for the door. He stared after her for a minute or so, then suddenly leapt to his feet, seized his bill, flung some money on to the table and rushed after her.

'Sophie! Sophie!' He arrived at her side a hundred yards or so up the road just as her bus drew up at the stop, panting and bending double for a moment as he recovered his breath.

'Sophie – that letter, the letter you said you had. The one you thought I had written. Could I see it? Could I have it?'

'The letter? I've kept it safe, Mr Hilden-Parker. I don't carry it around with me or anything, you needn't worry about that. It's all locked away and safe. It wouldn't do for anyone else to see it. Not the Bishop or anyone like that. But you did quite right to write. And I'm sure it was wise to stick it together with those letters the way you did, rather than do it in your own handwriting. And not sign it or anything. It was a pity it seemed to get some pooh on it from somewhere. No – I think it's better to keep it safe and private. After those little things you said about watching from behind the curtains. Prying eyes, you know . . .'

She jumped on the bus just as it was drawing away, and waved and smiled at Derrick Hilden-Parker as he stood there at the bus stop, still panting, his face now haggard and staring.

'I'll be in touch,' she shouted, then paid her fare and settled into a seat reserved for the handicapped and aged. Poor old thing, she thought. He's not well really. But he can afford to help me with some pocket money now that I'm out of work. Just for now, until I find a nice new job somewhere.

Just like Grandpa. I never knew the naughty old man had so much in his savings account. And he was sensible to be generous too. After I'd had my little private chat with him.

Chapter Forty-Eight

Colin was waiting for his father in his study at Eaton Place.

The new Portuguese maid, who had only been in the house for three days, had given him his tea in his mother's best Spode set. This was much to his satisfaction, as normally it was the blue nursery china that Colin was given by his mother, and the second-best at that, after an incident some ten or more years earlier when he had dropped a porcelain coffee cup and smashed it on the hearth.

His mother was in the country, however, and his father was now over an hour late for the conversation with Colin, the time of which he had himself fixed, with a cold instruction to his son to be punctual.

Eventually he came into the room. 'Colin. There you are. Sit down, for heaven's sake. Sit down.'

There was an uncomfortable moment when Colin, who had leapt to his feet on his father's arrival, then as abruptly sat again, in doing so spilling his full cup of hot tea all over his lap. But his father showed no sign of noticing, and Colin decided to leave well alone, desisting from any mopping operation which might irritate him yet further. For he was, unmistakably, in a powerfully bad mood.

'All well, Father? You well? Mother well? The dogs well, and all that sort of thing? The garden looking well?'

Sir Arthur rolled his eyes to the ceiling, and started rapping feverishly on the arm of his chair with his knuckles. When he replied it was with pedantic emphasis and articulation, as if he was giving a language class to a particularly regressive person of considerable age and very little English.

'Everybody is well. I am well. I hope you are well. I have had a very busy day. But now I am here.' He rolled his eyes upwards again, then stared at his son with a furious eye. 'The Bank has flown you back to England, at, I gather from Miss Humphreys, your particular and urgent request. To see me. I am very busy. Please say whatever it is you have to say. Clearly and succinctly.'

He glared at him, and Colin licked his lips, trying to suppress the grin coming to his face that he knew would annoy his father even more than he already had.

'Well – it's a little bit sensitive actually, Father. Rather delicate. That's why I thought I should see you personally. Good of you to see me. Most good of you. I really am most . . .'

'Colin. Please. *Clearly and succinctly.* What is it? What do you want to say to me? I have more people whom I have to see later on this evening, and papers to read for meetings in the morning. I really am very busy. What is it? Why did you fly home to England? Why, Colin, why did you want to see me?'

'Because, Father . . .' and as he started to speak Colin could feel, perhaps now to his pleasure, the familiar, heady prickle of anger come into him ' . . . because there's something that looks to me to be very wrong in what I am looking at in the Poonjee investigation. I'm beginning to find things that concern me. And mystify me.'

'And that, if I may say so, does not surprise me. I'm not in the least surprised that you are mystified. I knew you would be. I knew the whole matter was beyond you. I told Robert Luscombe that, and I told you that as well. You don't have the experience for it, and you don't have the—'

He hesitated, and Colin returned his gaze with a heady sensation of lack of fear.

'Intelligence?' Colin said cheerfully. 'Brains? Tact? Contacts? Breeding?'

He smiled, but there was now a clear tension between them, and after they had stared at each other for several moments, it was his father who turned away first. When he spoke, it was in a tone of voice that was noticeably less aggressive.

'I was going to say training actually. Training. There's nothing to be ashamed of in not having sufficient technical knowledge to undertake a review of something as complex as the Poonjee transaction. The Bank is training you as a generalist, not a specialist, and the Poonjee matter was a very specialist affair. That was why I told Luscombe I was not enthusiastic for you to tackle it. That's all. Now, what is it you want to know with such urgency?'

'It's not so much what I want to know, Father. I already know more than I had expected to do. I'm here because I think I ought to tell you about it, because I promised I would, if you remember – before I put any of it on paper. That's why I'm here. That's what you asked me to do.'

Arthur Ewing nodded several times, pulled a wry little face, which Colin construed as an attempt at an apology, then said: 'Of course, of course. So . . . what can I tell you? Or what are you going to tell me, or however you want to conduct this conversation?'

'Well, let's say that several things have emerged which have surprised me . . .' he held up his hand to stop his father commenting on this, as he saw the familiar look of sarcasm and irritation pass again across his face ' . . . and some of them concern you, and other senior members of the Bank. Perhaps I've misunderstood an aspect of the negotiations. Perhaps I've been misled. But I don't believe I have. And I feel I've got to the point where I have to brief you.

'I now have a good deal of information, and there are some important points of propriety and ethics amongst it all. And these have to be discussed with you before I take them any further.'

'What points of ethics and propriety? What on earth are you talking about?'

'Father – perhaps I've been cast into the real world for the first time. Perhaps my appreciation of how business works has been much too facile. But I am shocked by what I've come across in this affair. And surprised a little by how the business has been transacted. By us, mainly, it seems. By the Bank.'

'What are you talking about? If there have been improprieties or dishonesty in the way the Bank has conducted itself in this business, then that is exactly why we set up the whole system of these compliance and security audits. To police them, from within the family of the Bank. And by doing so to demonstrate to everybody in the Bank that our standards should be the highest of anybody's in the world. And that we all of us – senior or junior – have this heritage and culture to preserve.

'Now, Colin. I apologise if I was impatient with you before, but you've caught me at a most busy time, and I really do have other urgent things waiting to be done. What is it? What are we here to discuss? What exactly are you shocked by?'

Colin got up from his chair, and put his tea cup, which he had been clutching all the while on his lap, back on the tray on the corner table. When he went to sit again it was in a different chair, slightly to the side of his father, and with the evening light behind him.

'I went to see Marty Schwab, Father. You know that. You know about the letters?' His father nodded impatiently, muttering his confirmation that Robert Luscombe had told him about them. 'I went to New York to see him because whoever is writing me these letters told me to go there to ask various questions. I checked it with Robert Luscombe, and he thought there was something in it, and that it should be followed up. So I went.

'The letters had told me various things. Firstly, that C.P. Nerappan had defrauded the Bank of funds by taking a bribe to give Prasad & Prasad a very considerable loan at an artificially low rate of interest. That was one thing – but the letters also made two other accusations, and it was these I wanted to check against whatever version of events Marty Schwab put forward.

'These two accusations were firstly that we blackmailed the Chicago and Illinois Trust into letting us have a large position in their consortium by threatening to expose them for trading illegally with Iran. And secondly that the consortium negotiators bribed some Government of India officials into ensuring that we won the contract.'

Arthur Ewing was sitting quite still in his chair, his elbows on the arm-rests, his hands held before his face, the fingers lightly touching. He was staring at the carpet in front of him. Colin waited for some moments before continuing, to give his father the chance to respond at this time, but he didn't do so.

'And I got the confirmation I was looking for. Although when I had it, it came in a form that I was not expecting. It's clear to me that we did both, Father. We blackmailed Chicago and Illinois. And the consortium bribed their way to win the contract. I'm going to say so in my report; I don't feel I have any option. I felt I should tell you first. It's the truth. Maybe it's the way of the world. Maybe it's how everybody behaves. But it's the whole point of these compliance and security audits of ours that behaviour of this sort should be brought to light. That's what you told me. So I'm going to have to do it.'

Still Arthur Ewing did not respond. Colin got up from his chair, fiddled around with the tea tray, then returned, this time to his original chair. He spoke now very quietly and gently.

'Schwab indicated to me that it was you who was the prime mover behind the first business, Father. That it was you who personally negotiated our position, and that you used threats of exposure to do so. Explicit threats. Blackmail, in other words.'

There was a pause, then Arthur Ewing raised his head, and looked Colin directly in the eye.

'Who used the word "blackmail", you or him? I very much doubt that he did. Who used the word "threat"? Think back very carefully. Very carefully indeed. You're making an extremely serious allegation. At the moment it's in the privacy of our own home. No harm is done. But there will be if it goes any further.

'You see, Colin, what I believe actually happened is that you put words into Marty Schwab's mouth. That you suggested to him the way things were done, and because he didn't specifically deny the form in which your version was expressed, you took that to be a formal confirmation of it.

'Because that was what you wanted to hear. That's what you wanted very much indeed to hear; to have the thrill of catching me, if that's the right way of putting it, in a morally ambiguous situation. Catching me red-handed. The turning of the tables on your father. Some sort of delayed and rather tiresome adolescent revolt against a father with a position and reputation in the world.

'At least you'll find that to be Mr Schwab's position and account of your meeting. He telephoned me the moment you were out of his offices. He assumed you were some sort of a delinquent member of the family, as he told it to me. He guessed you were genuinely my son because of your physical resemblance to me, although he got his secretary to call my office while you were sitting there to make sure. But he was concerned for a moment that, my son or not, you might yourself have been a blackmailer. The moment you'd gone he was through to me. You behaved like a very stupid young man.'

There was an absolute silence between them for some minutes. Then Colin stirred in his chair, and when he spoke his voice was very quiet.

'I didn't make a tape recording of the meeting – perhaps I should have done. But I remember very clearly what was said. I remember every word that Marty Schwab uttered. Of course I attempted to make him say and admit things. Not because I was trying to incriminate you, but because I wanted to learn the truth.

'I have no motive in this to try to embarrass you, or to humiliate you in any way. Though . . . yes, if you insist, yes there *was* a moment of excitement when I realised that you were capable of behaviour as ruthless as anyone else when it came to securing the welfare of the Bank. There was a moment of excitement, and a moment of amusement. It's always fun to see the Emperor with his clothes off. Of course it is.'

'I think it was a little more than that,' said Arthur Ewing. 'Quite a lot more than that, according to what Mr Schwab had to tell me.

You lied to him. In order, I assume, to ensnare him and trick him into an indiscretion. Some cock-and-bull story about a government official who wanted to tell tales about the consortium to the Indian Prime Minister's office. The whole thing was a figment of your imagination. I checked it out with the people who would know. It was a lie. A lie, told in an attempt to mislead and ensnare Marty Schwab into an indiscretion. A lie. Am I correct? Yes? Am I correct?'

Colin was now red in the face and, as he had from a child, was forcing his fingernails into the palm of his hands and screwing up his toes in his attempt to hold his anger in check. Even so, his voice had a shrillness to it that indicated to him that he was in danger of losing his self-control. He realised that he should pause, say nothing more for a moment, and get himself poised and calm, but he couldn't stop himself.

'I'm not going to allow myself to be pushed on to the defensive like this. I'm not going to be treated like this. It's not me who's in the dock. It's—'

'Me? *Me* – in the dock? I beg your pardon! What is this insulting nonsense? Is that how you see your role in this business – as the High Court Judge? The Grand Inquisitor?

'Perhaps you were hoping, really hoping, for a genuine scandal, with all the excitement that goes with that. Police vans, and journalists, and the Serious Fraud Office and all the rest of it. Is that what you were after? Perhaps you've just given your position away.

'Because I think you wanted to see me disgraced. I think you're an inadequate young man, unsuited to your family's position in the world, and that you want to get rid of the shame of that by bringing me down. Like an adolescent. To make you feel better about yourself. I don't believe you're man enough for anything very much. And I think you know it.'

Colin sat motionless, his breath suspended; his eyes closed. All his life he had waited for this moment to come. The moment when his father would actually expose and reveal his contempt for him.

Openly, and stated. No hints, no half-statements, no obliqueness.

And now it had happened. Now the contempt had been displayed, and had been done so with a clarity and absence of dissemblance that they would both have to live with for the rest of their days. Neither of them would ever forget it. His father had, in his anger, gone very much too far. He had said what he clearly believed, but to reveal himself to this level of clarity was an act of viciousness and lack of self-control. And stress. And illness. And . . . perhaps? . . . guilt. At any rate, their relationship would never be the same again. And that was a very good thing indeed.

Colin looked across at his father, and stared at him. He had calmed down now, and his voice was back under control.

'No. I don't know it. And I deeply resent your speaking to me in that way. But let's stay on the point. I'd like you to answer my question. Did we, as a bank, put undue and unethical pressure on the Chicago and Illinois Trust by threatening to expose them for illegal trading? Did we, Father, or didn't we?'

There was a long pause before his father answered.

'I'm sorry, Colin. That was unforgivable of me. Those were unforgivable things to say. I'm truly sorry.'

Colin shrugged but said nothing.

Then his father said, 'To answer your question. No, that's not how I would describe the negotiations, and I'm perfectly certain the Chicago and Illinois people wouldn't either.

'There was a robustness in our discussion, certainly. We have traded together in a number of situations over the years, including, to be quite frank with you, in certain dealings in the Middle East, and I was irritated that they were talking to other British banks before they seemed interested in talking to us. So I stepped in. I hadn't met them myself before, or barely had, so we had no personal history together. In those circumstances it wasn't difficult for me to be straightforward and tough and get what I wanted for us. And I was tough – distinctly so. I did remind them that we had worked closely before. In the Middle East, yes, as well as several other places which some people might describe as . . . unorthodox.

And I did get what I wanted. Not for me, of course. For us. For the Bank. For us all.'

'And that's what happened?'

His father looked at him directly and, almost in the first time that Colin could recall in the long history of their relationship, with amusement and perhaps even a hint of affection in his eyes.

'Yes. That's what happened. Colin – I meant it when I apologised to you. I was crudely insulting to you, and I feel extremely guilty and . . . lessened by that. You asked a reasonable question of me, and I should certainly have answered it earlier. But now I have. That's my answer. You're right in thinking that I played a very tough hand with them. I did. You're wrong in suggesting that my conduct transgressed any rule. It didn't. And it was certainly not blackmail.'

'And it is blackmail that was suggested to me. By my correspondent.'

'Yes, I know. We'll find out who that person is, because the writer is trying to pay off old scores, and damage some of us for some motive or another, and that has to be stopped. You're being led along a route that's never quite right. It's always nearly right, but then doesn't get it exactly right. There's too much personal malice involved.

'You spoke of Nerappan. You know he's been in contact with me since your conversations with him in hospital? I believe the explanation he gave you of the Javed transaction is the right one. It has to me the ring of truth about it.'

Arthur shifted in his chair. Colin saw him look down at his hand as it lay on his lap, then, perhaps noticing the degree to which its shaking was obvious, he lifted it, and thrust it away in his pocket.

'And as for the letters that the lawyers have produced, I don't give them one jot of credence. None of them is a so-called original. All are copies, and thus childishly easy to forge. They are, without doubt, fraudulent.

'And the bribing of the Government of India negotiators? It could be. It may be. It might just as well be a matter of knowing the right people, and pulling a few strings. In, I concede the point, an Indian way. And – certainly – I am not so hidebound that I cannot personally see the virtue of working within the mores of the culture in which one is trying to operate. What does it matter? Where is the personal gain? There were the performance bonuses, of course, but . . .'

Arthur Ewing shrugged, and made a little grimace, as if in dismissal of the issue. He looked at his watch, then got to his feet.

'Colin – let me say it again. I'm deeply sorry that I said to you a few minutes ago some things that should never have been said. I apologise without reserve. Without reserve.

'Now – good luck with the rest of your efforts. You must get your report checked by Robert Luscombe, of course, before it's released, but as far as I am concerned you must say in it whatever you feel you need to. I certainly have nothing more I can add to it. Thank you for coming by, dear boy. Have we covered everything? Is that all?'

He smiled, and Colin smiled faintly back at him.

'Yes. That's all, I suppose. That's all.'

And as his father went out through the front door, and he went himself to gather up his coat and bags, he thought to himself that it wasn't really all, by no means was it all, but it was certainly all he could face at the moment.

'Sufficient unto the day,' muttered Colin to a portrait of his great-grandfather, which he passed on his way out through the hall. 'Sufficient unto the day.'

Chapter Forty-Nine

The top-floor flat, facing due west towards Fulham and the river, caught all the fading warmth of the sunset, and Robert and Alice were there alone, without lights, allowing the room to sink slowly into darkness.

Robert was sprawled at an angle across the sofa, and Alice sat on the floor before him. He was running his fingers through her hair, and stroking her head and the side of her face. Then he straightened himself a little and said: 'We must bring all this part of it to an end now, Alice. I want to be with you properly and openly. I want to tell Sarah.'

He adjusted his position so that he was more upright, then, after a moment's silence, he suddenly got to his feet, crossed the room, and sat down on an ottoman facing Alice directly.

'I can't live with this deceit, Alice. You know that. The guilt poisons my life. I've had a failed marriage in which I've been a failed husband, and I want to end it. The subterfuge of my behaviour disgusts me. I want to be with you. I can't spend another night with Sarah in these circumstances. I can't live like that. I want to go to tell her now, then come back here to be with you.'

Alice got up from the floor, and sat on the sofa beside him, leaning forward, her elbows resting on her knees. It was some moments before she responded to him.

'You haven't been a failed husband, Robert. You've been a very responsible husband to a very difficult woman. To say that of yourself is actually a piece of convenient dishonesty. It makes it all seem tidier and more logical and neater that you should need to split with her because you've failed and your marriage is irreconcilable.

'I don't believe that's true. The truth is that if it wasn't for me you would be staying with Sarah without a second thought. If you do break up your marriage, our relationship is the cause of it. You've fallen in love with me, and the excitement of that is such that you want to abandon your wife for it. I think we need to face up to that. You talk about deceit – I think that's deceit as well. I want us to face up to the truth. You want to abandon your wife because of me. I have to face up to that as well. And it's not a very comfortable proposition.'

Robert got to his feet, and looked down at Alice. He stared at her, and as he did so he thought that all the conventional clichés and aphorisms of popular romance were true. He *would* die for her, if needs be. He *would* love her for ever. She *was* all that the world could bring him.

'Yes. All right. That's the truth. And you're quite right, I'm not going to ease the position by pretending something that isn't true. But I'm going now to tell her. And then I'm coming back to you. And I'll never let you go.'

Alice held up her hand, shaking her head, and got to her feet too, now standing directly in front of him. She put both her hands on his two shoulders, and grimaced as she stared into his eyes.

'No, Robert. We must go much more slowly than this. This is much too fast, and much too impetuous, and much too decisive. I don't want us to act this quickly, and make important decisions this fast. I don't want to break up a marriage. Sarah exists, and she's your wife, and she's a wounded animal, and she's decidedly not a woman capable of taking this breakup without a colossal amount of pain. Which I very much doubt she can withstand. I want to think much more. I want to go very much more slowly than this. I want time to calm down, and act rationally, and think.'

When Robert looked at her now he began to flush, and there were beads of sweat suddenly on his forehead and lip. 'What do you mean?' he said. 'What does that mean – you want time to think? Does that imply that you want to . . .' He sat down on the chair behind him and looked up at her, his face grimacing.

'We've been through all this, Alice. I love you. We've been through it all. It's come to the moment now to be decisive and clear and positive in what we do. We can't go on living in this way. Things have to be brought to a head. We've done the thinking. That stage is over. We *must* bring all this to a head.'

He reached up, took both her hands in his, then stood again, and they faced each other. Frowning, she started to speak again, but he interrupted her, and pulled away from her.

'No. *No*, Alice! This has to be done. These things do happen. I have to go to her now. I have to tell her the truth, that I'm going to be with you.'

She started to say something more, but he had already turned away from her, and she stood there, motionless, as the front door of her flat shut behind him.

Chapter Fifty

Sarah stared at him. Her face had greyed, and she kept covering her eyes with her hands, then running them down her cheeks on either side in a compulsive, unaffected gesture of raw grief and panic. She kept up a rhythmic, distraught chant, her breathing heightened and panting between each word.

'No. No. No. No.'

Robert stared back at her. He stood there opposite her, absolutely still, holding her eyes directly in his. Then he spoke again.

'It's for the best, Sarah. It's for the best. It's what I want. I'm sorry it's happened. I'm sorry to hurt you. But I have to go. I have to be with her.'

'No, Robert. No. Stay with me. Stay with me. Stay with me.'

And now she was shouting, shouting, her voice hysterical, her hands clasped into tight fists and pounding at her stomach and chest and head. He went to her, and as he put his hands on her shoulders to try to steady her, she seized him and clung to him, then sank to the ground, her arms around his back, then his thighs, then his lower legs.

'Robert. *Please.* Stay with me. Stay with me. Stay with me.'

He bent down to her, and putting his hands under her arms he lifted her to her feet. She tried to cling to him again, but he led her gently to an upright chair and put her into it, then pulled up another and sat just before her, leaning forward, his hands straight down before him, his fingers intertwined.

She buried her face in her hands now, and the sobbing continued, but lessened as the moments passed and she began to gather some semblance of control. Then she blew her nose several times on the handkerchief she had been clutching, and wiped the sleeve of her dress across her eyes.

'I'm sorry, Robert. It's my fault. I haven't given you a proper marriage. I haven't been a wife to you, not a real wife to you. I would have liked to have been a real wife in a real marriage.'

She wiped her eyes again, and looked at him directly now, then sighed, the remnants of a sob still there in her breathing. There was a pause of several moments while she gazed at him.

'So really I haven't got anything. You've been my husband in name, but there hasn't been love. Nor respect. Not from you, or anyone else. I don't blame you. As my life has turned out, there's nothing much there to respect.'

She sat now completely still, her head in her hands. Robert crouched down beside her, and reached out to hold her forearms for a moment.

'Don't say that, Sarah. Never say that. It's been my fault, not yours. I've let you down and failed you. You haven't failed me – I've failed you. Please don't say these things. I haven't helped you enough. I haven't helped you.'

But she made no response either to his touch or what he was saying, and when she spoke again her voice had deadened and lowered, her head bowed down.

'I'd rather tell all the truth now. We've never done so before. I wish we had. It's one of so many things that we should have done. You know I've been unfaithful to you, but I don't think you know how much. Well, I've done it whenever the opportunity arose. I've never managed to hold a man for any length of time, but if I had I would never have been the one to break it off. If I could have held on to any of them, I would have done so.'

She shrugged, blew her nose again on her sodden handkerchief, and looked at him again, her whole body trembling and shaking as she did so. She made the same shrugging motion again, then grimaced in a wry, partial smile.

'And I never made a home either. I wanted to make a home for me and for you and for the children, but I never did, except perhaps in the very early days. I never could. It never happened. I wanted to, but I could never do it. We never had a home. The only home I ever had was with my father when I was a child. And that was not ... that was not ...'

She tailed off, and her eyes turned away from him again, as she locked and hugged her arms across her chest.

'Sarah. Don't say those things. Don't talk of failure like that. It's me that's failed. I never tried to reach you. I could have done so much more. I never helped you make a home. You think it's all your fault – it's not. I'm to blame. I never tried enough to make a marriage.'

Please don't say those things about yourself, he thought. Please don't. Please don't drown. Please don't drown.

But she was staring at him, her face open and expressionless and inert. In growing horror he listened to her as the words continued tumbling out, as if she was in therapy, under the effect of some relaxant drug.

'And I've told other people that I don't love you.'Other men. Particularly men. But other people too. Church people. I've told them that I don't love you. That I've never bonded with you.'

She reached across to him, and took his hands in hers. She had started to cry again, but silently, the tears running down her face as she gazed at him.

'I'm sorry for all that, Robert. Truly sorry. I half believed it was true – I half believed that I really didn't love you. But I did. I *did* love you. And you're my husband. I wish I was all sorts of things that I'm not. But please stay with me. Alice must be stronger than me. Everyone is stronger than me. She'll cope. I can't cope. I can't be alone. Stay with me. *Please* stay with me.'

He took his hands away from her, but slowly and gently, and

when he responded his voice was decisive but unemphatic. He heard himself speak as a third person would have heard him, and the words that he heard held a firmness and focus that he now by no means felt inside.

'No, Sarah. I've made up my mind to leave. It's what I need to do. I see a chance of having things I thought had passed me by. I haven't been happy. I want to go. I've failed, you've failed, both of us have failed. Me just as much as you. At this moment – certainly more so. Certainly more than you. But I'm still going to go. I'm too much in love with Alice to let this pass.'

She stared at him still. Then, 'Please understand. Please don't close the door on me. I can't manage my life without you. We've been together all this time. We've had two daughters together. We've been through so much over the years. Don't leave me. Please don't leave me.'

He got to his feet, and as he did so she first reached her hands out to him, then let them drop hopelessly at her side. She said no more, but looked at him and was silent.

'Sarah – Peter Rutherford will be in touch with your lawyers. You can have the house, of course, and half of the money. And the car, and half the pension and everything else you need. I'll make sure you always have enough, and Peter will keep an eye on you as well. I'll make separate provision for the two girls out of whatever I keep. You'll be all right. You've got your church, and your friends there, and Sophie of course.'

He went towards the door, then turned and looked back at her as she sat there, her hands now again held over her eyes. Then he went up to his bedroom, threw some clothes into a suitcase and took this out to his car before going back into the house again.

He found her squatting on the floor, hugging herself, her head bowed, tears running down her face.

'Goodbye, Sarah,' he said. 'I understand. I know how much I'm hurting you. I wish I wasn't. I wish I didn't have to. For all that we've done to each other, it's me now that's at fault. We should never have married. It's difficult to remember now why we did,

but we did, and, as you say, we've been with each other for a very
long time. We've occupied a major portion of each other's lives.
And had our children together. In years to come, try to remember
some of the good things. I will. I can promise you that.'

He stood staring at her, but she made no response, nor raised her
head, and after a moment or so he turned and left the house. He felt
in him a curious blankness of emotion and sensation. He was
leaving his wife of almost twenty-five years, and he realised that
his heart was empty of any feeling whatsoever.

He had reached his point of exhaustion when she'd invented
that evil story about him, he thought. When she'd told other people
that he'd had a sexual relationship with his daughters. That was the
moment. When he'd realised she was capable of inventing
something as malicious as that – and did so to tell the tale to
Hilden-Parker, in an attempt to win sympathy, or martyrdom, or
whatever she was doing. That was the real treachery. Whatever he
said to her, they both knew the degree of failure in that. The real
treachery was hers.

Alice was only one part of the truth. He was not leaving Sarah
just because he'd fallen in love with Alice. No one should do what
Sarah had done: the accusation of sexual dealings with his
daughters. That wasn't waving and drowning. That wasn't a
pathetic inadequacy of ability or fortune.

That was a degradation of the soul.

Chapter Fifty-One

'Well, I think Dad's a pig,' said Sophie, munching on her peanut butter sandwich. 'But then I always have thought he was a pig, so nothing much has changed. And a filthy one too. A filthy degenerate. If you knew some of the things that—'

'No, Sophie. No. Not now.' Sarah held up her hand to stop her, then looked across the kitchen table and tried to smile. She smoothed a stray strand of hair from off her forehead, then left her hand supporting her cheek, her elbow on the table.

'Not now, my dear. Somehow I haven't got much appetite for that at the moment. Or any longer, actually. I don't think it's true, Sophie, is it? It's not true, and you know you really must stop these stories and fantasies. They're bad for you, and they're bad for all of us who listen to them, and allow you to tell them to us without correcting you.

'Perhaps you need some help, Sophie – some psychiatric help of some sort. We should think about it. I'm sure we can find the money for it, if it would be a way of helping you find a little more confidence and happiness. Daddy and I would both help. I think we should consider it very closely.'

Sophie gave an attempt at a facial expression of injured, innocent, abused virtue, gave a little laugh, and took a final mouthful of her sandwich. Then she sucked the last traces of the peanut butter from off her fingertips, and flicked them dry and clean afterwards in her habitual delicate, genteel little gesture.

'I don't think that'll be necessary, thank you very much. I certainly wouldn't accept help from my father, even if I needed it. He's abandoned his home, he's abandoned his family, he's gone off with another woman, and I never want to see him again.'

She gave her sarcastic little laugh once more, then went to the fridge to get herself a large glass of milk, removing and pouring the bottle carefully, so as to ensure she secured all the cream from off the top. She came back to the table, holding her glass in her hand.

'You don't know what he gets up to. No idea at all. And the fact that he's gone off with a girl young enough to be his daughter seems to me to be exactly in character. Just what I've always said. That's what he likes – young girls. The younger the better. You ask his two daughters what he—'

Sarah buried her head in her hands, then looked up again at Sophie, and screamed, 'For Christ's sake, Sophie! For Christ's sake! Stop. *Stop!*'

The totally unexpected, unheard-of oath from Sarah, and the coarse, screamed delivery of it, seemed to shock and surprise them both equally. They gazed at each other in astonishment, both saying nothing for some moments. Then Sarah continued, this time in a more familiar, quieter voice, though her words and her determination were something Sophie had never before experienced from her.

'I mean it, Sophie. Stop it. Just . . . stop it. I've allowed this sort of thing for far too long. I'm trying to face the reality of my situation now, perhaps for the first time in my life, and this lying and falsehood from you doesn't help you or me. It doesn't help at all. I've got to find some courage. And some truth and some guts. You must pull yourself together, Sophie. You're a bad, vicious child when you say these things. Stop it. Stop it!'

Sophie was now flushed a bright pink, and she faced her mother in fury, her hands thrust deep into her dungarees pockets.

'A child, am I? It's not me that's the child, it's you, you stupid woman. You're the child. The bad, vicious child. You and your little cuddles with people. Cuddles with men. Leading them on. Trying to get them to have you, then sneaking on them to your foul prayer group. You're like a schoolgirl, that's what you are. A dirty little schoolgirl, with a crush on the vicar. The poor sod.'

Sarah was staring at her in horror, her mouth open, her eyes glazed with the ugliness of what she was hearing. Sophie stood there, her expression full of contempt and scorn, her eyes twinkling now with the pleasure of what she was doing.

'Still – it's in the family, isn't it? Your disgusting old father – you know what he does? He comes into my bedroom at night and looks at me with my nightie pulled up. You know that? He has a good look at my rude bits. And plays with himself while he's doing it.' She thrust out her groin and made an obscene pumping movement in front of it with her hand. She laughed, her eyes shining and her little white teeth and dimples showing.

'Surprised, are we? I don't expect so somehow. He's been doing that sort of thing for years, hasn't he? To you. Or *with* you, I should say. How lovely for you both. You're made for each other.'

She laughed again, and went back to the fridge to pour herself some more milk.

'Come on, Mum!' she cried 'Don't look so shocked. You look like you've swallowed something nasty. Cheer up! We were having a nice truth session together, remember? You were about to send me off to a psychiatrist, remember? But it's you who ought to go really, isn't it? That's what I told the newspaperman today, when I had my little talk with him. The man from the *News of the World*.'

She walked back across the room, and sat again at the kitchen table. She grinned at her mother happily.

'That was all news to me, that one was. The black man on the beach; the caution from the police for gross indecency. Sounds a bit of all right to me.'

She laughed again, this time uproariously, bending over double at the waist in her mirth. She then wiped her eyes with the back of her hand, and had another drink of her milk.

'Oh dear. You are funny, you really are. You really make me

laugh. Not a bit like you seem. Not a bit like you let on. But then nor is Grandpa, is he? It runs in the family.'

She gazed across at her mother, who was still standing there, her face racked with horror. Sophie held her hand out to her, then brought it back.

'Come on, Mum. You look really shocked and hurt. I'm only having a little joke. Just a little laugh. Come on, sit down. You'll make yourself ill. That's what I told the newspaper reporter, actually. That you were not at all well. Quite ill with the worry, I told him. With being abandoned by your husband and all that. Abandoned at this time of your life. And you a churchwoman. Head of the prayer group and close friends with the vicar. A very close friend of the vicar indeed. I told him that.

'He said he quite understood. He said the *News of the World* respected that sort of thing. Wouldn't want to make a mischief in those circumstances, he said, as he's a family man and a churchgoer himself. He was a real gentleman. We had a lovely talk. He asked me all sorts of questions. I'm sure he's going to write a lovely article on it all. Really moving, I expect. I can't wait to read it.'

Sarah put her hands to her face. 'You talked to him? A reporter from the *News of the World*? He asked you questions? He . . . told you? He . . .'

She slumped slowly to the floor and remained there, half lying, half propped against the radiator. She gazed at Sophie, then moaned and shuddered. When the weeping started Sophie got to her feet, and looked down contemptuously, dragging her anorak off the back of her chair and on to her shoulders.

'Oh, pull yourself together,' she said, now taking a bundle of banknotes from out of her mother's handbag and stuffing them into the pocket of her dungarees. 'Pull yourself together, you silly old cow. Show a bit of guts. That's what you were going to do, wasn't it? Show some guts. Courage and truth too, I think you said. You told me. You were going to show a bit of guts. For the first time in your life, I think it was, and I wouldn't disagree with that. Well – show them. Go on!'

Sophie was gone now, and Sarah could hear the front door slam behind her as she left. After ten minutes or so she got to her feet. She went into the little garden at the back of the house, and picked a single yellow bloom from the big Peace rose shrub that stood at the end near the lilac tree. She brought the flower back into the house, went to her bedroom up on the top floor, and laid it down on her dressing-table beside the only photograph she possessed of her mother, whose death those many years ago had left her alone with her father in the Folkestone vicarage, in circumstances not wholly dissimilar from those that Sophie had guessed at.

It was a dive rather than a jump that Sarah took from the bedroom window, and when she landed right down in the basement forecourt, her outstretched arms did little to break her fall.

She died instantly, of course, and it was Sophie who found her there, returning to the house for some purpose that was never divulged.

PART THREE

Chapter Fifty-Two

'Mr *Valiant-for-truth* was taken with a Summons... When he understood it, he called for his Friends, and told them of it. Then said he, "I am going to my Father's, and tho with great Difficulty I am got hither, yet now I do not repent me of all the Trouble I have been at to arrive where I am. *My Sword*, I give to him that shall succeed me in my Pilgrimage, and my *Courage* and *Skill*, to him that can get it. My *Marks* and *Scarrs* I carry with me, to be a witness for me, that I have fought his Battels, who now will be my Rewarder."

'When the Day that he must go hence was come, many accompanied him to the River side, into which, as he went, he said, *"Death, where is thy Sting?"* And as he went down deeper, he said, *"Grave, where is thy Victory?"*

'So he passed over, and the Trumpets sounded for him on the other side.'

There was total silence in the church. As Robert read from the lectern the final few sentences, his voice had started to crack on him, and his throat swell, and he knew that there were tears running down his face. He quickly brushed at them, and stood there still, his head bowed, determined to be completely in control of himself before he returned to his pew.

A few months before she had died, as if in intuition for what was to come, it came to light that Sarah had written a codicil to her Will. In it, she had directed that this particular passage from *The*

Pilgrim's Progress should be read for her at her funeral. As a statement, Robert knew, for what she would have liked her life and death to have been. He would not have guessed that she had so much as known the piece. But she had, and she wanted it read. In her memory.

How I wish I could have filled the church for her, he thought. How I wish that her Mr *Valiant-for-truth* could have been read to a thousand people.

But there were only eleven there in St Matthew's, and apart from Derrick Hilden-Parker, Robert knew none of them.

Douglas Tilton had retired to his bed the moment that Robert had driven down to tell him the news. He had wrapped himself in a blanket, turned to the wall, and seemed to be willing himself to death. Rowena could not be traced. Sophie said she was too upset to come. Sarah had no other family at all.

Chapter Fifty-Three

Sophie sat at the kitchen table in the same chair and the same place as she had been three weeks ago, on the afternoon of her mother's death.

She had in front of her a great heap of magazines and newspapers, out of which she was cutting words and part words and single letters, then pasting them on to a large sheet of writing paper. A can of Diet Coke was beside her, and every so often she took a drink from this, then wiped her mouth with the back of her hand before resuming the work, her tongue stuck out from between her lips, and her heavy, thick eyebrows furrowed in her concentration on what she was doing.

The whole exercise took some considerable time to complete, but when it was done she pushed the magazines and newspapers to one side and looked down with pride at her handiwork. She repasted and patted down one or two of the letters more securely, then read over what she had compiled, a dimpled, prettily happy smile on her pink, healthy cheeks.

Dear Alice Livingstone,

You are a disgusting lustful whore. You have seduced for your pleasure a man who is old enough to be your father, who until now has led a blameless life in the bosom of his family. His wife killed herself because of what you did. Girls like you are a menace to decent people. You are nothing but a common prostitute. His wife was a good, pure woman. You will rot in hell. You will hear from me again.

Sophie put this into an envelope, reflecting that she was particularly pleased with '*a blameless life in the bosom of his family*', which she had cut entire from page three of the *Daily Telegraph*. Then, having checked in the telephone book for the address of Alice's firm, she wrote it on the envelope in block capitals in a deliberately crude and disguised hand. Placing a first-class stamp on it, she then went to make herself a thick peanut butter sandwich, dropped the magazines and newspapers in the big wicker waste-paper basket in the study next door, went out through the front door to put the letter in the box that stood a few yards up the road, then came back into the house and went into the kitchen once more.

Munching her sandwich at the table, she reached out again for the telephone directory. Having found what she was looking for, she then dialled the number of the vicarage at St Matthew's, Wetherby Gardens. It was Mrs Hilden-Parker who answered the telephone, and Sophie's voice, assumed in response, was that of the stricken, grieving orphan in pathetic need of pastoral counselling and succour.

'I'm so sorry to bother you, Mrs Hilden-Parker. It's Sophie here, Sophie Luscombe. We met a couple of years ago. I do hope this is not an inconvenient moment or anything. It's just that . . . it's just that I'm all alone here. In my mother's house. On my own. And I would like so much to . . . Mrs Hilden-Parker, is the vicar there, please? If it's not inconvenient. Only if it's not putting him out. I can easily call another time. It's just that . . . Oh, thank you so much. So much.'

She took another large mouthful of her sandwich, and munched at it whilst waiting to be transferred. When at last Derrick Hilden-Parker came on to the line his voice was so hushed and taut that Sophie could hardly hear him.

'Mr Hilden-Parker? Is that you? Goodness, your voice *is* muffled. It sounds as if you're speaking from under the mattress or something. It's just that I was a little bit disappointed this morning, when the letter you promised me didn't arrive.'

'Sophie . . . Sophie, my dear, could we talk about this again? Just discuss it once more? I'm not a rich man, my dear, and—'

'Oh, Mr Hilden-Parker, I do hope you're not thinking of changing your mind. It's just a little loan I need, that's all it is. Just to tide me over while I recover from the shock of my mother's death. To help get me up and going once more. A little arrangement between friends, in memory of my mother. Think of it in that way.'

'Sophie, it's just that I don't have very much money, my dear. Not very much money at all, and I was wondering if—'

'Mr Hilden-Parker, I want my payment posted tomorrow morning so that it's here on Friday. If you do that everything will be all right. It'll just be a little loan. As I said – to tide me over while I recover from my mother's death. Then we won't need to worry the Bishop, or anything horrid like that.'

Sophie took the last mouthful of her sandwich while she was waiting for the response, then licked and flicked her fingers. She waited for him to speak again, which he did after a long interval, and she was taken aback to find that his voice now had a resilience to it that hadn't been there before.

'If I send you the money, Sophie, I would like the letter back. In fact, I would like the letter back first – then you can have the money. Not as a loan, as a gift. But I want the letter back first. I *must* have the letter back first.'

'That's not what we agreed, Mr Hilden-Parker. That's not what we said.'

'It may not be what we said, but it's what I'm saying now. It's absolutely what I'm saying now.'

There was a pause of several moments while Sophie considered what to do. She decided to threaten him directly, but even listening to her own words she had the sensation of losing control and initiative, and she knew she was making a mistake.

'I think I should go to the Bishop after all, then. I should go to the Bishop with the letter, and show him what you've been up to. I think it's my duty as a Christian, and my duty to my mother's memory. I don't think I have any choice.'

'All right then, Sophie. Go to the Bishop; take the letter to him. If that's what you want to do, go ahead. As a matter of fact, I'll call him first to say that you're coming.'

There was another pause, this for several moments, before Sophie said, 'Oh, Mr Hilden-Parker, this is just silly. Of course you can have your letter! Of course you can. We're both of us stressed and unhappy and saying silly things, because of Mummy's death. We're both so full of grief over that, we can hardly think straight, can we? Either of us. We're both quite numb with the grief of it all, aren't we? Of course you can have your letter. And thank you so much for offering me a little money as a present. I'm going to accept that before we have any more misunderstandings. And we'll make it a little more, shall we? Let's say a thousand pounds more? And then we'll never mention this business again.'

'Bring the letter here, Sophie. You must bring it here, Friday afternoon at four o'clock. The money will be waiting for you, as long as you bring the letter. If there's no letter, there'll be no money.'

Sophie replaced the receiver, and picked at her fingernails while she thought about what had been said.

He shouldn't be let off too lightly. It wouldn't be right. A clergyman like him, letting someone else's wife get all frisky and excited over him. He's supposed to be setting an example to people. Some example.

He must be wondering who actually did send the second letter to Dad, she thought, and grinned at the memory of it, and the hours she had spent in her bedroom at the Battersea flat, cutting and pasting on the floor. It might be as well to get a nice payment out of him on Friday, then call it a day. He's right, she thought. I don't expect he's got much money anyway. May as well take a nice bit now, then let it go.

She suddenly burped, then immediately put her hand to her mouth in her accustomed way, always the little girl with the nice, well-brought-up manners. And as she did so, she had a sudden vision of the formidable Vera Hilden-Parker, and her heart dropped. Perhaps it really would be better to get this out of the way, she thought. Too much potential for getting caught up with her, rather than him. Not an inviting prospect, thought Sophie, who had a feeling that her skills and talents were more promisingly directed as a rule against men than women. Particularly when it came to women like Vera Hilden-Parker.

What a cow, thought Sophie. What an unbelievable cow.

Chapter Fifty-Four

They were back in Peter Rutherford's office, with Alice once more seated on his left, and Robert, huddled and white, opposite her on the other side.

The private investigator, Albert Jenkins, had just been shown into the room to join them, and once the introductions and the handshakes were completed, he was waved by Rutherford to sit at the other end of the table. As he did so, he took from his briefcase two or three neat files, which he laid down before him, and then looked to the other end of the table, his expression polite and passive.

'So, Mr Jenkins,' began Rutherford. 'Regarding the anonymous letter which my client Mr Luscombe here received – the second anonymous letter – I gather that the fingerprint and DNA tests have been completed. Is that correct? What do you have to tell us?'

'Yes, sir. I have the results here. Would you like me to circulate copies to all those present? Or would you like me to present the findings orally in the first instance?'

'Orally in the first instance, Mr Jenkins. Orally, please,' replied Peter Rutherford, then, fearing that his repetition and tone of dry humour might be construed by Mr Jenkins to be sarcastic, he beamed a reassuring and warm smile to him down the table, and gestured to him to continue.

'Well, I can confirm that the position is this. The fingerprints are not those of Mr Hilden-Parker, and nor did the DNA tests suggest that the – er – other – er – source of evidence derives from him either. My contact within the Hilden-Parker household on whom I earlier reported, the cook-housekeeper, was able to provide other materials on which we were able to undertake our tests, and we are clear of the evidence. Mr Hilden-Parker did not send that letter. It's not what I was expecting, to be quite truthful to you. But it's certainly the case.'

Robert raised his head for a moment and nodded, then looked across at Alice. 'He said as much, as I told you. He sent the first letter without any doubt at all, but he was adamant that he was not involved in the second. I believed him. I'm sure you're right,' he said, turning to Jenkins.

'Yes, sir. We are right. I can assure you. We're right.'

There was a silence for a few moments. Then Peter Rutherford said to Jenkins. 'So – what do you propose? Is there any other line of thought you could share with us?'

'Yes, sir. We know now who sent the letter.' Jenkins turned towards Robert, and grimaced awkwardly. 'I beg your pardon, sir. I fear this may be painful. Forgive me, sir, but I'm afraid it was your daughter Sophie. Your older daughter, sir.'

Robert stared at him, and said nothing whatsoever. Nor did the others, and for a minute or two there was a taut, embarrassed silence. No one moved either, until Alice first put her head in her hands, then dropped them again, her face frowning in what looked like resolute, decisive anger.

Then Robert said to Jenkins, with growing incredulity in his voice, '*Sophie?* What on earth are you talking about? Why do you think it's Sophie? She's my child, for God's sake! Writing that disgusting letter to me? Sophie?'

'I'm sorry, sir. It's the fingerprints, you see. We've checked, then double-checked them. They're hers, all right sir. They're your daughter's.'

'How do you know they're hers?' said Robert, as much to prolong the conversation as anything else, as he tried desperately to settle himself down again. 'How on earth can you know?'

'Because, sir ... because the police have them on record. After that incident at the estate agents' office where she was working a year or so ago. And I have a source at the police who confirmed to me that—'

'So you suspected her anyway? You already thought it might be her?'

'Yes, Mr Luscombe. I had reasons to suspect that she was the possible originator of the letter. Once we had eliminated Mr Hilden-Parker from the enquiries.'

'What reasons? How could you have possibly thought that it was her?'

'Because, sir ... because there is another matter also. At the Hilden-Parkers' house. The vicarage. I know from my source that voices have been raised, and certain conversations continued in my source's hearing. Miss Sophie has been involved with putting certain threats and pressure on Mr Hilden-Parker. She's holding the other letter which was sent to you anonymously, sir. Two or three years ago, from the vicarage. And she has demanded money from him. Blackmail, sir. Failing which she's told him that she'll report the incident to the Bishop. And if she does so, my information is that this will cause great difficulties, because of the previous incident of this kind at the Hilden-Parkers' previous parish, which the Bishop had to deal with on that occasion as well.'

Robert realised that he had been staring at Mr Jenkins for some moments since he had finished speaking, and that they were all waiting for his response.

'Blackmail?' he said, so softly that the others heard it almost as a whisper. 'Blackmail? Sophie? Are you sure?'

'Yes, sir. I'm afraid so. She goes to the vicarage tomorrow afternoon to deliver the letter back to Mr Hilden-Parker in return for her money. Or so she thinks. Actually the police will be there, sir. To arrest her. My source, sir. She inadvertently overheard the arrangements being made. The police have been at the vicarage and interviewed both Mr Hilden-Parker and Mrs Hilden-Parker.'

Again there was a silence, and Robert looked around the table at the others in turn.

'Can't I stop this?' he demanded. 'Isn't there anything I can do? Why don't I go down to the Hilden-Parkers' and try to straighten the whole thing out? Explain that Sophie isn't well – in shock probably from her mother's death. Still in shock, and worried about the future and her financial position, I expect. Actually, I wouldn't be at all surprised if Hilden-Parker hadn't misunderstood the whole business. Got completely the wrong end of the stick. Misunderstood totally what Sophie was saying to him. I imagine that's precisely what's happened, actually. He's a very stupid man. Gone off in a panic, thinking the worst, when he'd simply failed to grasp what had actually been said to him.'

He looked around the table again, and then back to Peter Rutherford, who shifted uneasily in his chair, and nodded to Mr Jenkins to respond himself.

'No, sir,' he said. 'No – there's been no misunderstanding, Mr Luscombe. I think you'll find she was quite clear and straightforward in her demands to Mr Hilden-Parker. And then there's the letter, sir. The second anonymous letter that was sent to you. That was hers, sir. We have the evidence – fingerprints, and a strand of hair. There's absolutely no doubt about it. That letter was hers.'

Peter Rutherford now leant forward in his chair, and turned his gaze directly to Robert.

'Robert – I don't believe there's very much you can do at this point. Or should do. What we must all be extremely careful of is any suggestion that you're interfering with the police. Blackmail is a very serious offence, as you well know, and affairs must now be allowed to run their course. Do please understand that completely. And anyway, you don't really have very much choice in that, you know. It's the Hilden-Parkers who control all that side of things now, not you or us. If Sophie is arrested, then we'll have to do all we can at that stage to help her. That's the time to do it. And she'll need a good deal of help. Assuming of course after all this that you still . . .'

347

'Yes, of course I do. She's still my daughter. She's mine. Of course I'll help her.'

There was silence; then Alice, who had said so little in the meeting, turned to Peter.

'Do you think perhaps that covers everything, Peter? Perhaps we could let Mr Jenkins go at this point. I suspect we've covered all the relevant ground. I'm sure Robert needs some time on his own to absorb this awful news. I think that's best, and then we're here for you, Robert, whenever you want us. You must call either Peter or me whenever you want to see us again. Shall we leave it like that? I think we should.'

She turned now to Albert Jenkins and smiled, and in the bustle of the chairs being pushed back, and files being picked up, and the formulaic statements of prognosis for the weather, Peter reflected that it might be better, and sooner rather than later, to tell Alice that all the one hundred plus members of the law firm regarded her affair with Robert not so much as rumour as established fact. And that he would find it a good deal less embarrassing if she would simply announce it, so that they wouldn't have to go on with this farce of prevarication with her. But he was showing Jenkins to the lift now, and he missed witnessing the hand she laid on his arm as Robert gathered his papers slowly together and prepared to go. And neither would he have guessed what was actually in Alice's mind.

Please don't misunderstand me, Robert, she thought, as she did so. Please don't misunderstand what I feel. Please God I have the strength to do now what has to be done. I know what has to be done.

But her fear was misplaced. She knew what had to be done, but Robert did so too. There were no misunderstandings of any sort between them.

Chapter Fifty-Five

Sophie had sensed that something was wrong the moment she arrived at the house. Derrick Hilden-Parker was too confident when he opened the door; gloating almost in his manner as he took her through to the study, eager in his anticipation of some occurrence or other.

In the time that followed her arrest she cursed herself for not simply walking away at that point. She could have simply handed him the letter, and laughed when he tried to give her the money, saying that it was all just a misunderstanding and that the last thing she had wanted was to imply any threat to him, or anything of that kind. What made her pound her fists on her head in rage at the memory of it was that she could see that the door through from the study of the adjoining passage was not fully shut. A warning instinct had struck her then to back away.

But she hadn't. There was the money in front of her now, piled on his desk, all in nice new twenty-pound notes. She signed the receipt he was insisting on, and reached for the money and took it almost before she knew what she was doing. And then it was all too late.

Sophie gathered the spittle in the front of her mouth and spat at Hilden-Parker as she was led away, and as he wiped down the lapel of his jacket where it had landed he looked at her with a surprised, gentle half-smile.

'I don't know why you bothered,' she shouted. 'Why did you bother with her?'

He held up his hand, and the police sergeant stopped, waiting for him to speak. There was a silence, and then, as if wholly bemused, he said, 'Because, Sophie . . . Because . . .'

'Because what? Lost your tongue, have you? Too frightened to speak? Well, I'll tell you what I think. You should have let her go. She's nothing but a stinking cow.' Hilden-Parker stared at her, his mouth open. Sophie grinned, then added: 'Your wife, you fool. Your *wife*. Who did you think I was talking about? Your girlfriend? My mother?'

'I must take her along now, sir,' said the police sergeant, and started to move again towards the door.

But Sophie continued, 'Did you think I didn't realise that it was your wife who sent that letter, two years ago? That's what I can't understand. Why did you protect her? Why did you pretend it was you?'

And then they were gone, and Hilden-Parker could hear the police car's engine start and move off down the street.

How do I know why? he thought as he set off for the staircase, and Vera's bedroom above, where she was waiting for him. How do I know why? If I don't understand it, how could Sophie? Vera did these things. It was something within her. Something she couldn't control. Impossible to explain that to other people. The Bishop, all those years ago. That time then. He never would have understood. It had been easier to take the blame himself. Easier and fairer. You have to share in a marriage. Good times and bad times. The rough with the smooth.

So why had he done it?

Love? Loyalty? Habit? Weakness? Fear? Some of all those things, perhaps. But mostly something else. Gratitude. For the fact that she had spent her life with him. With him.

For I'm not exactly a catch, he reminded himself. There's not much there, at the end of the day. Not really. Not much there in me at all.

Chapter Fifty-Six

Robert Luscombe, the three other executive directors, the three non-executive directors and the Company Secretary were together now in the boardroom.

Coffee cups were in their hands, and they were gathered in two or three groups, uncharacteristically silent and tense. Above them the large portrait of Arthur Ewing's grandfather, Sir Colin Ewing, hung alone, in pride of position, on the wall at the near end of the room. A huge rectangular mahogany table stood in the middle, surrounded by twenty matching Hepplewhite chairs. On the side wall, opposite the three great windows facing out over the Thames, were more portraits, each of a deceased or retired member of the Ewing family. And at the other end wall, opposite the portrait of Sir Colin, was displayed, on a substantial Victorian plinth, a bronze bust of George Ewing, Arthur's great-great-grandfather, the founder of the family Bank.

All of the directors, including the executives, who had not seen Robert in recent days, had one by one touched his arm as they came in, or murmured a word or two of condolence in his ear. The news of Sarah's suicide had been widely reported in all the newspapers; scandalously so, and with considerable background flavour and detail in the *News of the World*. There had been, inevitably, a salacious interest in the story amongst the Bank's staff, and there was a good deal of curiosity in the eyes of the directors as they saw

Robert already standing there in the room as they came in.

He was most strikingly pale, and looked as if he had lost at least half a stone in weight, but he held himself upright, and looked controlled, and his expression carried the clear message that he was back, and still a force, and not to be sentimentalised.

An ornate and famously valuable Dutch clock, which stood on a Queen Anne table in the corner of the room, struck the half hour. Immediately, the coffee cups were replaced on the trays on the sideboard, a steward removed them from the room, and the directors made their way to their places at the table. The Company Secretary sat, as by tradition, alone at a mahogany writing table, which was placed at an angle to the board table, and slightly behind the Chairman's left side.

Robert moved to his place, the directors opened their folders, and there in each were copies of the agenda, the minutes of the previous meeting, and spare copies too of the various papers that had already been distributed in support of the individual agenda items.

Amongst these papers was the report which was to constitute the final agenda item; the Overview of the Poonjee River Dam Project Financing, prepared by Colin Ewing, who would be called in to join the meeting at that time.

There was unmistakable tension in the room at that moment, for the Poonjee paper had been distributed the previous evening in individual sealed envelopes by the Bank's own messenger, and all those who had read it were fully aware of the significance of what had been written. Or, as the majority of them sensed, *not* written, for the version of the report that Colin had finally submitted for this meeting was spare, and cold, and although in it were no accusations of misconduct as such, underlying it was a sense of matters left purposely unresolved.

Even Robert had a sense of unease and uncertainty about what was going to happen. Out of the office almost all the time in the last ten days or so in the aftermath of Sarah's death, he had not seen Colin at all to discuss what he was going to say. But for Robert the unease was mostly the irritating and unaccustomed sensation of being out of touch, and unable to orchestrate the consequences of what was to unfold. For the others it was something different, and the brittle attempts at humour around the table were a mark of the anxiety amongst them all as they waited for the meeting to begin.

Then Arthur Ewing came into the room, and despite the ponderous slowness of his movements as he went to his seat, they saw that his expression, in so far as the mask-like legacy of his illness would allow, was relaxed and good-spirited, and to some extent the atmosphere in the room eased at the sight of this.

Arthur laughed as he said something to his secretary, who had followed him in with a file, and he laid a hand on Robert's arm, who nodded and smiled at him in response. He gave a cheerful greeting to one of the non-executives, Lord Strathmere, who had missed the previous two meetings, following some riding accident or other, then he addressed the Board.

'Good morning, everyone. Good morning, and we must rattle along as there are a number of matters to deal with. Most importantly, of course, agenda items three and four, which cover the debate we must have on the half-year results. Specifically the interim dividend, and then the Finance Director's report on the revaluation of our property portfolio, and the provisional decisions we will need to make in the light of this on the carrying values on our balance sheet.'

Arthur looked down again at his agenda.

'And the final agenda item too, of course, which I'm very much looking forward to, although I have some doubts as to whether I should have allowed it on to the agenda. It will, however, give one or two of the non-executive directors the opportunity to hear and watch my son Colin more thoroughly than perhaps they have had the chance of doing so far.'

And as he turned now to the Company Secretary, and called for the minutes to be dealt with, and the matters arising from these to be called, Arthur's eye caught, for the briefest of moments, the gaze of Robert, who was sitting, as was traditional, immediately beside him at his right hand. And the look there, Robert thought, was one of conscious anticipation for the battle to be joined, and irony, and challenging, brutal engagement, and the sight of that alarmed him.

For Robert knew that, if handled badly, there was danger in the situation. The slighted, unloved son might well prove most unexpectedly tenacious and determined. He wanted Arthur to approach the moment with caution and awareness. For all their sakes. If there had been misconduct, then it would have to be properly dealt with. Whoever had done it. But if Colin was there to try to make trouble, whatever the circumstances, then this too needed careful and tactful control, particularly in front of the non-executive directors.

The problem for Robert was that, because of his recent absence, he had very little idea at all of what Colin was going to come up with. He had seen the report before anyone else of course, but only about a day before, and he had been dismayed to find that it had already been accepted as an agenda item – on the specific instructions, the Company Secretary told Robert, of the Chairman. Colin had been to his father and asked that it should, and Arthur, for whatever reason, had agreed, despite the fact that matters of this sort were traditionally dealt with by Robert's private committee.

Perhaps Arthur had done this to preserve Robert, so soon after Sarah's death, from the need to take on something so sensitive. But possibly – and this was more likely, Robert thought – there was another motivation altogether; one that Robert dreaded most. If his son intended to challenge him, then Arthur meant to meet that challenge absolutely head on. And if the boy was humiliated and scorned by the public confrontation that he had invited, then so be it. He would get what was coming to him. He had brought it on himself, and if he was bruised by the experience, then that might be a very good thing.

It was exactly this that Robert thought he saw in Arthur Ewing's eyes when he came into the boardroom. It was exactly what he didn't want to happen. Partly because he was in no fit state himself to do the clearing up of the bits and pieces afterwards. And partly because he didn't want the Bank, on the threshold now of some promising developments and opportunities, to be diverted by a quarrel of this sort.

But it was all too late now, and they had already voted on the interim dividend, and debated what to do with the balance-sheet valuation of their property portfolio, and Robert's cautious, prudent view had won the day on that.

Now Colin was being ushered into the room by the Company Secretary, and sat in the empty seat at the head of the far end of the table, immediately facing his father, and facing too the portrait of his namesake, his great-grandfather Sir Colin Ewing.

Robert looked down the table at him, and noticed that Colin's clothes were much less flamboyant than they usually were. His suit was quiet and dark and of an understated, nondescript cut. His starched blue shirt and foulard tie, together with his neat haircut, and the absence of the absurd bright red braces, gave him, in Robert's eyes at least, a quite unexpected aura of competence, and professionalism. He liked what he saw.

There was a silence as the directors put in front of them Colin's twenty-page report and fingered and leafed at it. While this was going on Arthur Ewing inclined his head to hear some whispered comment from the Company Secretary, then stared down the table at his son, who sat there, hands folded together on the table in front of him, looking down at the front page of his own copy.

'It's customary, I believe,' Arthur said, 'to thank the manager who has prepared the compliance and security audit report, and to congratulate him on his efforts. I do so now. Thank you. Congratulations on your efforts.

'This is, however, a rather unusual case for several reasons. In the first place you made a particular request to me that we should disregard our normal procedures and bring your report directly here to the board rather than through the Deputy Chairman's committee. I agreed, but I shall want to feel, at the end of this, completely satisfied that your request was well founded. Secondly,

I find that the report itself, now that we have seen it, is an unusually undetailed and unhelpful document. I'll need your explanations for that. And thirdly, we have the odd position here that the report that you were actually asked to do – on the South India Region overall – has not yet been completed. We'll need to understand the reasons for that as well.

'However, rightly or wrongly, we have accepted your report as an agenda item, and I invite you now to present it. And I ask you to do so in a succinct and articulate manner, and strictly to the point. Our non-executive directors have, no doubt, further engagements today to attend to, and we can give you no longer than thirty minutes to complete what you have to say. So I would ask you to keep it short.'

Robert found himself wincing at the rudeness and aggression of this statement, and when he glanced down the table he saw that Colin had flushed, and there were beads of sweat now on his forehead which, reaching into his pocket for his handkerchief, he wiped away. There was another short silence while Colin seemed to collect himself, and then he began to speak, looking first at his father, then around the table at the other directors.

'My report breaks down, as you've seen, into several sections. Part One deals with the conduct of the Bank's officers in India itself. I'll wish to discuss the relationship between the Bank and one of the major contractors on the Poonjee project, Prasad & Prasad, to whom we lent a good deal of money. I wish also to comment on the conduct of the Bank's officers with officials of the Government of India.

'Part Two looks at the construction of the banking consortium formed to finance the Poonjee project, and the method by which the proportionate breakdown of the consortium between its constituent members was set.'

As he talked, Robert watched him with a growing sense of security and confidence. He had never seen Colin so coolly self-possessed, and he admired him for it. And wondered at it, after the brutally insulting introduction he had received from his father.

He's a strong boy, Robert thought. He's an unexpectedly strong boy, and he looks as if he believes his moment has come. I don't know what he's going to produce, but the next few minutes are going to be extremely interesting. He's on top of himself, and he's in control, and his father failed to frighten him off.

'Part Three . . .' Colin was saying '. . . covers the effects of the Poonjee financing contract on the profile and market capitalisation of the Bank, and the resultant benefit to directors and senior staff, while Part Four examines the means this Board took to achieve individually the maximum benefit from the arrangements.'

Lord Strathmere turned his back on Colin, and facing Arthur Ewing said, 'And I, for one, am more than a little confused about this final item in the report. I've no idea what it could possibly mean. The report . . .' and he held it up, as if it was a piece of soiled clothing '. . . the report, if I may say so, is rather less than instructive on the subject. Rather less than helpful. I say so with the deepest respect. But I have no idea what your son is talking about, Arthur. No idea at all.'

'Then perhaps we should wait to find out, Peter,' said Robert. 'Don't you think it might be appropriate to give Colin a chance to say what he wants to say, whatever it might be? Isn't that rather the point of it all? Shall we give him a chance?'

And as he spoke, Robert noticed that his Welsh accent, in his irritation with Peter Strathmere, had accentuated, as it always did when he was angry, into a caricature of the boy from the Valleys, and he was not entirely displeased that it had. Robert, secure in his success, drew pleasure in the distancing of himself from those whom he considered his theoretical social superiors, but demonstrably his intellectual inferiors. And a very good example of this was before him in Lord Strathmere, whom Arthur had appointed to the Board entirely because he thought he could be trusted to support him in whatever he wanted his support on.

Strathmere turned to Robert to answer, but Colin was already speaking again, to Robert's pleasure without any reference to Strathmere's interruption, and still composed and cool. And more articulate than Robert had ever heard him.

'If I could ask you to turn to Part One of the report,' Colin said, 'and the overview of what happened in India itself. I would remind the Board that the Bank had two distinct areas of interest in India over the Poonjee Dam arrangements.

'First, with our twenty percent interest in the financing consortium, and our special experience and skills in the Indian market, we acted as the lead negotiators for the consortium with the Government of India officials in the securing of the financing contract, and the subsequent terms of it.

'Secondly, and unconnected with the fact that we were members of the Poonjee funding consortium, we supplied debt to Prasad & Prasad. Very substantial sums are involved in this – we agreed a facility for them equivalent in sterling to fifteen million pounds. We secured this by hypothecating the cash flow from the Prasads' Government contract, but the interest terms we levied, at only one and a half per cent over the Federal Interbank rate, was perhaps as much as one and a half per cent *under* the market rate for such a transaction.

'The resultant loss of interest received to the Bank is in excess of two hundred thousand pounds per annum, until the debt is repaid at five years. The total sum involved in loss of income is in excess of one million pounds.'

Tim Landesbury, one of the other non-executive directors, a Conservative politician who had at one time been in the Cabinet, had been flicking through the report as Colin had been speaking, reading well ahead of the section on which Colin was trying now to provide his commentary.

He now glanced at his watch, closed the report, pushed it out in front of him and said, 'To speed this process up a little, Colin, I see at the bottom of your second page that Mr Nerappan set this interest rate to match an offer the Prasads had already received from Javed & National. You talk about the market rate for this transaction – well, there it is, surely. The market rate is what people are prepared to sell at and buy at. There it is. Javed & National established the market rate. They offered to sell debt at that rate, and the Prasad & Prasad people were prepared to pay that rate to buy it.'

As Colin started to reply, Landesbury held his hand up, and continued: 'Yes, yes, I know what you're going to say, Colin. I appreciate that there's a suggestion that Nerappan was in some way outmanoeuvred or duped by Mohammed Javed in this. Here it is, you say so in your report. That may or may not be the case, but to make the point again, this is exactly the sort of issue that Robert's Deputy Chairman's committee is there to look into. That's why it was set up.'

Arthur Ewing nodded. 'Certainly,' he said. 'Precisely. All this should be dealt with by Robert's committee. And Tim's comments lead me to say something else. This entire part of the report – and you go on to mention some tittle-tattle about us bribing the Government of India officials on behalf of the consortium, and Nerappan being involved with something similar on behalf of the Prasads, or whatever it was – all this section seems to be based on a lot of hearsay and gossip. All totally unsubstantiated, of course. And it's particularly based, and this I resent and deplore very much indeed, on giving credence to anonymous letters, which some buffoon has been feeding you with. Vicious, half-baked, recriminatory anonymous letters. This Bank does not deal on the basis of anonymous letters. I can assure you of that. I'm absolutely appalled at the idea that you think it might.'

'Hear, hear,' muttered Lord Strathmere. 'Quite disgraceful. Disgraceful.'

At this, Robert turned to Arthur and said, 'Of course we can look at all this at my committee, Arthur, and we'll do so. But I want now to hear Colin through. I want to hear all he has to say – I believe we should. I don't take the same view as you do as to his reaction to the letters he received. I believe he was sensible to take them seriously, and to see where their trail took him. The letters appear in some respects to have misled him. I'm not, however, convinced that they misled him entirely.'

Strathmere looked across at Robert and said, 'That's not the point, Robert. With great respect. The point in my view is that—'

'May I move on?'

There was a look on Colin's face as he spoke of such resolve and purpose that Robert felt almost amused by it. The school fat boy suddenly become Head Prefect. The joker suffused by *gravitas*. Robert felt at that moment emphatically supportive of him. Keep going, boyo, he thought. Don't lose your flow and your nerve. Keep going.

As if he could hear him, Colin said again, 'May I move on?'

His father nodded slightly, and made a waving motion with the back of his hand, in a gesture of impatient assent.

'I'd like to progress now to the second area; the issue of how the banking consortium to finance the Poonjee project was put together, and how the proportionate share of it was arranged by its leader, the Chicago and Illinois Trust.

'The Board will see from the report that I had a meeting in New York with Mr Marty Schwab, a partner of Rosenbaum Siegel Schneider & Schwab. They are, for those of you who don't know, the New York law firm that represents the Chicago and Illinois Trust in these dealings. I went there – and I concede the point – because it was suggested to me by the person who was sending me the anonymous letters that I should . . .' Colin held his hand up as Lord Strathmere started to say something to him, then continued '. . . and I'm very glad that I did so, for I learnt from Mr Schwab some details of our dealings over the consortium that I'd previously suspected of being the case, but didn't know for sure.

'What I learnt was this: that we'd secured a place in the consortium by putting certain pressures, and it would seem unethical pressures, on the Chicago and Illinois people. Also that . . .'

As Colin was speaking, Robert watched Arthur Ewing for a moment, and saw that he had shifted his position so that he was sitting now slightly sideways to the table, gazing down at his hands as he tried to push them out of sight, the tremor in them that of an old man incessantly rolling a pill. But he was frowning now in his concentration at what Colin was saying, and Robert wondered how he would react.

'I don't understand from the wording of your report exactly what you mean by that,' interrupted the third non-executive director, a retired but moderately well-known industrialist, whose wife, a lady-in-waiting to one of the more minor royals, was an old friend of Arthur Ewing's.

'No, I don't understand what you're driving at, old fellow,' repeated Tom Houghton. 'I can't quite follow. Nor in what you go on to say in your report – that not only did we get into the consortium by threatening CIT, but we then managed to get our position in it increased by more of the same. I can't see what you're driving at, old boy. I don't understand what you're saying.' Houghton looked away to Arthur Ewing as he was speaking this last sentence, his back to Colin, grinning his yellow-toothed smile as he did so, anxious, as Robert perceived, to be making emphatically clear where his support and loyalties lay.

'I'll follow through on your question in a moment if I may, Mr Houghton,' said Colin. 'I want first to summarise the whole report, and then draw the conclusions from it that I feel I have to make.

'My belief is that we were so keen to be participants in the Poonjee financing that we transgressed the normal boundaries of acceptable business conduct to get what we wanted. And many would say perhaps that the proof of the pudding is in the eating. Which is what the final two parts of my report are designed to show: the point which I assume Mr Houghton was attempting to make.'

At this Houghton turned to face Colin, the banal, mirthless, yellow-toothed smile still on his face, but a look there now of puzzled resentment as well.

'Because our inclusion,' Colin said, 'as major players in the Poonjee consortium, and then the success of our consortium in winning the Government of India's contract, has had, as we all know, a most significant effect on the Bank's results, and thereby our Stock Market rating and consequently our market capitalisation.

'Let's start with our share price. Poonjee, and all the favourable publicity that surrounded it, served to put the Bank's shares up by eleven per cent, as you know, increasing our market capitalisation from one billion three fifty pounds or thereabouts to approaching one billion five. That was a very significant increase for our shareholders, who in recent years have not had a particularly satisfactory experience with our results, compared to those of our main competitors. We all know this to be true, I imagine. The City and the financial press certainly do.'

There was an almost imperceptible stir around the room at this, and several of the directors turned to glance at Arthur Ewing, as if hoping for a lead from him as to how they should respond. But Arthur said nothing, and remained looking down at his hands, which were now locked tightly together.

'And this is where I now want to be a little more explicit than I was in my report,' Colin was continuing. 'I said there that I proposed to examine the benefits of the Poonjee contract as they came through to the directors and the senior staff, and then the steps, if any, that the Board took to maximise those benefits for individual gain.

'And on that issue, I have first an argument to put to you all on the way that the Board handled and accounted for the Poonjee royalty income from the Government of India. The profits of the deal, if you like.

'You remember what the arrangements were. The World Bank lent India two billion US dollars, which has to be repaid, together with rolled-up interest, in twenty years' time. That will make approaching four billion dollars that India will have to produce at that time. And to defray the risk of them not doing so, the World Bank has provided for a consortium of international banks – our consortium – to underwrite the entire amount, in return for a royalty paid to the consortium by the Government of India of one and a half per cent per annum.

'Our share of this royalty amounts to comfortably over seven million dollars every year of the twenty-year span. And that income, in this first year of its receipt, has added over seven per cent to our profits before tax. Hence the good press, and the rise in our share price.'

Robert's arms were folded in that familiar position of concentration of his, and he was staring directly down the table at Colin. But Colin's eyes were all the time on his father, who was still in the same pose, slightly sideways onto the table, looking down, engrossed in thought. The other directors were in general gazing straight down at the papers in front of them, though Houghton, in particular, was continually turning his head to Arthur, waiting for his cue on how to respond.

Only Landesbury of the three non-executives was looking directly at Colin as he continued speaking, and Landesbury, thought Robert, might well be the only one of the three who grasped the true significance of what was being said.

'Well – my concern is that we have not taken proper heed about the risk of India defaulting on their repayment of the three or four billion dollars when the twenty years are up,' said Colin. 'If they do default, then the underwriters will have to provide the money for the World Bank of course: *within forty-eight hours*. Our share of that would be roughly five hundred million pounds at current exchange rates. That might not quite wipe us out, but it would certainly do the next best thing. We would be very badly damaged by it indeed.

'There are two issues here, in my opinion,' he continued. 'And it's worth emphasising that both would have reduced substantially the profit taken from the Poonjee deal in our annual accounts. And thus brought our share price and market value down. And thus reduced very greatly, or more probably obliterated, the extremely valuable bonuses and share options for the directors and senior staff that the rise in the stated profits had triggered off.'

There was a discernible tension around the table now, and the Finance Director's pink face, and his cough and his nose-blowing was like an actor's unsubtly played portrayal of a man discountenanced by guilt. There was no comment from him or anyone else however, as Colin went on.

'And I do feel there are principles here of prudence and conservatism and fiscal rectitude, and I feel that my report must deal with these.

'First, I don't believe that the Board adequately researched the possibility of insuring against the Government of India's eventual default. I imagine the premium cost would have been high, perhaps very high, but I cannot believe that we should have gone into this deal without insurance protection. And secondly ...' There was a murmuring around the table, which grew louder as the directors turned to each other and started to talk. 'And secondly ...' Colin had to raise his voice now to hold their attention. He tried once more, but then Robert held up his hand, and Colin gave way to him.

'No, I'm afraid you're not right in that, Colin. That point is not correct.'

'But I checked the board minutes,' Colin said, and he flushed a little now as he faced Robert. 'I checked the minutes, Robert. There's no mention at all of discussions about the desirability of insuring against India's default. None. There's nothing whatsoever in the minutes.'

Robert shrugged, turned around in his chair, and bending down to his attaché case on the floor behind his chair, took out the seven or eight slim manila files which were in there, sorted them through, found the one he wanted, and handed it across to Colin.

'It's all in there,' Robert said. 'All the details and correspondence are in there. You can see that I've been dealing with the issue myself in my office, and that I'm still exploring it. You'll also see that the problem is that the insurers will definitely require certain letters of comfort from the Government of India, and that the people there are not being cooperative – at the moment, anyway. I may in the end find a way of doing it, I'm not sure. I haven't so far. But I have been trying, and will continue to do so. Take the file.'

And as Robert said this, Arthur Ewing slowly turned so that he was sitting square to the table again, and stared straight down it at his son, who had been leafing through the file, and was now pushing it back towards Robert.

'Colin . . .' Arthur had begun to speak, but Colin interrupted and said, direct to Robert:

'I apologise. I asked the Company Secretary about this insurance point, but he simply referred me to the minutes. I didn't realise that you were dealing with it. I apologise, Robert.'

And now Robert said to him quickly, as if to get in before Colin's father, 'And your second point, Colin? You said there were two issues in here. You said you had two points of prudence, both of which would have had the effect of lowering the profits. What was the other one?'

'Provisions,' he said. 'Provisions against default. We should be providing against it each year in the accounts. We should set up some sort of reserve, which would, of course, be set against the profits until the twenty years are up, and India has repaid the loan to the World Bank.'

Again, it was Robert who answered him, and he did so with a slight grimace, and a smile of resignation.

'Oh come on, Colin. You tell us you've read the minutes. That comment rather makes me wonder if you have. If you read them you can see that I personally wanted us to make annual provisions, and that I proposed that very course of action to the auditors. And was in the end argued out of it. By them. Rather to my surprise quite frankly, but by the auditors. We had a long debate. It's all there in the minutes. I argued very strongly for provisions – actually very large annual provisions – but they took the view that it would be an artificial and misleading reserve, given what they told me they considered to be an infinitesimal chance of default.

'In the end we voted on it, and I didn't carry the Board. Though I did get everybody to agree that a strong warning statement should be carried every single year in the notes to the accounts, though obviously that's not at all the same thing. But the Board, advised by the auditors, who were present with us at the meeting, voted against provisions against profits. It's all there in the minutes, for heaven's sake. You can't have missed that.'

Colin looked back at him, and smiled too. 'No, of course I didn't miss the account of it all in the minutes. It's the first thing I looked for, after . . . after . . .' He shrugged as well, then continued: 'Let's say for now that it was the first thing I looked for. The minutes were perfectly clear. You were fighting a losing battle though, Robert. I assure you that you were fighting a lost cause.'

And now it was Arthur who spoke first, cutting ahead of Robert.

'What does that mean, Colin? What does that mean, for heaven's sake, that Robert was fighting a lost cause? Look – I'm embarrassed by all this. You've said nothing of interest, and your report says nothing of interest. You've made some absurd accusation about lack of fiduciary care and prudence over insurance coverage, which would have been cleared up in a moment if you had gone through the proper channels and raised the point as a query at the Deputy Chairman's committee. As would all your earlier points over C.P. Nerappan and the Javed & National people.

'Instead of telling you to go to Robert's committee, I agreed, mistakenly, but because you are who you are, and because Robert was away from the office, to allow you direct access to the Board. But you've said nothing except banalities, and I resent the way you misused your family connection with me to shortcut the normal channels and procedures. I resent that very much indeed.'

Family connection, thought Robert. What an odd, cold phrase to use to him. Why can't he bring himself to use the word son, for God's sake? Poor Colin has lost control of the meeting at this moment, poor boy, which is all the more reason for a little delicacy and gentleness from his father. Colin has kept cool, which surprises me, but he's beginning to make a fool of himself. In any normal family, his father would now move to protect him, and bustle him away out of trouble. In this case, it looks to me as if Arthur is just at the point where he's setting himself up for the kill.

He glanced sideways at him, then down the table to Colin, and they were looking directly at each other. Colin's face, typically so flushed and florid, was pale and drawn, almost white in its sudden, unexpected pallor. It was he who spoke now.

'Well – if I haven't as yet said anything of interest, then I am going to do so now, Father. And I believe you would be wise to be very careful indeed in how you respond.'

'What? *What?*' Arthur Ewing exclaimed, in a tone that was both brutally contemptuous and dismissive, looking at Tom Houghton and Lord Strathmere as he did so, as if to corral them in to his side. 'Careful in how I respond? Are you trying to threaten me or something?'

He grinned sarcastically around the table, the effect of it to accentuate to an uncomfortable degree the mask-like, Sinitic quality of his expression.

'You're witnessing a moment of history, gentlemen. A moment of history in the Bank. A little family drama, played out before your very eyes.'

There was a ripple around the table of tense, artificial laughter, led by the Finance Director, a man of middle years, only recently promoted up from the ranks of the Bank's accounting staff, and the obliging Tom Houghton. Robert Luscombe, however, unsmiling and silent, cut in on it immediately, so obviously angered, despite the quietness of him, and the calm, that there was an instant silence when he spoke.

'I'm beginning to find this an unfortunate conversation,' he said. 'I think what's happening is unwise and unprofessional. I don't believe that we should carry on with this debate any longer at this time, and I'll arrange for Colin to attend the next meeting of my committee to pick up the story there. That's the correct channel for this report, and I would ask, Arthur, if we could now move on. Before the meeting closes we need time for a preliminary discussion on—'

'The auditors, Father.' Colin spoke as if Robert had never been there, his eyes boring straight into his father's up the length of the gleaming, rich brown table, his voice cold, and acutely threatening in its tenacity, and its now chilling lack of deference.

'Let's first talk about the auditors. And then we'll talk about what you actually said to the Chicago & Illinois people – the exact nature of the threats you made to them. And then, after that, we'll deal with your conduct with the Government of India officials. Your arrangements that they should be paid to ensure that our consortium won the contract. The arrangements you and C.P. Nerappan made.

'Those three things, Father. The auditors. How we got our share of the consortium. And the bribing of the Indian officials. Those three things.'

There was complete silence in the room. Even Tom Houghton was motionless, and the disappearance of his habitual wet-lipped smile gave his features an oddly collapsed, forlorn appearance. For the first time since Colin had come into the room, Houghton was avoiding rather than attempting to attract Arthur Ewing's eye.

'The auditors,' Colin repeated. 'I want you to tell me about your dealings with the auditors.'

Arthur Ewing's demeanour was that of a man in control, but aware and contemptuous of danger. And, as he stared back at his son, Robert saw again that look of disdain play openly across his eyes.

'I have absolutely no idea what you're talking about.'

Robert watched them both in their mutual tenseness, so extraordinarily facially alike at that moment, quite unmistakably father and son. And great-grandson too, he noticed, glancing up at the portrait under which Arthur sat, then down the table again at the still, composed, determined young man.

There was a pause for what seemed to be at least half a minute, and then Colin said, 'Very well, then – I'll tell *you* what happened, Father.

'The senior audit partner came to see you privately at Eaton Place, the night before the board meeting at which Robert Luscombe was going to press for provisions to be set against the Poonjee income. The audit partner came to tell you that he agreed with Robert and that he would say so to the Board. Even given the fact that the provisions would largely cancel out the Poonjee income, as far as the profit and loss account was concerned, he agreed with Robert that the provisions should be made.

'And then you did, Father, what you are inclined to do when someone proposes some course of action which is inconvenient to you. You obliterated him. He's a weak man, terrified of losing the Bank's audit at a time when his firm has lost several other major clients. You simply obliterated him. You told him that unless he supported you, his firm would be stood down at the next AGM. And that you yourself would control the publicity giving the supposed reasons. You quoted an error they'd made in auditing the Bank two years back, of an embarrassing and serious dimension, which only came to light when Robert spotted it in the draft accounts.

'So the man gave in. He immediately caved in. And arrived at your board meeting the next day, and advised the directors to vote against Robert's provisions. And that's what happened. The directors decided against the provisions against profits which the Deputy Chairman himself advised.

'You won again, Father. You always do. You wanted the provisions out and the profits up, because you didn't like the fact that the financial press was commenting that our profits had flagged in recent years against the banking sector generally. So you wanted a stronger share price. Partly because of your personal bonuses perhaps, but that wasn't really the reason. That never would be the reason for you. It certainly would be for some of the others, I don't doubt, but not for you. It was your pride, Father. Your pride.'

The only man at the table who moved was the Finance Director, who for a moment put his face into his hands, as if in personal fear. The others, including Robert, sat there absolutely still, most staring straight down at their papers, Robert alone gazing directly at Arthur Ewing, awaiting his response.

And when it came, Arthur's face flushed suddenly a violent puce, and the hands in his lap, held there locked one over the other, now separated, and the shake in them was that of anger as well as the Parkinson's Disease, and the beginning of a loss of control.

'My pride, you say. My pride! It's not my pride for myself. It's my pride in the Bank. Your Bank. *Our family Bank.*'

He pointed up to the portrait above his head, then swung his now violently shaking hand to indicate all the others hung on the wall to his left, and when he continued his voice had risen to a near shout.

'The Bank you were brought up to succeed to – had you been good enough to do it.'

And then there was a pause before he finished: 'That's what my pride is. That's all I care about. That's all you should care about as well.'

It was almost a shock when Tim Landesbury, the Cabinet politician, spoke up, weathered no doubt by a lifetime of conflicts of this sort. Every head swivelled to him as he did so. He turned first to Colin, saying, 'That accusation of yours regarding the audit partner going to your father's house and being threatened: can you substantiate that, Colin? You do realise the seriousness of the charge?'

'Yes. I was at school with the son of the senior audit partner, the one Father saw. He was in the firm at the time, but he's gone out to New York now to join someone else, and he told me the story one night before he left. He was outraged by it. And he did more than just tell me the story. He gave me a formal, signed deposition through his lawyers. And I have that now under lock and key.'

Landesbury now turned to Arthur, the slightest and gentlest of smiles in his eyes.

'I think we should have all three, Arthur. Let's have them out on the table. The auditors, the threatening of the Chicago & Illinois people, and the bribery of the Indian officials. Let's talk about all three. And come clean on the lot.'

There was a murmur of assent to this from Lord Strathmere as well, and it was only then that Arthur released his stare from his son, swinging sideways suddenly to face Landesbury.

'How dare you,' he said, the face again flushing puce, and his hands shaking wildly. 'How dare you speak to me like that! "Come clean," you say, as if I were the tea boy with his hand in the till. And this from you, a failed, morally notorious politician, who is simply here for whatever fees you can pick up from us. What do you know about anything? What contribution have you ever made to us or our affairs or our lives – the lives of all of us who really care about this Bank?'

He turned then, and swung his head to face Robert, gesticulating at him with his hand, then back again to face Landesbury.

'Me. And Robert too. Us. The real Bank. The people who really care for it, and work for it, and make sacrifices for it.

'I'll tell you what actually happens. I'll tell you about single-mindedness, and determination for the Bank to succeed, and toughness of spirit, and having the guts and courage to fight for us out there in the real world, where it actually matters. The real world. Marty Schwab, and those very unpleasant people in Chicago. Government of India officials who wouldn't so much as bury their own grandmothers without being bribed to do so. That world where money is made. The world where the Bank actually has to operate. To survive and prosper in it we have to be just as tough and rough as the next people are. Tougher perhaps, because we're not as big as most who play in our league.'

As he paused, he appeared to notice for the first time how violently his hands were shaking, and he tucked them back again on to his lap, away from public sight and display.

Then Landesbury said, 'I have a contempt for that speech of yours, Arthur. I have a contempt for your inability to play anything in your life according to the accepted rules. Or even the basic, common-sense principles of decent behaviour. Decent, professional, *ethical* behaviour. I have a feeling that what your son has told us is absolutely factual. I think he's got it right. I believe you've made a fool of us all in your conduct in this. You've made fools of the whole Board.'

Then Arthur suddenly and unexpectedly grinned, derision in his eyes.

'Poppycock,' he said. 'Balls. Sanctimonious poppycock. You make fools of yourselves easily enough, with no help from me. I have nothing to apologise for whatsoever, to you or anyone else. Particularly you.'

Landesbury replied, 'All that's bluster, Arthur, as you well know. Everything you've said in the last few minutes has been bluster. You're not a well man, and that may be the reason perhaps why your reaction is not more considered.

'You're not addressing the issue, which is that this is a major public company whose Chairman looks as if he's gone off the rails. Bribery – blackmail – coercing the auditors; if these things are true you've behaved in a way that is a disgrace to the traditions of the Bank. And disgraceful for a public company that is responsible through its Board to thousands of shareholders. The Moorgate & Mercantile Bank is not a personal fiefdom. It's a public company of major stature. And the Board of Directors – the whole Board of Directors – has a legal and ethical responsibility for the way it's run; to the staff, the community, and the shareholders. And there are traditions of probity and fair play here that your behaviour over this seems to have made a mockery of. We each have our personal reputation and our personal legal status to consider, for what we're dealing with here is a matter of illegality. Illegality and fraud.'

Again Arthur flushed, and again the shake in his hands was there for all to see.

'Don't be such a pompous ass, Tim. Don't be the self-righteous, hypocritical fool that you are. Don't patronise me by telling me that I'm not well. And don't presume to lecture me on the traditions of my own family Bank. We made the traditions, not outsiders like you. The family made the traditions. It's the family's Bank.'

He looked down the table at his son, and Colin looked back at him, and Robert thought, as he watched them, that much of the tension between the two of them appeared to have been released and tapped off by the events and the anger of the previous few minutes. Then Arthur started to shuffle together the papers in front of him, as if the meeting was concluding, and when he looked up again to speak, it was directly to his son, and his voice was calm, and there was a stillness about him.

'I am what I am. I'm a determined, tough man. I had to be, because none of the other members of the family of my generation had the character and courage that were needed. None of them was good enough to come into the Bank. You know that, Colin. None of them was good enough. And neither were my father and my uncle. I was. I hope you are.'

Colin and Arthur stared at each other in the hush that followed. Even Landesbury was motionless.

Colin said, 'Those three points, Father. Let's just deal with . . .'

'Yes,' Arthur said, now seemingly absolutely calm and in control of himself, his voice steady and low. 'Yes, your three points – though I thought that you and I had covered at least two of them together the other night. Why are you doing so again? Are you trying deliberately to embarrass me? We covered much of this ground.'

'Not in front of us you didn't,' said Landesbury. 'And we have our own legal and ethical status to—'

'You didn't tell me the truth, Father. You tried to buy me off with some half-truths. And some apologies for what you said to me in anger. You didn't tell me the whole truth. You drew short of that. Maybe if you—'

'The auditors,' said Arthur, directly to Colin. 'Yes, what you describe is correct. That is what happened. I believed what I did was the right thing for the Bank. The Chicago & Illinois people. Again; what you suggested was correct. I told them that unless they gave us the share of the consortium that we deserved, then I would report them to the State Department for trading with Iran. And the Indian Government officials. Of course they were bribed! How else do you think the consortium would have got the contract? I didn't trust Nerappan, so I did it myself. I did it.'

Landesbury moved in his chair to face Arthur. 'All three of those actions are outside the law, Arthur. Well outside the law. You know that to be so. We'll have to inform the authorities, as you

373

know we must. There are very severe penalties indeed for someone in your position who—'

Arthur gathered his papers and, with painful, faltering awkwardness, left Landesbury to his speech, and got to his feet to leave the room.

And as Colin watched him, he suddenly experienced the exhaustion of what was supposed to be victory, but felt at that moment to be very like defeat.

Chapter Fifty-Seven

Two days later, Robert joined a private meeting in the boardroom, called by Tim Landesbury on behalf of the three non-executive directors.

Robert, as always, was precisely on time, but the other men were already waiting for him at the table as he walked in. They each rose to their feet as he entered, and Robert saw that they had with them Lord Worth, the senior partner of Worth Hanley, the Bank's private lawyers, and a figure of legendary connection and influence.

'Charles,' said Robert as he shook Worth's hand. 'I'm glad to see you here.'

The immense, gross, theatrically unstable and stooping figure of Lord Worth was precariously held in a standing posture by the support of a stout walking stick on one side, and a shaking, palsied hand pressing down on to the board table on the other.

He let his drooping mouth curve into a simulation of a smile, and his discoloured teeth were displayed for sufficient time as courtesy required. Thereupon his lips sagged again into an open, wet grimace, and his eyes popped in apparent panic at his instability as he was lowered back into his seat by Lord Strathmere, who had positioned himself beside him.

'So sad for you, my dear Robert,' Worth said, when safely settled again in his chair, which looked several sizes too small and fragile for his bulk. 'So very sad.'

The mild, breathless voice and the damp red eyes assumed an expression of impenetrable, terminal melancholy before, again after an acceptable interval, adjusting back to one of alert and dangerous intelligence. Robert smiled his acknowledgement back at him across the table, as guarded as he always was when dealing with Charles Worth, whatever their business together might be, and whatever side of the table he was on.

The Bank had used Worth on a number of missions over the years, each time at Robert's behest; Arthur Ewing had always distrusted all the trappings and casuistry of the medieval prelate about the man, and preferred a much more straightforwardly robust and unpleasantly aggressive firm in Upper Charles Street. But Robert disliked the style of these people, thought that Worth was the most effective lawyer in London, and brought him in increasingly now to work on the Bank's business.

For all the several years of their acquaintance, however, Robert had never felt that he knew Charles Worth to the very slightest degree. There was between them now a certain ritualised pretension of elaborate personal familiarity, but the truth of it was that there was no familiarity at all, and Robert knew that there never would be.

It was said that only his mother, still alive at ninety-five, was truly close to him. His mother, and just possibly the last but two Prime Minister, for whom Worth had conducted a service of indescribably personal delicacy, and was consequently ennobled in the resignation Honours List that followed two or three years later. Robert had tried to make friends with him, but had failed. He had found, as so many had before him, that all that was on offer from Worth was an affectation of intimacy, a privileged and rationed quota of exquisitely accurate gossip about the famous and the powerful, and the benefit of a feared and respected mind. And, most important by far, unrivalled access to a network of those people in powerful places whose lives are made the easier by the give and take of services and favours. This arranged by brokers of these things, of whom Charles Worth was the most effective in the land. And quite possibly amongst the most effective anywhere.

'We must lunch, of course,' Lord Worth was continuing. 'So sad. So sad.' But this said impatiently, and now with no pretence at melancholy or sympathy, his mind, as Robert from his long experience of him could see, on to whatever brief Tim Landesbury has presented him with.

Worth turned now his heavy, swinging jowls towards Landesbury, as if reading Robert's mind. And there was in his drooping eyes an instruction for him to begin whatever it was that had to be begun, and an expression of saddened, world-weary acknowledgement that there was business to attend to, and lives to move on their way, and that these things were best dealt with by the men of intelligence, and pragmatism, and sensible judgement who lived in the world that Charles Worth most comfortably and expertly straddled.

'Good of you to come, Robert,' said Landesbury, in his detached, competent way. 'Glad we could catch you at such short notice. This is a miserable time for you to go through. You have all our sympathy, as you can imagine. All our sympathy and respect.'

Robert half smiled his recognition of this, and Lord Strathmere, furiously flushed and plump as he always was, his habitual round pebble glasses giving him, quite inadvertently, and possibly for the first time in his life, an oddly modish and contemporary look, nodded too in response.

'Sorry we had to get in touch with you at such a time. But affairs of state, you know . . .' and Strathmere gave his sudden, curiously feminine little laugh, then pursed his lips again in a gesture that Robert had long found irritating.

Robert shrugged, and smiled again, and wondered when any of them would come to the point. Then, 'That was a miserable board meeting by any standards,' said Tim Landesbury. 'A most unfortunate occasion. You must have hated what you heard as much as any of us did. Hated what you heard, and—'

'Taken aback by what you heard, I imagine,' interrupted Tom Houghton, and as Robert looked at him, and his sloppy appearance, he wondered as he had in the past, how it was that in these supposedly meritocratic days someone as terminally second-rate and incoherent as Houghton, rich and well-connected wife or not, could have been Chairman in his time of a reasonably large industrial-holdings group, and a director of a handful of prestigious public companies.

But he smiled pleasantly, as if to deny his own thoughts, and responded, 'Taken aback, Tom? I was surprised by the way some things were put, perhaps, and some things that were said – but taken aback? Do I miss your point?'

Houghton turned for help to Tim Landesbury, who continued smoothly: 'I think Tom is trying to edge towards the issue which we feel we have to raise with you, Robert, and let me say once more how unhappy we are that we have to do so at such an extra-ordinarily unpleasant time for you.

'But that's rather what non-executive directors are there for, don't you think? As referees and ombudsmen for the shareholders when things go wrong. A disinterested, honourable, independent pair of hands – don't you think that's right? Wouldn't you say that's what we're for?'

And as Robert nodded his acknowledgement, he thought to himself that disinterest and honour and independence were not attributes that would have immediately sprung to his mind if asked to describe the three of the men before him. Experience perhaps, but at no time, in Robert's recall, since any one of them had been on the Board, had they made a single genuinely perceptive or helpful contribution to the Bank's affairs.

Arthur Ewing's private opinion of them had always been wholly dismissive and derisive, as Robert knew. He had regarded Houghton and Strathmere simply as voting fodder. Landesbury he had brought on to the Board in the mistaken belief that he would bustle around to provide some useful government contacts and access. All three of them ranked amongst 'the lame and the palsied', in Arthur's customary description of men of this sort, and he would have been shot of the lot of them, indeed shot of non-executive directors entirely, had he been able to persuade the Stock Exchange that he could do so.

But Arthur was wrong about Tim Landesbury at least, thought Robert. Wrong in one respect. He was indolent, and he had done nothing for them since he'd been on the Board, but he was nobody's fool. And he was an ambitious man, unpleasantly tenacious when on to the main chance.

'The point we feel we have to ask you,' said Landesbury now, 'is whether you knew what Arthur was up to. Clearly you didn't know anything about that business of the auditors being threatened, as you were very much fighting in the other camp. We acknowledge that instance, of course. But . . .'

Suddenly Robert realised why he was here. That phrase of Landesbury's – 'we acknowledge that instance, of course'. They're graciously going to give me that, he thought, because they're going to attempt to incriminate me on the others. That's why Charles Worth is here. They're after me as well as Arthur. Or Landesbury is. What is it he wants?

'. . . But we do feel we must explore with you the two other areas. And more too, if you think there are other points that we should know about, that Colin Ewing missed.'

Robert, for all his self-control and containment, flushed at the remark. Then he looked for a moment at Charles Worth, whose hooded eyes were gazing at him with a concentration that Robert knew of old meant that he was here to do a job; he knew precisely what it was, and he would get to it when the timing was just right, and the *coup de grâce* had been set up for him.

Robert turned to Landesbury. 'The other two areas,' Robert said. 'The bludgeoning we did to get into the consortium, and the bribery of the Government of India officials. No – I knew nothing of either. Arthur and I divided our worlds up very precisely, as you know. At the time all this was happening I was representing us on the Bank of England bi-annual consultative committees, and in New York for the Third-World indebtedness talks. Arthur handled all the Poonjee issues himself. On neither of these two areas did I have any direct input.'

'No direct input perhaps, but how about *in*direct input? Surely you must have been concerned and informed indirectly at least? Wouldn't it have been extraordinary if you hadn't?'

Robert gazed at Landesbury very closely indeed before he answered him. Then, 'No. No input, and no knowledge, whether we define it is as being direct or indirect. I had nothing to do with it whatsoever. Directly or indirectly. I had nothing to do with it.'

'Shouldn't you have done?' put in Lord Strathmere quickly, then laughed and pursed his lips again in the fashion that, Robert thought, would lead him to homicide were he too long in Peter Strathmere's company.

'Shouldn't have done, Peter? Again, I'm not sure I grasp what you mean. What do you imply by that?'

'He's not implying anything,' said Landesbury. 'He means this: that we do have a very uncomfortable situation on our hands.'

Landesbury remained staring at Robert for a moment, then shifted his position in his chair and said, 'Robert – we met Arthur earlier this morning, with Charles of course, and he has now resigned from the Chair and the Board. We made it clear that we would vote him off if he didn't. The non-executives have the power to do that, as you remember, by the Company's Articles of Association.

'There will be an announcement to the Stock Exchange at six o'clock this evening. Certain papers which we extracted last night from Arthur's files will be handed to the regulatory bodies tomorrow morning. It was the existence of those papers that made Arthur accept the need for his resignation. Under, it has to be said, some persuasion and . . . explanation, shall we say, from Charles. About the voting rights of the non-executive directors.

'There's illegality involved in this matter, of course, and I doubt whether we can avoid either the Serious Fraud Office people or the police. We depend on Charles's advice on how next to proceed. We doubt we have very much choice of action in the matter, however. Particularly as we now find that Arthur put some explicit threats in writing to the Chicago & Illinois people, which would make that side of things next to impossible to defend if it came to a court of law.

'On top of that there is the deposition from the auditor friend of Colin's, the knowledge of which makes us accessories after the fact. And we have Arthur's own statement to us about the bribing of the Government of India officials. As I say, I doubt we can do anything else now but to hand the matter over to the authorities, however serious that may turn out to be for Arthur.'

Robert glanced at Charles, who nodded to him in confirmation of what he had heard, then turned back to Landesbury.

'So that's what Peter meant,' Landesbury said heavily. 'There's a danger that the Bank is going to suffer a most unfortunate setback over this affair. And there's a school of thought that if you knew what was going on with Arthur you should have stopped it. And that if you didn't know what was going on, then you should have done. And – forgive me for being blunt – there's yet another school which suggests that not only did you know about it, but that you were active in it yourself.

'Your bonuses, Robert. Your executive share options and your bonuses. You did rather well out of them because of Poonjee. You made approaching half a million pounds before tax out of it yourself. So not everyone is convinced that your hands are any more clean in this affair than Arthur's. Not us, of course, not us . . .' and at this Robert could see out of the corner of his eye both Houghton and Strathmere shake their head vigorously in confirmation of their innocence and sadness about it all, whilst he recalled, ironically, that the bonus and share options had done little more than give him what he thought at the time would be a decent provision for Rowena and Sophie in their trust fund '. . . but I'm afraid you may find that some of your working colleagues feel that way. In fact, I can tell you that they do. I must tell you the truth in this. I'm afraid that they do.'

Whenever anyone announces to me that he is about to tell me the truth, thought Robert, the more certain I am that he is going to do the opposite. Would there really be this view amongst the others? McGregor possibly ... who knew I was never comfortable with him in the Finance Director's job. Higham, who had that run-in with me a few months ago about that business in Italy ... God knows. God knows. But whatever it is, it's not the truth which people are trying to find in this. It's the opportunity for personal gain and advancement. And the fun of the hunt. And the desire to put the boot into someone stronger and more powerful than them when they can see that he's damaged and reduced for a moment to their level.

Robert looked now as directly into Landesbury's eyes as he was able, staring at him, testing his will and courage, daring him to complete whatever there was to complete.

'I don't think you mean what you say, Tim,' he said in due course. 'I don't think that you've said yet whatever it is you brought me to this room to hear. Let's have it all out on the table. Tell me what this meeting is actually about. Tell me why you brought me here.'

There was a silence. Then, 'Just a chat,' said Peter Strathmere, and when the pretty, feminine laugh came, and the pursed lips, Robert looked at him with the narrowed eyes of overt loathing.

'Just a chat,' Houghton echoed in support. 'Just to mull things over with you. So sorry again that's it's such a rotten time to—'

Lord Worth took this opportunity to drop the walking stick he had been holding on to the floor, and then knock his glass of water over.

As he made his laboured, histrionic attempts to bend down to pick the stick up there was a flurry of chairs being moved, and apologies made, and arms held, and the green baize mopped, before all was restored, and Worth upright and seated again, and gazing benignly at Robert across the table.

The stage now was his. With a shaking, plump, strangely coarse and artisan hand, the fingernails irregular and dirty, the thumb vulgar and bloated, Charles Worth reached into the inside jacket pocket of his crumpled suit, and took from it a folded document on thick legal contract paper. He read quickly through its two or three pages, then folded it again, and laid it on the table in front of him, placing his hands on top of it.

Turning his friendly, innocent gaze upon Robert, he said, 'It often happens, Robert, we both know that. So often it happens in this way. A change of Government, the need for fresh faces, a new start, a new agenda, a new shot of energy. That's the way these things happen. It was rather that way with you, if you recall. When Arthur at last wrestled the chair off his father, he brought you straight in with him, and some heads had to fall to make room for you. That's the way these things occur. It's brutal in its way, but it's often for the best for everyone, as things turn out.'

Robert waited for what was to come. He felt a total stillness inside him, and an ironic, peaceful resignation, but he kept his eyes deliberately alive, and acute, and challenging, so that Worth would have to fight for his ground.

There was a pause while Charles Worth stared back, and then he shrugged, and said, 'It's bad luck, of course, that this all happened together. The business over Colin Ewing's report, and his challenge of his father, and all the unfortunate things that came out of that confrontation.'

Then he smiled suddenly, and confidentially, as if what was to follow was an amusing matter of personal confidence between two old friends.

'And then, of course, your private life on top of that.'

Robert felt a sudden nausea, and as Worth gazed at him, he knew that he was showing the wound.

'Your wife, my dear fellow, but I'm afraid the girl too. Your young girlfriend. And all that business. Your private life, my dear fellow.'

Robert felt the blood drain from his face, and his breath shorten and shallow. As he stared at Worth, that mocking detachment in Robert had gone, and there was fear there now, and the beginnings of considerable anger. He started to try to speak, but he was unable to collect and steady his thoughts and his composure, and now Worth was continuing.

'But it may all be for the best, old chap. Early retirement, you know. Many people do it nowadays. They make a virtue of it, and I can't say I blame them. Should have done it myself.' He made an imitation of a smile again, but just with his mouth, and stopped it as he saw the coldness of Robert's stare.

'You're a most intelligent and experienced man, Robert,' said Worth. 'You know these things can't be fought off when they come in this form. Tim is right, you know. There's no disputing the fact that the non-executives are able to put these things to a vote. And that, in these instances, they have special voting powers. That's the truth. They do rather hold the ring in matters such as these. Under your Articles. It's an unusual provision you have in them, but there it is. Goes back many years, to the time of that unfortunate business in the thirties. But there's no doubt the powers are still there. I'm afraid he's perfectly right in that.'

Robert waited mutely for him to continue.

'Rather than agree on severance terms now,' said Worth, 'I suggest that Peter Rutherford's firm, or whoever you want to use, contacts me in due course and we'll negotiate the severance arrangements together. But you have an excellent contract of employment, of course, and you're protected by that. Well protected. You should be – I wrote the contract on your behalf myself, if you recall. Acting for you.'

And there was another show of the humourless smile, before he said, 'Though there are provisions against you joining another bank, naturally. You are aware of that. The usual competitor provisions.'

All four men were now watching Robert, and there was silence for several moments.

Then Robert said: 'And the public announcement?'

Worth reached now into the other inside pocket of his jacket, and brought out a second piece of folded paper. He opened it, read it, then pushed it across the table to Robert. It was a typed announcement in capital letters, under a Moorgate & Mercantile Bank letterhead.

PRESS ANNOUNCEMENT MADE AT SIX P.M.
SEPTEMBER 8 1992

THE MOORGATE & MERCANTILE BANK ANNOUNCE THAT THE CHAIRMAN SIR ARTHUR EWING AND THE DEPUTY CHAIRMAN MR ROBERT LUSCOMBE HAVE BOTH RESIGNED WITH IMMEDIATE EFFECT; SIR ARTHUR FOR PERSONAL REASONS, AND MR LUSCOMBE FOLLOWING A DISAGREEMENT WITH THE BOARD OF DIRECTORS AND THEIR ADVISERS OVER STRATEGIC POLICY.

THE BOARD HAVE ACCEPTED THEIR RESIGNATIONS WITH GREAT REGRET, AND WISH TO PLACE ON RECORD THEIR GRATITUDE TO BOTH SIR ARTHUR AND TO MR LUSCOMBE FOR THEIR MANY YEARS OF OUTSTANDING SERVICE AND LEADERSHIP.

THE RT HON TIM LANDESBURY PC MP, WHO HAS SERVED AS A DIRECTOR OF THE BANK SINCE 1989, ASSUMES THE CHAIRMANSHIP WITH IMMEDIATE EFFECT.

Robert examined the paper for some time, before meeting Charles Worth's eyes.

'Is that it?' he said. 'My whole career here in the Bank, and that's it? And Arthur's whole career as Chairman? And nothing of his ill-health? Nothing of that?'

Lord Strathmere immediately started to say something in response, on the lines of Arthur's refusal to concede any ill-health at all, and specifically not in a public statement, but Robert brushed him aside, addressing Worth.

'Landesbury to take over – having done absolutely nothing for us at all from the moment he got here? And disagreements over strategic policy, for God's sake! What strategic policy? What disagreements?'

'Oh, I don't believe that's too difficult,' said Worth. 'As long as both sides stick rigidly to the same story. Third-World lendings would be the easiest. You wanted more of it, and the rest of the Board less. Or the other way around. You wanted less, they wanted more. Whichever you prefer. Big row; everyone right in their own way. That's the best line, I think. And then we must all stick to it. That's the trick to these things.'

As Robert watched Charles Worth say this, there came suddenly to his mind Lord Melbourne's comment after his dismissal by William IV. 'I have always thought complaints of ill-usage contemptible, whether from a seduced disappointed girl or a turned out Prime Minister.'

Its memory immediately calmed Robert, and cheered him, and released his humour, and recalled for him that inner world to which in recent years he had increasingly turned; chamber music, and his study, and Virginia Woolf, and Henry James, and the books of poetry, and the walks in the London parks.

He got up from his seat and walked to the door, then turned, holding the handle, and looked back at Lord Worth.

'I'll leave the Bank, Charles, because, as you say, I can't fight it. But Peter Rutherford or one of his partners will be in your office within the hour with my instructions.

'The severance terms will have to be decided this afternoon, or I won't allow the statement to be issued tonight. And the Stock Exchange regulations are such that you're forced to issue a statement to the City by tonight at the latest. And, having yourself written my contract, you know that the Bank is not allowed to issue any statement of this sort without my written consent, or there's breach of contract. And I'm not in the mood to be nice about breach of contract.

'And I tell you now that I won't anyway allow that statement as written to be put out. It's a dishonest nonsense. The Press and the world will see through it immediately, and then it won't be the Bank the rumours will be about. They'll be about us – about Arthur and me. Which is, I imagine, rather what you had in mind.

'If I'm going, then I'll do it in dignity. And there'll be dignity for Arthur too. Peter Rutherford will draft a new statement. On behalf of both myself and Arthur. And you will issue it.'

Chapter Fifty-Eight

Alice had arranged to meet Robert at Elm Park Gardens at half-past six, but she had gone home early so as to be able to collect her thoughts and steady herself before he came.

She sat slumped on the sofa, still wearing her outdoor coat, her hands pushed into its pockets, staring out at the rain that had begun now to fall in earnest, visible to her in distinct angled lines against the dark background of the buildings across the street.

Beside her on the seat cushion was the anonymous letter from Sophie, which she had taken out of her desk drawer to read one more time, before throwing it down again.

Filthy, disgusting anonymous letters, she thought. His wife's suicide. Crazy daughters. Darkness and filth in everything the poor man touches. It's not what I want, and it never was what I wanted. It's gone too far, and it's got too dark, and it's too threatening, and too intrusive. It must be stopped now.

She got up from the sofa, and went to the window to gaze at the wet, gleaming street outside, and off to the right, the traffic stationary and clogged on the Fulham Road.

The moment Sarah killed herself, I knew that the affair was finished. I knew even before that. And then the suicide, and that degrading, revolting letter. And the prospect of even meeting his children, after all that had happened . . .

It could never work now. I nearly stopped it immediately after our very first lunch in the Italian restaurant, before anything at all had got under way. But then we made love, and then again, and again, and by that point it was so much more difficult to do.

But that last time, when he was lying there beside me, I could see the soft sagging of his face, and the veins on his hands, and the looseness of the skin on his neck. I knew then it could never work. He looked at that moment so different. So much older. So much a stranger.

She checked her watch, and it was almost time now for him to be with her. Let me find the words to let him go in a way that he can accept, she thought. Give me articulacy. Give me a tone of voice and a phrasing that will give us both a chance to say goodbye in a way that avoids too much pain. Pain for him. No pain for me now really. Not any more. All I want is to be here on my own in my flat, and at the office, and in contact with Tom, and all the things that represent what my true life is.

Then there was a knock on the door, and she went to answer it, and as he stood there looking at her, there was a fatigue and a heaviness in his eyes that she had never seen there before. He reached out to hold her, as he always did, and after a moment she put her arms round him as well, but there was an unmistakable hesitation before she did so, and a lack of contact and commitment in her touch, and she guessed that he could sense this.

He disengaged from her then, and dropped his hands to his side, and stood there in the narrow hallway, staring at her, silent, his eyes shrewd and waiting.

And it was there that she told him. Standing there looking at him in the tiny hall. Quickly, and stumbling over the words, and speaking too fast, and first flushed, then drained and white in the face, and trembling.

But she told him, and whatever her delivery, she was clear in what she said, and he understood. And, as she finished, he managed to smile, and said nothing in response.

And nothing at all of what the rest of the day had brought him.

Then he nodded his head, as if in agreement, and smiled again.

He opened the door to leave, and the last sight she ever had of Robert was as he turned at the staircase, and gazed back at her. Tears now ran freely down her cheeks, until she brought up her hands, and pressed the heels of them into her eyes, and wiped the tears away. Robert stood for a moment absolutely still, then he smiled once more, raised his hand in farewell, and was gone.

'You made my life, Alice,' he said to himself as he stumbled his way down the stairs.

'You made my life,' and then the pain of it, and the pain of the whole day came to him, and he stopped, and for a moment stood there alone, one arm held as tightly across his face as he could force it, in the effort to contain and hold all that was within him.

'You made my life, Alice,' he said one last time, and the single memory of her he knew he would hold most closely was that of his last sight of her, as she pressed the heels of her hands up into her eyes, and wiped away her tears with the back of her fist.

Like a little boy gazing down at his father, on the footplate of the Howrah Express.

Chapter Fifty-Nine

The following Sunday afternoon, Robert went back to the Bank to pack up his personal belongings. The Sunday guard was there in the lobby to let him in, and there was a certain embarrassed awkwardness between them as Robert signed the security book and asked after the man's family, his son having worked for the Bank one school holidays as a messenger boy on Robert's sponsorship.

They exchanged a sentence or two, then Robert was able to take his leave of him and go up to his office. He shut the door behind him, and saw that they had put out for him, as he had requested, half a dozen or so plastic crates, into which he could load his private possessions.

He sat at his desk for a moment, taking stock and trying to settle himself down, then went to the filing cabinets in the corner of the room, having noticed that the special locking bar across each had been forced open.

Every one of the files had been removed. All the records he had held there during his period as Deputy Chairman. All the transactions he had negotiated, and the arrangements he had made, and the correspondence he had received and written, and the minutes and notes of the meetings he had attended and contributed to. All now removed from him. All now locked away, and taken from his trust. Before he arrived that afternoon. So that nothing, he imagined, could stray into a competitor's hands.

He saw then that his private papers, in the special little red cabinet at the end of the room, had clearly been looked through. His Will. His income-tax returns. Some miscellaneous bills and bank statements and documents. And the several files of his correspondence with Peter Rutherford's firm. Almost all of it dealing with the adventures of his family life.

Robert sat again at his desk and, folding his hands behind his head, gazed out unseeingly at the damp, leaden skies and the grey river beneath.

All gone now, he thought. Or almost all gone. My career, my wife, my daughters, and Alice. All gone. Just my inner life left. Just what goes on inside my mind. That's what's left.

And it was my marriage that brought me down. It was my marriage that poisoned my life, and poisoned Sarah's too. Stopped her from developing as a responsible woman. There was no malice in either of us; just different areas of weakness and failure. The incompatibility of the marriage cast a pall over both our lives.

Robert gazed for some moments around his familiar room then rose, went over to the red filing cabinet, and threw the files, one by one, into the plastic crates. He looked in the drawers of his desk, took out from them a pen or two, and his desk diary and address book, and put them on top of the files. He sat once more, this time on the edge of the desk, and stared out of the window.

My career gone. Sarah a suicide, on my behalf. Alice gone. Sophie a traitor to me. Rowena destroyed. And that's now the sum of my life, I suppose. That's what there is. How quickly one's life can crumble away to nothing. How relentless the retribution is for one's own mistakes. How unexpected that one can survive the pain of so much loss.

And, engrossed in these thoughts, he didn't turn at first, or answer, when he heard the tentative knock on the door, imagining that it would be a routine check from a security man, or the cleaning staff. But then he heard a familiar voice, and he swung around, and there was Colin Ewing standing behind him.

'Robert. I heard you were coming in to pick up your stuff,' he said. 'I hope you don't mind. I've come to thank you, and to say goodbye.'

Robert smiled at him. 'To thank me?' he said. 'You've nothing to thank me for. You know that.'

'Actually that's not what I meant to say,' Colin replied. 'What I came to say was that I was sorry for what happened. I'm sorry you got caught up in the Poonjee affair. None of that is what I meant to happen.'

The two men looked at each other for a moment, then Colin sat down in the armchair by the side table, but upright, and without ease.

Robert tried to smile at him again, then said, 'I don't think I fully realised what was on your agenda, Colin. Let's just say that. You found what you found. And there's a certain crude justice in the proposition that was put to me, I suppose. That if you could have found it, then I could have done so. Or that I *should* have done so. There's some sort of fairness in that, perhaps.' Robert made a gesture of indifference, then turned away to check one last cupboard in the corner before he left.

As he was doing so, Colin said, 'But I didn't find anything, Robert – you know that. I was led to every single thing I came up with. The business with the Chicago and Illinois people . . . The bribing of the Government of India officials . . . The Prasad & Prasad story . . . All of that came from the anonymous letters. The auditors' scandal came to me from my schoolfriend. The only thing I discovered on my own initiative turned out to be a nonsense. The insurance matter, which was all balls – as you pointed out.'

There was a silence from them both for a moment, as Robert came back to his desk, and threw some final few articles into the crates to join the others.

'The letters, Robert. It was the letters that did it.' Robert looked up at him, and Colin continued, 'And that's rather why I've come here this afternoon, because I don't understand what happened. If the letters had never been written, my father would never have been compromised, and nothing would have emerged, and you wouldn't have ... you wouldn't have lost your career. Nothing would have happened if the letters hadn't been written.'

'But they were,' said Robert. 'They were written, and they led you to wherever they led you, and whatever happened, happened. And now it's all over, my advice to you is to leave it that way. Whoever it was that wrote the letters enabled you to do the job you did. Whoever it was.'

Colin pinkened a little, then said, exasperation in his voice, 'Oh, come on, Robert. Come on – that's past now. Everything's over now. There are no more games to play. Of course you know who the letter-writer was, for God's sake! We can stop all that now. It was *you*, Robert. It was you. You wrote the letters. You led me along all the time. You were directing me all the time. From behind the scenes. It's the only explanation I can find. But what I *don't* know is why you wrote them. Why did you do it? What did you want? That's what I can only guess at. And try to understand. In some way – for whatever reason – you wanted me to track my father down. There must have been some score or another that you wanted to pay off. It misfired for you as things turned out. But the letters were definitely from you.'

Robert shook his head. 'No, Colin. The letters weren't from me. I thought somehow you knew. They weren't from me.' He remained looking at Colin. Then, 'They were from C.P. Nerappan – all of them. It took me longer than it should have done to realise it, but that's what happened. They were all written by him.'

Colin's face frowned in incredulity and bewilderment. 'C.P.? C.P., for Christ's sake? But ... but how? This is nonsense. It can't be true. The last letters were posted from England, for example. C.P.'s not in England. He's in India.'

Robert shrugged. 'His brother is often here in London. C.P. could have asked him to post them. Or made some arrangement with a secretary at the Bank to mail letters on for him. Or used some friend of his here in the Indian High Commission. God knows.'

Eventually: 'It doesn't stack up, Robert. There's an inconsistency in this somewhere. If you knew the letters were from C.P., why didn't you say so earlier? Why didn't you tell me earlier?'

'Because at first I didn't realise they were from him; not until I spoke to Arthur on the telephone the day after C.P. had had his heart attack. Then I suddenly realised what had happened. Something in what your father said stopped me clean in my tracks. Before that, I was absolutely certain who had sent the letters. In fact I was so certain of it that it never crossed my mind that I might have been on the wrong scent.

'I thought they came from Gupta. It seemed to me so obvious that they were from him. I knew that he was never comfortable with C.P.. He always disliked him and disapproved of him. To set about dismantling his career in that way struck me as being precisely what Gupta would do, given the opportunity that your audit provided.

'Initially I left the whole thing undisturbed because I thought Gupta would go on and on if we left him alone, and might come up with something really significant. I decided not to tell you, as I didn't want to risk you talking about it. Which, after your performance with Mohammed Javed, looked rather probable.

'But, as it turned out, I was wrong anyway. The letters weren't from Gupta. They were from C.P.. And by that point it was too late. You were so deep on the trail that I thought it best to leave you on it. Until I worked out for myself exactly what C.P. was up to.'

'Well – what *was* he up to, for heaven's sake?' Colin demanded. 'You said to me once that he was a dangerous enemy. Why an enemy of any of us? That's what I can't understand. Why should he do it? Why should he send the letters?'

He leant back in his chair, and shook his head in bewilderment.

'I don't understand it: I can't understand it. Why should C.P. do this? They were directly self-incriminatory. Why should he do that?'

When Robert replied there was a certain disinterest and fatigue in his voice, the tone of a man who wanted now to conclude the subject, and finish the debate.

'I don't know, Colin. And I'm not sure I care any longer really ... Look – let's say that the most obvious reason was straightforward spite against your father. He wanted to weave a web of complicity and guilt around him. Certainly he'd always believed that Arthur had promised him, when he and C.P. first joined the Bank together, that the pair of them would one day run it. And of course that never happened. That's not how it turned out.

'Perhaps your father was jealous of C.P., and never meant it to happen. Perhaps he changed his mind and decided to go with me instead, because that's effectively what he did. Perhaps he deliberately misled C.P. all along. Your father has a manipulative and malicious side to him as well, you know.

'So C.P.'s motive may simply have been spite and revenge. Or it may have been more subtle than that. It may have been a game for him. Just a game, the point of which was to destabilise the Board and the Company. Having sport with people he felt revengeful towards, for whatever reason that might have been.'

Colin shook his head, again in his gesture of bewilderment and disbelief. 'Games? Sport?' he said, then sighed, defeated.

Robert said, 'Well, maybe there's another explanation. Perhaps C.P. played around as a bear in the Bank's shares, selling shares he hadn't got, while the price was high, then buying them in, before he had to deliver them, when the price had dropped. That sort of bear-trading would not be untypical of a man of his temperament. For all his appeal, and there was plenty of that, he had such a cynical and sceptical temperament. Cynicism and scepticism, and raw intelligence. That was always what underpinned C.P.'s charm. Plus a certain dangerous, but seductive process of toying with people. Playing with them. An odd game of setting people up, in order to knock them down.'

Robert paused, fiddling with a pencil on his desk, before throwing it into the bin beside him.

'I have a feeling he would have tried, or perhaps was trying, something similar in my own private life,' he said. 'Creating mischief between me and Sarah. Stirring up the pot, and then further destabilising us. There was a very odd conversation we had in India when I was out there this last time. All about my supposed searching for love. He was looking to make trouble between me and Sarah in that, I believe. The opening serve in a pleasing little tennis match, in which the game was all about further subverting what he knew to be a flawed and pieced-together relationship.

'C.P. was addicted to that sort of manipulation in other people's lives. And he would have liked the joke that the share price dropped, perhaps to his gain as a bear-trader, when that had happened because of the destabilisation actually orchestrated by himself. That was just his sort of joke.

'But perhaps there were other reasons. Who knows? Perhaps loyalty to me. Perhaps he was trying to get rid of Arthur, so that I would be the beneficiary of that. Though of course exactly the opposite is what actually happened. So maybe it was the opposite that he was planning: creating an environment of such total disorder in the Board that I would be put aside myself.'

Robert half smiled, half grimaced at Colin then, and shrugged his shoulders.

'God knows, Colin. A bit of all these things perhaps. I don't know the answer. But the letters definitely came from him; I can assure you of that. He kept copies of them. I don't know why, but he did. Presumably because they amused him. His lawyer here in London has them; I went to his house this morning to see them. C.P. sent them to him by courier some time last week. Under the circumstances, the lawyer wanted me to see them.'

Robert seemed to have finished with that, and walked over to the filing cabinets, opening and shutting the doors, lost, it seemed, in thought. Then, 'I don't think you know. C.P.'s dead. He may have realised it was coming. He died yesterday afternoon. He never came out of the Delhi hospital. There was a second heart attack. He's dead.'

Colin put his head in his hands, and muttered something that Robert failed to catch. Then he got to his feet and went to the window and stood there gazing out at the river, and the rain that had begun to fall, and the first browning and bronzing of autumn now showing in the leaves of the lime trees lining the Embankment below.

'I'm sorry, Robert. I'm so sorry about C.P.. I'm sorry about so many things. I came here to apologise to you for getting your life caught up in this business with my father. Though when I did so, I thought that you had actually brought much of it on yourself. By the letters. But now I realise that I was wrong. What happened was that I brought you down too. I brought you down with my father. At a time when . . .' He stopped, then tried again. 'At a time when . . . your wife . . . And then your daughter in that trouble with the police. Arrested, according to the papers, then held in remand. And your other daughter too.' Again he hesitated, then, 'Office gossip, of course. But I know it's true. And I wish it wasn't. Particularly now that you've lost all this too. I wish I could find something to say that would mean anything. But I am so sorry.'

Then he said, 'So many of us would like to say goodbye to you, Robert. There are more people here than you can imagine who want to say goodbye, in whatever way you'll allow. But you're so private. And so contained, and . . .' He leant back on the window sill behind him, the sentence finished by a gesticulation of his hands.

Robert tried to smile at him, but could manage only a fleeting glimpse of it. 'Not so private really, Colin. And not in the least contained. The reverse of those things, at the heart of me; the reverse of that. Perhaps C.P. was right about me. Perhaps he read me better than anybody. I tell you what happens. When I find love, wherever I find love, I cling to it like a limpet on the rock. But I can never hold fast enough. In the end, I always lose my grip, and it's gone. And usually because I've chosen the wrong rock to attach myself to. Perhaps always because I've chosen the wrong rock to attach myself to. And yet . . . that's not it. That's not it.'

He threw the last papers into the crate, and took his jacket off the back of his chair. Then he turned, and looked over at Colin again.

'I'll tell you a story, Colin. Before I go.

398

'My father was a railway engineer. An engine driver, really. Most of his career was in Orissa, and that's where I was brought up as a small child. He was a man of great sweetness of nature, but dangerous when he drank.

'There was a bad night at home once, when I was six or so, and he knew that I'd run off to hide in the bushes, so as not to hear the shouting. In the morning, after I'd crept back to my bedroom, I saw my father wash himself under the shower in the yard. And when he walked back again into the house I could see that his face was screwed up in the pain of self-accusation at what he'd done.

'It was always like that. My mother forgave him each time so readily and completely, and he knew that she would again. But he'd seen that I'd run away from him, and he realised that I was old enough by then to comprehend the degree to which he had lost control of himself. And he wanted my forgiveness for that, no doubt. Not understanding that, just like my mother, I would always forgive him anything. Anything at all.

'So he took me off to Ranchi station to see the Howrah Express waiting to leave. Showing me off to his friends, and, by his public display of pride in me, trying to demonstrate to me his love. And his remorse. And his reaching out for my forgiveness.

'The whistles blew, and the train started to heave and grind its way forward, and there was all the noise and the shouting and the chaos of an Indian railway station. And suddenly – completely unexpectedly – my father threw me up on to the footplate of the Express, and ran beside the engine as it gathered speed. I thought he would never make it, and I was screaming for him, and holding out my hand, and reaching for him, and his fingers could never quite reach the bar to pull himself up, and I was stretching and stretching to help him, and then suddenly he had it, and he jumped and he pulled and he was there. Lying on the footplate beside me. Laughing with the driver. Laughing and laughing. And as I looked at him, I thought, young child as I was, that I would never feel love like that again.

'And I never have. I've never felt love like that again.'

Then Robert smiled, and walked across to Colin, and held out his hand.

'Goodbye, Colin,' he said. 'Good luck. Good luck with the family Bank.'

And, raising his hand in a final gesture of parting, Robert reached the door and set off for the rickety little second-floor lift, and the marbled, echoing pretension of the columned lobby, knowing that it was for the last time in his life.

Chapter Sixty

When Sophie was sentenced, she looked up immediately to Robert in the gallery, and held him for a moment in a piercing stare. Then the handcuffs were fitted to her wrists, and the officer beside her led her down out of his sight to the cells below.

Peter Rutherford laid his hand on Robert's arm. 'That was inevitable, Robert. You know that. That was always going to be the verdict. There was so little we could do. The Defence had nothing to work with. But we'll talk to Counsel about an appeal, if you like. The sentence was a good deal heavier than I was expecting, certainly. We might well get that reduced, I suppose. It might be worth seeing if—'

'No,' Robert said. 'No appeal. At least, I suppose that's for Sophie herself to decide. But personally I don't want to have anything to do with an appeal. We've all been through enough.'

Neither said any more for several moments, and they remained side by side in their seats as gradually the gallery emptied around them.

Then Peter said, 'I'm so sorry, Robert. I do feel so very—'

'I must go down to see her before she's taken away,' Robert said, again cutting him off in mid-sentence. 'I hope I'm still in time for that. How do I do that? Where do I go?'

He was on his feet now, and trying to get his arms into his overcoat, as always an awkward movement for him with his damaged shoulder. As Peter reached forward to help him he turned away and set off for the wooden stairs, calling back, perhaps in apology for his brusqueness: 'I must see her, Peter. You saw how she looked at me. There's nothing I can do for her, but I must try to see her.'

Peter followed Robert down the stairs, told him to wait outside the courtroom, then returned in a few moments with an official.

'You can have ten or fifteen minutes with her in the cell before they drive her off, but I'm told that's all the time there is,' Peter said. 'And I'm afraid there'll be a police officer with you all the time. But I've explained who you are, and I hope . . .' He shrugged, and smiled awkwardly. 'I'll wait for you in one of those seats over there in the corner. I'll be there for you when you've finished.'

Robert went with the officer; a kindly, courtly man who took it that Robert needed cheering up, and kept a running commentary of pleasantries going until they had reached the corridor of cells. A guard unlocked the door at the furthest end, and there was Sophie, sitting at the small deal table, her head in her hands.

The policeman sat on a chair in the corner of the cell, as far as possible out of both Sophie's and Robert's sightlines. The guard brought in a third chair for Robert.

'Fifteen minutes, sir,' he said, 'and I'm afraid that's it. Probably a few moments less. It depends on when the van's ready to leave.'

The lock turned behind him. Robert gazed at Sophie, who still had her elbows on the table and her head in her hands. He wondered what he could say. He turned to glance at the policeman, who was sitting there absolutely still, his arms locked across his chest. Their eyes met, and he gave Robert a ghost of a smile, as if in support and encouragement. Never mind me, sir, the eyes said. I've seen everything. Nothing shocks me, sir. Pretend I'm not here.

Robert turned back to the table. His daughter remained in the same bowed posture, and he stared at the top of her head. He noticed that the parting in her greasy, unwashed hair was showing not just dandruff, but signs of thinness, the white scalp beneath it gleaming through. As he had watched her in court over the days of the trial he had thought that her condition had deteriorated strikingly since she had been arrested. Her face now looked to him to have a waxen, pudgy quality about it, and her legs and ankles appeared swollen and engorged. The drive of life seemed to have drained physically from her.

He looked at his watch. Already two or three minutes had gone, and not a word had been exchanged. He had to say something.

'Sophie,' he said. 'Sophie. Let me know if I can do—'

She suddenly sat upright, stared at him, then shouted, her face twisted into an ugly, snarling contortion. 'Fuck off!' she screamed at him. 'Fuck off!'

The shock of the obscenity from his own daughter made Robert shrink back into his seat. But as she shouted it again a third time the surprise of it had already passed, and he was unmoved by it, or comparatively so.

Then, as abruptly, she was still, her face ashen, her expression closed and absent. He had expected, without much considering it, that their incongruous meeting in a courtroom cell would serve to bring them closer together; his daughter's life now so entirely broken that she would turn to him in desperation, and he to her from compassion and loyalty. At that moment he felt nothing of that at all. It appeared that Sophie didn't either.

'Sophie . . .' and as her face contorted again, and she started to scream her insults at him once more, he found himself shouting back at her, louder than her; 'Stop! Stop! STOP!' and at last she was quiet.

Robert turned to the policeman, who remained in the corner looking impassively on. Then he faced back to Sophie, and tried to find something more to say. In desperation almost, he began, 'Sophie. I'm not here to attempt some sort of—'

'Words,' Sophie sneered. 'Just words. You talk away at me, but nothing you say means anything. You can't say anything to me that means anything at all.'

Robert tried to speak again, but she immediately cut in on him.

'And another thing. For Christ's sake don't come to see me in

403

prison. I don't want your fucking visits. I don't want your fucking compassion. I don't want to fucking see you. I never want to see you again.'

It was the policeman who gave Robert his lead, moving in his chair in a way that indicated that the interview should now be terminated. Robert got slowly to his feet, put his hands into his overcoat pocket, and started to go with him to the door.

Then Sophie spoke, so softly that they nearly missed it.

'Dad.'

They both turned to her, and stood waiting for what was to come.

But she sat there still, her back to them, looking silently before her, and soon the guard had turned the lock, and Robert was gone.

Epilogue

After Robert had left Alice's flat on that final occasion, he went that night to a hotel in South Kensington, and moved the following day to another in Bayswater, where he thought, without giving it very much consideration, that he might as well remain indefinitely. It was there that he returned that evening, after his meeting with Sophie in the courtroom cell.

He had saved only a single love letter from Alice, which she had written him one evening in Elm Park Gardens, and that, for the rest of his life, remained with him. She had nothing of his at all, only the crude, blurred passport photograph that she had taken from the office files. But, for all her need in the end to terminate the affair, the memories of him remained with her, filed away in her clever, honourable, decent mind, together, if only in a dusty, rarely visited spot, with those of her mother, and in due course Tom, who died in her arms one winter night, the wind and the rain lashing at the windows of their Grange Road home.

And, as it happened, it was on that very evening of Tom's death that Robert drove his car up to Rowena's house in Plender Terrace at precisely a quarter past six, as the telephone message to the Bank that morning, relayed on to him by his previous secretary, had instructed him. He locked the car, then went through the open front door of the house into the hall, where the young man whom Sophie had encountered a few months previously was waiting for him.

'Christ knows why I'm doing this,' he said to Robert. 'But the truth is, I'm sorry for the kid. I'm sorry for the poor little bastard. Well – you're exactly on time. Rowena left the house fifteen minutes ago, as she told you she would. I've been with the kid until you arrived, in case the message hadn't got through to you or anything. I'll show you where to go.'

The door into Rowena's flat was standing open, and the two of them walked in. The playpen was in the middle of the room, which had been stripped of its carpet and all of its furniture. Jamie was standing in it, holding on to the bars in front of him, his hair brushed and flattened, his face and hands sponged clean, his blue sweatshirt and dungarees both pressed and fresh.

'Here he is,' said the young man, walking over to the playpen and running his fingers through the boy's hair. 'He's a sweet little sod, he really is. She cleaned him up for the first time in his life, I should think. Good luck to him. He'll be better off now. That's for sure.'

He walked over to the mantelpiece, took down a sheet of notepaper and handed it to Robert. 'Here you are. She asked me to give you this. She wanted you to read it, then keep it safe for the kid. To read when you think he's old enough to understand what she's saying to him. That was the message.'

He walked to the door, and raised his hand in farewell. 'Cheers, Jamie. Have a good one. Make it all work.'

Robert stood gazing at the child, who watched him in return, motionless and silent. He could see his own appearance so clearly marked there in his grandson. The ears. The shape of the head. The set of the mouth and the chin. The same tortured, piercing eyes. He was a Luscombe.

The letter was in his hand, and he unfolded it and read it. He saw that Rowena's handwriting, normally so heedlessly illegible, was for this occasion of meticulous clarity and care. Every word bore for him the mark of his daughter's deliberate, painstaking reach for communication and accuracy, and it chilled him.

Dear little Jamie,

You're so young and small now, and you understand so little. How could you understand? You've never seen anything else but the hell in which we live. The hell I have subjected you to. But there is another life, Jamie, in which good things happen, and the birds sing, and the light shines on the fields. I just can't lead you there. I wish I could.

But I've lost control of my own life now, and I know that I will never retrieve it. And because of that I'm incapable of being your mother, and looking after you, and bringing you up in the way you deserve. And showing you a real life. A life like other children have. Of happiness, and laughter, and sunshine, and hope. So I have to let you go. And leave you in the care of my father. And it will be for ever, Jamie. I can never come back.

And I just want you to know this, my darling. That you're the most blessed person of my life. I've loved you more than you'll ever imagine. When you moved in my womb it was to me like the quickening of a new world. I wanted you, and you were mine. My very own. And you always will be. And I'll never, never forget you. Nor forget how I have failed you.

Forgive me, Jamie. I wish you were old enough to remember me.

Mum.

Robert read the letter through again, folded it, and slipped it into his jacket. Then he leant back against the wall behind him, supported there until the moment had passed, and he had recovered his strength, staring all the while at the child in front of him.

As Jamie began to whimper, he stretched out his hands and held them up. Robert pushed himself forward, and went to him, and lifted him into his arms.

A selection of quality fiction from Headline